OF THE CURATRIX CODE

The Unanswered Questions Series

The Unanswered Questions
Of the Curatrix Code

THE UNANSWERED QUESTIONS

BOOK TWO

OF THE CURATRIX CODE

LAUREN D. FULTER

*To Saint Lawrence,
the patron saint of comedians*

PROLOGUE

All her friends were dead, and had been for ten years.

Sergeant Jessica Taryn Hunter stood amongst the ruins of her old office, reduced to charred walls, a caved roof, a mound of crushed rubble in place of a desk, and bits and pieces of scattered newspaper among the rubble.

She was brutally aware it wasn't the most ideal place to take her vacation from the rambunctious six teenagers that took up every waking moment of the past month, but it was the place she knew she needed to go.

She exhaled. The echoes of her uncle's last words aunted her. They couldn't be true. Dean had killed them. A tragedy the media had covered so gracelessly.

Something brushed against her ankle. The Sergeant jumped, spinning around, her fists clenched in a quick defense. Her eyes fell to a paper fluttering in the breeze, pressed between the ground and a crushed chair.

Taryn dropped her tense arms and laughed to herself softly. She dropped to her knees and pulled a fluttering article free. *"The Curatrix Team mur—"*

Not that stupid name again. Taryn quickly crushed the paper to a ball in her fist. *Curatrix Team. Curatrix Team.*

She stood up and threw it with all her force into the waves of yellow grass in the North Cordellian plain. It was pointless. Her search had been pointless. All along the murders had come from the Defending Department itself.

Most likely out of fear of a Council or the political power they had grown to have. That *Reyna* had grown to have, Taryn corrected herself, kicking through the rubble. Reyna Wents Aguirre had always been the star, whether she wanted to or not.

Taryn's eyes stung, her pulse pounding in her ears. *You're not here to loathe.* She turned back to the desk, tearing the drawer open and letting out a huff. The drawer was crammed full of notecards, adapters, stray screws, and audio chips. For once in her life, she couldn't be organized, could she? It didn't take long for her to navigate to the yellowed envelope. Her heart settled, feeling the worn paper between her raw fingers. She gently opened it, letting the black ring fall out into the palm of her hand. She held it up to the setting sun, the orange light glistening along the dark ring that once had glown bright when the wearer had lived. Taryn clasped her hand over it. At least it was safe. If Kordin had been right in his dying words, she'd be needing it.

She dropped it back into its envelope, tucking it away into her bag.

Taryn flexed her cold hands, ignoring the sharp freeze of the oncoming winter, and with a heave, pushed the desk over. It crumbled easily under her pressure, falling into shambles as it hit the floor. Taryn dropped to her knees, digging through the charred woods, till she hit a secure drawer. She unsheathed her knife from her thigh, tucked the blade in the crack of the woods, and tore away the wood. There in the compartment was a black box, untouched by human hands since it had been boarded away a decade ago.

Taryn's chest tightened, slowly shifting the box from its hole. She held it up, blowing off a thick layer of dust. It was a metallic black case, held locked by two titanium clamps and a DNA pad.

As if it had just been written, a small blue note was taped to the top in shaky handwriting: *To Jess.*

A lump formed in Taryn's throat, and she batted away the tears stinging her eyes. She set the case on the ground. She held out her hand to the scanner. She hesitated, realizing her hands were shaking.

There was nothing to be afraid of. They'd left something for her.

Why was it so hard to think maybe, just maybe, they weren't completely gone? Why didn't that make her happy? She was being absurd.

"Come on, Jess." Taryn grit her teeth and clenched her eyes shut, pressing her hand against the screen. She turned her face away.

A small click caused her muscles to tense, the hair on her neck standing straight up. She slowly turned her head to the now open case. A silver device stood proudly in its wake, with pristine black buttons for a keyboard and a lense in the center. A projector. Taryn sucked in her breath, reaching her trembling hand out to a silver switch. With one flick, the machine whirred to life. A light illuminated from the lense, slowly fading into the holographic recording. Taryn's body went rigid.

A familiar face, two piercing eyes, dark curling hair tied up, a piercing on the left ear, like she hadn't been dead for all this time.

Reyna smirked like she'd sensed Taryn's shock. "If you finally decided to open this, then what Kordin told you is correct, Jess. It has begun."

PART ONE

THE ESCAPE

1

"COME ON, TABS. TABITHA!"

Coleson Johnson took a sharp turn, nearly ramming into a woman with an arm full of produce crates.

"Sorry!" Cole called out after, sprinting around her and dashing down the street. The girl couldn't have gone far, but she had a habit of surprising him. He'd gone five minutes in a shop for the painkillers the Medics requested. *Five minutes.*

The small town #321 of the region of North Cordell was as busy as ever in the dead of what seemed like an eternal winter. Farmers loaded trucks on sidewalks, business partners talked with those out for lunch, bots advertised outside doors, and shop owners were kept busy inside their bustling shops.

A group of students made their way through town, always taking a chance to give their former classmate a second glance, or in this case, a wave.

Cole tried to wave back, but almost tripped over a bistro chair, awkwardly catching himself against the wall.

The group of girls giggled. "Tell Felicity I say hi!" one

called out.

"Sure!" Cole turned on his heel, darting across the street. "Tabitha Delorous!" She was in for it now. She needed to stop running off like this.

"Oh, hey Cole!"

Cole twirled around to meet a girl, with short stature and chopped blonde hair, walking out of the door of a shop with a steaming cup.

Cole sighed with relief, rushing to her. "What were you thinking?"

"I wanted coffee." Tabitha simply ignored him, taking a sip from the cup, starting her way down the sidewalk. "Did you get the medicine?"

Cole pat the leather satchel at his side. "I did, but then I had to chase after you."

"I'm seventeen years old, good sir," Tabitha laughed. "No need to be paranoid."

"Seventeen as of a month ago," Cole grumbled under his breath. Tabitha and the concept of age didn't really work well. Yes, she *was* seventeen years of age, but sometimes she had the maturity of a child.

"Well, Taryn's been making us do that training stuff, so I'm perfectly capable of defending myself." She smiled at him before taking another enormous gulp.

Cole pretended to be annoyed, rolling his eyes. He didn't doubt that. "You still refuse to spar me, though."

"Don't wanna hurt you, Goldfish." She flashed a smile and quickened her pace as they crossed the road. "So, next thing on the list?"

Cole brought up the list Taryn had sent him on his Comm. Tabitha pulled him away from a collision with a bot.

"Some eastside farmers are in need of food supplies," Cole said. "We can pick them up at the warehouse down the block."

Tabitha cringed. "Is the fever that bad there?"

Cole heaved a sigh, handing her the Comm to look for herself. "Apparently. Lincoln said they had a bad outbreak two years ago too."

Tabitha bit her lip, scrolling through the Comm. "There's a request for newborn supplies too." Cole's heart skipped a beat. "What?"

"There's families on the eastside, Cole," Tabitha shrugged.

"Right," he breathed. The fever on the eastside's high infection rate could have disastrous effects on the kids there. Parents were probably out, the psychological effects of the sickness probably frightening. And they were low on supplies. It made his stomach twist. "I hope they're okay." Tabitha tucked his Comm into her pocket and hooked her free arm with his. "Don't stress yourself."

Cole couldn't find it in himself. He tightened his grip on her arm. "But aren't we supposed to be helping people? Like, that's our whole...*thing*?"

Tabitha snorted. "We've only been at this for six months."

"Fair point."

"And after the Inn is finished, we should be able to have a bigger reach," Tabitha said, looking up to him. "It shouldn't be too long now."

Cole couldn't help a smile. "I don't think Nikki would let it be delayed."

"That thing's really been her brain baby, hasn't it?" Tabitha laughed.

"Be glad she's at least not trying to convince everyone to paint it yellow anymore." Tabitha shrugged. "Maybe it would have looked nice. And she hardly *tried*. She mentioned it like three times."

"Three times is a lot for her."

"True," Tabitha said, taking another gulp of the coffee. She led Cole away from the bustling, down the corner toward the warehouses that were set farther off from the center of town. "But it's something, isn't it? Anyway, with a base, we'll be able to do so much more."

"I sure hope so," Cole sighed. So far, he felt like they'd hardly done anything after Imperial. The kids who'd saved the great Imperial City when the Defenders couldn't had been reduced to running errands and morning self-defense drills.

Tabitha elbowed him.

"Hey! What was that for?" Cole said, rubbing his arm.

Tabitha didn't say a word. She froze, standing still, before raising her arm, pointing. Cole slowly turned his head to where she was pointing, his heart skipping a beat.

In the distance, a truck was flipped entirely over, engulfed in flames, another auto rammed into its side. Two men were trying to break through the window of the overturned truck, and a woman was standing to the side, screaming words Cole didn't even take time to process. He ran through the long grasses toward the crash, dropping everything he was holding. The smell of smoke was pungent. The woman ran toward him, tripping on the hem of her skirt. Cole caught her frail, shaking frame, gently helping her to the ground. She had a cut above her brow, blood trickling down her face to her lip, her hair was singed, soot streaked her face, and her body trembled violently. Besides that, she seemed alright.

"We—we have to go!" she cried out, stumbling over her words, trying to catch her breath, throwing her hands about. "No—no time! We ha—have to—to leave! Now! Go—go! No time—"

Tabitha dropped beside them, Cole's dropped bag in arm. "Slow down. Go where? We need to get you to a Medic." She tore out Cole's Comm. "I'll call Taryn."

"No!" the woman shouted, swatting the Comm from Tabitha's hands. She took a deep breath. "The fever. We— we have the fever on—on the—" she coughed, taking another breath. "—far ridge farm. Four farm hands are down. Riel William's daughter and Abigail Patton. They'll die—" The woman buried her face and trembled with cries.

Tabitha stared blankly at Cole, as she gently rubbed the woman's back. Tabitha's lips were pinched, her eyes wide with a worried uncertainty as her brows knit.

"What do we do?" Tabitha whispered.

Cole's lips parted, though unsure what to even begin to say. He looked to the growing flames of the crash, the smell of the burning, and the sound of the soft cries of the woman with him. He turned back to Tabitha. "We have the medicine, right?"

"Yes." Tabitha's eyes lit up. She jumped to her feet. "We have to go."

"Get to the truck. Call Lincoln. Tell him to finish the runs."

Tabitha grabbed the Comm from the ground and nodded, dashing back toward the town. Cole couldn't help but sit a little straighter.

Finally, he was needed.

Thwack!

The staff nearly missed Felicity's head. She stumbled backward. She balanced, digging her heel into the ground beneath. *Right hand was front, so next attack must next be left.* "Four, two," her opponent breathed as they made a light leap forward.

Felicity swung her own staff forward to block the next blow. With a cry, she pushed forward. Her opponent slipped out, sashing to the left. "Seven, eleven."

Curse her. Felicity swung for the heel. Her heart pounded in her ears. Her opponent jumped, twisting their body, and landed gracefully on their feet. They swung the pole for Felicity's face. Felicity ducked backwards.

"Three, two."

Felicity spun back upward, crashing her opponent's pole. Her opponent dashed away, having no trouble jumping onto the deck of the cabin, crawling up the railing, catching the edge of the group, and hoisting her light body weight up on top.

They plopped down, crossing their legs, with a satisfied smirk on their lips. Felicity gave an agitated sigh, throwing the staff to the ground. "Nikki! That's cheating!" The younger girl just smiled, wiping the sweat from her brow, reciting the numbers under her breath. "Four, two, seven…"

Felicity's anger cooled, the adrenaline draining suddenly to leave her feeling sweaty, and her muscles sore.

How long had they been at it? Half an hour at least. That would be her own personal record of keeping Nikki off her.

"I win," Felicity laughed. "You retreated."

Nikki shrugged, brushing her hair from her face. She threw her staff down to Felicity, who caught it swiftly, scooping up her own from the ground. She tucked them under her arms, and headed back to the barrel on the edge of their makeshift training grounds, which were marked with spray paint that was practically all rubbed away besides random splotches of blue across the ground.

The couple squarefeet had become a sanctuary to Felicity, where she spent nearly every waking hour waiting, watching, and whacking sticks around. It was truly a time.

She put the staffs back, accepted a washcloth from a bot, and wiped her face and hands. It all started with baby steps.

She hadn't been confident enough to even try sparring until a month ago, when Nikki offered to do it with her.

The biggest mistake in her life.

Nikki beat her every time, though she never mentioned it. Felicity had grown accustomed to bruises. She sighed. There was no doubt there would be a new one on her shoulder tomorrow. But being the only Council Member who didn't know what they were, learning to at least defend herself without losing it was the least she could do.

She'd never felt so stable in her life.

"Felicity?" A familiar voice called out.

Felicity turned on her heel to see the teenaged Aviduous boy walking around the back corner of the cabins, his face in a Comm, his mop of messy sand-brown hair fallen in his black eyes. He wore a worn forest green hooded jacket and a satchel around his shoulders, jangling every step he took.

Nikki jumped off the roof, landing with a thud right beside Lincoln.

Lincoln cried out and scrambled back, dropping the Comm. "Nik!"

"Hello Lincoln," Nikki said, with a small nod.

Lincoln clasped his chest, settling his breath. He looked to Nikki, then the roof, and then to Felicity. He frowned. "What were you guys *doing?*"

"Sparring," Felicity sighed, striding to him, picking up his fallen Comm.

"I didn't think sparring included roofs." He took his Comm back from Felicity.

Felicity chuckled, eyeing Nikki. "It's not supposed to."

"I don't see why not," Nikki retorted, softly.

"This is why I don't spar her," Lincoln said, cracking a smile. "I like keeping my dignity." Felicity raised a brow. "Dignity, you say? Ray has stor——"

"Eh-eh! We don't talk about that!"

Watching the subtle panic flood his face made Felicity laugh. The two boys fought and pranked each other to the point it was a weekly occasion, the damage only being a broken window and occasionally two damaged egos.

"Did you need something?" Nikki said, cutting off the conversation. She tilted her head, and her wide eyes were intent on Lincoln.

"Yeah, Cole sent me a message. Ray took my audio buds, so I can't read it." Nikki took the Comm from him.

"'We had to run and we'll be back late. Please finish our runs. List attached below.'" Nikki read, moving her finger across the words, Lincoln watching over her shoulder. Felicity's heart dropped. "They had—had to go?"

"It's probably nothing," Lincoln said, placing a firm hand on her shoulder. "There's not too much trouble you can get into in ol' North Cordell."

Felicity shot him a glare. "Oh, really."

"You can come with us if you want," Lincoln offered with a shrug.

Felicity's body went stiff. Going to town meant seeing people, and riding in an auto. The thought of riding in a bouncing auto over dirt roads to the tiny North Cordellian town made her stomach churn. She forced a smile. "I'm good. You two can go. I don't want to hold you back." Lincoln raised a suspicious brow, but she pushed him away, crossing her arms. "You two go. I'll keep practicing here."

"Okay," Lincoln said, reluctantly. He looked back to Nikki. "Meet me at the road in ten?" Nikki nodded. She gave a small nod before dashing off to the girl's cabin. Lincoln watched her go with wide eyes that softened to a small smile, and made his shoulders relax. He tore his gaze from Nikki and back to Felicity. "Last call, Felicity."

"I'm good, Linc. I promise." Felicity waved him off.

"Alright," he droned, and ran off with a glance over his shoulder.

She watched him go, letting out a sigh. She grabbed a staff, digging her fingernails into a crack of the polished wood. As long as she could stay out of the way, they wouldn't be able to see her break.

She wouldn't mess things up anymore. That was progress, wasn't it?

She slid into a stance. *It's progress,* she assured herself, and swung.

2

Nikki's eyes were blue, and it had confused Lincoln since the day he met her. She strode beside him as she moved along the side of the road to the stock warehouses. The sky was slowly sinking into the evening, the grey clouds painting the sky behind the four peaks that had begun to sprinkle again with green after the attack six months ago.

Her eyes were moving about, seeming to take in every new thing they laid sight on. Her light brown skin had grown darker as time had gone on, and the longer she spent all her days outside. Her hair now reached below her shoulders and was tied back, revealing her round, childlike face. She was a good couple inches shorter than Lincoln, but made up for it with her speed. And her eyes clashed with her appearance. Lincoln knew it was common for Ewyon to have startling features due to their adaption to illusion and outward appearance, but the life that radiated from them was almost...supernatural.

Why are you obsessing over Nik's eyes? Lincoln scolded himself.

"Do you think a storm's coming?" Nikki looked up to him.

"A—a storm?" Lincoln looked to the sky. "Nik, the sky's been like that for days."

"The Inn's uncovered," Nikki said. "And we're at such an important part—"

"Don't worry, Nik," Lincoln said. "The Inn will be fine. If it does come, I'm sure we'll be fine."

Her gaze didn't drift from the sky, her shoulders still tense. "I don't know…I mean, it's just—" she stopped, pursing her lips. She took a deep breath. "Yeah. It will be fine." She gave him a small smile.

Lincoln elbowed her. "A storm wouldn't want to even *try* you."

She rolled her eyes, but the tension in her shoulders relaxed. "What would you do without me?" Lincoln gasped. "Nik, was that sarcasm?"

"What's sarcasm?"

"It's a use of irony to mock or contempt."

Nikki took a few moments to process the new word before nodding slowly, then shaking her head.

Lincoln didn't give her a moment to confirm her thought before saying: "Do you think we have time to stop by E's on the way back?"

Nikki's face contorted at the mention of the blacksmith. "E?"

"The one and only."

"Why him, though?" she said quietly.

Perfect timing. Lincoln whipped out a small device from his satchel that immediately sparked Nikki's eye. A shiny cube….well, half of it. The other half was torn apart, alive with wires, cords, memory chips, and a few sparks.

"Meet my new project."

Nikki's eyes became wide, her lips parting. She looked to Lincoln, her eyes seeming to pry for an explanation, a silent look that he knew well.

He tossed the device from hand to hand. "Right now, it's just the cube, even though Ray wants to call it Super."

"Super?"

"I called it the 'super survival tool' *once*."

Nikki shrugged. "I like it."

"It's cheesy," Lincoln said, brushing it off. "You know how Taryn found that tracker from the Curatrix team, right?"

Nikki nodded.

"Well, I know I'm no Aguirre-Curatrix team genius, *but* I'm trying to implement a tracker of my own."

Nikki's brows raised.

"Less of a tracker than a sensor. Being able to *sense* people. That way the tracking could be even stronger." Lincoln settled the cube in his left hand, studying it. The hollow mind stared back at him. "My only problem is I have no idea what to use to build something that can track all kinds of humans."

"I'm sure you'll figure it out," Nikki said. "You always do."

"Thanks, Nik," Lincoln sighed. He tucked the cube away in his satchel. The cube was by far his most ambitious project, but if he could manage to complete it, he was sure it would be revolutionary. If he could even rival the infamous Lyell Aguirre's tech, he was sure to have a name for himself...besides the black-eyed boy that got crushed by the Glass Tower.

He cringed, trying to bury the thoughts away.

He *would* complete the cube. He just needed E's expertise to point him in the right direction for a source.

They approached the warehouse in silence, as it usually was in Nikki's company, besides her recent habit of reciting a string of numbers under her breath. Lincoln entered the passcode to the warehouse door, and it opened and they walked in.

"There's two containers reserved for 'Serg. Hunter,'" Lincoln said.

Nikki nodded. The two didn't take long to short through the shipments and find the corner reserved for Defending Department shipments, which were commonly scarce. "Any progress on the numbers?" Lincoln asked, inserting Taryn's I.D. into the scanner slot on top of the cargo.

"Four, Two, Seven, Three, Two." Nikki shook her head. "That's all I have."

"I wonder if it's a region area code," Lincoln said. The machine blinked green and he removed the card. Inside the cargo case, he found a surplus amount of small crates bound together by leather straps, which made it easier to hoist them out and fix onto his back.

"A region area code?" Nikki frowned, unlocking the second cargo.

"It's five numbers long," Lincoln said. He rushed to help her move the lid. "Maybe it's where you came from?"

Nikki froze, her eyes glowing. "Where—where I came from?"

"Potentially," Lincoln said. He hoisted another pair of crate packs from the cargo bin and handed them to Nikki. She snapped out of her surprise with a jump. She seemed unable to control herself as she quickly adjusted the packs over her shoulders and paced, with a bounce in her step, repeating the numbers more firmly.

"What else could they be?" she said, stopping.

Lincoln motioned her to follow him as he strode for the exit. She raced after him. "A room number," he said, once she was beside him and they left the warehouse. "Or maybe a Comm identification...It's a bit short for that though."

"Right," she said, biting her lip. "Don't you find it strange that I've only remembered it for a few weeks?"

Lincoln shrugged. "Something might have triggered it."

Nikki insisted she'd just been walking and the numbers had just hit her. Lincoln couldn't quite get to grips with that fact.

She sighed. "You keep insisting…"

"Insisting? That's a new word."

She shrugged shyly. "Not really."

"How many things do you have in that mind of yours we *don't* know, Nik?" He laughed. A light blush spread across her face as she shrugged.

"You'll never know...especially since we're going to E's."

"He's not that bad."

She gave him a deadpan expression.

"What? He talks a lot, that's all."

Nikki sighed, shaking her head. "If you say so."

"Hello! N! L!"

Nikki tried to avoid the eyes that E had drawn to her and bolted for the open doors of his workshop. The mechanic pushed the goggles from his eyes into his hair, which was pulled back into the tiniest ponytail, leaving marks around his eyes, the holographic screen shimmering away in front of him. "How're you doin'?" He asked, like he was dying to know. Nikki was grateful for Lincoln stepping in. "Alright, thank you. And you—"

"As usual, great. Don't you love the weather?" E said, jumping over the table, tearing off his gloves. He seemed to always be moving, not dissimilar from Taryn, who had a tendency to always have a foot tapping. He wiped the sweat from his face. "And you, N?"

"Fine," Nikki said, quickly, moving into Lincoln's shadow. "We're here—"

"To pick some stuff up. The Sergeant told me. Yeah, I know N." E said, jumping back over the table, rummaging through a nearby pile.

Nikki frowned. Taryn had called for something from the blacksmith with too much energy? "Do you mind if I look around?" Lincoln called, not waiting for a response before he began sifting through the closest scrap pile.

E threw something, and Nikki ducked as the wrench clattered behind her.

"Sorry!" He called.

Nikki picked the wrench up. She held it out in front of her. It was old and rusted, and it felt heavy in her hand. She turned it over, discovering something etched into it, but it was too rusted to make out.

"That thing's from the EarthShaker," E said, slamming a metal crate down onto the workshop table, some scraps falling to the ground. "I found it in the field by the mountains. They say it used to be an old war site back in the day. Apparently, someone in the camp cursed the land so it couldn't snow."

Nikki placed the wrench onto an overcrowded shelf. She looked over her shoulder to E, rummaging through the crate.

"Apparently, it snowed the night they laid siege on the camp," Lincoln said, appearing out from a scrapped stove. "Everyone died, and someone cursed North Cordell. It's a cool story, but not factually accurate. The lack of snow is most likely due to the altered climate here due the Earth-shaker."

Nikki rubbed her arms. The crazy local legend felt less and less like a legend as she'd lived in the region. "It's cold . . . all the time here," She said, going up to the desk as E hauled another crate to the table. "Shouldn't it...snow?"

"Wait till the summer," E said, wiping his hands on his pants. "That's when the upper region folk come and visit here. The weather's amazing. Too warm for me though." Nikki guessed so as E was wearing a short-sleeved T-shirt, with his doors open wide to the freezing degree weather. The shop was fairly warm, as E insisted on using early models of boilers. He had gone on about it one afternoon for no particular reason.

"Was there anything else the Sergeant wanted?" E said, looking up from the box. "I'm no-"

"Oh yes!" E shouted, running to the back of the shop. Nikki followed him to the corner or scrap metal in the corner of his shop. He quickly whipped his worn, leather gloves back onto his hands and began rummaging through, reciting the gibberish names and tossing them aside. He

finally pulled out a piece of molten metal. It was black and scratched. Nikki frowned curiously at it.

"Your Sergeant lady especially wanted this little thing," E said, tossing it to her. Nikki grabbed it, the metal rough against her hand. She held it up, examining it. It was nothing special. It looked like some sort of messed up abandoned metal work project. But Taryn did seem to like messed up projects.

"Keep it safe," E said. "Sergeant was keen on receiving it not anymore beat up than it already is." "What is it?"

"It seems like some old file case or something. Dunno," E said. "I found it when I went up into the mountains after the fires from the attack. Something probably melted in the fires."

Lincoln appeared at her side suddenly, looking over her shoulder. His eyes grew wide. "No way."

"What?" E said.

"It's classified," Lincoln said quickly.

Nikki slipped it into her coat pocket, the metal clinking with the Stone. E dropped the box in her arms. The weight caught her by surprise, and she stumbled back. Lincoln reached to steady her, but she caught herself. E laughed.

"Want a little help, N?"

Nikki shook her head.

"I got another box..." E said, placing his hands on his hips. He grabbed the other one, slamming the lid shut, smacking the sides. It slowly began to float from the ground. Nikki's eyes widened, her lips parting in surprise. E smiled, patting the top. "Got these special ordered from Manifest. Hand me the box, N."

She dropped the box to the ground, dusting off her hands. E placed the box on top of the floating one, sliding the lid shut, tapping the side. She got onto her knees, swiping her hand below the box and the ground. It didn't even falter.

"Watch this," E said. He pushed the boxes and they glided across the floor. Nikki stumbled back, cracking a small smile.

"What is it called?" She asked.

"Levitation?" Lincoln said. "It's when an object floats above ground."

"L-levitah-tion?" Nikki said.

"Lev-i-*tay*-tion," Lincoln corrected.

"Levitation."

"You got it."

E pulled a slick black remote from his coat pocket. He scrubbed the grease off with his thumb, and tapped it twice. The boxes slid gracefully back toward him. He tossed her the remote. "Return the boxes in fourteen days. That's the policy," E said, winking.

Nikki nodded. "Thank you," She said with a small smile.

E returned it with an enthusiastic grin. Nikki got to her feet, brushing the soot from her pants. She took a step back and the boxes slid toward her. E laughed at her astonishment. "Find anything you needed for your project, L," E said, turning to Lincoln.

Lincoln gave a weary sigh. "Nah. Nothing. I'll keep looking I guess."

"Your best bet is the woods," E said, slipping back on his gloves. "There's been freaky stuff going on there. They're growing at a wicked pace."

Lincoln laughed, though Nikki sensed an edge. She saw his eyes drift.

She hoped he wasn't actually considering it. The last time

they'd been in the growing woods they'd been attacked by vengeful, cloaked people known as the Oquelite. They hadn't seen the Oquelite in months, and Nikki hoped it stayed that way. She was in no rush to go accidentally stumbling across one in the woods.

"Still no development on a weapon for you, N?" E's face swelled.

Nikki's shake of a head caused it to fall. "I don't like weapons," she said, simply.

"Yeah, well you can go relying on your little arms forever," E said with a shrug. Nikki smiled. She intended on it, but E would never stop dreaming of the day she let him craft a weapon.

"Thanks anyway," Lincoln said, turning for the door. "We'll be back soon!"

E slid his goggles over his eyes. "Looking forward to it."

Nikki ran through the garage after Lincoln, back onto the road to the camp. "What's in my pocket?" she demanded, as soon as she was certain they were out of the eccentric blacksmith's range. They walked down a dirt path through the barren trees, the grey, swirling sky above them. A gust of wind brushed through them.

"You have the Stone with you, right, Nik?" Lincoln said.

She nodded. She didn't go anywhere without the Stone, a supernatural crystal shard and home of the ancient Ewyon spirit, Avalon. It had saved her life on multiple occasions, and Avalon was the only way she could learn about being an Ewyon, despite her resentment against the spirit. She withdrew it from her pocket, gently cradling it in her hands as they walked. A small flicker of light swirled under the surface, sending a small shiver down her spine. "Did it ever tell you *why* it has supernatural abilities?" Lincoln asked.

Nikki frowned. It hadn't. She'd never thought to ask. She shook her head. "Essence is immortal, and legend says, or at least whatever's been implanted in my mind, that the ancients created seven 'artifacts' as a resting place for the fallen essence," she said, casually. Nikki remembered Avalon mentioning the stone was one out of seven. She held the stone up with a newfound curiosity, watching the heartbeat-like glow closely in the dying light. "They created these rare materials of pure, material illiah, or essence, and harvested their artifacts from them. The Key Ring was the Oquelite's, and its abilities can only be used by the Oquelite Council Member."

Right. There was one of those. *If we ever find them*, Nikki thought.

"And the Stone is the Ewyon's. That's how we knew you were the Member, remember?" Nikki nodded, though all that flashed in her mind was the memory of the earsplitting explosion and the charred walls of the destroyed Defending Base. She clasped her hand over the Stone. It was dangerous, but at least she knew that now.

"The Ewyon royalty took pride in using the material to decorate their royalty," Lincoln scoffed. "Which *really* if you think about it, is a horrible waste of supernatural material. Did they not see the potential it had? I mean, just think…"

Nikki smiled and tuned him out. She removed the small scrap piece from her pocket. How did Lincoln think the little thing was artifact material? And if so, what kind? It wasn't golden like the Oquelite's, and definitely not the green crystal of the Ewyon. What did Taryn need it for? She slipped it away into her pocket, picking up her pace as they ran up the hill, then stopped for a breath, looking over the camp.

The camp was a ring of cabins, all set in front of a fire that was constantly tended to by the few local Defenders. A line of black trucks were parked behind Taryn's cabin, and a small tent was set up to their left, full of supplies, and served as a part-time mess hall. Not too far off was the wooden structure of the Inn, its outer walls beginning to be filled. The worksite had been abandoned for the day. Nikki again looked warily to the sky.

Taryn held the main, and largest, cabin, and Nikki and her friends held the farthest two opposite cabins.

The cabins were perfectly square. The bathroom took up a corner of the room, leaving a solid 'L' shape for them to work with. She, Felicity, and Tabitha Delorous had taken it upon themselves to divide theirs by sheets. Tabitha's corner was tucked away toward the front, Felicity's directly across, and Nikki's toward the back.

The little cabin, and the camp, had grown to be the only home she knew…or remembered. She had grown fond of it. She broke into a run down the decline, down the worn path, racing toward the camp. Lincoln called for her to slow down, but she simply pretended not to hear him. She spotted Felicity pacing toward the end of the path, her long red mane drawn to a braid behind her. She perked up on seeing them, and ran to meet Nikki.

"Taryn called a meeting!" Felicity shouted. She nearly rammed into Nikki, catching herself on Nikki's shoulders. "She didn't say why, so don't ask."

"It better not be one of her exercises," Lincoln groaned as he slowed to his pace, and stopped beside them. "Last time, it was an announcement and me and Ray had to do night watch, alone." Taryn's exercises, as she called them, ranged from handwriting practice to accidentally making Cole eat nuts, which he was allergic to, all in the name of preparation.

"It can't be anything too big," Nikki said, pushing past them, striding down the path. Lincoln groaned. "How I wish I could have your optimism. Sergeant didn't give a single hint?" Felicity shook her head.

"I hope it doesn't result in another night in the dirt."

"Suck it up. You lived in the woods for four years!" Felicity laughed.

"In a cave by myself, without Ray, who by the way shouldn't have that Shadow Blade. He figured out way too much that night." Lincoln shuddered.

"Ray and Cole can't be that bad," Nikki said.

"Suit yourself. You said barely sleep at night, Nik."

Nikki shrugged off the comment, though she fought back a wince. Sleep wasn't an issue once she was asleep, but the idea of becoming so vulnerable scared her half to death. They stopped at the camp entrance.

"I can take your crates, Nik," Lincoln said.

Nikki thanked him, unbuckling them from her back, handing them off to him. "I'll meet you at Taryn's," Lincoln said, with a small smile and nod to her. He turned and left with his arms full.

Felicity smiled, then looked to Nikki as they began to walk slowly toward their own, as the sun began to go down, the flickering flame in the center of the camp and the electric lamps becoming the dominant source of light. "How was the pickup?"

Nikki buried her hands in her coat pockets. "Good."

"It sure seems like Lincoln's happy you went along," Felicity said.

Nikki nodded. He was loyal. Maybe for saving his life after being crushed by a giant glass building. She liked having him around more than anyone else. He was her greatest friend after all.

"I wish he knew he didn't have to look after me."

"He wants to, Nikki," Felicity said, elbowing her. "So try not to do anything *too* dangerous or you'll kill him."

Nikki smiled. "I'll try."

Felicity gave her a nod, as they stopped in front of the cabin.

Nikki jumped through the door before it slammed shut from Felicity's entrance. "Have you seen Cole or Tabitha at all today?" Felicity asked as she pushed the sheet aside and walked into her room, pulling her hair down, and tying it up tighter.

Nikki guessed this meant they weren't back yet. "I saw Cole this morning." Felicity scowled, grumbling about how she already knew that.

Felicity always seemed paranoid about the amount of time Cole and Tabitha were away from camp. It wasn't like the two were running off doing pointless activities. They always came back, and always with something useful. It wasn't like they were going to die. Cole had the Illuminate, a sword with supernatural abilities. So Nikki could never tell what Felicity was so concerned about.

"You think I should take the spear?" Felicity said, turning her yellow-green eyes toward the weapon, leaning in the corner. In the Imperial City, their friend Jack Sallow had thrown her a strange spear he'd found on display as protection. Felicity had kept it as a memento, with limited experience of even knowing how to use it.

"Why would you need it?" Nikki asked, peeling gloves off her hands and stuffing them into her back pocket, bending her sore fingers and forcing feeling into them.

Felicity shrugged. "You never know what Taryn is planning anymore," She said, looking back to Nikki. "So that's a no?"

"Yes...I mean no. Yes, I say a no."

Felicity cracked a smile. "Yeah, good idea," She said, turning back, pulling open a drawer to her dresser, sorting through. Nikki lost focus, shoving her hands into her pockets, walking to the window and looking out to the camp that had become somewhat like home. The wind rustling through the shadows of trees, the few lanky figures sitting around the fire, the flames flickering and popping. It was the small things that had begun to make her feel truly alive. "Don't zone out now!" Felicity called, rushing to the door. "We have places to be." Nikki nodded, following Felicity out the door, shutting it behind them.

The sky rumbled above them, sending a shiver down her spine, the cold pricking at her bare arms. Nikki followed Felicity the short way to the main cabin that stood at the back of the camp. Felicity waited for Nikki at the steps, tapping her foot.

Nikki turned the knob to the door, pushing it open to a crack. So far no surprises. She opened the door wider, taking a step in.

A woman sat at a long table in the center of the room, her legs up, and her long dark hair up in a messy bun. She turned her hazel eyes from her tablet up to Nikki, swinging her legs down. "You're a little early, aren't you?" She said, smiling. She stood up, tossing the knife into a beat-up post.

Nikki nodded. Felicity trailed in behind her.

Almost as soon as Nikki shut the door, the door burst open, nearly slamming into her. A dark-haired boy shimmered into view, walking in and leaving the door wide open. Nikki glared at him and shut the door.

Ray jumped at the slam and whirled around. Noticing her, his golden eyes glittered. "Hey-lo, Nikki. Haven't seen you all day," he said. "And you know I could've closed it from here." Ray was an Oquelite hybrid, meaning he was the only one at the camp with supernatural abilities and he made that fact clear to everyone.

"I know," Nikki said.

Taryn scowled. "Mathews, where is your esc——"

A loud knocking came from the door behind her. Nikki turned around and peered out the window, opening the door back up. A few men and women who were helping at the Inn walked in. The Defending Offices sent help to Taryn ever since her entire Base was destroyed, but they'd only sent half the supplies and help Taryn had asked for. Most of the helpers were locals. Many donated lumber, their labor, and machines. The Inn hadn't just become their project, but all of North Cordell's.

Lincoln rushed in after them, shutting the door for Nikki. He paused and frowned, looking around the room, opening the door again, and peered out. He shut it and turned to Nikki. "Where's Tabitha and Cole?" He said in a hushed tone as Taryn cleared her throat and began to speak.

Nikki shrugged. They should have been back by now. It was unlike them. Taryn didn't seem to notice.

"We're making excellent progress. Sinni is in Rigia with the Oquelite studies. Outown and Sallow are on a search mission, and you're all making somewhat improvements upon your skill," Taryn said, clasping her hands behind her back. "But we still have an elephant in the room that I find needs to be addressed."

Lincoln leaned over, whispering into Nikki's ear, "There's a problem people are avoiding talking about."

She nodded in thanks. She'd been getting better at the whole expression and metaphor thing, but she was still thankful for Lincoln's help.

She thought back to the small scrap in her pocket. It no doubt had to do about that, right? "The Council—" Taryn cut herself short. She frowned for a moment, counting them silently. Her frown grew deeper for a moment when she got to four, but she brushed it off quickly. "—is a dangerous key. Something that hasn't been attempted to be formed in millenia."

"We know that already," Felicity said.

"Then you'll also be aware, you are dangerous," Taryn said, stepping forward. "Everyone informed is aware you are incredibly dangerous. With all twelve members, its ability is unspoken of."

Literally, Nikki thought. She'd heard the speech a thousand times, and had gotten a hint that's really what Taryn meant. No one really knew what a full Council could do. They were powerful and not to be formed in the wrong hands.

"We have to be more careful than ever. The woods are

growing and full of awakening creatures. I don't know which ones are intelligent or as savage as animals, but we need to be careful. We already have Officer Miriam Outown leading a small mission in search of more Members, but it's not enough for use here. We need a course of action. So by request—" Taryn took a sharp breath. "I've allowed another Sergeant and his troops to come to North Cordell, along with a Defending Agent from Court Illegia."

Almost immediately, there was a protest.

Ray groaned. "But why?" He said. "More people to watch us?"

"A Council is a fragile thing, Mathews," Taryn snapped, her brows furrowing. "And one made up of Members so young must be protected and trained properly. You of all people should know what happens when you're not protected."

Ray still didn't look pleased, but he backed down from starting another argument. Taryn took a deep breath. "Not only with updates on our Council situation, they come bearing news concerning the Curatrix team and their machine. Apparently... something Council related is causing trouble."

The room dropped silent, the air stiffening.

Nikki saw the hurt in Taryn's eyes, as she rapidly blinked. Taryn straightened herself. "They will be arriving in a little over 48 hours so you might want to get your act together," Taryn said, after a deep breath. She strode, steady now, to the far end of the table, placing a gentle hand on the black case that protected the ominous machine.

Nikki strained her eyes to try to see it.

Taryn looked over her shoulder. "And actually have all six of you show up on time. I'm afraid not all Defenders are in your favor."

3

"TABITHA DELOROUS! WHERE IN THE WORLD HAVE YOU been?!"

It was nearly midnight when the small blonde girl crept into the cabin. Felicity hadn't been able to sleep. She had been up worrying, fiddling with the spear and her cracked, falling apart tele. She was almost tempted to get up, grab a staff, and go search for Tabitha herself, but her mind had punched some sense into her. She wouldn't have been able to do it alone. For all she knew, she could've made things worse.

So she was infinitely relieved when Tabitha trudged in.

Tabitha didn't answer her. She just dropped her bag, pulled the curtain aside, and plopped face down on her bed. Felicity frowned, glancing over to Nikki, who sat with her legs crossed like a small child on her own bed. Nikki just shrugged.

Very helpful. Felicity huffed, jumping off her bed and storming over to Tabitha. "Where were you?" She repeated.

"In town," Tabitha said, through her pillow.

They didn't have time for Tabitha's stubbornness. No, not when she'd been gone for long without so much as a message. "Tabitha! Seriously! This is serious." Felicity crossed her arms. Tabitha shot up. "What do you want?!" She shouted.

Felicity jumped a bit, taking a step back. Tabitha's face was worn, not holding the cheery confidence it usually graced. Her hair was damp, her eyes red, and her jaw was clenched.

"What were you doing?" Felicity said, trying to remain sturdy and confident, though all of her anger began to slip.

Tabitha's eyes trailed off. "We were just... collecting supplies. Then... some idiot got into an accident. One was dead by the time we got to him, then—" Tabitha took a deep breath. "-there was this woman...she said there was a bad fever outbreak—" Tabitha choked up, biting her lip. Felicity froze, reaching to give a sympathetic hand on her shoulder, but Tabitha's glassy eyes glared at her.

"Anyway, we—we got there." Tabitha paused again, her eyes glistening. Both Nikki and Felicity remained completely silent.

"So many sick. Cole wanted to get Ray... a medic. There was a woman—"

Tabitha went silent again. "T-the kid died," She said, hoarsely, her eyes turning away. "The mother lived."

Guilt tugged at Felicity's gut. She's been so agitated and angry about Cole and Tabitha being gone and they'd been helping on a farm with the fever outbreak. Her face burned. She couldn't dare look up. And she'd been too afraid, staying behind as always.

"If only we'd gotten Ray..." Tabitha choked.

Felicity stepped closer. "There wasn't anything you could do," Felicity said, softly. It only seemed to make Tabitha worse.

"Death..." Tabitha muttered, burying her face in her arms.

Felicity looked to Nikki. Nikki wasn't paying attention to her, her deep blue eyes seeming to be lost in a way Felicity had seen a few times before. She was thinking back to times she'd never tell.

Felicity suddenly felt alone.

Tabitha wanted no comfort and she made it clear, closing

her curtain.

Felicity turned off the light.

All three of them lie in the still darkness, the only sounds being the steady rumbling of the sky above them, and Tabitha's quiet shuddering breaths.

Felicity was restless.

Seeing Tabitha miserable made her miserable too. *Death.* The word echoed through her mind. Tabitha's cries finally grew silent, her breathing returning to normal as she fell asleep. Felicity found little comfort in it. She rolled over on her side and squeezed her eyes shut. Should she have gone after Tabitha? No. She couldn't have. She would've frozen up and freaked out. She needed to stay where she was comfortable. The thought didn't make her feet better. Instead, it felt more like another punch to the gut.

It seemed only moments later when Felicity was jerked awake, not even remembering falling asleep. The thunder outside crashed outside as it always did, but this time... it was right above her.

Rain.

It was raining.

Nikki didn't hesitate a second. She swung off the bed, pulling her boots onto her feet as scrambled for the door handle. She didn't even bother to grab a coat. She burst out into the storm.

Felicity wasn't as quick. She woke up in a daze. Thunder. Rain, Nikki's running. She stumbled out of her back, tearing her coat from a chair, and struggled to tie up her boots over her sweatpants in the dark.

It was raining.

She turned to Tabitha's side of the room and paused.

Tabitha was exhausted. Mentally and physically. Felicity decided to leave her. Felicity ran out the door, trying to close the door softly, but the wind slammed it behind her. Felicity cringed.

Felicity darted off the steps and instantly slipped, falling into the mud. She spit out the dirt, groaning, and picking herself up. "Seriously," she grumbled.

She tried to remember the balance exercises she'd learned from Nikki, trying to imagine herself running with a pole. It was proving hard to run through a howling rainstorm in the pitchblack night with your only guides being the adults running past you with lanterns. The Inn wasn't far from the camp. If she traveled quickly, she'd be there in a matter of minutes. A howl shot through the night, sending a shiver down Felicity's spine.

Wolves? In North Cordell?

She shook it off. When had she even encountered a wolf? Lightning flashed, thrusting the towering silhouette of the growing woods against the sky. It already seemed closer than before. Felicity pushed herself to run faster, her heart beating in her ears, counting every slam of her food against the muddying ground.

She finally reached the Inn. The rain was falling harder, and her long hair was sticking to her face. She should have put it back up. Felicity made out Nikki's small figure already on top of the Inn, balancing with ease on the frame.

The workers from the Inn were rushing in, grabbing tarps, throwing them to each other, trying to save as much as possible. Felicity ran to help. She grabbed a discarded lamp, holding it up trying to help aid the others.

Ray, Lincoln, and Cole seemed to make their appearances out of nowhere. Felicity felt an urge to confront Cole on what had happened, but she yelled for them to grab tarps instead. "We don't have enough!" someone yelled. "Too much to cover! It's done for!" Lighting cracked, sending another shiver down Felicity's spine. All their work would be set back.

Then she heard something bark.

Then a howl.

Wolves were the first thing to flash in her mind. They were coming. They were real. She held the lantern out in the direction of the barking, her hand shaking. If a wolf jumped out and tried to rip her face off, what would she even do?

Running across the field toward the Inn wasn't wolves, but farmers, the men, a few women, and the farmhands, running toward them, a pack of *tame* dogs running alongside them. "We're here to help!" One shouted.

Felicity broke out into a grin and cheered. They swarmed past her, grabbing supplies and tarps, doing whatever they could to help. Felicity guessed there were over thirty of them, all hurrying and working fast.

Felicity grabbed another lantern, running around the site trying to be as much of a help as she could. These were the citizens of North Cordell. The ones who'd chosen the beat-up, neglected region over all others. They were just like the farmer who'd crashed in the accident. They were suffering through a fever, and they'd come to the Inn?

Felicity felt something burn in her chest.

She was completely drenched, but she didn't care. She just kept screaming, waving her lanterns and throwing tarps. It felt like a life or death situation. They were making some progress. Where the heck was Taryn? It might have been helpful for an experienced Defender to keep things in order, but Felicity didn't see the Sergeant anywhere. It was up to them, just like in Taryn's crazy exercises.

Felicity rushed to help the men unravel the heavy tarps, leaving them to hoist it up. She spotted a new group arriving, and ran with an upright stride toward them. "Felicity!"

The cry tore louder than Felicity had ever heard Nikki use her voice. She whirled around just in time to watch her slip.

Felicity probably was the one who screamed. Felicity's heart skipped a beat. It might as well have stopped altogether. Felicity ran as quickly as she could, slipping multiple times in her panic to Nikki, who just laid there in shock.

"Nikki! Get up! Are you okay?" Felicity shouted, grabbing Nikki's shoulders. Nikki blinked a few times, beginning to push herself up.

"I'm fi- Ah!"

Nikki crumpled back down, grasping her arm in pain.

Felicity's heart dropped. "What's wrong?" Felicity demanded. Nikki didn't need to answer. Felicity could see clearly for herself. Nikki's hand definitely twisted in the right place. Nikki pressed her useless hand against her chest, taking in deep breaths.

"I-It doesn't matter!" Nikki yelled. "We just need to save the Inn!"

"You're a little more important than a building," Felicity said. It was only slightly relieving to find Nikki's *mind* was still in its place.

"Can you sit up?" Felicity said.

Nikki tried, but every time, she slipped in the thick of the mud. Felicity tried to assist her with her good arm, but she suffered the same slipping fate.

Felicity looked around desperately. She tried to cry out, but her voice caught in her throat. She could feel her muscles tensing.

Out of nowhere, a boy fell to his knees beside Nikki. He had round glasses around his large, dark eyes, his thick dripping curls falling into his face. Felicity could barely make much more out in the rain. "Are you okay?" He shouted.

Nikki growled, holding her hand closer.

"Your hand..." the boy started. He didn't take the time to finish. He shouted for Felicity to put her arm under Nikki's left arm, and he rushed to her right. They hoisted Nikki to her feet, and guided her away from the commotion.

"Your hand doesn't look great," the boy said. "It needs attention. Now. Is anything else broken?" Nikki shook her head. Felicity hoped she was telling the truth. Thunder rumbled. Lightning flashed. In the light, Felicity saw Nikki's eyes look toward the Inn, squinting and glassy. The boy made Nikki sit down on one of the crates, no matter how much she insisted she was fine. The boy knelt in front of her.

"Can I see your hand?" He asked, though it sounded more like a demand. Nikki hesitated, then slowly extended her arm out toward him. The boy's fingers barely brushed against her wrist, and Nikki pulled her arm back, wincing.

"Sorry."

"I-it's fine." Nikki's breathing was rushed and shaky.

"Do you have a medic here?"

"Not officially, but we have a guy trained in HCS. Raphael Mathews. He's somewhere in the Inn though," Felicity said. She started toward the Inn, but the boy called her back.

"It's no use if he's up there," he said, with an agitated sigh. "I'm going to try to turn your wrist back."

Nikki's eyes grew wide, but she kept her mouth shut, letting the boy take her arm into his hands. He looked up to her and nodded. "This is going to hurt a lot. Feel free to scream." Nikki seemed unphased, not moving her eyes to meet the boy's.

Felicity stiffened, forcing herself to watch, her heart beating against her chest. She could stay strong, if Nikki could.

The boy turned Nikki's wrist suddenly, wincing as he did so. Nikki didn't scream, but she did make her lip bleed and nearly swung her good fist into the guy's face. The boy stumbled back. "Sorry," he said with a hard laugh, getting back to his feet. "Should've warned you." Nikki glared, looking back down to her disfigured hand, then back up to the boy. "Stay calm," he said, moving back to his knees slowly.

Nikki took a deep breath, handing her arm back to him. He looked her firmly in the eyes and nodded, turning her wrist around again. Nikki bit her bleeding lip harder. The boy let go of her slowly, and Nikki jumped up. She stared at her hand, now turned at least the right way, and let out a shuddery breath of relief.

"You need to get help from someone more professional from this point on," the boy said, looking to Felicity.

Felicity nodded, though she couldn't move her eyes from Nikki, wondering how much Nikki had wanted to scream. She didn't know much about Nikki's past. All she'd told them was that she'd

been a test subject of sorts. Felicity wondered how many times she'd had to keep herself from crying out before.

"T-thank you," she said, facing the boy.

The boy didn't smile, nodding, then turning around to Nikki. "Need help getting back?" She shook her head, but Felicity spoke for her. "Please. We—we're at the camp." Nikki cast her a lips-parted, horrified look, but Felicity didn't care.

The boy nodded.

"We can't-"

Felicity grabbed Nikki's shoulder, though her friend winced. "Nikki, I said it before and I'll say it again, you're more important than a building!"

Felicity and the boy steadied Nikki. Felicity gathered herself, forcing forward through the wind. She led them up the path, trying to control the ramming of her heartbeat. They pushed their way up the hill in silence, the lights of camp growing nearer, settling Felicity's churning stomach. She broke out into a run, hoping Nikki and the boy could keep up. They reached the ring of cabins after what felt like an eternity. Felicity turned on her heel to the other two trudging after her. She could see the boy more clearly now in the dim light. He had fair skin, dark eyes magnified under the round-rimmed glasses. His coat was battered and worn, the sleeves too short for his arms, and his books seemed held together by tape. Nikki wasn't paying any attention, just looking longingly over her shoulder toward the Inn. The camp seemed deserted. It seemed as if everyone had run to help. Felicity hoped she was right about her assumption of Taryn never leaving.

She turned to run to the main cabin, when she stopped. She turned around and nodded to the boy. "Thanks for your help."

He nodded solemnly back, slowly turning to leave.

"What's your name?" Nikki asked suddenly.

They didn't have time for this. "Nikki—"

"Lawrence," the boy said, quickly. He gave her a harsh nod. "My name is Lawrence." With that he ran off back into the storming darkness, leaving them alone. Nikki stood and watched him go, only to be nearly ripped off her feet by Felicity.

They ran for the main cabin, only to find it empty.

"Nik, wait here," Felicity ordered, pointing to a seat under the cabin porch roof. "I'm going to find Taryn. I'll be right back."

She expected Nikki to protest, but she nodded, staying put and wiping the blood from her mouth, and took a seat, muttering her numbers under her breath.

5

LINCOLN BURST INTO THE MED-TENT, COMING FULL STOP, nearly tripping over his feet. Nikki sat on a table with her legs crossed, looking up unphased by his breathy display, and turned to glare at her bandaged wrist like it was the bane of her existence. A wave of his relief overcame him. "You're okay. I heard you fell and I assumed—"

"Just my hand," Nikki murmured, holding up her arm for him to see.

"How bad is it?"

"It's broken?"

"Yeah," Lincoln sighed. "Nevermind. I'll ask Taryn later. Nothing else broken?"

Nikki shook her head, but her shoulder fell as she let out a heavy sigh. "Is the Inn okay?"

He moved to stand beside her and nodded. "We got it all covered... literally. There's nothing to worry about."

She looked at him through the damp strands of her hair, and studied him with her large eyes for a moment. She finally gave a tiny smile and nodded.

Lincoln felt he could breathe a little easier. "Are you sure you're fine?"

"Yeah," Nikki said, though her voice felt shallow. Her gaze fell back to her wrist.

"Come on, Nik," Lincoln said, finally. He strode the tent flap. "You should get your mind off this."

She slipped off the table and followed him reluctantly.

Outside, the world was wet. The sky was dark, and the cold air was ruthless, pricking at his exposed face. The worn ground of the cabin was muddied, and tired defenders and farmers were littered around the fire, all reciting their dramatic retelling of the storm the night before. Nikki looked toward them longingly, but Lincoln urged her away.

"I should have been there," she said, quietly.

Lincoln led her up the porch of the boy's cabin, grabbing his bag he'd discarded by the door. "Don't beat yourself up over it, Nik."

"I shouldn't have fallen," Nikki said, looking up to him. She blew a hair from her face. "I had to distract someone to help me too."

"I heard about a farm boy."

"His name was Lawrence."

The two began along their usual trail to the storehouse. "What'd he look like?"

"Light hair, maybe blond. It was dark. Light skin." She bit her lip. "He had metal on his face." Lincoln frowned. A cyborg? "Metal? Like in his skin?"

Nikki shook her head, drawing lines with her fingers on her face to explain. "It was bent all up smooth to sit on his nose, and bend around his ears."

Lincoln laughed. "Nik, those are glasses."

"Glasses?" She frowned, taking in the new word.

"Yeah. They help people see," Lincoln said. When was the last time he even saw someone with a pair? "Most people can get their eyes fixed now. Some can't afford it."

"His eyes are broken?"

"No—I mean, kind of?" Lincoln rubbed his temples. "It's probably just blurry or something without them. I don't know."

"I'm going to ask him," Nikki said, quickening her pace to match Lincoln's.

Lincoln raised a brow. "You think you'll even see him again?"

Nikki shrugged. "I hope. I owe him."

"Then so do I," Lincoln said. He also now had a few questions concerning glasses. Nikki seemed more like herself. The fresh air and conversation had perked her up. The storehouse was a small garage building tucked away in a patch of trees a ten minutes walk from camp where Taryn stored most of their extra supplies, and where she'd sent Lincoln to grab extra blankets for a shipment for the farmers.

Nikki's one working hand status proved to be unhelpful, which while she brushed it off as nothing, Lincoln noticed silently frustrated her. She sat on top of a shelf, waiting for him to tie the bundle together.

She slipped the Stone from her pocket, beginning to flip it in her fingers.

"You should really keep that thing hidden," he said, startling her. "Especially with the new Defender troop coming tomorrow."

Nikki nodded quickly and put it away in her pocket. "How much longer?" she said. Lincoln picked up the bundle. "Till what?"

She jumped down from the shelf and rushed to assist him. "Till we don't have to hide anymore."

Lincoln whistled under his breath. "I'm not sure how long," he said, eyeing her open arms, then glaring at her broken wrist.

She sighed, dropped her arms. Though she didn't say it, the pinched expression on her face showed her feelings well enough.

"One day your wrist will heal, and one day, we'll be able to stop hiding," Lincoln said, handing her a singular blanket. She took it graciously, tucking it under her good arm. "It just takes time, I guess."

Nikki suddenly laughed under her breath as they trailed back outside.

Lincoln frowned. "What?"

"You should take your own advice," she said, with the closest thing he'd seen her get to a smirk. "What do you mean by that?"

"You are always moving... quickly," Nikki said, turning to meet his eyes. "Like you don't trust there will be time."

Her words came like a slap to his face. His tongue tripped on itself. "Maybe there won't be, Nik," he sputtered out. "Anytime it seems like I might be good, everything comes crashing down." Literally in some cases. The scars littered throughout his body were enough to prove for that. If he didn't move quickly, it would give him too much time to think. The boy who he shared a cabin with six months earlier tried to kill him. There was no time for sitting and thinking... for his own sanity.

"Trust a little more," Nikki said, with a shrug.

"Says you," he retorted, pointlessly.

"I trust you," she said, simply.

"I trust you too, Nik."

She sighed. "No. You don't."

Lincoln frowned. "What do you mean?"

She didn't answer him.

6

THE SOUND OF SCREECHING, GEARS AND ENGINES ON THE edge of blowing up, I promise you, isn't a great way to start the day.

"Is that some sort of dying animal?!" Ray shouted at the top of his lungs. He clamped his palms over his ears.

The older, blond boy had already swung the door open. Cole turned to Ray, yelling, "One loud dying animal then."

Ray groaned, flopping from the cot onto the floor, making his way to the door. He laid by Cole's feet, straining his eyes. The source of the Sound of Death wasn't in sight. It seemed as if the entire camp had been aroused by the sound. "You know, I'm gonna check it out!"

It took him approximately half a minute to grab his coat, secure the Key Ring on his thumb, and run down the steps… only to be jolted to a stop by the back of his collar.

He looked over his shoulder and met the glaring eyes of his older brother. "Are you crazy?" Cole scowled. "You're hardly dressed. And you are *not* taking the Key Ring with you."

Ray pouted. "They're just sweatpants, and the Sergeant entrusted me with it, so I'm just doing my duty, grumpy."

Cole reeled him back into the door. "Taryn doesn't trust you with anything. You know full well the reason you have it."

Why'd he always have to remind him? On top of never being allowed to leave the sight of a Defender outside of camp, Ray was also the temporary keeper of the Key Ring only because of his Oquelite blood. Non-Oquelites couldn't stand its power, like Nikki's Stone, so therefore their only choice was Ray.

Ray took it as a step in the right direction, and to proving himself back to Taryn. Protect the stupid little ring till they found the Oquelite Member. It was simple.

"Blah, blah, blah," Ray said, rolling his eyes. "You sound like Taryn."

Cole raised an eyebrow. "You sound—" Cole cut himself off, his eyes growing wide, his gaze drifting from Ray to behind him. He let go of Ray.

Ray frowned, turning to see what he was looking at.

Through the entrance of the camp was the strangest machine he'd ever seen... on wheels. It seemed to be a sort of tank, with beat and scratched tinted windows, holes lined in silver above each window. The wheels seemed to be almost half as tall as Ray himself... which wasn't astounding recently. His height was becoming a sore subject, especially since Lincoln now had three inches on him.

The machines stopped, the noise stopping too. They were hideous, but Ray expected no less for anyone who dared to ride into their lovely region.

The back of the vehicle opened, a few Officers jumping out.

A group of workers from the camp had formed in the center of the camp. Taryn appeared from the crowd, walking toward the newcomers.

"See, Taryn's here," Ray said. "Not dangerous."

He sprinted off before Cole could grab him again. He could feel the energy and air bend around him as he ran, taking a slight leap, and the next moment, landing softly on the ground behind one of the vehicles. A small smile curled across his lips, the excess power tingling in his fingertips. He loved the feeling of the essence as it ran through him, though he was still getting used to the occasional dizzy spells and nausea that came with the whole thing. That and the flashes of guilt. He tried to be positive about the whole "you're part of the race which has for the most part collectively decided to wish death upon everyone you love" thing. The bonus was he got abilities... even if they were limited, and Taryn forbade it.

He looked back to Cole, who still stood on the steps of the cabin, his arms crossed, with a disapproving glare, tapping his foot.

Ray waved to him.

Cole threw his head back, most likely groaning. He looked around, taking the moment of distraction as Taryn called out to one of the newcomers to run to Ray, skidding to the ground beside him.

"You and Tabitha both need leashes," He grumbled under his breath. "If this is what brothers are like..." He trailed off into inaudible muttering.

Ray smiled. He liked the idea of Cole being his older brother, but it sent a sick feeling through his gut every time someone mentioned it. It didn't feel real that the guy, who seemed to be everything he wasn't, was his half-brother, who his father had been hiding away for his own protection. Ray shook off the thoughts, crouching beside Cole and watching Taryn walk up to a man in a Defending uniform.

Her expression was dead serious, but then suddenly her eye twitched, and a smile burst out across her face. "It has been a few years, Dow."

The man nodded, holding his hands behind his back. "A good decade, Hunter. Good to see you in your right mind, despite the rumors."

The Dow-man towered above Taryn, which was an accomplishment in and of itself. His dark skin compliment-ed the charming golden brown color of his eyes. The man's broad shoulders were pulled back, holding his head up in confidence. All Ray could keep count of was how muscular the man was. He immediately took note not to get on this guy's nerves.

"Hopefully things haven't been too rough," he said, smiling and looking around the camp. Taryn crossed her arms, looking up to him, shrugging.

Dow's smile was short-lived as it quickly melted into a thin line of his lips. "Our main priority is the Council. I expect they are awaiting our arrival."

Ray saw Taryn cringe in the slightest. "They will be prepared to make your acquaintance soon."

"You haven't greeted me yet!" A Defender strode up to Dow and Taryn, his face contorted in a frown. IT looked like his ride hadn't been pleasant. His dark hair was mussed, his strange Defender uniform disheveled. He had light brown skin, similar to Nikki's, dark brown eyes that seemed to pierce into Ray's soul without him even looking, and a neatly trimmed moustache. "Where should I unload your belongings, Agent?" a young officer rushed to the man's side. Ray's eyes widened. This guy was a Defending *Agent*, a fairly rare position.

"Do I *look* like I'd know?" he snapped.

The Officer cowered.

"He can take the empty cabin left of the main one," Taryn said, quickly.

The Officer nodded and scurried off.

"You seem to be in a lovely mood, Lopez," Taryn said, turning on him.

"Oh don't act like I don't have dozens of fair reasons to be, Jessica Hunter," Agent Lopez said. He paused. "First a whole block fatally losing power and then Dow's assistant's terrible driving." "He's not that bad."

Agent Lopez glared at Sergeant Dow.

"We'll have time to discuss your concerns later," Taryn said. "Right now, I think you should unload your supplies and get your troops settled, and we'll meet in the main cabin, with the Council."

"You mean the bunch of kids?" Agent Lopez sighed.

"You do forget we weren't much older than them in our prime. Jessica here was sixteen when she passed the trial, with her infamous teammates." Dow elbowed her, but Taryn didn't seem proud. She forced a smile, and nodded.

"From what I've heard these ones are a mess. Tried to kill each other or something." Agent Lopez raised an eyebrow.

Ray cringed. *Hard.*

"After you unload your supplies are unpacked, and your

troops settled—" Taryn pressed. "—We'll discuss this."

She seemed to keep to official composure, but Ray had been around her enough to know the strain in her eyes meant she was on the verge of panic. Ray shook Cole's shoulder. "We gotta go," he whispered, harshly. Cole didn't argue.

They got to their feet, and Ray grabbed Cole's arm. Cole's eyes widened as he opened his mouth to protest, but Ray already sent them through the fabrics of the space around them and crashing through the door of the girl's cabin. He hadn't meant to go first.

He scrambled to his feet, getting hit in the face with a pillow.

"Knock first, you morons!" Felicity snapped.

Nikki nodded as she walked up behind Felicity. To his surprise, they were fully awake and dressed. He couldn't say the same for himself and his sweatpants.

"Okay, okay!" He said, waving his hands in the air. "But we have some serious company!" "You think we haven't noticed?" Nikki said.

Oh yeah. There had been a giant sound of a dying demon of sorts.

"They're the new Defenders. They're crazy. You know—the ones Taryn's been freaking her head off about? And they want to meet with the Council... us, in like, I don't know, ten, twenty minutes if we're lucky."

Felicity gasped, grabbing her head and beginning to rant. "Where is Lincoln? Like how ruthless? Oh gosh, like right now? What did Taryn even say about us?"

Nikki's pupils constricted in horror, but she didn't say anything. Ray hoped they'd go easy on the whole Ewyon thing... and even more so with the Oquelite-hybrid.

"Where's Lincoln is actually a good question," Cole said, stopping Felicity's rant. "Nikki and Ray should go find him. Felicity, stop panicking."

Felicity didn't seem to hear him. "B-but Tabitha! Gosh, she's still not awake. She's gonna hate me," she said, turning to Tabitha's corner of the room.

Cole caught her by the shoulder. Felicity whirled around. "I'll get her. You go on ahead." Felicity raised an eyebrow, but then took a deep breath and nodded, rushing out the door after Ray and Nikki.

As soon as the door shut behind Felicity, Cole sighed, turning his eyes to the sheet that marked Tabitha's section of the cabin. He pulled the sheet away, stepping inside the dark corner, the morning light trying to spill through the cracks of closed blinds on her windows. Tabitha lay, knees curled to her chest, her short, frizzy hair scattered across her face. Not even the ear-bleeding sounds of the tank-like vehicles could wake her up.

He'd seen her mood yesterday. Tired and miserable. From the way she held herself, he knew she felt entirely responsible for the death of the child. She'd blatantly avoided conversation all day, and disappeared into her room early.

He didn't want to give her another reason to mope around all day.

He leaned to her ear, whispering, "Come on, Tabs. Wake up."

Tabitha made small groaning sounds, rolling over and burying her face into her pillow. "Oh, come on," Cole said, in a playful tone, sitting down on her bed, trying to roll her back over. She just slumped back over with the same tired groan.

Cole gently shook her shoulder. "Hey, Tabs."

As of the sudden, Tabitha began to toss.

"Tabs? Tabitha, are you okay?"

She muttered something under breath, and she began to wrestle the blanket. Cole grabbed her shoulder. She threw a fist. He grabbed it. "Tabitha!"

Her eyes burst open, in a daze, searching the room. Her breathing was heavy. "They're still here. I can see them. They're coming."

"Tabitha, what are you talking about?"

"Blood. The mountains are on fire." Tears began to stream down her face as she tried to wrestle away. "They're on fire!"

Cole grabbed her wrists. "Tabitha, listen to me! It's not real! It's okay."

She froze. She stared at him for a long moment. She suddenly crumpled against his chest, trembling.

He jumped, surprised, but he quickly wrapped his arms around her. "Hey, it's okay. It wasn't real."

"They were on fire," she choked.

Cole rubbed her back gently, waiting till she slowly uncurled from him, sitting back. She blinked a few times, before flushing red. "S-sorry," she croaked. Her eyes had dark lines underneath, her eyes red from tears. "Ni—nightmare."

"It's alright," Cole said, gently. After all they'd been through, it was only natural, but it still tore at his heart to see her in pain. He'd completely forgotten how hard Tabitha, a girl raised in the priviledged regoin of Liberty, would be so shaken by the horrors of the world he'd known since a young age.

"The mountains..." She took a deep breath, wiping her face. "They... they were soaked in blood. I could smell it. Just like—" Her face fell.

Just like the mural in the Hall Of Heroes six months ago...

"It's not your fault," Cole said, knowing those words weren't enough. He would never be able to say anything to heal her from the horrors a few days ago.

Tabitha forced a smile, her eyes growing wet again. "Yeah. I-I know," she said. "I've been told." She stared up at the ceiling, taking in deep breaths. "I saw North Cordell burn, and it was our fault. There were these... feather." She laughed hoarsely. "They were on fire."

She turned to meet Cole's eyes. He watched her intently.

She swallowed hard. "I'm sorry," she said, her face falling.

"Tabs, you have nothing to be sorry for." Cole lifted Tabitha's chin to meet his eyes. Tabitha pulled her face away, biting her lip to keep from lashing out. She suddenly turned back to him, falling to his chest. Cole froze, hoping she wouldn't see his face redden, then wrapped his arms around her. She was trying to keep her tears silent, and her shoulders from shaking, but she couldn't help it. He rested his chin atop her head, curling her fist against his chest, trying to catch her breath. They just stayed in the dim silence.

Cole could've held her forever. She was safe with him, in his arms where no one could touch her and hurt her ever again.

But Taryn was waiting for them.

Cole began to pull away, but Tabitha stopped him. "Not yet. Please don't go." He felt his heart ache. Soon enough he'd have to. They'd have to go back to acting like everything was fine, and face the new Defenders and their fate. Tabitha finally crawled from his arms and slipped off the bed to her feet. She wiped her face with her arms and put her hands on her hips.

"Great way to start the morning, don't you think?" She said, smirking a little. Cole laughed softly, relieved to see her in better spirits.

She looked down at herself, still in her night clothing, and frowned. "So, how long do we have?" "At this point, maybe five minutes if you're lucky."

Tabitha's eyes grew wide, dashing across the room, grabbing her iconic red tennis shoes. "Meet me outside!" She shouted, pushing through the sheet, trying to tear her fingers through her hair at the same time.

Cole ended up pacing impatiently outside the cabin door, counting the seconds down in his head. But his thoughts constantly were distracted by Tabitha. He knew he would never have let go of her if it wasn't for the stupid Defenders and their big, important meeting. But he also knew Taryn would be furious if they missed another gathering.

He'd never seen Tabitha so... broken inside. And he couldn't help blaming himself. He'd made them go to the farm. He hadn't gotten a Medic. He hadn't protected her.

Tabitha burst through the door, her hair tucked into a red beanie, though some hairs had already escaped. Her eyes were still red, but with her grin, it could easily be ignored. "We're gonna be late!" She shouted, grabbing his arm, pulling him down the path to the main cabin. "Do you have your necklace?"

Cole glared, but she just smiled. She refused to call the Medallion by its real name. "I never take it off," he said. He knew she knew that. He wondered why she asked. They stopped in front of the cabin, catching their breath. Tabitha turned to him, tugging at the chain around his neck, the Medallion coming out from under his shirt. It was a gold plated circle, engraved with various designs, which he later learned was linked to the Illuminate Blade. Tabitha seemed happy with her work, grabbed him again and dragged him through the doors. He held his breath, bracing himself for a scolding.

But to his surprise, they seemed to be on time. Or maybe they'd all been waiting for them. Lincoln raised his eyebrow to them, seeming to ask where they'd been. Cole ignored him. The other sergeant, the one Taryn had called Dow, stood beside her, seeming to be inspecting the room.

The door slammed open from behind them, and a younger, stout man, who seemed to be made of nothing but muscle, strode into the room. He couldn't have been much more than a year older than Felicity. His hair was dark auburn, and fashioned into a mullet. His face was freckled, and his muscular arms showed off an array of scars. He gave a deep frown, his killer black eyes gleaming.

Cole tensed. He was an Aviduous. Another full-blood?

Dow turned to Taryn. "These are all of them?" Dow asked, turning to Taryn. Taryn nodded.

Agent Lopez scoffed, mumbling something about a dozen deaths that did not give Ray a nice feeling.

Cole felt like they were some sort of spectacle, forcing himself not to scowl under the new Aviduous's glare. Dow took a step closer, his eyes seeming almost sympathetic, giving a soft smile.

"The Illuminate, and the Outown protege," He said, nodding to Cole.

He turned his head to Ray. "The Holder of Shadow Blade."

Ray nodded, though his side was empty from the blade... another thing suspended by the Sergeant.

"He's the Oquelite hybrid we've all been hearing so much about?" Agent Lopez said, wrinkling his nose.

Cole's lips twitched to defend him.

"I am," Ray said, boldly.

Dow smiled. "It's good to see you standing with us. And you two are brothers?"

"Half-brothers," Cole said, quickly. The whole idea of having a "brother" still felt a little too fresh with him to come to terms with. It felt like his mind and heart were fighting over it. In one sense, he loved Ray, knowing the kid was his younger sibling, but his mind was determined to be angry with his father for lying for eleven years.

Agent Lopez chuckled. "This is why I failed Impure genetics. The Illuminate's a Unidentifiable, and our friend who's currently giving me the nasty eye, is an Oquelite."

"Fate controls what essence is passed down and created," Dow sighed. "Why was that so hard for you to understand?"

"Because it doesn't logically make sense."

"Logically on our terms." Taryn rubbed her temples. "Not on the supernatural realm. Now would we get back on track?"

"Humanic," Dow said, walking past Tabitha. "Aviduous."

Lincoln's gaze fell away.

Dow nodded to Felicity. Felicity nodded back. Apparently, Felicity was supposed to unlock what she was on her own, and if she was told outright, she wouldn't be able to access her essence. But Dow was stumped when he reached Nikki. "Wingor?" He guessed.

Nikki shook her head in the slightest. Dow frowned.

She turned head away in shame, shifting as she muttered slowly, "Ewyon." Instead of gasping in horror as Cole expected, Dow's smile grew wider.

"Ewyon," he murmured, like the name of the illegal race enchanted him.

Agent Lopez went still, looking to Taryn, and they shared a silent exchange. Cole frowned.

The other Aviduous scoffed. Dow looked back to him, like he just noticed he was there. "This is my right-hand officer, Armstance Giles," Dow said, holding his arm out to him. "He will be helping with our observation of your Council."

"Armstance Giles. Manifest. Nineteen," the officer said, a thick accent on his tongue. And what about his eyes? Cole wanted to ask. How many other full-blooded Aviduous were there?

"It seems like you'll need it," Giles grumbled.

"Now, Sergeant Hunter," Agent Lopez said, the title stiff on his tongue. "Must we discuss the *Mors Vis* in front of your... Council?"

"I don't see why not," Taryn said, gesturing for them to sit. "It does concern Council affairs. And as you've been telling me, it has led to a multitude of deaths."

Lopez eyed them suspiciously. "Alright, Jess. I trust you. Don't make me regret it."

The man's disdain for them was uncomfortable. Cole itched to jump from his seat and leave, taking the others out with him, but he kept his head cool and sat obediently at the conference table. But if any of them dared trash talk another of them, Cole might not be so merciful. "Might as well get on with it. A force has caused a total of twenty four deaths just this week, took fourteen last week, and who knows the week before, in Court Illegia," Agent Lopez said. "And I believe it's linked to the *Council*."

"Last time I went to Court Illegia, I was four," Tabitha said, her face pinching. Lopez ignored her.

Cole shook his head to Tabitha. She only rolled her eyes at him.

"In Court Illegia—" Lopez flicked on a hologram, projecting in the center of the table. "—we were able to only get one image of this force. And from matching it to images we have in Impure research, we believe the name is *Mors Vis*."

From the image, Cole could only see a cluster of shiny feathers. They hardly looked dangerous. Was the Agent scared of magic feathers?

"Wow. Feathers," Lincoln said, looking bored as ever.

Lopez growled. "Mors Vis means Death Force."

That got their attention quickly.

"We have little to no ancient text talking about it, so we're left to our own," he said, swiping left on the hologram, revealing a series of notes and images of feathers under pressed glass and gloved fingers. "It appears that the Mors Vis appearing is directly connected to the awakening of the Council, and from the looks of it, can't be good. It's led me to believe a Council Member might be in Court Illegia, and this thing is after it. Considering its feather like shape, it's not hard to deduce, the member is most likely a Wingor."

A Wingor... like the Outowns.

"It hasn't found it though," Tabitha said. "And if it's some magical force, don't you think it wouldn't need to keep looking?"

"It might be waiting for the Member to reach their breaking point," Taryn said, stepping forward. "A breaking point is when a full-blood's essence 'breaks' per say, and activates its supernatural capabilities. So far, I assumed Nikki was the only one to have one, since her connection to the Stone, but she hasn't been able to harness any abilities... so I might be mistaken."

"With the awakening, its essence could break any time now," Lopez said, landing a hard fist on the table. "For who knows how long that *thing* will go on its supernatural rampage glitching out bridges and scrapers. If it causes too much ruckus, there will be more casualties, and might as well lead the darn Oquelite right to them!"

"Which means there's an unguarded Member some-where, and the remaining Oquelite's location is *completely* unknown to the department," Dow sighed. "Two problems. Stupid feaher force—" Tabitha snorted at this comment. "—and the loose Oquelite with a vulnerable Member." Taryn's eyes drifted to the case at the end of the table. "And so that's what you came for the machine for."

It was somewhat common knowledge at least among the Members, thanks to Lincoln's skill of eavesdropping, that the mysterious Curatrix machine was coded to be able to track people based on their essence type.

The only problem?

"It's locked by a DNA code," Taryn sighed. "It isn't mine. It was clearly meant for us, so it couldn't be either of the Aguirre's."

"Well then who?" Dow said, rubbing the hair on his chin.

Taryn's shoulders sagged. "That's the issue. We don't know who."

Nikki suddenly perked up. "Williams," she blurted out.

As soon as everyone turned to stare, she dropped her head.

"What'd she mean by that?" Agent Lopez grumbled.

"She doesn't like the fact you're all watching her," Cole said, straightening in his seat. The Defender, Giles, glowered at him and rolled his eyes. Cole tightened his fists.

"Caroline Williams." Taryn gasped. "Kid, you're right!"

"Who what now?" Ray frowned. "I don't know no Williams."

Taryn swiped away Agent Lopez's Mors Vis presentation, drawing up a file saved to her database. The screen now projected an image of a woman with fair skin, blonde hair curling on her shoulder, a hint of a kind smile on her lips... and two startling blue eyes. "Caroline Williams, sister of Agent Reyna Wents Aguirre," Taryn explained. Cole frowned, focusing on a singular, bold printed word at the top of the file, that caused his heart to sink. "But how can she be the one? She's dead."

He caught Nikki flinch out of the corner of his eye.

"So we have a dead end," Giles grumbled. "How genius your oh-so-awesome Council is." Cole took in a sharp breath, glaring at the bold Officer, who didn't care to look at him.

"She might be dead, but her children aren't. Both of them were born at least seven years before Reyna herself." Taryn began to pace excitedly. "And they live in North Cordell. All we have to do is locate their residence and request them to come here."

"I can do that for you." Lincoln jumped from his seat. "It'll only take me a day or two at most."

Taryn smiled. "Excellent."

Agent Lopez raised a brow. "You rely on children to do your tech work?" Taryn didn't respond, acting as though she didn't hear it, but Cole did, as did everyone else. There was an awkward tension in the air.

Dow cleared his throat. "How about we give the boy a chance, and see what becomes of it? We'll regroup in a few days and see the progress."

"Sounds like a plan," Taryn said, forcing a smile.

"If these Williams might be our only chance of preventing an Oquelite attack before it happens, especially one concerning a Member, then I'm all for it," Dow said cheerfully. Agent Lopez rose from his seat, stretching his arms. "Always a great time, Jess. I'm going to get some rest after that... delightful journey." He cast a quick glare in Giles's direction and strode from the room.

"I'll meet you in the back room so we can catch up," Dow said, with a pat on Taryn's shoulder and a reassuring smile.

He slipped through one of the side doors, after giving them a wink.

Taryn spun on them. "Tabitha, try to calm your random—" Taryn shook her hands trying to form the words.

"—bursts of making other people feel stupid, and I'd say it went somewhat smoothly."

"Well, they said stupid things," Tabitha said, leaning back in her chair, with a shrug. "So I felt the need to point it out."

Cole face-palmed. Of course she did.

"Great, but not *now*." Taryn took in a deep breath. "Try and stay out of trouble. I have to meet with Rayd—Dow. Behave yourself."

"You got it, Serg." Ray saluted her.

Taryn didn't look impressed. She adjusted her jacket and rushed into the room after Dow. Cole rose to his feet, avoiding the prying eyes of Officer Giles. "Let's go." No one argued. Cole held the door open as they filed out in silence.

"So you're the Ewyon they've been talking about?"

Cole whirled around to see Giles towering over Nikki.

His tone didn't seem impressed, edged with disgust.

"Leave her alone," Cole snapped.

Giles looked up, searching around the room before settling on Cole. "Oh, sorry. Didn't see you." Pathetic. "Come on, Nikki. Let's go."

"What happened to her hand?" Giles frowned.

"She fell." Why did he answer?

"You fell?!" Giles snorted.

Nikki clutched her good hand. A small frown creased her forehead, her eyes honing in on him. Her body had tensed.

"Let's get one thing straight, *boy*. I was never fond of your Sergeant," Giles said, his gaze set firmly on Cole, taking a heavy step forward. "She doesn't seem to make the best decisions, the lunatic, does she? I wonder why they didn't execute *her* with the rest of the Curatrix team."

"Shut up," Nikki said through her gritted teeth.

His voice screamed through Cole's ears. It took every ounce of will power to control the instinct that told him to pull out the Illuminate. "Nikki, let's *go*."

"Go. Probably better to keep your spirits up anyway. I know all about you too, 'Illuminate.'" Giles crossed his arms, lifting his chin with an irritating sense of authority.

Cole had enough. He stormed right up to the Defender. "Whatever you know about me doesn't make your actions any more valid."

"What actions? I haven't done anything to you."

Nikki stepped forward, but Cole held out his arm.

Giles shrugged. "All I know is your father is an Oquelite, and personally, I have no trust for them—" His expression darkened. "—or their offspring."

Out of nowhere, Giles was knocked off balance, crashing into Cole. Cole twisted away. Giles grabbed him. Cole twisted the grip off. Giles was on his feet, and Cole ducked a grab, whirling around to see Ray caught in Giles's grip, swinging his fist around aimlessly. "Don't you dare speak to him like that you big... fat... oaf! I will end you! You hear me?"

Cole groaned mentally. Was Ray trying to get them killed?

"Let him go," Cole snapped.

"He attacked me, and so did you," the officer spat.

"Well you initiated it."

"Oh hazzah, the shrimp of an Aviduous has arrived to scare me too. I'm honored." Giles rolled his eyes.

Cole turned to find Lincoln standing protectively in front of Nikki, pointing an accusatory finger. "Not helping." He looked back to Giles. "Let. Him. Go."

The officer snorted, dropping Ray to the floor. Ray let out a curse, and would've pounced right back on Giles, if Cole hadn't caught him.

He took another step toward her. "Better keep your language to yourself," Giles said, a smile flickering onto his lips, his hand going for the gun in his belt. "Might I remind you, your fate lies in my hands."

"Listen to the little thing of an Aviduous," Giles said, crossing his arms.

Lincoln didn't flinch, but Nikki looked offended

"Ignore him," Cole demanded, squeezing Ray's arm. "Let's go."

They left the cabin, Cole making sure to slam the door.

So much for their best behavior.

"We're in for it," Felicity sighed, leaning against the back of one of the cabins. Nikki hid her face in her hands. She felt sick even thinking about it. Taryn would be furious. She should've listened to Cole and just ignored him. "This is my fault."

"It's that Armstance Giles's fault. He's worse than

Conrad," Ray said. He sat beside her, having gotten a lecture from Cole about his actions. Nikki guessed he got them often. He didn't seem the least bit ashamed. "I mean, who does this guy think he is, waltzing around like he already owns the place?"

Lincoln knocked the green hood from his head, frowning. "He's an Aviduous," Lincoln said, keeping his voice down. "With black eyes. A full-blood. That's incredibly rare." That had come on Nikki's mind too. What were the chances another full-blood Aviduous was the right-hand officer of Sergeant Dow, a close friend to the Curatrix team? "It doesn't matter. Taryn's still gonna kill us," Tabitha groaned, breaking the prolonged silence with the optimistic thought.

"Well, we didn't *hurt* him?" Ray pressed, with a grin.

"Oh wow. Yay. We did something." Tabitha glared at Ray, and shook her head. The new Defenders had just arrived and they'd already managed to screw it up. Taryn was working so hard to make sure that the world wasn't going to kill the Council. They were never going to hear the end of it.

"Maybe... we can tell her about Giles?" Ray suggested. "I mean, he literally seemed to try to get Nikki and you to fight him."

Nikki shot him a glare. "I could've taken it."

"Yeah," Lincoln said, rubbing his forehead, sighing. "We know that, but that's not the problem." "Taryn will probably believe us," Felicity said. "But you know if we're the Council." She went onto doing a bad imitation of what was supposed to be Taryn's voice. "We have to be stronger beyond all odds. If we're the Council... all that. And with this new '*Mor Vis*' thing, we have to be careful."

More silence.

"I'll just stay out of Giles's way," Nikki shrugged.

They agreed.

"And Ray's gotta stay away too," Cole said.

Ray frowned, whipping his head up. "Wait? What!? Why me!?"

"So you don't accidently cut off his head."

Ray paused, thinking over what Cole had said. He nodded, satisfied. "Doesn't mean I won't decapitate him," Ray said.

"Well, at least try," Cole said, looking to Nikki. "Both of you... and me."

His face fell, Nikki noticed a small furrow in his brow. "I'm sorry I acted so rashly."

"Without you, we would've probably really screwed up," Ray said. "Don't be too hard on yourself." Cole nodded, though his thoughts seemed far away, his eyes firm on the ground. He abruptly got up and left.

They all fell silent, exchanging glances. Nikki had an empty feeling in the pit of her stomach, tapping her fingers against her knee. Something had to be done and quick. Their reputation depended on it, yes, but so did her friends.

She wouldn't let anything hurt them again.

"I've searched through countless records, Nik. Wherever the Williams are, they're well hidden." Lincoln rubbed his sore eyes and leaned back in his seat. He removed his earpiece as it read him the text on the search, and turned to Nikki. She sat on the arm of the chair, reading over his shoulder with unbroken focus, her lips pressed firmly together.

The rain pounded down against the tent, seeming to have gone on for hours. The heaters glowed in the corner. The long tables of the mess hall sat empty, except for Ray, who had happily surrounded himself with as much food as he could manage to take from the kitchen. He was supposed to be helping them with their search, but Ray seemed to have other plans. "How's it going over there?" he called out when he noticed Lincoln's gaze.

"Poorly." Nikki sighed. "Williams is a very common last name."

"So is Mathews," Ray said, opening a new bag of chips. "I always wanted a cool name like Ray Thunderstorm or something."

Lincoln snorted.

"Like you could do better, Black Eyes. Chips?"

Lincoln waved it away. "I'm not hungry."

Ray frowned. "That's weird."

"Don't eat and talk."

"It's multi-tasking, genius."

"Lincoln, can you go back to Caroline's file?" Nikki asked.

They'd already studied it word by word, which there weren't many of. But Lincoln slipped his earpiece in and drew it up anyway. "What about it, Nik?"

"There. The man. Her ba—something..." She waved her hands, stumbling over her tongue. Lincoln frowned. "Husband?"

"Yes. That!"

"Wait, Nikki has a point," Ray said. He jumped up from his bench and rushed to Lincoln's other side. "There. Riel Williams."

Lincoln clicked on the name, bringing up a new file.
REIL WILLIAMS.
Deceased.

Ray groaned. "Well, never mind on that lead, then."

Lincoln frowned as his earpiece continued to read. "No, wait. He died a few days ago. It says he died in North Cordell."

"So the Williams have to be here." Ray's eyes widened. "And look, it lists their children!" Instead of names, long IDs were given under *"children."* When Lincoln accessed one of the files, it was blank besides a birthdate, genders, and links to parent files.

"The eldest is twenty," Lincoln said. "That means she would have been ten when Reyna died. Plenty of time for Reyna to choose her DNA."

"How about the second?" Nikki said, leaning in closer.

"He's seventeen. Still plausible." Lincoln clicked through to the third child's file before frowning. "The third's five years old."

"And?" Ray looked back and forth between Nikki and Lincoln, confused.

"Caroline Wents Williams died ten years ago."

"So, it's not her kid. Great," Ray shrugged.

"But there's no listing of a second wife." Lincoln scanned over the file, driving the poor earpiece crazy as he scrolled, stopping at "residences."

One was listed. That was something Caroline didn't have. The small house was located a few miles away in the north farm lands, but Reil Willaims had sold it ten years ago. A decade ago sounded like a horrible year, and one Lincoln so desperately wanted to know more about. If only he could find a way to hack the Aguirre machine…

He brushed off the idea. His cube would be able to recreate its tracking qualities. Maybe he'd be able to get Taryn to let him help with the Curatrix case with the device once it was complete. His chance to prove himself.

"So if he sold his old residence a decade ago, but died only a few days ago nearby... then his kids can't be too far off," Lincoln decided.

"If we're lucky." Ray sighed, taking another chip. "For all we know, they could've been sent away. Or left."

"We're thinking positive right now," Lincoln growled. But Ray did have a point. Both Williams children were old enough to leave if they wanted.

"We can show Taryn what we learned tomorrow," Nikki said, with a hopeful shimmer in her eyes as she jumped to her feet.

"If they are here, they can't be far," Lincoln said. He shut off the Scroll, attaching the magnetic earpiece to the frame. And if they found them, that might loosen Taryn's anger when she inevitably learned about the Giles scuffle... most likely from the nasty Officer himself. Nikki nodded, taking her oversized coat from the bench. "Tomorrow then."

"If it was that easy to find Williams, then it's a wonder Miriam and Jack haven't found a single eligible Member yet," Ray said.

"Not like there's just hundreds of members handing out," Lincoln sighed, getting to his feet. "The last report in looked hopeful."

"That was a month ago," Nikki reminded them, zipping up the coat.

Right. Miriam Outown hadn't sent a message in four weeks. Taryn said it wasn't unusual, and Lincoln tried not to stress over it.

Lincoln led Nikki to the door, which was more of a weighted tent flap. He peered out. The world was pitch dark, except for the camp lights. Not that it bothered Lincoln. The dark wasn't usually a problem for him. The rain seemed to come down in a heavy curtain, and it hadn't stopped for hours. Thunder crashed above them. The wind howled, trees swaying and bending in its wake.

"It doesn't look good out there."

Nikki squeezed in beside him, looking out. "The Inn?"

"I'm sure it's fine, Nik. I was more worried about you."

Nikki gave him a quizzical look. "A storm hasn't stopped me yet."

She had a point there, but this one was far worse than the ones they'd experienced when they first met.

She tied her hair up, and hid it underneath her hood. "I'll be fine," she assured him. Linoln didn't argue, but everything in him wanted to.

"Just don't get blown away." Ray laughed.

Nikki shook her head at him. She slipped out the tent flaps, waving to Lincoln before disappearing into the shadows of the night.

He closed the flap and turned away, looking to Ray who'd stolen his seat on the sofa, watching with full interest and a new bag of chips. "You really should stop worrying about her. It's a bit pointless, Linc."

Lincoln scoffed. "If it only were that easy."

Felicity heard Nikki enter with heavy boots, a jacket dripping with rain, and a swift slam of the door against the wind.

Felicity had lain still until Nikki had passed, closing her eyes as the dim light shone between their sheet walls. She knew they'd been researching the Williams. They'd asked if she wanted to come, but she'd brushed them off, saying she was tired and here she was awake at... what time was it?

She pulled her tele from her dresser, *"2 AM GQ"* shining through its cracked screen.

Really, there was nothing that should have held her back. There was nothing remotely dangerous about meeting in the mess hall, doing a task Taryn had assigned them, so why had her stomach suddenly twisted, and her sweat became cold?

She buried her face in her pillow and resisted the urge to groan.

A few moments later, Nikki's light flicked off.

Not that that meant she was sleeping, of course. Felicity swore Nikki slept maybe five hours on a good day, and if she heard Felicity making sad, pathetic noises, would she come in to check on her? Felicity heaved a silent sigh.

Maybe it was a good thing she didn't go. She didn't exactly have a complex skill set, unless you maybe needed a drawing done or something.

She should quit worrying about it. She turned onto her side, drawing her blanket over head. She needed to get some sleep.

Felicity Bentsworth.

Felicity slapped a hand over her mouth to hold back a cry. She glanced around the room, slowly. It couldn't be.

Silence your mind.

But it was. It was the same voice from all those months ago. The one that took control of her body. No. No. No. "Please, no," she whispered, squeezing her eyes shut.

You're delaying the process.

What process?

There will be consequences.

"Go away," she murmured, tangling her fingers in her hair. "I don't care. Go away." I don't care. I don't care. What consequence? What did the voice want? Why right now? I don't care. I don't care. Silence her mind? That was impossible. It was louder than it'd ever been. I don't care. I don't care.

"Wake up!" Felicity jumped up, turning to face the window, where a silhouette of a figure in the dim light through the curtains banged on the window. She glanced at her tele. 5 AM GQ. That couldn't be right. She jumped from her bed, pulling on a sweater, and flung the door open. Cole rushed to greet her.

"Where have you been?" she gasped.

Cole was drenched head to toe, muddy up his waist, and an uncared for cut on his lip. "I—I was doing runs," he said, leaning against the door frame, taking in deep breaths. "I—I was at—at the east side's H-HCS center."

He took a deep breath, settling himself back up straight. He met Felicity's eyes. "The rain..The mountainside... A warning went out..."

The mountainside? Felicity's heart skipped a beat. The storm. "Oh no. A—a flood..."

"Then what are you waiting for? Get out of my way!"

Without warning, Tabitha shoved past Felicity, already dressed, hair tucked in her red cap, a belt around her rain coat, a full pack on her back, and dark lines under her eyes.

Cole stared at her with wide eyes, his lips parted. He shook off his shock quickly, turning to Felicity. "We don't have much time."

"We should get Taryn," Felicity stammered. Usually her first thought would be Miriam, since she would probably more easily join them over the Sergeant, but they didn't really have a choice. They couldn't handle an upcoming flood on their own. Could they?

"It'll take them too long," Tabitha said, rocking nervously on her heels. "Anyway, I don't want to cross that Giles again."

Right, *Giles*. Taryn wouldn't trust them with this if she'd heard about that mishap. Maybe it wasn't a good idea to go...

Felicity looked to Cole. "What do you think?"

She saw his pupils narrow, and he swallowed hard. His brows furrowed. "I—I—" Another body pushed past Felicity out onto the porch. "There isn't time to stand around," Nikki said, looking more alive than all of them, leaping effortlessly over the railing and dashing across the camp to the boy's cabin.

"We go, then," Cole decided, though there was hesitance in his voice. Tabitha dashed down the steps before he could even finish. Cole scrambled after her. "Meet us at my truck. Hurry!" Felicity let out a shallow sigh. She glanced at the main cabin, in its powerful height among the rest, it's curtains closed and peaceful.

They were a Council, weren't they? They were supposed to be helping others. Even if she was a wreck though? She had a weird voice telling her stuff in the middle of the night. What could she judge? She laughed harshly to herself, and slipped back into the cabin. She quickly changed into more sustainable clothing, stuffed a bag full of extra jackets, and ran from her door, before something caught her eye.

She froze, her hand on the door handle, staring at the spear leaning in the corner. She didn't need a weapon. It was just an evac mission—

Felicity snatched it from the wall and flew out the door,

and tore through the mud, and the light rain. She reached the truck where the other five were already piled in. Ray, Lincoln, and Nikki occupied the truck bed, finishing up fastening down new supply crates. Cole beckoned her into the passenger's seat, shouting at those in the back to get down.

Tabitha sat snugly in the back with three seats to her and her pack filled to the stretched seams. Cole started the truck with the press of his thumbprint. Taryn's old pickup truck shuddered to life. Cole had purchased it from the Sergeant with the money he earned on runs, and Felicity doubted he got his money's worth.

The inside smelled of gasoline, the paint was chipped and rusting, and had a charging system two generations out of date.

She prayed they'd make it down the road in one piece.

She clenched the sides of her seat and squeezed her eyes shut. Her only relief was the bouncing truck didn't feel, or sound, like a regular auto. She forced her fear down her throat, taking in deep inhales like she'd been taught.

"And you really thought you could teach them to drive in this thing?" Tabitha laughed of the banging.

"Learn in the worst, thrive in the best, Tabs."

The truck bounced.

"I want to learn. Why don't you teach *me*?"

"Legal reasons, Tabs."

Felicity's stomach settled at the comforting sound of their usual banter. "Well you don't have to tell my parents. Not like they'd even care."

"Breaking the law just isn't my thing."

Tabitha snorted. "Right."

"What'd you say?" Cole shouted as rain began to pelt the windshield.

"I said I hope Nikki and Lincoln know how lucky they are to not have any legal guardians!" "Just don't talk, Tabs."

Nikki and Lincoln had both turned sixteen over the months, though no one knew either of the amnesiacs' actual birthdates. Nikki had thought it was customary for everyone to just update their age by new year, which didn't give them much leads on where she came from, except for that they didn't really care for accuracy.

Lincoln was without a birthdate entirely, so they'd

dubbed him one. The second day of the year. She smiled at the thought of it, settling the tossing and turning of her stomach. She cracked an eye open. They were on the main road now, rain beating down harder on the windshield, keeping the little wiper busy. Tabitha leaned forward between the two front seats, her eyes wide at the sight out the windows.

The storm had come swiftly, and it was taking every ounce of courage in her to trust the extent of Cole's driving.

Once they hit the first road, her stomach tried to reach her throat, and her fingernails drove into the sides of the seat.

The hill led down into the fair fields near the base of the mountains. Coming down from the top gave Felicity a clear, watery view through the windshield. Trees and yellowed grasses were scattered across the plain, swaying in the harsh wind. Streams branched off down the mountain, along the red boulders till the base of the river... that was growing.

"Slow down!" Tabitha shouted.

Cole's eyes narrowed, his brows furrowed. "I am!"

Cole took a hard turn.

"Ray almost fell out!" Tabitha took hold of Cole's seat.

"Good for him!"

"You doing okay, Liz?" Tabitha said, her voice switching to a more gentle tone. Felicity gave her a queasy smile.

Trucks had already pulled up the Med tents. Medics, doctors, and patients were flooding out. Many civilian farmers were gathered around, most likely for a family member of the usual supply pickups. Cole pulled to a stop at the end of the road.

The director, as Felicity quickly identified by the flapping badge on his jacket and his blue armband, raced up to Cole's window. "You made it!" he said over the rain as the window slid away. "Our priority is evacuation. Top of the ridge till we can get further pickup. Can any of your friends drive?"

Felicity began to raise a shaking hand before Tabitha swatted it down. Probably smart. She hardly remembered the last time she'd driven, and the thought was more terrifying than controlling her anxiety riding in an auto.

Cole shook his head, getting out. "But they have good composure under pressure, and a large skill-set."

"Good." The director ran an anxious hand through his soaked hair. "Most of our equipment shorted out—"

Lincoln jumped from the truck bed, his hefty messenger bag clanging with him. "I can fix it." "I'm sorry, but you can't. Not this quickly. They're busted."

Lincoln snorted. "Show me."

"Bring him," Cole reassured. "We'll lead the evacuation."

The leader gave a firm nod, surprising Felicity with his assurance in them. "Thank you." Felicity took a deep breath, and lept from her seat into the second emergency they'd faced in the storm. How long could it last?

"Someone stop Nikki from using her hand!" Ray shouted right before he illegally glinted out of sight and appeared at the tent doors, and rushed in.

Nikki just glared at where he stood.

"Just do what you can," Felicity said, even though she knew it sounded pathetic. "Guard the truck!"

"Who's going to steal it?"

She had a point. "Just stay put."

Nikki heaved a sigh, but did as she was told, climbing swiftly to the roof of the truck and plopping down.

Felicity took off toward the evacuating crowd. Some were taking the trek up the hill toward the ridge, and others were loading into trucks and trailers. Over half the crowd had the drooping pale eyes and dragging feet of the fever. She suppressed a shudder. She knew it wasn't contagious. It was caused by North Cordell's unclean water and sources out in the farms, but that didn't stop her nerves.

She pushed forward into the crowd. Out of the corner of Felicity's eyes, she saw a patient trip and stumble backward, torn from the person they'd been clinging to for support. Felicity didn't even realize she'd reacted till she'd caught the frail frame of the young teenager from hitting the muddy ground. She quickly thrust them to their feet as the caretaker tore against the current of the ground to recollect them.

The young, pale eyes stared back at Felicity in wonder, giving a breathless "thank you." "There's a truck loading up right over there!" Felicity said, her heart hammering against her chest. She pointed to a truck that had just parked its trailer a few feet away. "You'll be safer getting to the ridge."

The caretaker gave her a nod and turned for the trailer.

Felicity ran out of the crowd, running up the hill beside them. No doubt they'd be in need of immediate assistance there. She pushed herself faster, silently thanking Taryn for all the early morning laps around the camp.

A sudden pain shot through her thigh, sending Felicity flying face first to the mud. She scrambled to her feet, trying to wipe her face clean and ignore the new nagging pain in her leg. She must have fallen on it weird or something earlier. She didn't have time to check. She only paused a moment to catch her breath and pick up her trail uphill, pushing the pain to the bottom of the list of her ever-growing problems.

8

TABITHA WAS FAR FROM A RULE FOLLOWER, BUT FOR ONCE SHE wished the law was on their side. Taryn would know far better what to do than they did.

She stood holding the door of the Med tent open. Anyone could've done that. She wasn't like the world's unrenowned doorstop. Why was she here instead of a Defender? She should really start thinking things through.

Ray burst from the tent, a small group of Medics barging out after him. He caught Tabitha's eyes, turning on his heel, and rushed to meet her. "The tent's empty. We should be all clear." Tabitha breathed with relief. "Good."

"Lincoln got the generators working so they have something to work with for now." Ray's shoulder's heaved, his eyes drifting to the mountains, like the inevitable flash flood would be stopped just with a glare. He swallowed. "We should get out of here."

"You go," Tabitha said, letting the door fall shut. She scanned the crowd, staring her eyes for a familiar blond head. "I'm going to find Cole."

Ray frowned at her for a moment. "Alright. Stay safe. Don't die."

"I'll try."

With that, he took off after the evacuation. Tabitha ran through the field, spotting the truck still parked. Nikki was gone. Good.

At least she was out of harm's way.

She raced across the field, mud beginning to weigh her every step. Where was he? Maybe Cole had gone to the ridge and she just hadn't seen him. But would he really leave the truck behind? "Cole!" Her voice hardly resounded against the storm. "Coleson Johnson! Where are you?" She stared nervously at the mountains.

"Tabitha Delorous!" Cole's cry tore through her mind, echoing against her skull. She whirled around, seeing him standing, drenched to the bone, without a jacket, his eyes intent on her. "Cole!" She began after him when he began shaking his head wildly and pointing.

"Tabitha, look!"

Tabitha turned, feeling as though the air had been torn from her. A small boy, in only a wet knit sweater, shorts, and socks, in the downpour, standing proudly on a boulder. How did he get there? She didn't really have time to figure that out. She raced to him, not daring to look toward the mountains again. Just a flood... deadly flood. No blood. The grasses pulled at her legs, the rain seeming to seep into her bones. She trudged faster. Who cared if her fingers fell off?

She reached the boulder.

The boy looked down to her. "Hi!" he shouted, with a beaming smile full of chattering teeth.

"Hello!" Tabitha called up to him. The boulder wasn't too big. She could scale it awkwardly if she had to. "You need to come down. There's a flood."

"I can't leave!" the little boy said, shaking his head, plopping down. He couldn't be older than five, from the youthful fat on his cheeks. "I'm looking for a doctor."

"The doctors are all gone, lil' guy. Come down."

"No!" he shouted back to her. "Bel's very sick and sick people need doctors!"

Tabitha's heart skipped a beat. "Bel?"

"Yes." He sat, firmly staring forward before his eyes

glanced back to her. "Where are the doctors?"

"They're not here," Tabitha said, beginning to fit her footing on the crevice of the boulder. "You need to come down *right now*, lil' guy—"

"No!" he shouted. "I can't! I need a doctor!"

They had maybe ten minutes to spare. *Maybe*. She didn't have time for this. "I know a doctor!"

His eyes lit up. "You do?"

"Yes," Tabitha lied, nodding her head enthusiastically and plastering an exaggerated smile. "I do. Now if you'll come down, we can go to Bella."

"Bel."

"Oka, Bel! Come on!" Tabitha slipped backwards, landing back into the mud. "Please!" The little boy stared at her curiously before sliding down the boulder in a tumble, rolling through the mud beside her. "O-kay," he said.

Tabitha breathed a sigh of relief. She grabbed the little boy's hand, pulling them both to their feet. She dared a glance back at the mountains. She ran toward Cole, who seeing her with the boy, ran for the truck.

The small hand in hers was like trying to keep hold of a dancing fish. The slippery little hand kept slipping out and stumbling back. Tabitha finally gave up, scooping the tiny boy up in her arms, and ran. It was either leave him behind or go a little slower.

The truck's front lights brightened to life, beginning in Tabitha's direction. Cole met her, rolling the window down. "In! Now!"

She ran to the passenger door. "You don't have to tell me twice." She scrambled inside the truck, slamming the door shut. It bounced back. She cursed, pulling it shut harder, locking it. "Go!" Cole took a wide turn, sending her left. She grabbed the seat in one hand, and the kid in the other.

The truck gave a loud grunt, and Tabitha held her breath as they tore up the road. Another grunt. The truck slowed, and suddenly began to roll backward.

Tabitha's chest clenched. This wasn't happening.

"No. No. No!" Cole banged on the pedal. The truck whirred and pulled forward. "Only a few more feet," he announced through gritted teeth. The creaking truck pulled forward, taking what felt like forever before it slowed onto level ground. Cole didn't stop for a breath of relief, but Tabitha could see it in his face as they drove forward, his entire body relaxing, looking as if he might collapse. "If this wasn't a Defender truck..."

"Defender?" the little boy exclaimed. Tabitha had almost forgotten about him sitting on her lap. He'd been so quiet through the truck affair. "You're a Defender?"

Cole turned, seeming to have the same realization, before turning back to the road. He cracked a smile and a hoarse laugh. "No, but I have friends."

The boy's face lit up, her jaw hanging open, looking like he might burst. The boy, Tabitha was sure, was around five, and small at that. His skin had a subtle tan, and his hair was a dark brown and riddled with drenched curls. His eyes were a brilliant green as they turned to stare up into Tabitha's.

"I need a doctor," he said, his face becoming solemn.

"A doctor?" Cole said, a brow raised.

"Bel is very sick!" the little boy shouted, his eyes beginning to brim with tears. "Where is the doctor?"

"Hey, it's okay." Tabitha said. Her mind scrambled to try to comfort the kid, settling for a pat on the head. "We're going to make sure er—Bel is okay. Where do you live?"

"By the lots of trees."

Well... very helpful. "Um. Where in the trees?"

"The farm."

"He couldn't have run far. The closest farms are the eastside." Cole's voice was hollow, and his eyes stared hard in front of him.

The eastside. That would explain his sister. The sickness was raging there. Her heart hammered against her chest, echoing to her ears, as Cole took a harsh turn in the fork of the road. "Hey buddy, do you mind getting in the back? You'll have more room."

The boy happily jumped from Tabitha's lap and tumbled into the beaten leather backseat. He sat with his legs crossed, staring with a smile forward. "My name is Charles."

"I'm Cole."

Tabitha took her focus away from them, humming. She hummed when she was nervous, thinking of her beloved binder back in her cabin to calm herself.

Out the window, the vast wheat fields began to show

themselves. No doubt they wouldn't survive. Huge, U-shaped machines were parched halfway, usually manned during a good day. The field went on forever, swaying to the rhythm of the rain. It sent a shiver down Tabitha's spine. Barns spotted the fields. She spotted a few heads rushing to them. Some had stopped to stare at the solo truck trekking through the road.

"Any messages from Felicity?" Cole asked.

Tabitha picked up the Communicator, clicking the screen. "Nothing."

Cole nodded, starting down the road. Tabitha zoned out for a moment, staring out the window into the grey sky above them. They ran over a bush, jolting Tabitha back into focus. She looked around, a sick feeling creeping into her stomach.

"Which house is yours, Charles?" Cole asked.

Charles hopped up between them, pointing to a few roads down the fork. "There." Cole nodded, turning in as instructed. Tabitha frowned. The crops here lie limply. The long road overgrown with weeds as if hardly driven on. The dying trees looming on the side of the road, the broken fence.

It was all so familiar.

She wanted to scream.

In the distance she knew lay a grey, beaten house, one she never wanted to see again.

Nikki had rushed to Lincoln's aide, as he laid underneath a farmer's auto, banging away. She cradled his bag in her arms.

The rain hadn't let up, but the patients were safe from the flooding fields, though being out in the storm no doubt didn't have a good effect on their conditions.

"Nik! Can you hand me the shock-wrench?"

Most of Lincoln's tools were made by himself, and so far, Nikki had been the only one to properly remember all their names.

She handed him the metal bar, tipped in metallic blue.

Nikki turned to scan the ridge, watching the crowd push for a new trailer. The farmer had to forcefully push through the crowd, to lock the doors shut, and apologize about his lack of room. The crowd backed away reluctantly.

The blankets from Cole's supply proved to be the most useful, though there was hardly enough for everyone. Hopefully they wouldn't have to wait too long in the rain—

"Nik! Handle-driver! One without the rubble handle."

She found it under his spare hoodie, and tossed it to him. "Do you think we should call for more help?"

"They probably already have." A buzz of electricity came from under the auto. "They're tough people, Nik."

He had a point, but it didn't soothe the ache in her chest as a group of young women huddled on a boulder out of the mud.

Once they finished the new Inn, they'd be able to help these suffering families get back on their feet, Nikki told herself. She was going to do it. If only she was ready now. For the past six months, it felt like they were stuck at a standstill. They stayed at the camp, where they were comfortable, trained a bit, and listened to some lectures, but they never moved much past the guidance of the Sergeant.

What would it take?

Lincoln's head appeared out from under the auto, his face smeared with mud and oil. He held out the tools, and she took them. "Should be working smoothly now."

"Good."

He frowned at her, crawling out from under the auto, kneeling beside her. "You look worried, Nik."

"I am."

"You want to talk?"

Nikki shook her head and buckled his bag closed. She handed it to him.

He eyed her, putting it over his shoulder. "You sure?"

She nodded and stood up, Lincoln following up after her. Not that her growing frustration could be solved by her complaining.

She only hoped Lincoln could find his worth himself.

A bearded farmer turned the corner, his eyes brightening on seeing them. "Is it fixed?"

"Better than new." Lincoln wiped the mud from his hands to his pants. "The storm doesn't seem to be letting up—"

"Thanks, kid," the farmer chuckled. "I'll get a move on."

He clambered into the front seat, and as expected, a few

moments later, the auto burst to life. "Amazing how destructive some mud and water can do to these low manufactured autos." Lincoln sighed and shook his head. "*You* could probably even fix them if I taught you." NIkki wasn't sure whether that was an insult or not, so she decided on the latter. Lincoln and Nikki walked toward the buzzing crowd, where the sound of the new upstarted auto had sparked new life, many rushing to the doors in hopes of getting a seat.

"Are you sure they'll have enough?" Nikki asked, unable to train her eyes away. A young woman pulled away, clutching an elderly man, her face falling with disappointment as the door closed. "The sooner we get back, the sooner we can get Taryn, but right now we have the west side organization on our side," Lincoln said.

"E's father's farm is there, right?" Felicity appeared between them, an umbrella in hand. It was a peculiar mechanism that shielded them from rain with a solid hologram. "Yep," Lincoln said. "Best scrap fields in the region."

Considering his blacksmith son, Nikki didn't doubt it.

"And lowest infection rate of the fever," Felicity sighed. "Good thinking."

"Good thing we have your indestructible Liberty tele... wait where is that thing?" Lincoln frowned.

"Ray has it," Felicity said. "He's helping someone contact their auto shop employee back in the town."

Lincoln's shoulders heaved, grabbing his temples. "Good. An auto shop's help would be great. Everything we can do seems covered. Maybe we'll have some spare time to stop in town ourselves."

"We'll have to be quick." Felicity's eyes drifted upward to the stirring sky. "We don't have a great ride back to camp."

Nikki stopped. Where *were* Cole and Tabitha? Now that she thought about it, she hadn't seen them for hours.

Her heart hammered. They couldn't have gotten caught in the flood, could they? He hand went to the Stone in her pocket as if it would have an answer.

"I'm going to find Ray," Lincoln said, starting into a run. "Meet you back in a few."

"Got it," Felicity said, with a nod and smile. She turned

to Nikki and cheery expression faltered. "Is everything alright?"

Nikki's eyes drifted to the flooding field below. "I—I think Ta—"

Someone grabbed her arm from behind. Felicity shrieked. Nikki swiveled and landed a swift kick to the ankle of... Ray?

He winced hard, but didn't give a moment for words before they were thrust into a pixelated darkness, feeling as though every piece of her was torn apart and thrust back together suddenly, landing with a thud in the muddy grasses.

Cole saw Tabitha freeze up. He ached to apologize, but they needed to go back. "Please no," He heard her gasp, pressing herself into the seat.

"Tabitha," Cole said, his voice firm.

Tabitha took in a few shaky breaths, seeming to try to pick up a hum, but she quickly dropped it. "I just-" She cut herself off with a gasp for air.

Cole glanced over, seeing her staring at her sweaty, shaking palms. Why, of all places the boy could've lived, was it this one? The only thing that had ever made him see Tabitha cry. That scared him more than anything.

"It's so real," She muttered. "Never before did I think life was something so... real."

Cole's eyes widened. "That's what's been bothering you?"

Tabitha shifted in her seat, turning toward him, her arms wrapped around herself. "It's like... if someday... if I had children, I couldn't watch them die," She gasped for air. "I couldn't. Life that was caused by me... killed so easily."

"That—that wasn't your fault." He couldn't even think

straight. He told himself to focus on the road, his mind fighting against him to turn to her.

Tabitha was afraid of the gruesome reality of watching her own children die. In this day in age, young death was common in lower regions, but it must not have hit her till then. The thought *scared* her, and this was the place that reminded her the most. "Tabs... you're still young-" "I'm 17! Most kids my age are married by now in the lower class. I'm a Liberty reject!" He couldn't argue that, his stomach becoming a pit. From the little he knew about his mother, he knew she'd been young when she met his father for the brief time they were together. For all he knew, she could have been his age when she had him and Felicity's age when she died. "Tabitha." He forced her name out. "You're strong, Tabs. A lot stronger than most people I know."

"Death has its way. It sends you two inexperienced kids to slaughter your child." Cole gripped the wheel harder. "You'll never be alone in this situation, Tabs," he said, turning his eyes to her briefly. "I'll make sure of it."

Tabitha tilted her head, leaning across the divide between them. "Really, how?" "Somehow," Cole said, with an awkward laugh.

Tabitha placed her hand onto Cole's shoulder. "I'll keep that in mind, Goldfish." "I'll be with you too!' Charles said.

His compassion was heartwarming for a kid who'd they'd known for maybe a total of twenty minutes. Cole tried to force an uneasy smile for him.

The truck jolted again. Cole sucked in his breath, watching leaning grey houses grow closer. Some of the torn shutters whipped wildly against the house in the wind, the crops in the distance swaying. Tents were set up all around the main tents as they were per their last visit. The truck came to a stop, Tabitha flying forward, Cole slammed his arm in front of her. "This thing needs seatbelts," he hissed under his breath.

"I think it's fun!" Charles exclaimed.

"Glad you think so," Tabitha said, unblinking.

Cole set a gentle hand on hers. She surprised him by squeezing it to the point it seared with pain. "I can't do this," she whispered.

"Yes, you can," he assured her.

She let go of his hand, and he climbed out of the seat, letting Charles free from the back, in which he practically backflipped into the mud. Tabitha trudged from her side to them, holding her jacket close. The rain hadn't lightened. The sky only grew darker. Cole glanced back to the mountains. He hoped the others were safe. Guilt panged his gut to think he'd left them alone. He didn't have time to self loathe. He grabbed Charles' hand and they both rushed urgently to the door.

It was wooden, a rarity these days, probably used to be decorated with carvings before they'd eroded to lumps and chipped white paint. The door handle, another classic, was practically hanging by its screws. "You sure Bel isn't in one of the tents?" Cole asked.

"Cain wouldn't like that." Charles fearlessly kicked the door a few times.

The door suddenly cracked open, Tabitha and Cole jumping back. Charles leapt through the door pushing it open, crashing into the older boy that stood in the doorframe. "Cents! I got a doctor!"

The older boy looked to them, then his eyes widened in horror. Dark lines were under his similar green eyes through the thick lenses of his glasses, his dirty shirt not fully buttoned. The end of his trousers were nothing but beat rags.

A dark frown settled on his face as he dropped to his knees and he grabbed Charles' shoulders firmly. "You ran off without telling me?"

"Bel needs a doctor."

"Charles!" The older boy let Charles free, pinching the bridge of his nose, before taking a deep breath and turning to face Cole and Tabitha. Despite his ragged appearance, he had a fearlessness in his eyes when he faced them and got to his feet. "You're from the camp. The ones who came after the accident."

Tabitha froze under his glare.

Cole nodded. "We are."

Tabitha pushed forward. "How is the man?" she asked, reminding Cole that there had indeed been a farmer caught in the wreck.

"Dead," Lawrence snapped, his words harsh and cold.

There was a moment of stunned silence.

Tabitha fumbled over her words. "I... I thought he was at—at the Med—"

"He died on the way there," Lawrence said. A whimper came from the boy behind him. That seemed to soften him, as he turned and scooped Charles into his arms. "We've managed alright without him, if that's what you're going to ask. Condolences appreciated truly and surely, all that. Very nice."

Tabitha gulped.

Cole ignored the brashness. "Charles brought us here because of someone named Bel. A fever victim."

Tabitha fought back shooting Cole an outright glare. Why did they have to stop here and help these people when so many in North Cordell were suffering? She wanted to get away as quickly as possible.

He lightly kicked her foot, and she turned her head back and the answer was blown back in her face, watching as the two brothers stared back at her.

They couldn't say no.

Lawrence opened his mouth to speak, when the younger boy pushed past him and shouted. "She's in bed. Cain says no one's allowed to touch her though. He says she's gonna make it, but Cents said he lied. So I got a doctor," Charles said proudly, looking up from his brother's shoulder.

Lawrence's face flushed red, his fists tensing.

"Cain *is* a liar, Charles," he growled under his breath.

Charles wrinkled his nose, nodding. "He's gone in town, Cents. Miz says he'll back tonight." Lawrence raised an eyebrow. He looked up to them, beginning to quiver. Decision reached between his brows. He stepped back. Cole's heart began to fall.

Lawrence looked up from the ground, his eyes dark. "Come in, quick," he said, stepping aside. "We don't have much time before he gets back."

10

They had all crashed into a field. Nikki didn't even try to process it and just laid on the ground trying to catch her breath.

Lincoln was also there, looking nearly recovered, though he still looked a bit dazed, and wobbling upward.

Felicity on the other hand, shot to her feet, turned, and vomited.

Ray cringed, gripping his ankle. "Sorry. Jeez, Nikki. That kick *hurt*."

Felicity moaned, shooting him a weak death glare. "You deserved it."

"Ask next time," Nikki said, getting up to her swaying feet.

"Sorry," Ray muttered again, though the apology was more rushed than sincere now. He pulled out Felicity's phone from his pocket, tapping the screen repeatedly till it burst to life. "Cole told me to come here."

"At least be more specific," Felicity said picking herself up, seeming a still little shaken, clenching her stomach trying to simultaneously wipe the mud from her arm. "Some girl is dying from the fever."

"Oh." Felicity solemned, her eyes falling. She paused a moment before picking up her voice again. "I don't want to be insensitive, but-but tons of people die. What makes this so different that he wants to save her and specifically us?"

Ray looked to Nikki, and it clicked. She gulped, holding her good arm to her chest.. She knew he meant the P9F Healing File that was in her bloodstream. If things came to it, her blood itself could be a saving factor through a complicated transaction.

Lincoln looked back and forth between Nikki and Ray before his own eyes lit up with realization. "It can't be that bad."

Ray cringed at the mention of it. "It can't help to be prepared. I trust Cole." Nikki nodded. Cole knew what he was doing, right?

She looked to the eerie house in the distance, took a deep breath, and ran. There was no way she was going to let Ray teleport them again. Nikki looked over her shoulder to Lincoln and Felicity, who seemed to have recovered from her shock, following her.

They finally reached the front door that had been left wide open, the inside doormat soaked with the rain pouring in, the wind blowing it wildly. Nikki hesitated to walk in uninvited, but Ray had no such courtesy, waltzing right in like he owned the place. Nikki followed after him. Stepping inside, Nikki was thrust into a wall of smells. Musty, sour, and heavy of dirt, and a stench of smoke, explained by the discarded cigarette butts lying in the corner, by a pile of muddy work boots and coats.

Lincoln slammed the door shut against the wind behind them. The walls rattled. The four of them exchanged glances.

"Cheery place, isn't it?" Ray said.

Felicity elbowed him.

The hairs on Nikki's neck pricked up. A clatter of footsteps suddenly filled the air. Everyone froze.

Nikki quickly dropped into a stance.

Two people turned the corner to the entrance hall, stopping in their tracks. "Cole!" Ray cried with relief.

The second boy stared through the thick lenses of his glasses to Nikki, his frown faltering. *Lawrence*. She nearly burst out into a smile and rushed to greet him, when she stopped herself. The mysterious farm boy lived... here?

She glanced around the dirt smeared walls and rickety floors once more. That didn't seem right. He must have sensed her confusion, as his face instantly hardened, giving her a shaky nod. She returned it.

"Where is the woman? What's going on?" Lincoln demanded.

"We don't have much time—" Cole began.

Lawrence, on the other hand, didn't hesitate, turning and running.

They all dashed after him. She ran up a flight of squeaking stairs into a disastrous hallway. It was a mess with random clothes, the wall smudged with more dirt and fingerprints. Lawrence led them to the end, opening another door down another flight of stairs, and burst through a door, to a dimly lit room that smelled awfully strong of a cigar. The room was nearly empty, except for a cheap bed frame, and a small, frail figure curled on the mattress. They all froze. The air was still and stale.

Nikki slowly took a step toward the woman. She was deathly pale, and slim. Her face had a grayish tone to it. Her long matted blonde hair was strewn about her, a handful of it clenched in the woman's fist. Ray approached her, gently rolling her onto her back. Nikki saw the panic begin to rise in his eyes as he examined her.

"Why haven't you gotten a Medic sooner?" He asked, whirling around to Lawrence. Lawrence's jaw clenched. He didn't answer Ray, just turned his focus away, walking to the shutters, closing them.

The woman coughed, her body jolting, a pained groan escaped her mouth. "She's been sick for months. It was just mild then. They thought they'd just recover," Lawrence said, looking back over his shoulder to the door. "But it's gotten worse, ever since she's been pregnant."

Nikki felt as though something had slammed her in the chest. She held her breath, her mind trying to recollect itself. It was hardly noticeable now, the woman midress covered by her legs. "She's what?" Ray's jaw fell, his eyes anxiously glancing from face to face as if they'd have answers. Ray pressed his hand against her forehead. "She needs to be at a H.C.S Center." "There's not one for hours," Cole said. "The closest thing we had is the pop-up camp, and that's come."

Nikki's heart skipped a beat. "There's a Medic center at camp."

Lawrence's eyes grew wide. "She can't leave!" he shouted.

"She's dying!" Ray snapped.

Lawrence's face hardened into a glare. "Look, we agreed."

"Your terms aren't working out," Cole said.

Ray sighed. "Well come up with something we can work with. Nikki, get yourself over here. Cole, the Medic kit's in the back of the truck," Ray snapped.

Cole nodded, darting out the door and up the stairs. Nikki walked over to Ray, beginning to remove her jacket. "Isn't this dangerous?" She said. "You said only if-"

"This is an emergency," Ray said. "Just, do you think you can handle it?"

Nikki nodded, folding the jacket neatly, setting it down on the table beside the bed. Of course, it depended on how much of the File Ray needed to extract from her blood stream. Too much taken too fast would be dangerous. Ray had been able to do it once with his Oquelite abilities, but after the whole Lincoln incident, Taryn thought it was safer in the future not to perform the procedure, though it didn't stop Ray from acquiring an official transfusion machine from his other, and figuring out how to keep Nikki's mental state stable while doing so with his abilities. If it actually worked? Nikki had no idea.

Cole came barreling back into the room, the kit in hand, tossing it to Ray, who caught it without fail.

"What are you doing?" Lawrence asked, frowning.

Ray didn't answer him, pulling Nikki's arm forward, searching through the kit. "Cole, come hold this thing," Ray said.

And that's how Cole's arms became Ray's table.

Ray pierced Nikki's arm, pulling the sharp tool slowly through her skin, blood beginning to slowly emerge from the wound. Nikki shifted her focus away to the woman lying on the bed, her chest rising and falling rapidly. She coughed again, her body curling, letting out another pained moan. Out of the corner of her eye, Nikki saw Lawrence wince, turning his head away. Without warning, Nikki's body jolted, almost like she had been shocked. She shook her head. Ray muttered an apology, as he began to quickly look the other side to the woman. He turned to Nikki. "You need to sit down."

She shook her head, but as soon as the machine was flicked on she regretted that decision, her entire mind going blank. Various sounds around her, vague bits of knowledge wandering past. Pain searing from every part of her arm.

The world burst back, and she found herself leaning against the wall and the bed, the tips of Ray's fingers on her temples. She gasped for air, pulling back from him. Ray fell back, gripping his head in pain. "Thirty whole minutes," he groaned.

Nikki grabbed the end of the table and the frame of the bed, pulling herself back to her feet. She looked down at the woman again, still restless and pale. It seemed as if nothing had even happened. Nikki shuddered. Ray got back to his feet, his face visibly drained from the amount of essence he'd used to keep her stable. Dark lines had formed under his eyes, his hair a strewn mess, worried lines creased on his forehead.

"It didn't-" Nikki began, looking to Ray.

Ray shook his head, brushing his hand through his hair. Lawrence stopped pacing by the door, glancing back and forth between her and Ray.

"Any more than this, it could be dangerous," Ray said, again, his voice weary and drained. The door burst open, slamming into Lawrence.

"You have to!" A child's voice called out. "You have to save her!"

Charles stood in the doorway. He began to choke on sobs, tears streaming down his face. Lawrence looked to him in horror. He picked up the boy, who wrapped his arms around his neck, crying into his shoulder. "Cents, save her!" The boy yelled into Lawrence's shoulder, his fists tensing. For the first time since they'd arrived, Nikki saw Lawrence's face genuinely soften, running his fingers through the boy's hair, holding him tightly against him. "Hey, Charles, she's gonna be fine," Lawrence whispered, softly. "Calm down. She's gonna be okay."

Tabitha burst into the room, out of breath. "Sorry. He just-"

Tabitha froze in the doorway. She turned her eyes away from the woman back to Lawrence, her hands growing shaky. "I-I'm sorry," she muttered.

Lawrence shook his head. "It's fine."

Cole went swiftly to Tabitha's side. Nikki, being hooked up to a machine that gave her about a three foot radius to move, was grateful. Nothing scared her more than the night she saw Tabitha break. It ran quite close to Lincoln's bloody, beaten body from being crushed. Lawrence attempted to set Charles down, but Charles refused. "Charles," Lawrence said, calmly, but stern. "You need to go with them. Can you listen to me?"

"You have to save her," Charles choked.

Lawrence whispered something into Charles' ear, the boy looking up, brushing the tears from his face. Lawrence set the boy down, and he reluctantly went to Tabitha. She followed him out from the room, closing the door behind them.

"Your brother?" Cole asked.

Lawrence's face hardened again, nodding. He strode to Ray, looking to the woman. "Give her more."

"More? Have you not heard a word I've said?" Ray called out, giving a frustrated scowl.

"I don't care!" Lawrence snapped. His eyes widened, seeming surprised with himself. He pushed the glasses in their place. "Do anything. Anything you can do here. Please." Ray sighed, a frustrated, reluctant one. "You alright, Nikki?"

She nodded. Ray motioned for Cole to begin, pressing his fingers against her temples. He looked her hard in the eyes. "I can tell you lied," he muttered.

Nikki could feel her mind being pulled. "Alright is a general question," she murmured, feeling the world being pulled again into the lonely, cold abyss of her mind.

"Ray! Wake up!"

Someone hit him in the face. Ray shot up. Nikki and Cole leaned above him. He began to sit up, his head piercing in pain. He put his palms over his eyes, groaning. "Which one of you slapped me?" He moaned.

"She did."

Ray opened his eyes, frowning through his fingers at Nikki. "Lincoln is a bad influence on you." Cole and Nikki helped him to his feet. Ray froze, the woman that only a few moments in his memory prior was lying on the bed looking like a ghost, was sitting up on the bed, her face still pale and sweaty, but she was very much alive. And now that she looked at him with those eyes, she was... beautiful. Everything about her was absolutely flawless. Her round face, the light freckles across her face, even her matted hair now seemed immaculate.

Cole nudged him, and Ray immediately felt embarrassed, shaking the realization away. Lawrence stood beside her.

"H-how are you feeling?" Ray managed to say.

"M-much... better," she said, her voice worn and scratchy, as she pushed sweat from her eyes. "T-thank you."

She squeezed Lawrence's hand, looking up to him. "Water?" She choked out.

"I can," Nikki said. Ray realized someone had removed the machine from her arm. She took the cup from the table, running swiftly into the small bathroom beside them. The woman leaned against Lawrence. "Girl?"

Nikki came back quickly, sitting down on the end of the bed and handing the glass to the woman, who gave her a grateful nod. With shaking hands, she drank it like it was the last thing she'd ever have. She marveled at Nikki. Her face shifted to a slight, pained frown. "Your eyes," she muttered. "Blue?"

Nikki nodded. The woman's face softened. "Isabel," She said, weakly placing her hand on top of Nikki's. She then leaned into Lawrence. "Brother, Lawrence."

"We've met," Nikki said, nodding to Lawrence.

So the woman was Lawrence's sister. It explained a lot of things. Not so much the mess or the abundance of a mess. Was every farm like this?

"Nikki," Nikki informed her, turning to Cole and Ray. "Coleson Johnson and Rapheal Mathews." Ray pointed to his brother. "Cole-" and then to himself "-Ray."

Isabel nodded, rubbing her lips together. She looked up

to Lawrence. "Does Cain know? Is he here?"

Lawrence's eyes shifted around the room. Isabel's face grew grave. "It'll be alright. Won't it?" She looked to Lawrence. "Pater?"

Lawrence opened his mouth to speak, then shut it again. "B-bel."

Isabel looked away, letting go of Lawrence's hand, her eyes wide. She coughed, grasping her chest in pain. Tears glistened in her eyes. "What... happening?"

"Not a long story," Lawrence said. "But a lot. A lot's happened."

Isabel looked to Nikki, tightening her grip on her hand, with a weak, but dazzling smile. "I can tell."

11

First things first, Lawrence was relieved to get away from the stuffy, crowded room. The rain had begun to let up.

Isabel insisted he go get some air and find Charles. He knew he wasn't being much of a help either, standing there, not having a word to mutter beside an occasional comment on the situation. The constant reminder of time was nagging at his mind.

You don't have time.

He turned around the corner, the two towering metal barns coming into sight, their shadows casting down over the fields.

The guy, Cole, had been right. Isabel couldn't survive there. He knew it. It was obvious from the moment she woke up.

On the side of the house, Charles was curled up, his legs pulled up to his chest, watching the other small boys run and fight in the dirt yard that extended from the house to the gate that allowed you to enter the fields. The boy, Lincoln, sat next to Charles quietly. Charles looked up for a moment, blinking, a smile burst on his face. He scrambled to his feet and launched himself at Lawrence.

Lawrence grit his teeth in pain, having to hold Charles back a bit. Stupid side. His little brother stared, wide-eyed with innocence, up into his eyes.

"Easy," Lawrence said, catching his breath.

Charles flashed him a smile, patting him gently on the shoulder.

Lincoln got up, seeing Lawrence, but almost as soon as he did, the swarm of the younger boys rammed into him, Lincoln becoming their new target. Lawrence rushed to help him. "It's fine," Lincoln said, smiling. He pushed through to Lawrence, ignoring the mud-clad boys clinging to his legs and fighting each other around him.

Lawrence's nerves settled a little, catching a swift glance at the boy's eyes. They had been dark. He knew that, but they were black. Lawrence swallowed hard. So Lincoln was the other one from Imperial.

Lincoln pushed the abundance of messy, soaked hair from his face, then shoved his hands into his pockets. "How'd it go?" he asked. "Is she—"

Lawrence nodded. "She's awake."

Lincoln's eyes widened, and Charles leaned into Lawrence again, more gentle this time, hugging him tightly. "She's awake, Cents? You did it. Didn't you, Cents?"

"So you're Cents?" Lincoln said, tilting his head. "He kept talking about this... Cents." Lawrence sighed, looking down to Charles, who gave him another big smile. The kid really refused to call him anything else, didn't he?

Lawrence looked back up to Lincoln. "Yeah... it's a name," he said, shrugging slightly. The back door swung open, a few more children running out, the door slamming shut behind them.

"Are they... all your siblings?" Lincoln asked, frowning as he watched the newcomers run to play along the fence.

Lawrence smirked. "Heck, no. Only Charles and Bel," he said, crossing his arms. "They're from all the other farms, and people in the tents. Most of them are picked up from town and legally owned by the eastside farm."

Any household with more than two children received a monthly delivery of money per child. Lawrence knew it wasn't uncommon for people to pick orphans up from the side of the streets and register them as your own. He'd seen it throughout almost all the farms to train them as farm hands.

Lincoln nodded, seeming to know it all too well. "When I was younger, I had two farmers try to bring me in as a farm hand," he said, his voice lowering.

Lawrence frowned. "You were on the streets?"

Lincoln shrugged, his eyes shifting away. "For a time," he said. "I ended up moving into the mountains."

"Huh." The mountains? Did he ever cross paths? He couldn't possibly have. The boy would've said something by now, no doubt. He'd seen the Sergeant's urgency.

He'll say yes if you tell him. Ask him now, idiot.

"Is your family in the mountain?" Charles asked.

"No," Lincoln sighed. "Don't remember."

Lawrence didn't have a chance to ask, as the amber eyed boy skidded around the corner. He was out of breath, his face flushed.

He nodded quickly to Lawrence.

"Have you seen Cole?" He asked Lincoln.

"Saw him with Tabitha. She's probably having another breakdown of sorts," Lincoln said.

Ray sighed. "Again?" He grumbled, folding his hands into his jacket. The wind began to pick up again. "One moment they're arguing over paint colors, and the next they're comforting each other like a married couple."

"Did you come out here with an actual purpose?" Lincoln asked, raising an eyebrow to Ray. "Besides looking for Cole? Uh, yeah. Not useless, Black Eyes," Ray said, crossing his arms with a smirk. He turned to Lawrence. "Your sister is all caught up. Felicity's with Nikki in the front. She wants to talk things over with all of us. You too... Laurel? Right."

"Law*rence*," Charles corrected.

Ray nodded, not looking to the small boy. "Yeah. She wants to talk things over, and see what the plan is for the future to get more help... for your sister. Then of course, head back."

"Go back?" Lawrence said, immediately regretting the words as soon as they'd left his mouth. He shook his head.

"Yes, of course. Go back."

Make a decision.

Charles squeezed his hand. He looked up to Lawrence longingly, biting on his lower lip. Lawrence let go of Charles' hand and pat him on the head. "I'll be back. Get inside and change into something warmer. Got it?"

Charles nodded. "Yes, Cents. Can I hug you real soft?"

"Sure."

Charles gently wrapped his arms around Lawrence's waist and hugged him. "Bye, Cents."

"Get inside. Hurry up," Lawrence said, pushing Charles along.

Lawrence turned and rushed to catch up behind the two others. He tried to put confidence in his step, but it had long past failed him.

He was running out of time.

The conversation itself was short lived, arriving to the quick conclusion of coming back in a few days with new medical supplies to further help Bel. They'd found Tabitha, who seemed to be stable at the moment, and Cole. Lawrence could barely focus on what was happening around

him, nodding pointlessly, his vision going in and out of focus in thought. "It's settled then," Cole said, finally, looking up toward the sky that had begun to dim in the past few minutes, the air growing colder. "Two days."

Lawrence nodded. *Hurry up. Do it now.*

"We better be getting back now while the storm's under control," Felicity said. She gave a tired smile and a nod. "You'll know how to find us if you need to."

You're going to miss your chance. Now! "Yes," Lawrence said, with as much enthusiasm as he could force into his words.

There was a moment of awkward stillness, and an awkward "bye" from Tabitha, when they finally turned and began to walk down the driveway toward the truck in the distance. Lawrence turned on the heel of his boot, back toward the house. It was too late.

He took a step toward the wretched house.

Each moment they were getting farther and farther away.

He stopped, clenching his fist, cursing under his breath, turning around running after them. "Wait!"

All six of them stopped in unison, spinning around wide-eyed to him running to them. He stopped right in front, his fingers shaking. He tightened his fists.

"Is something wrong?" Lincoln asked.

Yes.

Lawrence hesitated. He'd made a mistake. He'd been a fool to believe that this would actually work. He should just turn back around and forget anything happened. He almost began to turn away, till Nikki took a step forward, her eyes meeting his.

They were oddly blue.

But the idea was ridiculous. She seemed to be trying too hard to understand him, her face frowning like he was speaking another language.

Then she turned to the rest of them. "We can't go," she said, suddenly. "H-his sister. It's only the first night. She still might need someone... someone to keep watch... if something happens." She looked over her shoulder to him, almost for confirmation.

Lawrence nodded, his mind in a panic trying to understand. Why had she tried to help him? "Y-yeah. Exactly."

"Why didn't you say something earlier?" Felicity said, relief washing over her face as her shoulders relaxed.

"We can't all stay," Cole pointed out. He squeezed Tabitha's hand, who seemed to have gotten paler at the mention of staying.

Felicity looked over the faces of her companions and sighed. "Well them... Nikki and Ray. If she needs another P9F transfer."

Lincoln cleared his throat.

"Sorry, correction," Felicity sighed. "Nikki, Ray, and *Lincoln.*"

Nikki looked over to Lawrence. "Is that alright?"

Lawrence swallowed, and nodded. He was actually quite relieved with those who they ended up choosing.

"Ray, anything happens, contact me. Right away," Cole said, with a stern glare toward Ray. Ray nodded with a small smile as he and Lincoln stepped away to join Nikki and Lawrence. "I won't disappoint you."

"That'll totally convince Taryn not to kill us seeing you without a chaperone," Cole sighed, giving Ray a firm pat on the shoulder.

Ray shrugged, turning back to them. Lawrence controlled his panicking heart, keeping his breath steady, keeping a stone face.

Charles needed him.

He couldn't let him down. Lawrence turned, leading them back toward the house. The sun had almost set now.

He had hours at most.

12

"No one can see you." Lawrence slammed on the large rusted silver button of the elevator door repeatedly. "Not even those kids."

"Why not?" Ray said, pushing forward.

Lincoln didn't say a word. He scanned around the massive interior of the barn, the walls lined with packaged wheat and empty crates and packaging. The U-shaped hover harvesting machines were locked in place, charging for the next day's work. His eyes finally settled, staring straight at Lawrence, awaiting a solid answer.

Lawrence froze for a moment, but then went back to slamming his fist against the button.

"Do you really think we believe you wanted us to come all this way just to make sure your sister was alright?" Nikki said.

The door finally burst open, the shaft making a shuddering noise that made a shiver go down Lincoln's spine as he watched Lawrence stop, looking into the elevator. A sign on the opposite wall indicated caution, and that they were rising up to the barn's storage unit. "I need help with my sister," he said. "Not just her health. I-I want you to get Isabel and Charles out of here."

Lincoln's eyes widened. "You mean, like bring them to camp? There are other places they can get help. The west side for example—"

"It isn't that easy," Lawrence snapped, shaking his head, stopping the elevator door from closing. There was a moment of hesitation. "I'll explain inside."

Lincoln hesitated. He didn't like the idea of being trapped without an explanation, but when Ray and Nikki followed Lawrence inside, he didn't have much of a choice. He crammed in with the others, the elevator door slamming shut behind them.

Lawrence turned to them, running his hands up through his hair, tightening his fingers around his curls. His eyes stared hard at the ground, not a flicker of emotion passing his eyes. "Look, it's not safe for them here. None of us. There's a man, Cain—" Lawrence's eyes lifted, darkening, his lip curling to a distasteful scowl. "Isabel's husband. He's off. Everyone here is. We don't belong here. They don't. They're getting hurt. It's only a matter of time..." Lawrence's voice dropped off, pressing his lips firmly together as he pinched the bridge of his nose.

Lincoln couldn't deny the iffy feeling he got, and Lawrence was being incredibly vague, but it seemed to physically pain him. The thought of his sister staying behind. The man, Cain, who Charles had referenced a few times, was her husband, and feared.

Lincoln blinked at the realization. The stoic boy in front of him was afraid. Suddenly, the thought of the man made Lincoln's sweat go cold.

"He will be furious if he finds Isabel was healed by outsiders," Lawrence said, his voice trembling. "I need to get her out of here. Tonight. And Charles. And you can't say no. You have to take her to the camp."

"Lawrence, I—"

"No, you don't understand!" Lawrence shouted. "I'm a Williams!"

The name echoed in the shaft, leaving a dead silence in its wake.

Lincoln's lips parted, unable to form a coherent word. Williams. How did he know? Here? At this place?

"How do we know you are?"

"Cut me open and inspect my bloody DNA right now if you feel it," Lawrence growled. "You need a Williams to unlock your Curatrix machine. *I'm* a Williams, and I have Isabel. Charles might not be of my mother's blood, but you can't leave him behind. That's part of the deal." "And you." Nikki crossed her arms. "You're coming with us."

Lawrence shook his head. "The only way for this to work is if I distract the field hands. I've been planning this for months ever since I heard about your unsolved Curatrix code."

"Your father?" Ray asked. "He hasn't intervened—"

Lawrence shot Ray a cold look. "He's been walking dead for ten years. So, are you in?"

He'd really waited to ask that when they were halfway up an elevator shaft with no ride back. Lincoln hardly knew anything about Lawrence's father, besides what he'd found on file. But it was no doubt the reason no location showed up on the file was because Reil Williams had been living with someone else for the past decade... here.

"I'm in," Nikki jumped in.

"Me too," Ray agreed,

If Nik says yes, we basically all do. Lincoln would have chuckled at the thought if he wasn't in a crammed compartment with Lawrence's never changing death glare.

"What's your plan?" Lincoln said, the elevator coming to a stop. The door slid open, cold air bursting in from the room. Enormous metal boxes lined the space. The smell of melted rubber filled the air.

Lawrence stepped out first, the others following. The elevator door shut, submerging them into darkness.

"I'll send Charles up to get you, and you'll take him. The priority will be getting into the house to get Bel out."

"Won't someone see us?" Ray said.

"Usually everyone's asleep by at least midnight. The hands stay in the lodging farther down on the property, and they're gone for tonight. Our main issue would be Miz's—" When they cast him uncertain stares, Lawrence explained with a heavy tone. "Charles' mother. My father's... wife. She's too mad to comprehend anything fully... someone might have to distract her."

"We should contact Cole," Ray said. "It may take a while to walk the whole way to the camp."

Lawrence sighed. "Do that. If you can trust them."

"Trust me," Ray said, whipping out his Comm. "They're trustworthy. Far more than we are." "Not helpful," Lincoln muttered. He shifted, turning his focus to Lawrence. "You could have said something earlier."

Lawrence laughed softly. "Trust me. I wish I could've."

Lawrence tapped on the button for the elevator. "I'm sorry... for this. Thank you for agreeing to help."

The light burst through as the elevator door opened.

Nikki nodded. "Good luck."

Lawrence stepped back into the elevator, a small hint of a smirk on his lips. "I don't believe in luck."

"It's an expression," Nikki said, looking almost proud of herself for knowing. "But you're going to need it anyhow."

The door began to close.

Lawrence clasped his hands behind his back, giving a small bow. "Thanks, but I insist. The only thing in this world I can trust is myself."

With that, the door creaked shut.

Lincoln couldn't stay still. Half because his nerves were on edge, and the other half because it felt if he stayed still for even a moment, his blood would freeze. Every time the barn rattled slightly, all three of them jerked their heads toward the door, their hearts beating into their ears, until nothing came through the door, and they were able to settle again.

Ray had propped himself against the door, his weapon out across his lap. Lincoln caught him dozing off a few times, but Ray denied it. Lincoln now sat on top of one tower of crates, his legs crossed, his hands in the pocket of his hooded jacket, fiddling with the cube. Knacks of being Aviduous. The dark didn't bother you as much. The only downside was everything had a dim black and white tint to it.

A bang jolted Lincoln up. He turned his head in the direction of the sound, his chest settling a bit, seeing Nikki struggling to pull herself up one handed to join him.

He turned to her, extending his hand out. She grabbed it with her good hand, and he helped pull her up atop the crates. The top of the crate wasn't wide, Lincoln nearly toppling off helping her. She quickly grabbed him by the jacket, pulling him back into balance. He nodded thanks to her.

They fixed themselves into a safe sitting position to keep from knocking the other off. Nikki tucked her legs up to her chest, pulling her coat over them. Lincoln could see the air of her breath. It was slightly warmer with her pressed next to him.

"What're you up to?" Lincoln whispered, finding it somewhat necessary to not speak loudly. Nikki shrugged, clasping her hands together.

"Thinking," she said, also keeping her voice to a whisper. She turned her head to him suddenly. "What do you think about Lawrence?"

Lincoln shrugged. That had been nagging on his mind. "I don't know. He's not exactly friendly." "Like you?"

Lincoln frowned. "I am very friendly."

Nikki stifled a laugh. "If you say so."

Lincoln raised a brow at her. "Well, what are your thoughts on him?"

Nikki immediately solemned, her eyes drilling into the opposite. Nikki's face scrunched up at the mention of the boy, like she was trying to focus. Then her expression became uneasy. "N-not full."

"What do you mean by that?"

Nikki bit her lip, thinking. "There's something missing about him."

"Incomplete?" Lincoln suggested.

"Something like that."

Lincoln shifted, flexing his fingers. "How come? Feelings? Like the rain?"

Nikki set her head in her hands. "Kind of. I don't know. Something about him just... seems so trustworthy? I don't know him. I don't think..." She began to repeat her numbers. "It's like the numbers, Lincoln. I know it's there, and how I *feel* about it, but I don't know how to think about it."

Lincoln watched her and she cupped his face in frustration. He wished he knew how she felt. He'd never found a trigger for his amnesia in the past six years he could remember, and he doubted he ever would. The least he could do was at least try to help Nikki figure out hers. "Did you feel something when you fell off the Inn?" Lincoln said, suddenly.

Nikki jerked her head in his direction, glaring. "I didn't fall," she snapped. "I was pulled off." She shrugged.

Lincoln frowned. "You mean pushed?"

She shook her head. "No. Pulled." She leaned her back against the wall, looking up toward the ceiling. "Something pulled me off. Like something pulled me to North Cordell. And to the woods, after… you. Then it just held me, until… until Lawrence helped us."

Lincoln tilted his head. "Lawrence. Did you feel something different with him then?"

"Only a broken wrist," Nikki said, holding up her hand.

"Do you think... it's Oquelite?"

She shook her head.

"The *Mors Vis?*"

The mention of the death force Agent Lopez brought up, perked Nikki up. "That's visible," she sighed. "And hopefully we'll never cross it. The fact it pursues a Council Member... that's terrifying."

Lincoln agreed. They already had enough problems in North Cordell alone. Nikki stared in silence. Lincoln turned to see what she was looking at. Nothing had changed besides Ray leaning against the door, jerking himself awake. He felt a small tap on his arm. He looked back, wincing at the sudden glow that flowed from the small Ewyon Stone in her hand. A light flickered inside, causing Nikki to flinch. She looked up to him, the light reflecting in her eyes.

"How's the rock friend doing?"

"She didn't like that," Nikki said, frowning. "She called you a stuck up black eyed cow." She frowned for a moment. "What's a cow?"

"I'll explain later."

Nikki nodded. "She doesn't like you," she said, lowering her voice. "Or Ray. Him being Oquelite and you being Aviduous."

"So, correct me if I'm wrong, but in the rock there is a

fallen Diones, who has the power to give you flashbacks, pretty much attack people, and has the power to blow stuff up, took her decent time to let you know she hates me?"

Nikki rolled her eyes. "All the time."

Lincoln couldn't help feeling a little honored.

Then the walls of the barn shook.

They jumped. Ray scrambled from the elevator door and rolled to his feet.

Nikki and Lincoln nearly toppled from the top of the tower of cargo bins again. Ray tore out the knife from his sheath.

Nothing happened.

A minute passed in frozen silence. Finally, they sank back down into a sitting position. "Just a machine?" Nikki said.

"Probably," Lincoln said, though he doubted it.

Ray scowled. "You know, if Taryn would just give me my darn sword back, I'd feel a lot more confident here."

"You'll get it back eventually," Nikki said, scaling down the crate tower to the floor. She stood tall and alert, her eyes on the door.

Ray snorted. "Eventually sounds more like never in Taryn's rule book."

"You sneaking out without a chaperone's not going to look good on getting the sword back," Lincoln pointed out. The poor Defender assigned to Ray had endured far too many an embarrassment when his charge took no heed to any of his instructions... which was almost a daily event.

"But if we get a Williams to unlock the Curatrix-Aguirre machine—" A smile settled on his lips, his brows turned in determination. "—our entire Council reputation will be saved."

Lawrence had left the elevator feeling confident, but with every step he'd taken toward the house, he grew deeper and deeper into despair. Charles was waiting patiently on the step outside the door for him, his eyelids drooping. On seeing Lawrence, he jumped up and ran to him, seeming to hold himself back from jumping up onto him.

"You can't tell anyone," Lawrence snapped, keeping his voice down, her eyes darting back and forth between the house and Charles' face. "Promise."

"Dollar promise?"

Lawrence raised an eyebrow at his brother, but couldn't help but smile as Charles put his fingers in between his, twisting their hands up and down twice. It wasn't part of Charles' made up promise handshake, but Lawrence fell to his knees and pulled his little brother into a hug anyway.

Charles carefully put his arms around his neck. Lawrence squeezed his eyes shut, trying to calm down his raging thoughts, hiding the utter terror on his face. He had to be confident. He had to be strong. He always had to be strong.

He held Charles by his shoulder as he pulled away. Charles' face was solemn, giving a small nod. Without a word, they walked to the back door. Lawrence opened it, Charles running inside to the staircase. He froze only for a moment, his eyes locked on Lawrence. Lawrence waved him off and he ran up the stairs, out of sight.

The house was unusually silent.

The floor boards creaked underneath his feet as Lawrence walked slowly through the house, past the stairs into the room that consisted of mainly chairs with sheets of them to substitute as a sitting room. The sheets were stained, some chairs fallen. Dirt trailed on the ground, an abundance of shoes, trash, and food scattered around the room.

"Where has the boy been?"

Lawrence jumped back, whirling in the direction of the frail, grimy woman standing in the doorway leading to the kitchen. Her hair was a frizzy mess, her face thin and bulging, her eyes glancing around his general direction. Not today. Not now. He didn't have time for this.

"The fields," Lawrence said, beginning to turn.

She began to hack up a laugh, beginning to cough. "Come here, boy."

Lawrence froze, his hands balling to fists, every bone in his body burning to turn. But he obeyed, walking to the woman, his eyes trailing along the floor.

She suddenly grabbed his face with her clammy hand, pulling it up to her own, squeezing it. Lawrence kept his eyes away, a scowl deepening. His heart hammered against his chest. She let go of his face, shouting on her drunken breath. "Look at me!"

She hit him across the face. Lawrence held himself still, hardly flinching. His glasses caught themselves by his ear. He adjusted them back over his face.

"I am alone now, boy. She doesn't want no trouble from the boy. Does he hear?" Lawrence grit his teeth. "Loud and clear."

"Don't sass Miz, boy," she snapped, adjusting her bony hand to hit him again, but her stern expression dissolved into a crooked smile, her arm lowering very slowly to her side. A small giggle escaped through her gritted teeth, her shoulders shaking as she turned back to the kitchen, leaning against the door frame. "In all good time, in all good time," She muttered over and over under her breath. She pushed herself laughing into the kitchen.

Lawrence controlled his breath. Tonight, he was getting them out of here. That would be far more rewarding than screaming into the drunk lady's face.

A clatter of laughter broke through the room.

"Williams!"

Lawrence's stomach lurched, his entire body tensing. His heart beat fast against his chest. He didn't need to look over his shoulder to know that the man was storming for him, his heavy

boots hitting against the floor with a thud every time they hit the ground. The group behind him stepped lighter, their voices drained out in Lawrence's head.

This changed everything. He wasn't supposed to be back till tomorrow at least. *No. No. No.* It took every bit of patience and courage left in him to force himself to turn around and take a step back to face Cain.

The man stood at Lawrence's height, something that always seemed to bother him, his eyes were sunken, his dark hair getting long like the stubble on his chin, and the drawn out sneer. The farm hands behind him looked no better. They had wide smiles on their faces, accompanied by rubbed red eyes, glancing toward him every so often as they jeered and joked amongst themselves.

"Miz, I'm home!" he shouted.

Miz cracked a laugh from the kitchen. Cain wrinkled his nose in disgust, like Miz was another thing that inconvenienced him. He took a heavy step toward Lawrence.

"I know what you did, kid. You brought a *Medic* here?" He cussed, his words clumsy. "What do you think you are?" He shouted, stomping his foot to the ground, the weak floorboards below Lawrence shaking.

Lawrence held firm. *Don't show fear.*

His fists were clenched, not taking his eyes from Cain. His heart bounded into his ears now. Someone cut him off, grabbing the collar of Lawrence's shirt, jerking him harshly forward. The farmhand's dark brown eyes basked in the yellow whites of his eyes, red veins reaching to them, the other eye growing more swollen by the minute. He shook

Lawrence. "Can you obey 'im? You undisciplined—"

"I didn't ask for your intervention!" Cain snapped.

Anger overtook the farmhand and he spat into Lawrence's face, and slammed him against the wall, thrusting him off his feet. The other jeered with laughter.

Cain cast a dark glare down on him. "Honestly, shouldn't have expected any less." He kicked him. Lawrence bit back a cry.

Cain stormed from the room, leaving Lawrence alone... with the group of smiling hands, looking down on him.

Lawrence scrambled to take his glasses off before someone grabbed hold of the back of his shirt, beginning to pull him up.

He was practically blind without his glasses. He tried to find his footing to pull himself up, but he was jerked off balance every time. He heard the door swing open. He was kicked over the steps, toppling into dirt. Lawrence scrambled to his knees, but a meaty hand grabbed him, lifting him to his feet and pulled him into the darkness.

He could fight them like he always did. Try to run, and try to prevent any further scars to his back, but tonight, it was different.

This is for you, Bel.

Blood was an old friend. Lawrence was acquainted with its smell, its feel, and its stingy stain. But usually, he never noticed it till he could think straight lying in the dirt the next morning. He became suddenly aware of it far too soon. The world was still dark. He lay in the mud, it clinging to his clothes and face.

"The barn door's open!" a farm hand's voice echoed out.

He could see their blurry silhouettes in the distance lit by a raging fire pit. *The barn.* He slurred a curse. Lawrence tried to move up, but his head rocked forward, his mind begging him to give in. He turned his head, flinching at the blaring flickering light. He heard the farm hand's inaudible yells grow farther away.

There wasn't much time.

With his arms, he pushed himself up from the floor, his body searing with pain. His ears rang, his head swaying. He forced himself to focus on the flames, the heat growing warmer and warmer, almost beckoning him. Something about their disoriented, yet brilliant movement called to him. It wanted to lead him far away.

He wanted to feel its burn.

He lifted his shaking hand toward the pit, pulling himself closer. The flames tickled his fingers. The warmth was more comforting than unbearable. He pulled his hand out slowly, a glowing shape flickering in his palm. Lawrence's eyes widened, though it didn't give him much help to see.

He must have been going crazy.

He shook his hand, the flame falling to the dirt, diminishing to nothing.

"Hey! Keep an eye on Williams!"

Lawrence jerked his head in the direction of the voice.

Lawrence tried to hurry to his feet, but pain seared through him at the sudden movement, and he fell forward. He cursed himself.

He jerked his head back to the fire. He squeezed his eyes shut. He was crazy. "There you are."

Lawrence's eyes burst open, lunging for the flames, grabbing a hold of whatever heat that collected in his hands. He turned and threw, letting out a cry of pain. He tried to breathe. They screamed.

This gave Lawrence a sense of delight. He turned, filling both hands. Another scream of terror, followed by a series of curses. Lawrence threw the second one, followed by a boom. He'd missed, but he hardly cared.

"Someone! Help! Help! One of the Purizies! They're back! They're back for the region! Help!" Lawrence ignored them and burst into a run. The burning pain caused tears to crowd his eyes, his shirt growing more damp by the moment. Without his glasses, Lawrence constantly stumbled, tripping over his own feet. His back was slathered in blood, and his body in mud. Lovely.

He collected himself only to slam into a post that knocked him back. He pulled himself back to his feet and ran to the blurry lights in the distance. He ran into the fence, but he caught himself against it, pulling it open.

He ran up to the wall of the house, pressing himself against it, searching for the door. His hands reached the dip in the wall and landed against the wood of the door. He turned the knob of the door with his slippery hands, collapsing inside.

He couldn't hear Miz's insane humming, so that had to be a good sign.

He crawled across the floor, searching blindly for his glasses. He scrambled around the room, searching for the right wall. Finally, his hands reached something metal. He gave a relieved laugh, pulling his glasses back over his face, everything bursting back into focus.

A red smudge was on his left lens. He frowned, looking down to his hands, finding them blackened and bleeding, though not burned. He flexed his fingers.

He heard a door slam.

He didn't take time to see who'd come in and ran for the stairs, running through the hall. He stopped to catch his breath before bursting into the small room he shared with Charles and a few of the other boys. If any of them woke up, their plan was done for and Tom would have another fit.

He opened the door slowly, trying to wipe off the remnants of the blood with the mostly clean back of his hand. He closed it slowly behind him. As usual, the wild children had scattered themselves asleep across the room and the multitude of bunks, and the small mattress in the corner. Lawrence crept over to Charles' side. The Communicator laying beside him blinked *11:48*. Charles was bound to get up soon.

Lawrence didn't have time to even change his bloodied and muddied clothes, much less care for the wounds. He searched through the closets and the heaps of discarded clothes. His hands met a scratchy felt material. He pulled out a long, heavy, dark coat. It was sized a little big, but it was enough to cover the wounds. Lawrence wiped his hands, wincing.

The Communicator went off buzzing.

Lawrence saw Charles shoot up, tapping the machine off, looking around. His eyes passed Lawrence, but then he froze, looking back to his brother. Charles' jaw dropped, and Lawrence gave a small wave, walking swiftly over to Charles, who grabbed his boots from beside the mattress and pulled them over to his feet. He picked up his own coat from the end and ran over to Lawrence, his mouth wide open.

Lawrence signaled him to be quiet.

Charles shut his mouth and nodded. Lawrence opened the door slowly, looking both ways down the hall. It was empty.

He motioned for Charles to follow him out.

Charles did as Lawrence instructed. Lawrence led him down the stairs, seeing no sign of Miz or Cain. They ran to the door, running outside into the cold dark night. A glowing light still raged by the barn. The thought of it made Lawrence's head rock. Charles looked up to him with a frown.

"You look so surprised to see me," Lawrence said, raising an eyebrow.

"Why is there blood on your face?" Charles said, his voice small and strained, as he touched his own cheek.

Lawrence reached up, feeling the sticky substance against his face. Charles' eyes were wide with horror. Lawrence didn't answer the question, grabbing Charles' hand, rushing them through to the field, keeping his eyes out for Tom's grand reappearance.

"I thought you weren't coming," Charles said.

"Change of plans," Lawrence said, wincing as he quickened his pace, dragging Charles with him. Charles suddenly ran ahead, jerking Lawrence with him. Lawrence had to control himself from yelling at his younger brother by biting his lip, and squeezing Charles' hand.

"Were you hurt?" Charles asked. "Is that why?"

You have no idea.

"Isabel can't get out on her own. And Cain's back... a little angry. We're going to need more hands to help distract him," Lawrence said, quickly, a sick feeling creeping over him, reminding him he was being selfish. He should stay behind, but everything was in jeopardy if he hadn't stopped them from getting to the barn. But now he'd caused a scene. He'd held *fire,* for mortal's sake.

He could be accused of being one of the cloaked persons who'd ravaged North Cordell a few short months ago.

Now, they had every legal right to kill him.

14

"It's a whole freaking three minutes after twelve," Ray groaned, banging his head against the elevator door in frustration. Lincoln shushed him.

He pulled away from the door, crossing his arms, looking over his shoulder to Nikki and Lincoln, who had made his way down from his crate tower, all prepared to be met with an opening elevator door, and yay! They rushed out, saved this Williams boy's sister and all the heroic stuff that came with that.

It was quite disappointing to find the door still shut when he turned around.

Ray let out a deep sigh.

What if the Lawrence guy had summoned them here to die? I mean, the guy wasn't exactly all warm and cuddly... or agreeable.

You're one to question someone's loyalty, he snapped at himself.

"Still nothing?" Lincoln asked.

"Wanna blow it up, Black Eyes?"

"Wish I could."

The past six months had left Ray with very little sleep thanks to Lincoln and his obnoxious projects. Also because about half of the little gadgets were perfect for tormenting Ray with. If Taryn wasn't as strict as she was about Ray using his Oquelite abilities, he would have had some serious payback planned.

Sadly, Lincoln hadn't made any explosives, which in Ray's mind, was pretty pointless. "Did you bring something useful?" Ray asked, looking back to Lincoln.

"Can't you teleport?"

"Three people?"

"You did it with me and Felicity," Nikki pointed it out.

Ray rubbed his temples, groaning. "You and *Lincoln* are different. You're both full-bloods. Teleporting one full-blood is fine, but two? I don't know if I can even take that. It was tiring just to teleport you and Felicity," Ray said, looking to Nikki.

Lincoln sighed, muttering something about being a 'hybrid.'

Ray crossed his arms. "Well, if you were a real full-blooded, essence-broken Aviduous, you could tear down the door or something, or call a rabbit or something."

"Why a rabbit?" Lincoln asked.

"A cow, then?"

"What *is* a cow?" Nikki said.

Ray looked to Nikki, then back to Lincoln. "She doesn't know what a cow is?" Lincoln groaned. "She's going to get super confused, so let's just wait to explain basic life things when we're out of the life threatening situation."

Nikki frowned at him.

"Hey, Nikki." Ray pointed to the far wall of the barn. "Do you know what color the wall is called?"

"I'm not stupid," She muttered. There was a moment of silence, before she answered, "It's gray." "Brilliant," Ray said.

Lincoln looked like he was restricting a groan, but his face allowed Ray's nerves to settle with a smirk.

"I think you're getting better, in all seriousness," Ray said. "Learning what things are and all. Linc here is a great teacher."

"Taryn's been there too," Lincoln added, shoving his hands into his pockets. Nikki's face scrunched up like she'd just eaten something sour, shaking her head. "Taryn's a terrible teacher."

"Can't be that bad," Ray said.

Nikki shuddered, nodding to him.

"That bad then," He sighed, looking to Lincoln. "All right Linc, guess this one's all on you."

Lincoln gave a sigh. "Thanks, Ray."

The elevator door Ray was leaning back rolled to the side. Ray fell off balance, crashing backward and landing hard on his back. Ray flinched at the light blaring in his eyes, throwing his hands up. Two faces came into focus above him.

The little boy, Charles, began laughing behind his hands, and Lawrence just looked... tired. Was that blood on his face?

Ray sat up, grabbing his knife that he'd dropped. That was not exactly how he planned to enter as the whole epic hero thing.

"Is that yours?" Charles gaped, his eyes wide, his fist clenched in excitement. Ray brushed his hair from his face, looking down to the knife. He noticed Lawrence's eyes were also trained nervously on the blade.

"Wanna hold it?" Ray offered. "I have a way cooler one back at camp."

Charles' eyes lit up. "Are you kidding?"

Lawrence looked from Ray to Charles and left the elevator like the whole affair was barely worth his time. Ray glanced over his shoulder to Lawrence, who was still watching him, and he very carefully let Charles grab hold of the hilt of the knife. The hefty knife was awkward in the hands of the small, malnourished kid, but his lips parted in pure awe and a type of innocence Ray couldn't miss. It was something he'd seen in his younger, seven-year-old brother, Adam. Ray hadn't seen him in over a year, and it seemed to weigh at his chest, but he stood up, trying to brush the feeling off.

He turned to Lawrence, and his eyes narrowed on the cut on Lawrence's lawline. He opened his mouth to address it. Lawrence shook his head and mouthed *not here*, with his eyes shifting Charles, still distracted by the knife.

Ray nodded, reluctantly.

Out of the corner of his eye, he caught Charles raising the knife above his head, his head focused above him, and his body teetering off balance. Panic seared through him as he turned to warn him from falling back.

Out of nowhere, Nikki grabbed the boy's shirt, and he dropped the knife. He looked a little surprised at first, then extremely smug with himself, and he straightened himself up. "Thanks," he said to Nikki.

She smiled. "You're welcome."

And he went right back to the knife.

Lawrence stepped forward, his lips tightened to a scowl, but Nikki held out her hand. "I'll deal with him," she said.

Lawrence froze for a moment, stepping back, giving a defeated sigh. "We don't have much time." "I thought you weren't going to be here," Ray pointed out.

"Change of plans," Lawrence muttered. "You know that guy I was talking about."

"Cain. Isabel's husband?" Lincoln said, his forehead deepening into a frown. "You said he wasn't supposed to be here…"

Lawrence nodded, his eyes shifting to Charles, who Nikki had knelt down beside, adjusting his fingers to better grip the knife. He looked back to the ground between them. He held out his hands.

Ray's eyes widened. They were smeared black, and blistered, but no blood. It couldn't have caused the blood on Lawrence's face. Lawrence quickly hid his hands in his trenchcoat. "I did something stupid."

"Yeah. You burned your hands," Ray pointed out.

He saw Lincoln shake his head, like saying *not right now*.

"Look, people are going to come after you. No doubt they've already started figuring it out. And I don't really want to die just yet."

What could he have possibly done worthy of death?

Nikki apparently had no such doubt or thoughts.

"Then what are we waiting for?" Nikki called out.

"We don't have a plan—" Lawrence said, but Lincoln grabbed his arm and dragged Lawrence reluctantly for the elevator. Ray noticed Lawrence flinch, and Lincoln must have noticed too, letting go.

Nikki, Charles, and Ray were right behind them, the doors slamming shut. Something crashed, causing them all to jump. They all turned their eyes to Charles who still held the knife. He gave a guilty smile. "Sorry?"

The elevator jerked to a stop, slamming them all to the ground. Sirens went off, the light turning red and flashing. Ray sat up, the elevator shaking.

"Charles, what did you do?!" Lawrence snapped.

"It wasn't me!"

The entire elevator box shook. "No one move!" Ray yelled.

"Go figure?!" Lincoln snapped back at him.

Below them, Ray began to hear banging and shouting. Someone was in the elevator shaft below them.

Someone had hijacked the elevator.

"We can't stay here!" Ray yelled over the roar of the siren, which was getting obnoxiously louder.

"This is why we needed a plan!" Lawrence said.

Suddenly, Ray's eyes widened. "I have a plan!"

"It's going to be something really dangerous and stupid, isn't it?" Lincoln groaned from somewhere.

"It includes teleporting."

"TELEPORTING?!"

Lawrence probably had no idea *how* weird of people he'd recruited to help him. "Weren't you just saying-"

"Yeah, but then we weren't possibly going to die!" Ray said, cutting Nikki off. "Is he serious?" Lawrence said.

Lincoln laughed. "Man, you have no idea."

"Everyone grab onto me!" Ray shouted. The elevator shuddered, and Ray wasn't sure if it was from them all scrambling to grab hold of him or because of their attackers below. Neither was fantastic.

Ray slowly got to his feet, the elevator swinging when he moved. He clung for his life to a safety bar bolted to the side of the elevator. "Come on, hurry! We don't have all night!"

The other hurried off the ground, the elevator creaking, swinging back and forth, the flashing lights beginning to give Ray a headache. Charles crawled over to him, making sure to give the weapon back, and hugged him around the waist. The other three were much more hesitant, and he ended up with Nikki around his neck, and Lawrence and Lincoln on either arm. Ray tried to act confident, but he'd never carried *five* people before.

Just two was a stretch.

The elevator shook.

"Now!" Lincoln yelled, right into his ear.

Ray squeezed his eyes shut, pulling at the energy and essence around them, trying to focus on each of the others who clung to him before he let himself lose balance and fall into the senseless abyss. Everything pulled at him. Not just Charles' tightening his grip around his waist, or the weight of the other three holding to him.

The very essence felt like it was pulling at his seams.

He clenched his jaw, holding his breath, hardening himself. He couldn't fall apart. His head felt light. It felt like it was hours before the world burst back around them, as they all rammed into the ground.

They all laid there for a moment, then Charles groaned.

"I feel sick." He coughed.

Ray rubbed his temples. He'd forgotten to warn them about the effects. His whole body ached. He wanted to curl up and fall asleep. His eyelids grew heavy.

And Lincoln smacked him in the face.

He shot up. "Ow!" Ray yelled, holding the side of his face. "I was fine!"

Lincoln raised an eyebrow. "Sorry," he said, with the least 'sorry' voice Ray'd ever heard. "Can't have you passing out on us."

Valid.

Lawrence suddenly gasped for air, shooting up, feeling his face, then his chest, examining his arms, falling back, covering his face, laughing harshly under his breath.

"Oh gosh," He gasped, shooting up to a sitting position, staring wide eyed at Ray. "You—you teleported. He *teleported*!"

"Yeah, yeah. I know I'm fabulous, but we don't have time for this."

"Into the fields!" Charles yelled, before Lawrence quieted him.

The little kid was onto something. Nikki reached to help Lawrence to his feet, but he waved her away. He finally shook his head and managed to get to his feet, running with them into the fields, in between the tall stalks, through the damp paths. Ray nearly tripped over Charles when the little boy stopped and dropped.

Ray smiled at him, nodding. "Good idea, buddy." He looked over his shoulder, nodding to the others as they crouched down into the safety of the shadows of the crops. "Alright, plan?" Ray said, looking to Lawrence.

"We have to get Bel out. C-can you teleport?" Lawrence suggested, shrugging. Ray sighed, suddenly missing his older brother and his bossy ways. So Lawrence had lost all sense of his original plan.

"Dude, if I try to teleport again, I could pass out or run out of essence or something worse. Even that was dangerous."

"We have to get her out ourselves," Lincoln said.

Lawrence heaved a sigh. "Miz is usually awake at this time."

"You didn't tell Mom about this?" Charles said, like it was the most horrible crime ever committed.

Lawrence ignored his comment. "We need to distract her. She's easy to distract. And, I think I know who would be the best viable option for the job."

His head turned to Nikki, who frowned, looking at him then to the others, seeming to try to see if they were all looking at her.

"You're a girl," Lawrence said, cringing a bit as he said it.

"What does that have to do with anything?" Lincoln asked.

Lawrence began to study his scorched fingers. "She's an unreasonable woman," he said, keeping his voice down.

Charles cowered behind Nikki when he spoke.

"She won't question it. Isabel's the only other girl here, and you showing up will keep her in one place. And you have a broken wrist."

"Won't she report it to someone?"

Lawrence laughed softly. His heart wasn't in it, as it came harsh and deep. "I'd be surprised if a soul believed her on a night like this." He looked up to Nikki. "But that's only if you're up to it." Nikki looked around to each of them and sighed, her eyes falling to her wrist. "Not like I can do much else," she whispered.

"Someone needs to deal with the farmhands."

"I volunteer," Ray said, slamming his fist down as soon as the words left Lawrence's mouth. He didn't ever bother to

ask *why*. "I've been waiting *months* to get back at this."
"I'll go," Lincoln said. "It's dangerous if Ray goes alone."

"Aw, come on Linc, I can handle them."

"Yeah. The only problem is how well you can handle yourself."

Ray glared at him, and Lincoln gave a triumphant smirk.

"You'll need to hide your faces," Lawrence said. "If they don't get your faces in their heads, the better, when they run around screaming about this later. Beware of Cain."
"On it." Lincoln pulled the hood of his jacket over his head, pulling on the strings. Ray undid his scarf, tying it up as a mask. It sent a subconscious shiver down his spine, reminding him suddenly of the stiff Oquelite uniform he'd dawned.

That's over now. He assured himself.

Lawrence looked from Lincoln to Ray. "Good," he said, taking a long exhale. "Charles and I will get Isabel and take the path to the camp."

"Through the woods?" Nikki frowned.

Only months ago, the thick trees and brush had been nonexistent, but they had sprouted from the ground and grew rapidly. Jack had told them it was due to a new awakening, where the creatures in the woods were coming back so the woods was growing as more of the supernatural past returned.

It was a lot to take in and process. Ray still didn't fully register it all. He'd stick to what he believed to be reality.

The supernatural that lurked within was only recounted by Felicity, and he had no desire to witness it himself.

"Of course through the woods," Lawrence said, staring hard at the shadows of them. There was an unsteady silence.

Ray gave a harsh sigh. No need to waste any more time. "Alright, it's settled." Lawrence nodded, lifting his eyes. "Let's go."

15

NIKKI HAD TO ADMIT THAT SHE WASN'T EXACTLY THRILLED with her position as a distraction. She stood with her back pressed against the wall to the side of the open door of the kitchen, listening to the woman hum and sing to herself, her words scratching against her throat, as she banged against the table every so often.

Nikki took a deep breath, peering into the light, watching the woman. She looked like she could be well into her late thirties, will the wear of one far older, running around with her dirty hands and her twitching eyes. She grabbed a pot from the running sink and banged it hard against the cupboard. Nikki flinched.

The woman hummed, slamming it against the counter.

The woman stopped suddenly, her humming growing quieter. Her eyes came to the center. Nikki's heart skipped a beat, realizing the woman was staring straight at *her*. The woman laughed harshly under her breath, setting the strange amber bottle down on the counter with bang.

"Little girl," she muttered, like it was a joke. She turned

inside, Nikki hesitantly following her. Everything told Nikki to turn and walk away, but she took the step into the kitchen. The stench from inside the kitchen was terrible. She wouldn't be surprised if there was a rotting animal hidden in the cluttered, greasy shelves. The smell made Nikki not even want to breathe. The woman rushed forward suddenly, her wet hands grabbing Nikki by her arm, shoving her toward the murky sink.

She held her breath, and fished out a pot.

Miz frowned, leaning closer, her yellowed eyes narrowing. "Girl's eyes," she hissed. "They are... hideous."

Nikki pulled the pot tighter like it was her only friend now. But even the woman tore that from her, shoving her toward the sink.

"Dishes for the boys..." she mumbled, like she was lost. "The boys."

Nikki didn't hesitate to turn to the overflowing sink. She looked over her shoulder to see the woman watching her with her crazy eyes. Nikki turned back, removing her coat, tying it around her waist, pushing her hands through the mountain of the dishes into the murky water below. Her hand laid against the bottom of the sink. The sensor must have detected her, as the water began to drain.

She pulled her hand out, wiping it against her pants. She would much rather be out with Ray and Lincoln right now.

"Another one," she heard the woman mutter, cursing suddenly in anger. "I thought I had all of them. Miz will have all of them."

That sent a shiver down Nikki's spine.

"Hideous eyes," the woman hissed again.

Nikki tried to ignore her, grabbing a bowl, though it nearly slipped from her fingers. It proved to be a difficult task with one working hand.

"Those eyes are supposed to be dead."

Nikki froze, the water running over the bowl. *Dead Eyes.* She tried to shake it off, running the bowl under the bowl, setting it aside. But the words lingered in her mind. What was wrong with her eyes?

Yes, they weren't violet like normal Ewyon full bloods, but the old lady certainly couldn't be talking about that. How could she have seen them before? And think they were dead?

The woman spoke about the eyes over and over under her breath, looking back to Nikki every so often with a look of nervous anticipation.

Nikki set another plate aside. Maybe if she just focused hard enough, the woman would ignore her. Maybe these guys deserved clean dishes…

The sooner they could get out, the better. She couldn't blame Lawrence for wanting to get out. She wondered why he hadn't run away years ago.

Something grasped her side. Nikki jerked away, whirling around up against the corner, the woman's glossy eyes staring straight at her. Nikki looked to the woman's hand in terror, where the green Stone was held between her fingers. The woman brought the Stone closer, though it slipped from her grip, clattering against the ground.

Nikki dropped down, skidding out for the Stone. She grabbed it, pulling it against her chest. The woman kicked her in the side. Nikki winced.

"You don't own that!" she shouted.

Nikki was tempted to curl up into a ball and stay there. But that wouldn't be very heroic of her. She scrambled up to her feet, and the woman grabbed her shoulders, shaking her. For such a frail figure, she sure had a grip and power. "Give that to me!" the woman screeched, letting go. Avalon vibrated in the stone against Nikki's clenched hand. Nikki took that as a go ahead. She softly unclenched her fist, slowly pushing her hand forward.

The woman's eyes widened, licking her lips as she snatched it from her hands, holding it up to the light. She noticed Nikki watching and growled. "Little, ugly Caroline girls do not deserve pretty little rocks," she said, smiling as if were clever.

The Stone sparked.

The woman shrieked, crumbling down to the floor, beginning to twitch and curse. Finally, her body fell limp, the Stone falling from her hands. Nikki grabbed the Stone from the ground, slipping it into her pocket.

Your pocket is proving not to be the most secure location.

Nikki sighed. The supernatural Stone's occupant, an ancient Ewyon, Avalon Emberson, had a habit of giving her advice at the most inconvenient moments. *Any better ideas? In my time, they would carry the stone in circlets or around the torso or... I can tell you don't like that idea.*

Nikki wrinkled her nose at Avalon. *I think the pocket's fine for now.*

For now.

Nikki crept to the door of the kitchen, glancing back at the woman over her shoulder back at the woman. She quickly looked away silently running from the kitchen. She looked both ways before darting her way up the stairs. A step creaked under her foot.

She might as well have shouted to the whole house she'd arrived. She crept farther up the stairs, reaching the halls. She moved slowly through the dark hallway to the last door. She grabbed the doorknob, finding the metal cold to her touch. She tightened her grip, slowly turning the handle. She pushed gently on the door. It let out a creak.

She winced, pushing it further, till there was enough room for her to slip in. There was a sigh.

Lawrence's entire body was tense, his fists clenched, looking like at any moment he would've pounced before it washed with relief.

Charles' face lit up. "Nikki!" He shouted in a whisper.

Isabel, bundled in jackets sizes too big for her, clung to Lawrence's side. She gave her a weak smile.

"What are you doing here?" Charles asked, frowning.

Nikki looked up to Lawrence, away from Charles. "Your... Miz will be out for the night," she said, rushing down the steps from the door to help support Isabel from the other side. "How are you feeling?"

"Oh, just great," she said, with a hoarse laugh.

At least she was still in good humor. It settled Nikki's nerves slightly.

Lawrence sighed, tightening his grip on his sister. Nikki wished for the others. It would be so much easier with the older Members. Most of which had common sense. Seeing the siblings they were trying to help in such despair and hopelessness made her begin to doubt. They were the Williams siblings, and Isabel's baby's, only chance, and the Williams siblings were the Council's. It didn't take too much to screw it up.

She wanted to see the young, optimistic Isabel somewhere other than a musty basement bedroom, and Charles perhaps in something other than rags. The feelings pulled strong at her mind again, just as they had with Lawrence before.

Charles ran up the few stairs, then opened the door to the hallway, urging them to follow him. Lawrence looked to Nikki. She nodded to him. They moved Isabel forward and up the stairs which proved to be a struggle.

Isabel could barely find her own footing.

Charles acted as their guide, showing them down the hall. They reached the steep steps downward.

Nikki heard Isabel release a shaky breath from her trembling lips, shuddering, her hand going to her stomach. "We're good," she whispered, casting Nikki a forced smile and pushing forward. Getting down the stairs consisted of *many* close calls. Charles tried his best to support Isabel from the front, but as soon as they reached the last step and Isabel tried to balance, she crumbled down. Lawrence and Nikki fell to their knees with her. Isabel's head hung forward as she gasped for breath.

"Bel? Bel. Please-"

Isabel shook her head, turning her face toward Lawrence. "I-I'm... too tired." Tears welled in her eyes. "I'm sorry, Cents."

She almost fell forward, but Lawrence and Nikki kept their hold on her.

"Bel!" Charles cried out a little too loud.

Isabel shook her head, shushing him. "I-it's okay," she mumbled.

"We need to carry her," Nikki said, looking up to Lawrence. He frowned, his gaze falling to her broken wrist.

"Are you sure you can-"

Nikki raised an eyebrow. "I can handle it."

Isabel was quite light, especially with Lawrence's help. Nikki could tell she was dangerously underweight, but she pushed the thought from her mind.

Focus.

Charles ran to the window, carefully peering out. "No one," he informed them. He was right. The world outside was dangerously still. The good news was that there was no sign of Tom. The kind-of bad news was that it also meant no sign of Lincoln and Ray. They crept to the back door, which Charles opened with ease. Nikki felt Isabel tense, holding her breath as they stepped out the door.

They rushed to the gate entering the fields. Once they passed, Charles led them to a hiding spot behind a work truck.

"I can take her from here," Lawrence said.

Nikki hesitated, slowly letting him fully take his sister into his arms, her head falling weakly against his chest.

"We're free," Isabel croaked, with a tired chuckle.

"Almost, Bel." Lawrence looked up to Nikki.

Screw proving themselves to the Defenders by cracking the Curatrix code. Nikki only wanted to get them out. Her heart ached.

"Get to the woods," Nikki ordered, as loud as their safety would allow. "I'll look for the other two. A-and I'll take Charles. You can't defend both him and Isabel if something goes down." Lawrence frowned, his brows furrowing, not seeming to like the idea of being unable to protect his siblings. "Well, you have a broken wrist."

"Still have one more hand then you will."

Lawrence sighed in defeat. He gave her a harsh nod. They rose and parted. Charles grasped her good hand, and she squeezed it back.

Charles kept his chin up and his shoulders straight, though she could feel him trembling, his teeth barely chattering from the cold. She admired the little boy's bravery. They approached the light of the barns. Still nothing. Her chest began to feel tight. Where were they? Rows of barns went down as far as she could see. She gulped, thinking of how far they could have gone. Cain couldn't hurt them.

Hadn't Lawrence said something about farmhands too?

Ray was part Oquelite. But he was also weak from his teleporting experience earlier. "M-miss N-Nik-Nikki?"

Nikki looked down to Charles, who stared up, horror stricken across his pale face. He slowly pointed upward, his lips trembling.

"Th-they're on the roof."

16

Lincoln hadn't meant for it to come to this.

"Next time, remind Lawrence his plans *suck*!" Ray shouted.

"If there is a next time!" Lincoln shouted back, just barely avoiding a fist to his face. How he and Ray had entirely ended up on a roof, he wasn't fully sure of. Why Lawrence hated the Cain guy, Lincoln understood entirely.

The farm hands were convinced they were witches. Ray didn't help with the fact he was very literally an Oquelite, and was using any moment to flaunt his supernatural superiority. They went on yelling about them being allied with a fire wizard or something.

Once they'd got to the roof, only a few dared follow them, led by a hard faced man of little words whom they addressed as Cain.

Lincoln balanced perfectly along the edge of the roof, on a sliver flat through the center. It was in his very nature. He easily avoided another sloppy blow, kneeing the attacker in the gut, and shoving him to Ray, who sent him flying through a portal.

Ray looked tired, like at any moment he'd drop down. His eyes zoned out for a moment. A cry caught Lincoln's attention. A man barreled straight for Ray. In a tired haze, Ray flashed away. The man nearly lost his balance, waving his arms like a lunatic. He caught his balance, and began swatting at the air.

The man's foot slipped.

Lincoln's heart skipped a beat, rushing to the edge, grabbing hold of the awful man's arm. Tom almost took Lincoln down with him, sending his arm searing in pain, trying with all his might not to fall.

"Get me up! Pull me!" he screamed. "Pull me."

With a cry of desperation, Lincoln pulled. He slipped forward, pain threatening to tear his arm from his socket. The man's frantic panic didn't help. For a moment, Lincoln was tempted to let go. He'd seen the blood on Lawrence's face.

He shook off the tempting thoughts, begging himself to hold on. Sweat began to build on his grip. He could feel himself slowly pulling forward.

The man screamed.

Lincoln's hand against the roof lost grip. Lincoln squeezed his eyes shut as he fell over the edge. Pain shot through his opposite arm, as his fall came to a harsh stop. He cried out. "Pull us up before I don't have an arm!" he shouted, feeling as though he might be torn in half.

"Working on it!" Nik's voice.

Lincoln grit his teeth, refusing to breathe as he felt himself, and the man, slowly being pulled back up to the roof. The man grabbed hold of the sweet steady safety, and took the opportunity to swing his fist for Lincoln's face. Nikki rammed him hard in the back of the head, and a portal came to take him away. Ray nearly collapsed, lying himself down to catch his breath. Lincoln grabbed Nikki and pulled her into a tight hug. She hugged him back. He didn't let her go until he felt like he could breathe again.

"Thanks," he said.

She shrugged.

"We need to go," Ray said, sitting up. Charles sat beside him, his eyes full of nervous energy glancing back and forth between all of them as he hugged himself.

"You okay, Ray?"

"Uh-huh. Just … sleep. Yeah, that'll be nice," Ray said, nearly slumping forward, before jerking himself up.

"What happened to Cain?" Charles inquired, his eyes widening.

"Don't worry," Ray said, rustling Charles' hair. "He'll be fine. He'll wake up, screaming about witches or something."

"Poor Isabel," Nikki muttered, his eyes wandering off.

They didn't dare speak further on the topic with the younger, seemingly oblivious, boy around. Lincoln guided Ray to the ladder and off the roof. Charles hitched a ride on Nikki's back. Nikki informed them she'd told Lawrence to head for the woods, so they quietly made their way there. Ray insisted he was fine, keeping himself farther than the rest. Charles rushed to join him. Nikki remained dead silent.

"You good, Nik?"

She was quiet.

"Nik?"

She jumped, turning to him. "Yes."

"That's not true."

She shook her head. "I'm confused."

"About?"

"I-I feel… strange," Nikki said, her brows furrowing. "Something familiar again." She paused. "Something painful."

She was quiet again. "Do you think they made Lawrence bleed?"

Lincoln took a deep breath, waiting for an answer to come to him, but nothing came. His mind felt numb, and tired, and horrified. Her cold fingers brushed up against Lincoln's. He hid his surprise.

He grasped her hand, entwining his fingers with hers.

It felt good to feel her grip tighten as they approached the dark frame of the woods. Though they trooped forward without hesitation, the woods gave Lincoln a daunting feeling. Something he couldn't understand.

And what he couldn't understand frustrated him.

The woods grew without mercy, reason, or explanation. They burst from the ground, growing as they pleased, raining down from the mountains. He held his breath as the darkness swallowed them, only patches of moonlight on the ground serving as light. Even though the dark barely bothered Lincoln's eyes, everything about the shadows screamed out as supernatural. "Lawrence?" Nikki whispered.

No response.

"Do you see him?" she said, turning to Lincoln.

The woods were crowded with towering trees and fallen brush. Entangled chaos of shrubbery, but no sign of a boy in a trench coat and his sickly sister.

The ground trembled beneath their feet.

Nikki gasped.

It stopped. They waited a moment. Nothing further. No earthquake, only a small shake. Supernatural.

They moved farther. Where had the boy gone?

He needed to stay to the border of the woods, or they'd be lost and they'd never find their way back.

"Lawrence!" Nikki cried out.

Lincoln joined her.

"What if they have him?" she muttered. Her eyes began to search around frantically, her pace picking up.

Lincoln tried to keep up. "Who?"

"Creatures. Monsters." She began to shake. "Lawrence!"

"Nikki?"

"Lawrence!"

Nikki let go of Lincoln's hand, pulling up Charles into her good arm and took off in the direction of the voice. Lincoln was stuck with Ray, who looked like he might pass out if he tried to move any quicker.

Lincoln saw Nikki fall to her knees, reach down into the dip in the earth, and pull Isabel's lanky figure up and out. Lawrence climbed out after her. They were dirty, and their clothes caked with mud and brush.

But they were alive.

Lincoln ran to Nikki's side. Ray groaned, muttering a curse under his breath as he slowly followed.

"Are you okay?" he asked.

Isabel nodded. Lawrence looked like he might as well have seen a ghost. "Did you feel that?" "What?"

"The quake."

Nikki nodded.

"We need to get the camp," Lincoln said, before they

could get further off track on it. "It's only a fifteen-twenty minute walk away."

"T-the camp?" Isabel stammered. Her eyes rolled back for a moment, but she shook herself. "C-camp?"

"Just relax, Bel."

At Lawrence's command, Isabel only seemed to tense. He scooped her back into his arms, though he clenched his jaw, almost as if it pained him. Nikki picked Charles back up, who was too tired to process much of anything that was happening, his head falling to her shoulder. Lincoln tried to offer Ray help, but he brushed him off.

"I'm fine," he said, though his words slurred, and he nearly tripped on his own foot as he said it. Lincoln led the group. He knew how to navigate far better than the rest of them, even in the frustrating, stupid woods. He swore he'd figure out their algorithm.

There had to be a pattern to them.

If they headed directly north, they would reach the camp. That's how the farmers always reached them so quickly, but with the woods always growing, it already looked different than the day before.

Little red eyes peered from the darkness down on them, a scatter through the leaves, and the eerie melodic breeze. Their trunks hung with bark, spiraling and embracing each other, their branches braided to an awning above them.

The ground was hardly wet. Lincoln doubted much of the storm made its way in. After what felt like an eternity, the trees began to thin. The familiar flicker of the camp's central bonfire flickered in the distance. "We're here!"

They all took off running, even Ray. It was a downhill run, but Lincoln hardly cared for the stumbles.

Someone jumped up from the fire. "They're here!"

Cole's voice.

Cole ran to meet them halfway. Tabitha, who'd been at the fire beside him, ran after them. Cole rushed up to them, just in time to catch Ray from falling over. Cole's eyes widened, clinging his groaning brother upright. "What happened?"

"He teleported five people," Nikki said, quickly moving to the camp. "Drained him."

"Immafine," Ray grumbled.

Tabitha scoffed, her attention snapping to Isabel. "Is she alright?"

"She's still unstable," Lincoln said, quickly. How close to death had she been before the Exil Libium injection if she was still this weak? "We need medical attention."

"Tabs, get Taryn. Now!" Cole shouted.

Tabitha ran ahead of their descending group.

They reached the circle of cabins, just in time for Felicity to burst from the cabin. Her face flashed with relief, but quickly tightened with worry as she bounded to meet them. "He has blood on his face," Felicity said.

Lawrence scowled.

"When we get Isabel situated, go see a Medic," Cole said quickly.

Lincoln hoped for an explanation, but all Lawrence did was nod reluctantly, and gave no words. Taryn and Tabitha came from the main cabin. "Get the girl to a bench! Lay her down! Don't hesitate!"

The night guards scrambled from the benches, giving them space to do as the Sergeant instructed, laying Isabel on the log bench near the fire. Isabel was too drowsy to be considered conscious. Taryn brushed the hair from her face.

"Fever. Awfully malnourished," she said. Her face deepened to a frown. She looked to Lawrence. "Is—is she with child?"

Lawrence looked away and nodded.

Taryn sucked in a breath, holding back a patch of sweaty hair from Isabel's head. "C-can you help her?" Lawrence said, looking up. His face strained, eyes wide and fists clenched.

Taryn looked up to him, her brow raising. "Can I—"

"I'll do anything," Lawrence said, his voice quivering. The stone face flashed away for a second, breaking with desperation before he caught himself. "I—I'm a Williams. My name is Lawrence Williams, son of Caroline Wents."

Taryn froze. The entire group around them went still, the only sound being the slow cracking of the fire.

"How—how did you know I was looking for a Williams?" Taryn said, her disbelief slowly shrinking to a hardened confusion.

"The Curatrix machine isn't exactly a secret," Lawrence

said, regaining his indifferent composure.

Taryn stared at him wordlessly before clearing her throat and nodding. "We will discuss this later," she said, giving Lawrence a firm nod. "From the looks of it, her main source of illness is malnourishment... Did she recently have the fever?"

"Nik and Ray gave her an Exil Libium injection," Lincoln said, cringing as he did so. They were just asking for a lecture later.

To his surprise, Taryn didn't bat an eye. "Her body isn't recovered from the shock, nor strong enough to take it. No doubt the pregnancy is another factor." Taryn gave a breath of relief. "It will be an easy healing process considering her injection, thankfully."

She turned her attention to Ray. "Is Mathews okay?"

"Teleported too much," Cole said.

Taryn didn't even look phased. "I'm going to send another Medic to treat her. But she needs a place to stay. Our Medic tent is no place for a long term stay. Especially not for a Williams." The Defenders around them again seemed to shrink at the mention of who was in their midst. How esteemed *were* the Curatrix team to have simply those related to them be held so highly? Lincoln wasn't well-versed in popular culture, but now he made a mental note to do some research.

"Do we have an extra cabin?" Tabitha asked, looking around.

A Defender shook her head. "Not since Dow's troops arrived."

"She can have my bed."

Everyone turned to Nikki, causing her to flush. "I don't sleep much," she admitted quietly. Lincoln smiled at her, as if to comfort her, but she didn't meet his gaze.

"I'm fine if she stays in our cabin," Felicity said. Tabitha agreed.

"Now, what about the Williams boy?"

"My name is Lawrence," Lawrence repeated.

"Oh yes." Taryn brushed it off quickly. "Alright. His only options are the boy's cabin or I hear Giles has an extra-"

They all immediately cut her off with assurances the boy's cabin would be fine. "Is he your brother?" Taryn said, turning to Charles, curled up, asleep, in Nikki's arms. "Yes," Lawrence said, quickly. "He's hardly five."

Nikki piped up. "I—I can take him."

Lincoln watched as Lawrence's face hardened on his little brother. His eyes met Nikki's and they softened slightly.

"He can stay with you tonight," Lawrence agreed, reluctantly. "He's comfortable." Nikki gave him a small, reassuring smile and a nod.

"Now that it's all settled," Taryn said, rising to her feet, turning to the Defenders. "Get the Williams girl situated in their cabin, and someone get him to a Medic tent."

"I can find it myself," Lawrence assured.

Taryn opened her mouth to object, but Lawrence was already hurrying away. She frowned. "What a strange boy."

Lincoln agreed, but he didn't say a word out loud. He had so many questions. Why hadn't Lawrence addressed them earlier? If he knew they were looking for the Williams, why hadn't he come right then and there? Where had the blood come from?

And what had the boy done to make the farmhands want him dead?

It was near two in the morning when the Medic finally let Isabel alone in Nikki's bed. Felicity peered through the dividing sheet to the girl asleep. She was peaceful and still. Her vitals were weak, but steady.

She was alive.

Felicity gave a sigh of relief, letting the curtain fall closed.

She knew Tabitha had wanted to stay up to see how Isabel was doing, but she hadn't made it past twenty-four hours.

Tabitha seemed to be more at peace, now that the girl was safe. Seeing another fall victim to the fever in their hands, no doubt, would've crushed her.

Felicity finally turned back to her own bed, where Nikki sat, Charles asleep against her. The little boy was almost an exact, mini replica of his older brother, minus the blond curls. Nikki seemed lost in thought. Her hair was undone, grown to below her shoulders now. Felicity sat down beside her. "You look tired."

Nikki jumped. She registered Felicity and sighed, shaking her head. "No. It's going to be morning soon."

Felicity rolled her eyes. "Exactly. So a little sleep wouldn't be a wouldn't be full night's commitment, now would it?"

Nikki bit her lip and frowned at her.

"Oh, come on," Felicity groaned, plopping down. "Just lay down."

Nikki gave her a tiny frown, but did as she directed. Charles murmured in his sleep, repositioning his tiny body. "Are you happy, Felicity?"

Felicity. Nikki rarely called her Liz.

Felicity smiled and nodded. "Yes. I am."

She turned her eyes to the ceiling. Was she happy? She wasn't the anxious girl tripping over even breathing, but she was far from confident. Obsessing over everyone else's wellbeing seemed to help.

It was easy when she was surrounded by them, but what happened if she had to face something alone? Would she crack? Why couldn't she be as fearless as the wide eyed, curious girl, who was always asking bold questions beside her?

Felicity pushed the thoughts away. She was happy.

She was.

A hum of pain settled in her leg as she turned. "Nikki, do you ev-" She turned and stopped, and almost laughed at the sight.

Nikki's arms were wrapped around Charles, her cheek up against his hair, her eyes closed. Asleep.

"Too hard to resist, huh?" Felicity tucked a loose piece of hair behind Nikki's ear. She smiled and closed her own eyes.

But this night must have been her turn to be unable to sleep.

PART TWO

THE DAUGHTER

She must have eventually fallen asleep. For what? Two minutes? She grabbed her tele from the table. 9.00.

Her body ached with exhaustion. There was no use of trying to fall back asleep. She sat up, the cold morning air catching her off guard. She shivered, looking to Nikki and Charles, both of whom were both fast asleep. Felicity wondered for a moment if she should wake them, but decided against it.

Nikki needed the rest.

Felicity got up from the bed, the cold pricking at her skin. Her ankle was sore under her weight, but Felicity brushed away the thought. She rummaged through her dresser, finding her sweater. A groan came from Isabel's side of the cabin. Felicity jumped up. She was awake. Felicity ran and tossed the curtain aside, seeing Isabel struggling to sit up with the tubes connected to her skin. Felicity rushed to help her.

"Thank you," Isabel croaked.

Felicity nodded with a small smile.

Isabel brushed her sweaty hair from her face, her pale green eyes searching the room as a crease formed between her brow. "Where am I?"

"The construction camp," Felicity said, kneeling beside her. "You arrived with your brothers last night."

Isabel's face lit up. "We made it," she said, a grin slowly spreading over her face. "Cents really did it."

"You need to rest," Felicity said, glancing at a hologram displaying Isabel's vitals. The last thing she wanted was for the excited woman to lose any of her progress.

Isabel nodded, leaning back. "What is your name?"

"Felicity."

"You're the Bentsworth girl." Isabel closed her eyes.

Felicity's face flushed. The Bentsworth girl. That was her, wasn't it? "Yes. That would be me." Isabel smiled and turned on her side. Felicity left her alone, closing the curtain after her. The girl was twenty.

Only a year older than herself.

And she probably had seen more hardships than Felicity could even imagine. Yes. The anxious Bentsworth girl.

She kept her thoughts occupied with trying to get dressed, and contain her hair that, in the rain, had decided it was a brilliant time to frizz to the ultimate capacity.

The cold showers didn't help either.

She stuck a bobby pin in her teeth, and began to twirl her hair in her hands. Suddenly, a horrible, twisting pain seared up her leg.

She opened her mouth to cry out but she couldn't force it out. She couldn't breathe. She collapsed to the ground, grasping her leg. It felt like it was burning, her skin tearing, her bones twisting.

She shut her eyes, falling into the darkness where suddenly her screams became audible. She tried to open her eyes. To escape.

It wouldn't work.

The pain. The darkness. The *fear.*

Do not delay the process.

Shut up!

She screamed again, the echoes racking off her brain, pain searing through her head. *The lady is coming.*

The lady is coming.
The consequences are yours.
Leave me alone!
The lady is coming.

The words echoed on loop. Felicity was dying. That had to be the answer. The world was ending her.

Her eyes suddenly shot open, the world completely silent. She gasped for air, choking and coughing. She felt her face. She was alive.

No one had come to her screams. Not even woken up. She grabbed her tele. Only a second had passed.

Her heart beat faster.

What was happening? Was she going insane? No. This had happened before. But then, it'd taken complete control of her.

She tried to push it all away before it ate at the protective wall she'd formed in her mind. No. No. No. She was better. She would stay calm. It was fine. She was imagining things. Felicity stared down at her throbbing leg. She carefully pulled back the fabric of her leggings. A swelling purple bruise crawled along her ankle, blotted with red.

She must have fallen. Really hard?

She held her breath, checking her opposite leg. The same bruising.

Felicity clasped her hands over her mouth to hold back her screams.

The pain seared for a moment, cutting off her air, then it fell away, leaving her head swinging. She shook her head. What was happening to her? She hid her ankles with the ends of her pants. It would go away. It was nothing.

"Liz?"

Felicity jolted her head to Tabitha, who stumbled from her side of the room. She looked like a disaster, her short hair pulled up into a ponytail, the abundance of loose pieces sticking to her face, and the ponytail sticking straight up. Dark lines were carved under red eyes. She rubbed her eyes. "Something wrong? I heard something fall. I think it was you."

Felicity jumped to her feet. "Tripped," she said, hiding a foot behind the other. Not like that did anything.

Tabitha seemed too tired to be suspicious. Her eyes

suddenly widened. "Is Nikki-"

"Yes, now shush!"

Tabitha flashed Felicity a smile, and quickly slipped back behind her own curtain. Felicity pulled her hair up into a bun and quickly laced her boots, then turned for the door. A yawn halted her to a stop. She turned on her heel to the little boy, who now sat up, looking around his familiar location. He found Felicity's eyes, and waved. "Hi."

"Hi," she said, with a small wave back.

"My name is Charles. I'm five now."

She smiled, holding back a laugh. "I'm Felicity. I'm nineteen."

His mouth fell open. "Nineteen? You are really old."

Nikki turned over, and almost immediately sat up. She blinked a few times before she realized what had happened. Charles hugged her. "You're awake!"

Nikki's panic melted. She gave Charles a small pat on the head.

"Where's Bel?" Charles asked, jumping up.

"Behind that curtain." Charles scrambled off the bed. "Don't run. She might be sleeping, Charles—"

He completely disregarded Felicity, disappearing behind the curtain with a plop that very much woke up his sister.

Felicity sighed. She looked back to Nikki, who'd pulled her legs up her chest and rested her chin on top. She began to open her mouth to speak, but Felicity cut her off.

"Don't tell me you're sorry, Nikki," she laughed.

And Nikki didn't apologize.

Lincoln had a habit.

Slapping Rapheal Mathews. Not just for fun, of course.

That would be cruel.

Only when all other causes failed to wake him. Today happened to be one of those days. It was nearly noon, and Ray woke up with a start, nearly toppling out of the cot, before he realized what had happened. He scowled, facing both Lincoln and Lawrence. He rolled out of the cot, his dark black hair a disastrous mess. "What time is it?"

"Twelve," Lawrence said simply. His face was hard and solemn, but his eyes danced with amusement. That was an accomplishment to Lincoln.

The boy refused to be friendly. The closest thing he could get was a tolerated ally. He'd been in the Medic tent nearly till morning, and didn't answer a single question of Cole's regarding it. But it was still a success. The Williams children were now in their camp, safe and sound. A direct link to the Curatrix team.

This was a new opportunity. A chance to not screw everything up, and get squished by a building. He could show Taryn he was valuable once he finished the Cube and guided the Williams boy. So far, Lawrence seemed to be hanging around.

Well, technically it was because he probably had nothing better to do than watch them make fools of themselves before his inevitable meeting with Taryn later, but Lincoln was trying to be positive for once.

"Twelve?" Ray gasped, scrambling from the floor, digging through the colossal mess of the floor. "Already?"

"The teleportation knocked you out."

Ray shrugged, pulling on a shirt. "But look, Linc. I was able to handle it." He held out his arms. "No trembling. I'm alive. I woke up. It's pretty great." Lincoln knew what he was trying to communicate. *I haven't gone crazy.*

He hadn't gone mad since Imperial, but Taryn had also forbidden him from doing anything extreme. She obviously hadn't been too pleased with this one.

Ray grabbed his jacket and rushed for the door. "Any food left?"

"Plenty," Lincoln said, following him out. Lawrence trailed after them.

Ray seemed to just notice Lawrence, and he whirled around, then began walking at his pace. "So, thoughts on the camp? Us? The Sergeant? We don't call her Sergeant, though. So don't bother. It's usually just Taryn."

Lawrence nodded solemnly. "It's nice."

Ray glanced at Lincoln. Lincoln shrugged.

"What happened to your hands?" Ray asked, suddenly.

Lawrence's hands were indeed scorched black. He closed them to fists. "They're fine."

Ray cleared his throat. "I'll head to the kitchen. You and Linc here can go enjoy the fineries that are our lovely camp," he said, rushing forward, grabbing Lincoln by the shoulder and turning him around. "He's like Nikki with his few words."

"Nik was worse."

Ray smirked. "She still is. Look, you warmed her up. Maybe we can do the same?"

"I don't think it's the same scenario," Lincoln whispered quickly. "Nik was stuck in a lab for as long as she can remember, but Lawrence? He remembers a lot."

Ray scowled. "I'll be optimistic and hope it's less awkward in a week."

"Do that."

Ray winked and ran off. Lincoln turned back to Lawrence. He walked silently by his side. Lawrence didn't seem to have intentions of staying long. He was here for the safety of his brother and sister, after all.

"Yesterday, when I asked you about siblings, you said something about amnesia." Lawrence's comment caught him off guard. Lincoln blinked. He had said that, hadn't he? That conversation seemed like eons ago.

He nodded. "Woke up in a river when I was eleven. Haven't remembered anything since. Just random facts and information, nothing much."

Lawrence's eyes were wide as he studied Lincoln. "Do you miss it? Having memories of your family?"

A lump formed in Lincoln's throat. "Can't miss what you don't have."

"CENTS!"

Charles came racing out of the girls' cabin. He lept into Lawrence's arms with a full on force that nearly knocked Lawrence off his feet. "Careful, Charles!"

"Sorry." Charles still hugged his older brother tightly.

Charles caught sight of Lincoln, giving him a shy wave. "Are you going to talk to the sargen too?"

"Sergeant," Lawrence corrected.

Lincoln shook his head. "I don't think so."

Charles took that as his cue to give his full attention to Lawrence. "Bel's coming real soon, Cents. She's gonna see the sargen too."

Lawrence frowned, brushing back a patch of hair from Charles' eyes. "She is?"

"Yes. Nikki is helping her."

Lawrence blinked rapidly for a moment. "That—that's great news."

"It is very great," Charles agreed.

Lawrence turned his head for the main cabin, staring with unspoken words whirling in his eyes. "We better be going."

"Good luck," Lincoln said with a nod.

Lawrence scoffed. "I don't do luck, remember?"

18

Lawrence didn't like the feel of the spacious cabin. It smelled of fresh polish, and the walls were empty, besides two doors leading to opposite rooms. A long table occupied the room, and a small armour at the end. It was surprisingly homey for a Defending Sergeant's cabin. Isabel squeezed his arm.

She sat beside him, bundled in blankets, and a strange medical tube inserted in her arm attached to bags connected to a pole on wheels. Lawrence had never seen such a contraption, but it seemed to be keeping his sister alive, so he had nothing against it.

Isabel's hair was a frizzed, greasy mess, but it looked as though she'd tried to make herself look somewhat presentable, putting it up in a messy bun, her face cleaned from sweat and grime. She looked at the Sergeant of North Cordell discussing quietly with two other Defender men. Isabel's expression was soft, almost far away. She looked to Lawrence.

"Why did you tell them?" she whispered.

Lawrence's face hardened. "There wasn't much of a choice."

Isabel pursed her lips, giving a slow nod. "Cain won't be happy, Cents."

Lawrence contained a wince. "I have that covered, Bel," he lied.

How could he tell her otherwise? How could he tell her straight to her gentle face that he had no idea what he was doing?

Isabel relaxed back into her seat. "I trust you. You've gotten us this far."

Lawrence swallowed hard.

"What do you think of them?"

"Who?"

"The other children," Isabel laughed. "Well, hardly children. Council members, I heard them referred to. The ones who saved Imperial."

Right. These were those kids. "They're tolerable."

"Why must you be so harsh?" Isabel laughed softly. "I think they're fine…" Her gaze drifted.

"Is something wrong?" Lawrence asked.

His sister shook her head. "Cents, something about that girl feels so familiar." "What girl?"

"Nikki," Isabel clarified, staring him in the eyes. "You have to have seen it too. You had to have seen her eyes."

"Her eyes?" Lawrence's gaze faltered.

"Look next time," Isabel said. "I *know* her, Cents. Somewhere. Somehow—"

"I'm sorry to interrupt, but we're prepared to speak with you now." The tallest man, with dark skin and a brilliant smile, turned to them. His pin labeled him as "Rayder Dow, Sgt." The two siblings turned to face the three Defenders. Dow was by far the most inviting. Taryn Hunter seemed awfully distracted by the void of the table, and the other, Agent Nigel Lopez, looked as though he didn't want to be there.

Taryn turned her head suddenly. "From the test performed last night with Lawrence in the Med tent, your lineage is confirmed. You *are* Williams, meaning you're descended from the Wents of your mother's side. And your aunt…"

"Is Reyna Wents Aguirre," Isabel finished for her. "We

are well aware."

"Why haven't you approached us sooner?" Taryn said. "I am a Curatrix team member." The only one left at that too, Lawrence noted.

"You haven't exactly been readily available in the past," he said. He wasn't lying.

But if they had, would he really have gone to them?

Agent Lopez opened his mouth to rebuke.

"Our situation is complicated," Isabel hurried. "But we're here now."

Maybe Lawrence really should leave the talking to Isabel. So far, he was only getting a Defender mad at them.

"When was the last time you saw Agent Reyna Aguirre?" Dow asked, widening a scroll with a stylus in hand.

Isabel frowned. "My memory is murky from our time with them."

"Three weeks before their assasination," Lawrence said. He wouldn't forget the day his mother broke down on hearing the news. Her younger sister had been murdered in her own home. He remembered her saying, "only three weeks ago" over and over till the words were painfully ingrained in his mind.

"That's good news," Lopez said. He perked up a bit, as Dow scribbled on his Scroll device. *I'm glad my mother's sobs are worth something to you, Defender.*

"Did either Aguirre ever give you something of importance, have you touch something, or any information you might remember?" Dow looked up.

"She was ten. I was seven. So no."

Isabel shot him a warning look.

"Fair, I suppose," Taryn sighed. "Now, I guess the only way to confirm is to go ahead and try it." "Try what?" Isabel asked, frowning.

Lawrence already knew what was coming.

From the armour, Taryn brought out a metal case. She set it on the table, and with a light tap, the sides fell away, revealing a peculiar lean rectangular machine that sprouted holograms left and right.

"This," Lopez said. "Is the Curatrix machine. Sergeant Hunter was given it by the Officers after Agent Reyna Aguirre's death."

Taryn nodded. "We believe it's a sort of tracking mechanism, and no doubt you know of the force who attacked North Cordell."

Who didn't?

"They're called the Oquelite, and there's six other races like them, but it'd take years to explain it all," Lopez huffed. "We suspect they discovered a machine to track Oquelite at the very least. There's a missing piece. A chip, is it?"

"Yes," Taryn said, tapping on the side of the machine. "But to activate it, DNA is needed. We've already all tried. Our last resort is someone related to the Aguirres."

Isabel sat straighter. "I'll go."

Taryn cast Isabel a smile. They brought the machine around the table. Lawrence had to step aside to give the Defenders space. Watching Isabel prick her thumb caused his whole body to tense.

She pressed her thumb against the pad.

It was an agonizing thirty seconds of watching the circle on the screen turn and turn, mocking him with its indecision.

Then, it flashed red.

Isabel pulled back. Dow offered her a bandage.

"I guess it's not me, then," Isabel said, with a small laugh.

All heads turned to Lawrence. He made sure not to look a single one in the eye. They moved Isabel in her chair away, making space for him in front of the machine. He pricked his finger effortlessly, but stared hard at the pad below him, carved perfectly for a finger. Come on. Do it. It wasn't hard. Just put your finger on the stupid pad.

He thrust his finger against the pad, squeezing his eyes shut, waiting the painful moments. Why wasn't there a sound? Was it confirmed? He held his breath.

Finally, he dared to look up…

… and was faced with the grim red screen.

No.

For a moment, no one said a word.

Lawrence stepped back from the machine. It wasn't him. It didn't matter who they were now. They weren't the key of the Curatrix machine.

Taryn's face faltered. Lawrence could've swore he saw her eyes grow glassy, as she stepped back against the wall.

"So, Kordin was wrong?" Lopez's voice faltered. "He

said the Aguirre heir was still alive. If it's not the Williams, then where are they?"

Taryn squeezed her eyes shut. "Right in front of us."

"I agree with Ray. Super sounds cool," Nikki said.

Her teasing skills were improving and Lincoln glared at Ray who sat beside him, inspecting the unfinished cube.

"Yeah, Black Eyes. The cube sounds so unoriginal." Ray set the cube back down and pushed it back to Lincoln.

"Yeah, well, Super sounds super *stupid*. It's just a random word."

"I like it," Nikki insisted, cradling the warm mug in her hands.

Lincoln gave a dramatic sigh to contain a laugh. The rain had begun to pour again, and once again the older three Members had rejected their invitation to the mess hall. "How do the trackers fit?"

Ray slammed his foot up under the table, showing off the metal anklet. "Your tracker-thingies aren't very fashionable, Linc."

"Maybe they should be yellow," Nikki suggested, stirring her broth with a spoon. "Nah. Yellow'd look weird. Maybe gold or something."

Lincoln groaned. "It doesn't matter what they look like. They're *betas* right now. If they work, it'll be way easier for us to keep track of each other."

"Or for you to stalk me and Nikki," Ray said, taking his foot from the table. It was unusually quiet. Charles Williams stayed back at the girls' cabin, having fallen asleep after a long afternoon of Nikki and Tabitha training with him. He'd served much more as moral support than anything.

Nikki looked tired, taking careful sips of the broth, but far from unhappy. A small smile rested on her lips as she watched Ray argue his case for the Super name that Lincoln chose to drone out.

They hadn't seen Lawrence since he'd been summoned to the cabin. Lincoln couldn't imagine why it was taking that long.

"You look tired, Black Eyes."

Lincoln blinked, then scoffed. "Me? Tired? Never."

"I'm a Medic, idiot."

"I'm an Aviduous, genius."

"You use that excuse for *everything*."

Lincoln smirked. "It's because it's true—"

The door suddenly banged open. All three leapt to their feet. In the doorway stood a small, drenched group of Defenders.

Lincoln's first thought was *Miriam's back* until the Defender paid Lincoln and Ray no heed, the group charging right for Nikki.

Nikki was frozen in shock, panic seizing her.

Lincoln's heart skipped a beat, and he tore toward her. "What are you doing?! She's done nothing wrong!"

The Defenders ignored him.

Nikki's eyes looked to him, wide in terror. One cuff clamped around her fist. That set her off, bursting back into focus. She tore free, kicked one in the ankle, and began to run for Lincoln, before she was jerked back. The Defender hoisted her up and off her feet. Lincoln's face burned as he stormed forward. "Put her down."

"I'd like to see you try," one huffed.

Nikki kicked them.

Ray scowled. "You can't just-"

"Sergeant Hunter's orders."

Lincoln whirled around.

Giles.

Of course, it was Giles. This had to be his doing. His revenge on them.

"There's no need for brutality," Lincoln tried to not waver under Giles's gaze. "She's not going to hurt any of you."

Giles shrugged. "I didn't give the order. And she just kicked my fellow officer. Better safe than sorry. I was told specifically we were to retrieve the Ewyon, and only the Ewyon. I was also warned you'd try to interfere."

Lincoln sank his hand into his pocket, his fist tightening around the cube. They wouldn't get away with her.

"If you won't let her go, I'm coming too," he said, stepping forward.

Giles eyed him. "No-"

Lincol tore out the cube, the corner crackling with electricity at the press, and jabbed Giles's shoulder. Giles jumped back. His sleeve smoked, a small hole in the fabric formed.

He looked from Lincoln to the hole. "This is an *Officer* uniform."

Lincoln smirked. It worked. "It is."

"Where the *heck* did you get that?"

Lincoln twirled it in his hand. "Let me go with you, or I'll do far worse." "Simple threats won't-"

Lincoln pressed the button, the blue bolts cracking at the end. Giles scowled. "Fine. But I will make sure you owe up." Lincoln met Nikki's trembling eyes. "Looking forward to it."

19

The wait felt like hours.

Two Defenders guarded her, seeming to not even blink, waiting on the steps outside Taryn's cabin in the rain. She'd pulled her legs up to her chest, cradled by her magnetically bound hands, and she proceeded to have a glaring contest with them.

Lincoln hid his nerves.

Why Nikki? She'd nothing wrong. If anyone deserved to be punished for their most recent escapade, it was most likely Lincoln. He was the most capable of contacting the Defenders for help, but he didn't.

Giles stormed into the tent. "Sergeant Dow and Hunter are ready. Bring her." The two Defenders hoisted Nikki to her feet, as she struggled to pull from their grip. Lincoln followed them out beside Giles, who gave him an unsettling smirk.

They entered the main cabin, where Dow sat at a table, a tablet firmly in his hands. The walls were crowded with whispering Defenders. Tucked away in the corner sat Lawrence and Isabel, whose faces were stricken with confusion as they walked in.

Taryn was pacing, her face sweaty. She froze on seeing them enter. Her hands were shaking. She looked at Lincoln. "Why is he here?"

"Insisted."

To his surprise, she didn't give him a death glare. She looked far too pale and nervous to move. Giles shoved Lincoln aside, and Nikki was placed forward, the two Defenders on both of her sides. Her face was unphased. Lincoln couldn't read it.

Taryn looked up, her eyes widening. She jumped to her feet. "Why is she chained up? Officer Giles-"

"Resistance to arrest."

"She wasn't supposed to be *arrested*—" Taryn looked ready to charge when Dow placed a strong hand on her shoulder.

"What is your name, Ewyon?" Dow said.

No response.

"*Her* name is Nikki," Taryn answered, shrugging him off. "And she has no reason to be treated as a prisoner. Our new … suspicion doesn't suddenly make her a criminal. Remove the bonds. Now, Giles!"

With the click of Giles's wristband, the cuffs fell from Nikki's wrists.

"We have been informed of a claim that cannot be ignored," Dow said. "So, if it's alright, we need to ask you a few questions. Will you answer truthfully?"

Nikki nodded. "Yes."

Taryn took a deep breath. "Please answer yes or no."

"Are you sixteen years of age?"

"Yes."

"Did you escape from an unknown facility in Imperial?"

"Yes."

"Do you remember your purpose at this facility?"

"No."

Taryn bit back her breath, and hesitated.

"Are you the child of Curatrix Members Reyna Wents and Lyell Aguirre?"

20

The world fell quiet. The names of the Curatrix members echoed off the walls. Crashing into the fear and terror in Nikki's face.

"Yes or no?" Dow said.

Lincoln couldn't breathe. His thoughts fought each other, tearing and beating at his mind. He didn't understand. How had they gotten to this point?

Nikki stood in front of a silent staring audience, trying to keep from trembling, her eyes on Dow's.

It shattered, the room erupting. Voices shouted, demanding for answers, and confusion. Lincoln couldn't speak. He wanted her to look at him.

She didn't move.

Reyna Wents and Lyell Aguirre.

Two Defending Agents he barely knew about. Just that they were internationally acclaimed Agents, and murdered over a decade ago.

Why was everyone panicking?

He tried to keep his composure and breathe.

"Yes or no?"

Taryn's expression was not all shocked. Her nerves and shaking had even settled a bit. "They killed their full-blood before it was even born!" an Officer shouted. Nikki's face flared with panic and confusion as she tried to turn, but was shoved back forward. She hid her face in her hands.

Full-blood?

Lincoln was tempted to run to her, and command them to stop shouting at her and Taryn. But it was pointless.

"Silence." Dow's voice thundered through the room.

They all fell silent.

"Please, Nikki. Hearing the answer from you would be far better than running the tests," Taryn said, quietly.

"Run tests? Are you insane?" Lincoln stood up.

Taryn met his eyes. She obviously wasn't happy he was there. "We've known about a full-blood since it was conceived. There was a trial to determine whether Lyell and Reyna's full-blooded child lived. They lost." Taryn bit her lip. Lincoln noted she used her friends' first names. It made it sting a little. "The public knows nothing about it. Dean made sure of it."

"That's why a test might be vital. The full-blooded Aguirre should've been dead sixteen years ago," Dow said.

Dean. The name placed itself to belong to the Assistant Executive of the Defending Offices, Cadissa Dean.

What did she have to do with Nikki?

"I'm still here."

The tiny voice could have been easily missed. Again, attention shifted back to the small girl in the center. Lincoln knew she hated it.

His face grew warm, realizing he probably had only brought more to her humiliation. Dow cleared his throat. "It's crucial information. Some you might hold. Whatever activity Aguirre was working on is yet to be revealed, we believe—"

"NO!"

The whole room startled.

Nikki never yelled. Her good hand was clenched in a fist, her face forming a scowl. Taryn moved forward. "Nikki—"

She tore away, whirling around, and ran. A Defender tried to stop her, but she slipped past them and out the door.

Officers began to rise to their feet.

"No," Taryn said, sinking to her knees. "Leave her. Give her time. She'll come back." A few Officers grumbled. Lincoln caught a few. None were in Taryn's favor. They still thought her the rumored Sergeant who'd lost her mind. A lunatic.

Dow began to crouch beside her, but she shooed him off.

Dow walked off. Lincoln turned to follow. He needed to find her.

"Lincoln."

Lincoln whirled around.

Taryn was staring at her hands pressed firmly against the ground. "You have to understand the importance of this."

He glanced at Lawrence, whose hard face now represented everything Lincoln felt. Lincoln nodded, turning to go out the door. "That was horrible."

Taryn sighed.

"I know."

"Lincoln!"

Felicity burst from the flaps of the mess hall into the early morning air. Her eyes were clouded with worry as she tackled him with a hug. His mind was too scrambled to give her as much as a hug back.

All he could do was stumble back.

Felicity frowned. "Is everything okay? Is it finally Miriam?"

He stared off to find the faces of Ray, Cole, and Tabitha all watching him as well. He tightened his fists.

"Nikki's parents are probably Lyell Aguirre and Reyna Wents." It escaped as hardly a whisper, but Felicity caught it with a muffled gasp.

The others rushed over. Felicity told them, and immediately, all began showering Lincoln in questions. He ignored them, meeting Lawrence's eyes who had followed after him.

"Did you know?" Lincoln demanded.

Lawrence shrugged. "Why do you think I would?"

"Taryn did this after your meeting. It *can't* be a coincidence."

Lawrence clenched a fist. "The Curatrix machine failed us. The Sergeant said there was still one option."

"So she jumped from you, Williams on File, to Nikki, an amnesiac lab runaway?" Lawrence didn't cower from Felicity's accusatory finger in his face. "She mentioned something about a guy named Kordin saying something."

"Kordin?" Felicity's face paled. She stumbled back.

"The executive of the Defending Offices," Cole breathed. "Taryn's uncle." James R. Kordin had been killed by the Oquelite prince, Silas, in the Imperial attack. Lincoln had only caught a glimpse of him when he was carried out to safety after the collapse. He'd died soon after, but apparently, not after delivering a message.

"I think your Sergeant has suspected it for a while," Lawrence said, beginning to walk away toward the kitchen door. He paused. "When we failed the test, it was like she knew that confirmed it."

Lincoln had seen the defeat in Taryn's face as she'd crumpled to the ground. The way she'd been so cautious and accusatory of Nikki stung his memory.

There *had* been record of a full blood in the past sixteen years, and they were supposed to be dead.

But the daughter of two Curatrix heroes?

That was all too much to throw on someone's shoulders.

"Where is she?" Ray said, turning to Lincoln.

Lincoln didn't even take time to respond. He spun around and burst out the door, down the steps, and for the woods. He had to find her.

The Defenders might want their answers, but he wanted his friend.

21

NIKKI TRIPPED OVER A BRANCH, SENDING HER SLAMMING against the ground.

She picked herself up and ran, tearing through the light rain.

The woods was alive and dark.

It was watching and moving.

And she was utterly alone to be in a place as confusing as her own thoughts. She fell again, the world tilting downward, and she tumbled downhill. She tried to slow herself, but only cut her finger. She landed with a thud in the fallen branches and brush. Pain swelled in her thoughts, cuts stinging all throughout her body. She tried to push herself up, but her injured wrist crumpled her back down.

She gasped for air, her eyes stinging with tears. She couldn't cry. She wasn't allowed to cry. But every second, her mind reminded her of the blurry past.

A past that she couldn't understand.

Tears broke free.

She lay on the ground of the forest and cried, feeling so

small and vulnerable. She could hear the rustling of the woods growing quietly.

She shouted, sitting up, and then curled up, hiding her face between her legs.

She could feel Avalon trying to ease her mind, but Nikki refused to be taken. She squeezed her eyes shut and let herself sob.

Time was nothing. Everything blurred. Faces. Voices. Words. Horrible, terrifying words. Loving words. But memories. So many memories.

Something pressed gently against her shoulder. She didn't look up.

"It's alright, Nik." *Lincoln.*

A sinking feeling crept into her stomach. Guilt. He'd cared enough to come all the way into the woods to find her.

And *Nik.*

Oh, how it stung.

He didn't say a word, sitting beside her. Close enough that their shoulders touched, so she knew he never left her side.

That's all she wanted.

Finally, she managed to peer out, her eyes swollen, though Lincoln looked at her no differently. "Th-thank y-you," she stammered. She couldn't breathe through her nose, and she was shaking so hard it hurt. She bit her lip to keep herself from crying.

Lincoln gently pressed his hand against her shoulder. "You would've done the same." Would she? Her mind was reeling. Everything spun. Everything ached.

"You feel ready, Nik?"

She broke back down. Whatever dignity and pride she had crumbled away. Tears burned at her face, stinging in the cold. "M-my ma c-called me N-Nik."

She remembered it.

It hurt and it tore at her life, needling at her mind. She wanted to embrace them so badly, but at the same time, was scared of what they were doing.

"Oh." Lincoln's eyes softened. "Do you want me to stop?"

She shook her head.

She loved the nickname.

She felt nauseous. She curled up into a ball, clenching her legs to her chest. Lincoln remained beside her. Was she taking advantage of his loyalty?

He didn't need to be there. Why was he there?

Why did she want him there?

Friends.

She choked. She felt Lincoln's hand against her knee. "Do you want to talk?"

She looked back up to him and sniffled. "Not-not to Taryn."

"No," he said, his voice gentle and calming. "Not to Taryn. Just to me. Only if you want to." Nikki wiped her face, scooting closer to Lincoln. Her friend held her gaze, unbreaking and sure of himself.

She tried to search through the mess of her mind. "E-Emil and Jeana."

"Who are they?" Lincoln asked.

Nikki forgot the word. "L-like Is-Isabel and Lawrence."

Lincoln's face paled. His voice was small. "Siblings."

Siblings. Her eyes burned and she nodded.

"Jess," she squeezed her eyes shut.. "T-Taryn's real na—name is Jessica."

"That's right," he whispered.

His warm hand slipped over hers, with a slight, subconscious squeeze.

Fear seized her chest. "F-fire."

"Fire," Lincoln repeated, his eyes studying her.

"'Run and don't look back,'" her voice didn't crack as she recited the words that had never left her mind. "'Don't let them touch you.'"

Last words.

A warm tear slipped down her face.

"I never got to say sorry," she choked out in a small voice, curling back up. "Nik, I'm sure you have nothing to-"

"I feel it," she choked, a horrible pain of guilt weighing on her chest. She wanted the feeling to stop coming. Not enough images and voices to go with them, only horrible, painful feelings. She couldn't stop the new set of tears that began streaming. "I-I didn't un-understand w-why I could-couldn't go with-with them."

She laughed, though it hurt. "I never said sorry," she

whispered.

"You were… six," Lincoln said, his voice gentle and quiet. "They probably already forgave you." Nikki turned and hugged him. It was sudden, but she wanted to.

He paused, before wrapping his arms around her.

Affection didn't suit him, but it made her heart swell at how much he tried. She finally moved back, wiping her face clean of tears. "W-we should go-go back," she said, trembling.

He tightened his hands around her arms. "Nik. Are you ready?"

She stared at him taking in deep breaths to control herself.

"It's okay if you say no," Lincoln said.

Nikki leaned her head against his chest. She didn't know the words to describe her feelings. The sensation of her tense muscles relaxing, her breathing so quick, her heart seizing up. It felt so good, yet so painful.

They didn't speak for around an hour. They situated themselves to lay on the forest floor, staring up through the mangled canopy of branches of the woods to the incoming morning sky. The sky had grown dark, but it was no usual North Cordell night. The air was cold, but the sky wasn't black, with a smudge as the moon. Tonight the moon parted through the clouded atmosphere, almost an entire circle. Its light shone down through the branches, sending shadows dancing throughout the forest.

Her thoughts were finally calming down, but she didn't dare attempt to revisit them. She'd never cried so hard in her life.

She was grateful for Lincoln's silent company.

"When you die," she whispered suddenly, "do you see people who died before too?" It didn't feel like they were truly gone… or was that just the lack of her memory? She turned her head to his.

He frowned at her, then his face softened, his eyes turning back upward, laughing under his breath. "I wouldn't know."

"A place maybe?"

"I don't know how that would even work. When you die, your body just shuts down. It stays here."

"But where does your mind go?"

Lincoln tapped her forehead. "Your mind is right here. Part of your body."

Nikki frowned, swatting his hand away. "No."

"No?"

She pulled out the Stone. "Explain this."

Lincoln opened his mouth to argue, but shut it, and shook his head and sighed. Avalon snickered.

"We live in a world beyond what we can see," she said. "We can't control everything." "Maybe we're just not advanced yet."

Nikki turned onto her side. "You're scared."

Lincoln flinched. "Why would you think that?"

"You want control," she said. "You think that'll make you feel better. Understanding." Lincoln heaved a sigh. "A lot goes through your head when you see your life flash before your eyes."

Avalon vibrated in her pocket, but Nikki ignored her. A slow, shivering realization came upon her. "Are you afraid of death?" she whispered.

Lincoln met her eyes. He didn't answer. For a moment, his lip quivered like maybe he'd break and tell her, but instead he turned back at the sky. "Everyone you loved is dead, Nik."

"That isn't true," she said, sitting up. She balled her good hand to a fist. The heavy feeling still hung at her chest, the sudden movement making her sick to her stomach. He was right. People she loved were dead.

But that had been ten years ago, but for some reason, she hadn't had time to fully come to terms with it until a decade later.

Lincoln scoffed. "Why not?"

"I mean I love you."

Lincoln shot up, giving her a quizzical look, before his face softened, and he laughed. "I love your innocence, Nik."

"Well, I'm telling the truth!" She elbowed him.

He nudged her back. "Fine. I guess I love you too. As a friend."

"Is there another way?"

Lincoln laughed again, and she continued to stare, confused.

He smiled at her and touched her hand.

Nikki squeezed it. She saw Lincoln's eyes shimmer with tears, but she knew he'd never let them spill.

"I'm not going to let anything happen to you, Nik," he said, quietly.

"We're all born to die, Lincoln," she responded. "And if anything does happen, it will never be your fault."

He gave her a shaky smile, before getting to his feet and dusting himself off. For a moment, she feared he would direct her back to the camp. Back to Taryn, and confronting the rest of the camp.

But to her surprise, he froze.

A shiver went down Nikki's spine. She scrambled to her feet, falling into sloppy form. The eerie shudder overcame her. She hadn't felt it in months.

"Nik," Lincoln whispered. His dark eyes met her eyes.

Her senses sharpened, but her throbbing head, swollen eyes, and running nose didn't exactly suit her coordination. It couldn't be possible. But Dow had warned them... She heard a rustle in the branches above.

She took a quiet step back, swallowing hard.

Lincoln's eyes darted to the side. Nikki followed his gaze to the dark thick brush. She strained her eyes through the tangle of branches. Her heart skipped a beat, realizing the ground sloped down.

She looked back to him, and he was already counting down on his hand. She braced herself.

His final finger fell, and so did the caped attacker from the trees.

"Nik! Run!"

Did he really think she was going to *run*? She appreciated the thought, but by the way he was fumbling for his bow out of his bag, she decided to take it into her own hands. She dodged for the Oquelite, and as expected, they avoided the full-frontal impact. They appeared behind her, fully masked and hooded, their hands aflame, swiping for her. She dodged easily, taking her petite figure to her advantage. She lunged for a strike at the heavily body-armored uniform.

They teleported, appearing opposite of the clearing.

Good. Nikki had their attention.

Dashing, she ran for the trees. She quickly glided up through the branches, struggling to pull one-handed. As expected, she heard a snap above her, the Oquelite now entangled in the trees. A blast of purple flame fell toward her. She leapt out of the way. The flame collided with the branch, blasting it into flame.

Nikki stumbled out of the tree, hitting the ground with a thud.

"Nik!"

"I got you a distraction." She scrambled to her feet. "Shoot!" she shouted as she ran past him into the thick of the woods. The Oquelite burst from the trees.

Lincoln tore out an arrow, shooting. The arrow hit the ground, sending an explosion of dirt and rubble.

The Oquelite shook it off, racing toward them.

Nikki pulled an arrow from Lincoln's pack, and ran out between them, letting the tip ride with electricity. Her heart pounded in her ears and they came closer. And closer. And—They exploded into dust.

"Let's go!" Lincoln shouted. "Hurry!"

Nikki breathed with relief, swiveling to chase after Lincoln through the woods. Every sound blasted, her nerves vibrating on edge.

The Oquelite were back. The Oquelite were back.

Lincoln stopped, Nikki slowing beside him. "There's a river that way," he said, his eyes darting around.

"How can you tell?"

"I hear it."

He could *hear* it?

"This way," he said, turning and breaking into a run, leaping over the fallen, moss dressed tree. Nikki took a deep breath, allowing her nerves to calm, the adrenaline burning at her chest, before breaking out into a run after him.

Tabitha's scream shattered the silent night.

Cole instantly snapped from his dozing gaze, keeping watch in the fields for Lincoln's return, to Tabitha who'd fallen asleep beside him.

He grabbed her shoulders, holding her down from thrashing, shaking her. "Tabs!" he shouted. "Tabitha! It's okay! It's just a dream."

She continued to thrash and pull helplessly, her eyes squeezed shut.

Cole's heart hammered into his ears. "Tabitha!"

Her eyes flew open, staring straight up at him. For a moment, she stared blankly, in a daze, before she frowned and kicked him off of her.

She sat up and wiped her wet eyes. "I fell asleep again, didn't I?" she grumbled. Cole's chest ached as she turned her worn face to him. He nodded. This was the second nightmare he'd intervened in. How many more had she had, that he hadn't been there for?

"You good?"

She chuckled hoarsely. "Yeah, just great."

Wow, thanks Tabs.

She must have seen the hurt in his eyes, as her smirk softened. "It's fine, Cole. I promise. It was a stupid dream anyway. I don't know why I even freaked out."

"I'm sure it wasn't stu—"

"I was back in Liberty." Tabitha's head fell.

Cole waited in the dark for her to continue, but not another word came. He watched her stare at the dancing grasses, her eyes glassy and so far away.

She hardly spoke of her life back in Liberty. He didn't want to press her on it. Anything that made the girl cry out in her sleep was enough to scare him. He turned to the woods, trying to push the growing warmth and thoughts of Tabitha away.

It had been nearly an hour and Lincoln still hadn't returned.

It couldn't be anything serious. Lincoln knew what he was doing. Right? Cole tapped his foot. They always managed to get themselves in a mess and he was responsible for cleaning it up. He didn't want anyone else getting hurt.

Maybe he should go after them.

No. Wait for Lincoln.

Get the Defenders. Tell Taryn what's happening this time.

But Cole had it under control. He didn't need Taryn's help... right?

"Cole!"

Tabitha's cry sent him to his feet. "What? Another nightmare?"

But he turned to find her standing too, her hand pointing

toward the woods. He frowned. "What, Tabs?" Was she going crazy now too?

"You didn't see it?" Tabitha said. "The flash?"

"Tabs, a storm is probably coming, it could've been lighting—"

"There!"

This time Cole caught it. A tiny flash, hardly a glint in the woods. His senses suddenly became overwhelmed, slamming into him like a door and he stumbled back, goosebumps rising onto his skin.

It was just a coincidence. They were just seeing things.

"Oquelite."

"No, Tabitha—"

Tabitha's face hardened, swiveling on him. "I know what I saw."

"Tabs, what if it's just a glint? Or something else... like the *Mors Vis?*"

"What makes the murder feathers any better?" Tabitha growled. "Dow said they were heading south. Back *here*. Cole—"

"If it is them, they would've come back months ago." Right? They wouldn't wait this long. No, they wouldn't. They couldn't.

Tabitha snorted. "I'm going after them." Before he could even take a breath to rebuke, she tore toward the camp. Cole ran after her, struggling to keep up as she barreled up the hill to the cabins. The morning light was beginning to breach through. The smell of rain was strong. And the nauseating feeling of energy was rolling through him.

He'd felt it once before.

He was going crazy; this wasn't happening. "Tabitha! It's too dangerous in there!" She burst through onto flat ground, bursting into the line of cabins. "So you'd leave Nikki and Lincoln there in the name of danger?"

She got him there. He glared at her and she flashed him a nervous smirk as she tore through the door of the girl's cabin. Cole chased after her up the steps, only to nearly collide with Felicity running out the door. She was fully-dressed, her face eager, a satchel packed, and her spear in hand.

Cole crossed his arms and sighed. "I guess everyone had

the same idea?"

"If it's going after those two, then yes. Same idea," Felicity said.

"Because the Oqu—"

"The what?" Felicity cut Tabitha off with a shriek.

"Nothing!" Cole said, quickly. Way to go, Tabs. "Nothing at all is confirmed. We're just being prepared."

"Yeah, sure," Tabitha said, shimmying past Felicity and Cole, as she adjusted a backpack over her shoulder, which was stuffed to the very seams so it stuck straight out from her back. He was surprised the weight didn't topple her over.

Cole turned on Felicity. "Are Charles and Isabel situated?"

Tabitha smirked, putting her fists on her hips. "We've had it covered."

Cole frowned. "What did you do to them?"

Felicity rolled her eyes. "They're fine. They've been asleep for hours. We should be back before they wake up since it's only a quick thing, right?"

"Yes," Cole said before Tabitha could butt in. "And Lawrence?"

"That was supposed to be Ray's job." Felicity looked back to the boy's cabin directly across the camp.

"You left him alone with the Williams boy?" Tabitha raised an eyebrow.

"He hasn't spaced out in months, Tabs," Felicity said. "Besides, Taryn's even weaning him off the 'at-all-times supervision' thing."

Tabitha shrugged, not saying a word. The uncomfortable tension grew in the silence. Ray was trustworthy. Cole had taken a good month to see Ray's effort and loyalty, but it always shone through in the end with his obnoxious personality and all.

But Taryn was still suspicious, and anyone who'd heard of the Imperial instance avoided him. "Do we need to discuss this again?" Felicity said.

"No." Tabitha walked out the door, hooking her arm in Felicity's and pulling her outside, grabbing the handle and swinging the door shut behind her. "Look. Ray is well intentioned, but we've already established the fact he didn't have control over his mind then. We don't know what caused it, or when it could happen again."

"Tabitha Delorous? Cautious?"

Tabitha punched Cole in the arm.

They began a slow walk to the boy's cabin. The moon was bright, showing their shadows against the ground, but the air had no mercy with its cold.

"I lost control of my mind too, remember? When I went into the woods," Felicity said, her voice tremoring.

"But you didn't even remember that. You had no conscious control. And we know Ray remembers, and some part of him must have had to accept it." Tabitha crossed her arms. "And from what we know, Oquelite do *not* have mind control."

"Ewyon do," Cole said, blinking a few times. He remembered Taryn mentioning it. "They're master illusionists. Manipulate thoughts."

Tabitha frowned at him. "All I'm getting from this is you think *Nikki* of all people is behind it?"

"I mean, she apparently is an Aguirre," Felicity grumbled, her eyes falling. "There's a lot we don't know."

That fact was still fresh. It stung.

Cole cleared his throat. "No. Maybe there's someone else out there."

"Another Ewyon?" Tabitha's jaw fell.

"Maybe," Cole said, with a quirk of a smile. Could it be possible? "Or *Nikki*'s been fooling us along."

Tabitha rolled her eyes. "Very funny, Johnson."

They reached the boy's cabin, and Cole skipped up the stairs ahead of them and opened the door.

"I'm coming." Lawrence jumped down, right in front of Cole. Cole stumbled back. Where the *heck* had he jumped from? "How- Wait, What? Where's-"

"He won't listen to me!" Ray said. Cole looked up to Ray standing on the ceiling. Cole shouldn't even be surprised anymore.

Lawrence gave the closest thing Cole could call a smile. A quite smug one at that. Ray crossed his arms and glared.

"Are you stuck on the ceiling?" Cole sighed, stepping out under him.

"Why would I be stuck on the ceiling?"

"Because you're not coming down."

"Maybe I like it up here," Ray said. He paused for a moment. "Yeah, I'm stuck on the ceiling." "Ray's stuck on the ceiling!?" Tabitha pushed past Lawrence and Cole into the cabin and burst out laughing. "I thought you were kidding."

"Har har. I know, hilarious, Delorous." Ray stuck his tongue out.

"Knock it off," Cole snapped, walking to where he stood directly below his younger half-brother. "We have places to be *now*."

Tabitha snorted. "How'd you get up there in the first place?"

Ray looked to Lawrence. Lawrence shrugged.

"Anyway, I think I overestimated my ability," Ray grumbled under his breath. It was common knowledge among all of them Ray wasn't one to ever speak ill of his ability to control himself. It was always "I'm fine. I have perfect control," or "watch me, I can teleport this-number of times." Cole sighed. At least it was just something simple like this.

Not going crazy or taking down a tower.

"I'm going to pull you down."

"Are you kidding me?" Ray frowned at Cole.

Tabitha shook her head. "No. Cole has a point. Remember, your essence doesn't affect him. He can dis-charge it. Like a cancelling effect."

"Fine." Ray reached his hand out for Cole's.

Cole grabbed it, and almost immediately, Ray fell. Cole caught him with ease. Ray scrambled out of his arms and onto his feet, and brushed himself off.

His stare went straight to Lawrence.

"I'm coming," Lawrence repeated.

Cole almost forgot he'd announced it. He sighed. "Lawrence, you can't come. You need to stay here with your sister. Your family-"

"Nikki's my family too."

The room fell silent. Cole's gaze itched to fall, but he kept himself confident, staring into the boy's dark green eyes that refused to tear away. "We'll bring her back," Cole promised. "We know her. She won't hurt herself. It's hardly anything at risk."

"Then I can come."

Tabitha groaned, tossing her hair from her face. "This is for your own good. And really? You'd be willing to go out for your *cousin* that you didn't know before, like, a few hours ago, and perhaps put your siblings at risk?"

Lawrence's face twisted. "It's not that simple."

"How do we even know you're related?" Tabitha said, circling around him. "You're as pale as a sheet, and Nikki's obviously from the Southern Regions."

"You can't rely on looks," Ray said.

Everyone looked to him.

"Whose side are you on?" Tabitha said.

"The side that gets things done," Ray said. "Look if we can't get Lawrence to stay, why stand around pointing out the differences of our complexions?"

Lawrence looked to Tabitha. Tabitha sighed. "Doesn't mean I'm convinced." "Wasn't asking for your approval."

Cole could see Lawrence meant no offence. Simply stating his thoughts, and from what Cole learned, weren't often too positive.

"If you're done, we need to get a move on," Cole said.

Everyone's attention snapped in their directions, their faces blank like they'd forgotten for a moment what they were really here for.

Cole scowled. "Alright, small children. Let's *go*."

They all followed him from the cabin. He signaled them all to be silent as they crept from the camp, down the slope overrun by the tall weeds that pulled at their legs. The grass was too loud for Cole's comfort. It wasn't like they'd be caught. Unless it was Taryn, no one could exactly stop them. It wasn't like he was anxious for himself. Taryn could yell at him all she wanted, but the others?

A pain seemed to sink into his insides just thinking of it.

He didn't have time to contemplate it when the truck suddenly burst to life, the headlights nearly blinding him.

"And where do you think you're going?"

Cole didn't even need to be able to see to recognize Dow's second in command's voice as his silhouette stepped into the light.

Cole's shoulders slumped and he scowled. "Everyone, get in the truck. Giles, mind your own business."

The others listened, happy to ignore Giles's direct command.

"Your business is my business," Giles snapped. "Delorous, don't make that face at me." Tabitha dropped the face too quickly for Cole to catch her, but he just shook his head, and she shrugged with a smirk.

"Now, I repeat, where are you going?"

Giles took a step forward. The shadows that danced over the Officer's face, and the pitch black eyes that seemed to want to pierce into Cole's soul, didn't phase him. Maybe it was adrenaline. Giles and Cole stood at the same height.

Yes, Giles was far more muscular, but then Cole could just beat him with agility- wait. Was he really sizing Giles up for a fight?

"You're going after the two other Members, aren't you?"

Cole prayed Tabitha wouldn't choose now to shout about the possible Oquelite. "If you knew, why did you ask?"

"It's amusing to see your skinny little face grow so agitated," Giles said with a smile. "Very satisfying."

"Glad you live to bathe in other's misery," Cole said, starting to walk past him. Giles grabbed him by the shoulder. Cole tore away.

"I'm here to offer you my assistance."

"Oh, go flex yourself somewhere else, Armstance Giles!" Tabitha shouted, sticking her head out the window of the auto.

"Tabitha!"

She reluctantly slipped back inside.

"Fine," Cole said. "You can help."

"What? I thought we were in a rush!" Tabitha's head was out the window again. "First you let Lawrence, and now *Giles*? Are you insane-"

"Do you not trust Cole?" Lawrence appeared from the bed of the truck.

Tabitha turned to face Lawrence. "Not his judgement."

Cole blocked them out. "But first, why would you offer help?"

"A perfect opportunity to observe. Let me tell you what Executive Cadissa Dean will think when she hears the full-blooded Ewyon *ran away*."

"That's a terrible lie," Cole said. No one was that sick and twisted...

The blank expression of Giles's face seemed to prove it. "What do you know about liars, Johnson? Just get in your darn truck. I'll meet you at the border of the woods." Giles stormed off in a hurry, and Cole rushed into the driver's seat of the truck. Felicity sat in the passenger's seat, and Tabitha in the seat in the back, between Cole and Felicity. Cole came to the quick conclusion that Ray and Lawrence were in the bed.

He wished them luck as he started the truck. The engine began to shake and groan. Cole flinched, but it burst to life.

His grip was firm on the wheel as he made his way through the terrain. He edged to go faster, but didn't want to risk totally damaging the truck, or Lawrence and Ray. But Nikki and Lincoln... they needed help.

Only to agitate him further, Giles sped by on a motor bike. New Defending Officers tech. Tabitha groaned. "Show off."

22

Cole stopped the truck, jumping out. The trees had taken a new shape since he last saw them. The trees were too closely entangled together for a vehicle. Giles stood by the parked bike. They all unloaded from the truck and rushed to meet Cole.

Cole cleared his throat. "Alright, so-"

"I say we go in directly. I have equipment. We can find them with light. Even these mangly trees can't hide from it," Giles said, patting the bag slung over his shoulder.

"But that will cause too much commotion," Cole said. He caught Tabitha's eyes. Her brow was raised, waiting for him to announce their theory. "We don't know how creatures in there react to light-"

She frowned at him.

Giles laughed. "Johnson, this is my job."

"Yeah, well, Cole's the leader. And he has a functioning plan."

Cole was totally caught off guard by Ray's comment, as

he shoved himself between Cole and Giles. His younger brother had a scowl etched into his features as his eyes stared at Giles's, and he glanced at Cole with a prideful smile. Cole tried his best not to smile back. Giles laughed. "You? You're a University boy, from Sulfur. Some prodigy pianist. Taught yourself to read. Reading isn't going to find them."

"Searching will," Cole said. "Knowing Nikki, who Lincoln followed, she couldn't have gone far. From what it sounded like, she just needed to clear her head."

"Or she wanted to run away with valuable information to be used against the Defending Department. Ever occured to you?" Giles took out his spotlight lantern. "I thought you'd know what a traitor looked like when you saw one."

The silence was deafening.

Ray's face fell as turning his head away.

Giles pressed the sensor on top of the lantern. The light burst on all at once. The light was strong, reaching out for yards.

Cole winced. "So, take my advice," Giles said. "Let's go."

Cole clenched his fist, taking several deep breaths before following Giles. It took a lot for someone to get on his nerves, but this Giles guy had set a record of three days. The six of them entered the trees. At first, it seemed bearable. The ground below Cole's feet was familiar and steady, but then the trees grew thicker, beginning to twist around each other, the floor began to become thicker with debris, creatures scampering under the leaves.

No sign of Oquelite so far. Good.

Tabitha and Giles had taken to calling for them, and Felicity seemed to be too distracted to think straight, a line etched between her brows as she studied the world around them. She shivered. Ray had drawn his blade, but he was entirely unfocused, his face flushed.

Lawrence just moved forward, his face unchanging, his eyes unblinking.

Suddenly, Felicity stopped.

Tabitha nearly crashed into her from behind. "Liz, you-"

"Sh!" Felicity snapped.

Everyone went quiet. The woods was perfectly quiet. Not a rustle of the wind, the scamper of a creature, or even a breath. Cole held his breath. Was he right? Were they really about to encounter the infamous Mors Vis and their deaths? Preferable over Oquelite, though. Then a howl shattered the silence.

"Everyone! Run!" Felicity shouted.

They all broke out and ran.

"We can take on some wolves!" Ray shouted after her, his plain sword in hand.

"No! Not these wolves!" Felicity shouted, stumbling but not even daring to back down, her face streaked with terror. "These woods are enchanted. And so are those creatures."

"How do you know?" Giles hadn't even broken a sweat, not a sign of fear in his voice. "I don't know. I can just feel it. I've been in—"

"Lyntox?" Tabitha butted in. "If they're Lyntox, they're part human, so they won't hurt us." A horrible echo of howls and crashing came to disprove Tabitha's theory. Cole made the mistake of looking over his shoulder, seeing dozens of glowing red eyes. No bodies in the darkness, only catching glimpses of the gigantic creatures in Giles's swinging light.

"Go! Go! Go!" he shouted. "Faster!"

Tabitha screamed. Cole stopped and whirled around. Tabitha was on the floor, scrambling away from the vicious beast that towered over her, her satchel in its teeth. She growled back at it. "Give that back, you-"

Ray appeared from thin air, grabbed Tabitha, and disappeared. Cole barely had a moment to process, when he was slammed to the ground. He whipped out his blade, and the wolf screamed, jumping back in pain, stamping out its feet. Cole jumped to his feet.

Right. Magical creatures had a problem with touching him.

"Everyone GET OUT!"

The others didn't hesitate, all but Lawrence, whose eyes remained frozen on Cole's for a moment. "Go!" Cole shouted.

Lawrence twitched and ran.

A wolf growled, the creatures beginning to howl and bark as Cole whirled around to see Ray in the middle of the commotion. The creatures jumped at him from every direction as he flashed in and out of visibility and portals, swinging his blade uselessly against the wolves. Cole charged them.

A brave one charged him. He slashed with the Illuminate but tore back. The sword fared no better than Ray's dummy sword weapon.

The wolf's hide was impenetrable.

The wolf scowled, jumping with its mouth wide open. Cole jumped out of the way, rolling on the forest floor. He scrambled to his feet. He reached for his second option. His stomach dropped. The holster in his belt was empty.

Great.

Ray landed a kick in the wolf's skull. It reared, howled, and slammed down on Ray. The sword slipped from his grip.

"Ray!"

Ray met Cole's eyes as the wolf clamped its jaw down over his shoulder. Ray cried out in pain. Cole's mind went to auto pilot. He raced to Ray, slashing at the wolves who dared even get close. He grabbed Ray's sword, and hopelessly struck at the wolf.

Ray cried out. Cole froze for a split second to see Ray's gold eyes begin to glow, an unsettling glower covering his features. The sword had nicked his ear.

"Snap out of it!" Cole cried. In desperation, he seized the Illuminate and kicked the wolf in the skull.

The wolf whimpered. Ray slipped from its grasp. Cole grabbed him by the arm and tore him to his feet and ran. Ray blinked the glowing eyes, and Cole slapped him just to be sure. Oh mortals. Please don't let him slip.

"Can you teleport?" Cole shouted, glancing over his shoulder to see some of the wolves beginning to recover from the fight.

"I can try." Ray came to a stop.

Cole grabbed his shoulders, his stomach lurching when his left hand was met with wet. Blood.

Ray's eyes were unfocused, dazing off.

"Come on, Ray. Please-"

"I-I'm trying." Ray squeezed his eyes shut. "I-It's hard to teleport to certain people." The world began to pixelate, then fell back to normal.

Ray shook his head, and tried again.

The world fell away, flying back into focus. Cole collided

with Felicity. She nearly screamed, scrambling back, but when she recognized him, she threw her arms around him. He gave her a quick squeeze before returning to the more urgent matters. Tabitha's eyes were wide on Ray's shoulder. "Does this mean he'll turn into a werewolf?" she said. Her eyes were wide with total seriousness.

Felicity laughed. "No, Tabs. That's ridiculous."

"Well, he'll be a lot worse than that if we don't treat it!" Lawrence called out. Giles scowled. "They'll be catching up."

"They already are."

"Where do we go?" Tabitha said. "It's not just like there's a—"

"Will that big castle thing do?"

Everyone whirled around to where Lawrence was pointing. Cole's jaw dropped. Lawrence was not even making an exaggeration.

The towering stone castle was covered in shrubbery, slipping in the cracks in the stone. The door had a large log fallen over it, eroded by time.

"That's convenient," Felicity said.

A howl broke their stares.

They didn't waste another moment to barrel toward the doors. All six of them heaved at the log guarding the entrance, tossing it aside. Cole grabbed the rusted handle, and threw his entire weight down to even budge it open. They all squeezed through the crack, and pulled the heavy door shut.

Cole was out of breath. Moonlight escaped from the cracks in the ceiling, falling over the torn and thrown regal wooden furniture. Age had worn at them, but man made weapons had made the hacks in their delicate designs.

He and Giles began pulling the biggest pieces to build a barricade against the door. Finally, he stopped, fell to his knees, and breathed.

The room was incredible. The ceiling towered above them in a circular dome. Vines crawled up the walls, a single tattered banner swung in the wind. Painting of an ominous figure on the wall, slashed and torn at. A shiver went down his spine.

What was this place? He knew the woods were growing supernaturally fast, but taking castles with them? That was new.

He got to his feet, and silently helped the others gather scraps to make a fire. Thanks to Tabitha's overpacking habit, they were supplied with a lighter.

The fire burst to life, the warmth calming Cole's raging nerves a little. The warm yellow light was far more comforting than the unsettling cold silver light that shone down from the night sky.

It was only when Ray passed out into Cole's arms, they remembered his wound. "You're really starting to make a habit of going too far," Cole said, quickly lowering his unconscious brother to the floor.

They removed his jacket. The wound was uglier underneath, once they'd torn the sleeve away. Felicity gasped, covering her mouth.

"Water?" Lawrence said. He was surprisingly relaxed at the sight. "To wash the blood away." Tabitha searched her bag, coming up with a water bottle. Her eyes didn't shift down to the blood, keeping her eyes trained anywhere else. Her mouth was pressed into a thin line, handing Cole the bottle and turning back.

They washed the wound quickly, lucky it was still only about fifteen minutes fresh. But blood kept coming.

Giles, of all people, pushed his way through. He grabbed Ray's jacket and pressed it hard against Ray's shoulder.

"Bandage? Anyone?" he shouted. "I can't hold pressure on it all night."

Cole blinked away his surprise, turning quickly to Tabitha, who had come up with a bright multi-colored shirt. He didn't ask questions, took it, and tossed it to Giles. Cole applied pressure to Ray's shoulder as Giles ripped the shirt to clean shreds, and wrapped them tightly around Ray's shoulder.

Giles stepped back, and without a word, retreated to the shadowed corner where he'd set up his own camp.

None of them spoke.

No one but Cole dared to even watch Giles go. Cole felt sick, almost. Heavy and confused. Ray had almost died because of him. Everyone was stuck in this creepy castle in the middle of an enchanted wood because of him.

Had he been wrong?

Of course he'd been wrong. He shouldn't have come out in the first place. Nikki and Lincoln were smart. He told himself that over and over. It had been nothing more than a feeling and a flash.

He moved Ray closer to the fire and instructed the others quietly to try and get some rest. He sat alone in the flickering light, awake, fiddling with his Medallion, and with no intention of falling asleep. He glanced over to Giles, his head hidden behind his bag, but his chest moving rhythmically to his heartbeat. Asleep.

Cole tightened his fist over the Medallion.

"Are you okay?"

Cole jumped, Felicity's voice catching him off guard. She laid on her side, opposite him across the fire. The shadows danced along her face, her eyes radiated with concern, a line etched between her brows.

Cole nodded. "I'm fine."

"Is it about Ray?" Felicity sat up, wrapping the thin blanket around her shoulders. Another thing that Giles had provided.

Cole looked to his brother, asleep beside him, his face pale and his shoulder bandaged. At least he looked calm and at peace. No idea what was going on around him.

Then his eyes subconsciously moved to Tabitha, but he caught himself and turned back to Felicity, who was still watching him with the same motherly expression of concern. "A bit," he admitted, loosening his grip on the Medallion.

Felicity's shoulders relaxed. "You never mentioned where you got your medallion from." Cole never mentioned much in general. Talking wasn't his favorite thing in the world. He much preferred to listen, but Felicity seemed genuinely interested, and he didn't want to let down anyone else today.

"I got it from a peddler when I was seven."

Felicity frowned. "That seems a bit coincidental, don't you think?"

Cole managed a tiny smile as he drew his knees to his chest. "When I was seven, I got lost," he said quietly. "I lived with a friend of my father's at the time. He came back for visits. I never knew where he went."

He looked back to Ray, with a heavy sigh. "Well, now I

do."

Felicity tucked a lock of hair behind her ear, an apology forming on her lips, but he cut her off. "I liked it. I thought it was normal. I was seven. I didn't see anything out of the ordinary. But one day, the friend just … disappeared. I went into town looking for him, and then I got lost, and some elderly woman reached out. She ran a little shop and lived alone. She helped me get in contact with my father, and I stayed with her until he came to take care of me."

"And the friend?"

"Killed," Cole said, a lump forming in his throat. He moved on quickly. "I always went back to her shop everyday. To help her and visit. And one day, she gave me the Medallion. It was brand new to the shop. Some stranger had dropped it off."

Cole pieced together the bare minimum of what had happened. When he was seven, the order was given for the infamous Curatrix team to be killed.

Aaron Outown was the previous owner of the Medallion.

Somehow after he'd died, the Medallion made its way to Sulfur, into the old woman's shop, and as he was ever learning, must not have been a coincidence.

"And I'm sure there's a reason you never take it off," Felicity said, with a breezy laugh under her breath. "Did the old woman say so?"

Cole shook his head. "No one told me."

Felicity's face softened.

Cole's eyes fell away from hers. "There's only so much you can do when you're lonely."

Silence followed. Cole didn't meet her eyes again. He let go of the Medallion, feeling suddenly ashamed for reaching for it as comfort.

"You should get some sleep," Felicity said, finally.

He nodded, not willing to argue.

"But know this, Cole. You're not alone anymore."

23

"YOU'RE NOT LEGAL HERE. GET OUT, THIRD-BORN! I SAID, GET
out!"

No. It's not true. You're dreaming.

"Get out before I call the Defenders!"

I'm your daughter! Please. I'm your daughter—

"Tabs, wake up!"

Tabitha shot up. She scrambled back, Cole's features
coming into focus before her. Gray ... stone walls. Daylight
shining down on her through an eroding ceiling... when was
the last time she'd seen daylight?

It rushed back to her.

She relaxed her muscles, sitting up and tearing her fingers
through her tangled hair away from her face. She turned her
head, looking around. Everyone was awake.

Felicity, Cole, Lawrence, Lincoln

Wait, *Lincoln*?

Nikki was there too. Tabitha jumped to her feet. "Wait.
Wow. H-how you'd get here?"

Lincoln shrugged, tossing his cube machine hand to

hand. "Not that hard."

"He used a freaking device to track *me*," Ray said, also awake, and looking as moody as ever. He pulled up the fabric of his pants to reveal a metal anklet. "Nik's got one too. Don't let his smug face fool you."

"You ruined the magic," Lincoln said.

Ray rolled his eyes. "There wasn't any to begin with."

At least, Ray was acting normal. Nikki was sitting, silent, and her eyes focused on Ray's shoulder. "They're back."

They all fell still. Tabitha's breath caught in her throat. She'd been right. The flashes in the woods. The way Cole reacted. She'd been right.

Now. They were back now. They were too late to track them. They were on the move. They were after the Council. Why were they in the woods? Why did they always have to run themselves right into danger?

"Who's back?" Lawrence asked, shattering the silence.

"Oquelite," Giles said, unphased, as he tore at a piece of beef jerky.

So that destroyed Cole's *Mor Vis* theory.

Cole huffed, meeting Lawrence's eyes. "Do you remember the people who burned down the town and destroyed the road?"

Lawrence's eyes widened. His body tensed. "Oh."

"Are you sure it was them?" Tabitha said, her own thoughts seeming to trip over themselves. She had so many questions. Why now? Why not sooner? Why hadn't they attacked the camp? They were supernatural beings who had no fear of the Defenders. What were they doing back? It was no doubt because of them.

But what about them had *changed* for them to come back?

"Now that we finally got the runt awake, we can get out of here," Giles said, wiping his hands on his jacket and getting to his feet. "The Sergeants have to be informed of this."

Runt? "Hey, I'm not-"

Cole nudged her. She rolled her eyes and shut her mouth, her face flushing as she grit her teeth. She tried to meet Giles's eyes, but Giles only looked above her.

"We found the Aviduous and of course, the Aguirre child," he said. "We can head back to the camp for further questioning, and maybe I will make this little mishap less of a trashfire to Dean than it really was."

Oh right. Nikki was an Aguirre. Tabitha had nearly forgotten. The Oquelite were back *and* the whole Aguirre issue *and* the Curatrix machine *and* them trying to prove their worth to Agent Lopez and Sergeant Dow. What next?

She felt like her brain would explode.

Nikki was an Aguirre. The daughter of political legends Tabitha'd heard the names of since she could remember. *That* was too much to process right now.

It made Tabitha both thrilled and sick at the same time.

And Nikki didn't seem to like it either, as she quickly jumped to her feet as quickly as possible and rushed to the doors.

Tabitha gathered her things and met up with the others.

"Now," Giles said, stopping before his hand brushed against the metal handle. "I want no nonsense. Or running off, or getting bitten."

"Technically wasn't my fault," Ray grumbled.

Giles shot him a look.

"Stay close to me, and listen to me."

No one looked happy with it, but no one spoke up. Giles grabbed the ringed door handle and pulled.

Nothing.

Giles frowned. He tried again, throwing his weight and pulling, till a grunt escaped his lungs and he stumbled backwards. He scowled and spat.

"Need a little help?" Ray smirked.

Giles wiped his hands on his pants. "It's just stuck a little. I probably loosened it. It'll open now."

"Are you sure?" Lawrence said with a frown.

Giles ignored him. He grabbed the handle and heaved.

This time Cole helped him, grabbing hold of the enormous ring. Not a budge. A creak or crack. "Harder, Johnson!"

It was pointless. Nothing happened.

"The able lot of you, help!" That meant all of them, excluding the broken wrist and the wounded shoulder.

Tabitha wrapped her arms around Cole to keep him from sliding, her feet up against a jagged cut in the stone floor. She could barely breathe, focusing all her strength on keeping him from sliding. He was heavier than her, and she was not the strongest person.

Her foot slipped, sending both her and Cole crashing down to the ground. Giles stepped back and cursed. "It's stuck! The darn door sealed!"

Tabitha scrambled to get off of Cole as quickly as possible, taking a few steps back, looking over the towering scene of the doors. A shiver overcame her body. She couldn't breathe. A sense of dread overcame her.

And she wasn't the only one.

Everyone froze.

It left almost as quickly as it came.

"We have to get out," Cole said, looking to Giles. "As quickly as possible."

"Don't look at me, Johnson. No defending trial or training prepped me to be stuck inside a magic castle," Giles said. He paused and then laughed. "A magic castle," he murmured under his breath.

Cole swallowed hard. "Alright then. We search this place, and find another way out. A window. A back door. A hole in the wall for crying out loud. Any possible exit."

"Sounds plausible," Giles grumbled.

Cole nervously took the lead, the others following him without hesitation as they moved in the nearest corridor. A long hallway, the entrance arching high above their heads, reaching down far into the darkness.

"Light?" Cole said.

A light burst on. Everyone jumped, turning to Lincoln, who held a small rectangular device, now glowing up in his hand.

"Don't tell me that thing can taser people *and* glow," Giles said.

Lincoln smiled. Apparently, he took this as a compliment. "Now, it can do other things too. I created my own hotspot. Tabitha, can you get the box in your bag?"

Tabitha frowned. Box? She opened her backpack, and dug through it before her hand met cardboard at the bottom. She drew it out and handed it to him, but not without a glare. "I made trackers for Ray and Nikki, but they're far too complicated for me to replicate for everyone right now, but"—he opened the box to reveal nearly a dozen... ear buds? "—how about ear comms? If we get lost again, we can communicate... well, if it works."

"I can't believe you're using this as an experiment session," Ray said, and then he eagerly took one of the earbuds.

The others followed. Tabitha inspected it first, and became certain they *were* regular earbuds, but modified Lincoln-style. Which meant they weren't really lovely looking. Really, he needed to paint his inventions or make them look cool or *something*.

"Great," Giles grumbled. "You all have new toys. Let's get a move on!"

The group made their way down the hallway. It smelled of mold, the air growing moister the farther they went down the hallway. Along the walls, moss had begun to creep along the stone, abandoned cobwebs hung from the ceiling, but the most terrifying was the portraits coated in dust that hung on the walls.

Tabitha forced a swallow.

Many of the faces portrayed women. Immaculate, and utterly perfect in every shape and form. Chiseled, even jaw, small petite noses, broad shoulders pulled back into perfect posture. And strictly violet eyes.

"Ewyons," a voice gasped from behind her.

Nikki stopped, her eyes glued on a portrait. Tabitha looked from Nikki to the portrait. No resemblance. The Ewyon's fair, pale skin, and golden curls were in stark constant to Nikki. Nikki pursed her lips, and Tabitha stepped beside her. The hall grew darker as Lincoln's light drifted away, but Nikki didn't move.

"You don't look related," Tabitha said, with a small nudge. "Guess this creepy mansion isn't yours."

Nikki didn't acknowledge the joke, and Tabitha didn't blame her. It had to have been one of her weaker attempts, but there wasn't much to make light of in this situation. What choice did she have? It wasn't the end of the world. They'd find a way out of this *Ewyon* manor. She snapped back into focus on hearing Nikki repeat her usual string of numbers under her breath. "Did you ever find out what the number are?" she asked.

Nikki shook her head.

"Don't drill her, Tabs." Felicity appeared behind her.

"What are the numbers?" Tabitha asked.

Without hesitation, Nikki recited: "42732."

"I bet I could turn that into a song."

Felicity groaned, but Tabitha just smiled. Anything to lighten the heavy mood. She caught a glint of amusement in Nikki's eyes, and Tabitha's smile became genuine.

"Four my friend—" Tabitha started.

"Oh no," Ray laughed from ahead of them. "Is this song just a bunch of puns?"

"You bet, Mathews."

The girls rushed to catch up with them, Tabitha's mind whirling with the numbers. "Four my friend. Two too much. Seven One... No, Eleven. Seven and Eleven rhyme."

"Ingenious," Ray teased, and Tabitha was tempted to swat him in the face.

"Seven Eleven... Three we... Two do. Perfect!" Tabitha held back a laugh at the ridiculous rhyme she'd formed, but it brought smiles, both amused and those trying to hide it, to their group. "Now whenever you all are nervous you just remember... Four my friend. Two too much. Seven Eleven. Three we Two do."

"Kinda catchy," Ray said.

"You gonna sing for us, Ray?" Lincoln said, sending a smirk to him over his shoulder. "I'll spare the mirrors."

"Aw, you're not even bad—"

"Guys, hurry up!" Cole waved to them, and they ran back to catch up.

Four my friend. Two too much. Seven Eleven. Three we Two do. Easy enough to remember. It was a fine distraction from the terrors haunting her mind. They'd started so suddenly. Right after... the death. *Four my friend. Two too much. Seven—*

"New plan!" Officer Giles shouted, halting.

Ray groaned.

"At this rate, we'll be too slow. I suggest me and your—" he wrinkled his nose. "—Aviduous go ahead and scout. Johnson, take the light and guide the rest behind us. Can you see in the dark, shrimp?"

Lincoln pinched his face, seeming to try to hold back a scowl. "Yes. Perfectly fine." He handed his light to Cole, and went after Giles down the hall.

"Stay closer," Cole said, his eyes meeting Tabitha's. "Don't stall."

"Dead end!"

Nikki jumped at Officer Giles's voice. Cole ran, the others rushing after him. Nikki was small enough to maneuver her way to the front. Lincoln and Giles stood in front of a stone wall. No new turns or openings.

Nikki sucked her breath in.

This place is far more cursed that I imagined, Avalon huffed.

Nikki's heart jumped. *Cursed?*

The Void has twisted this place beyond imaging. Dark things had come about here.

"It can't end here," Lincoln said. "There's no way a structure like this would have such an awkward ending to a corridor."

Cole held the light up, casting shadows along the walls. It seemed no different from the others. Same moss, and weathered age, though no decoration hung on its walls.

"I don't know. It looks like a wall to me," Ray said.

Lincoln rolled his eyes.

"Everyone! Step back!" Giles shouted.

He didn't wait for them to follow his order, as he backed up and then jumped into a run, barrelling straight for the wall. He slammed right into it, bouncing back onto the floor. A small groan escaped his lips. "That's a wall alright," he scowled through gritted teeth. *Do you recognize it?* Nikki asked Avalon.

For a moment, there was no response.

Perhaps.

The word was short, and final. And extremely unhelpful. She was on her own. Lincoln pressed up against a stone. He frowned, trying another.

"Oldest trick in the book, scrawny," Giles said, still planted on the floor, with arms crossed. "Good thing this place looks pretty old."

Ray snickered, and Giles glared.

Lawrence crept closer to the wall, his dark green eyes strong in the light through the thick lenses of his glasses, as he studied the wall. Nikki decided maybe it would be best for him to try. He was the North Cordell native of them all.

He frowned, placing his hand against the wall, and pushed.

Like Lincoln, nothing happened.

He stepped back. "Maybe it's not a push-brick code sort of thing."

"Then what is it?" Felicity asked.

"The place is full of Ewyon portraits," Tabitha said. She turned excitedly to Nikki, a large grin on her face. "If there's anything there, shouldn't she be the one to activate it?" Nikki hated when everyone looked at her. It made her feel small, and want to cower away and hide. Especially right now. Even their looks taunted her with the name. "I-I don't know," she murmured.

She turned to the wall anyway, and studied it. She looked up. A rusted lever jutted from the wall. She frowned. That hadn't been there before.

She blinked, and it was gone.

She shook her head. She'd gone crazy.

Illusions, Avalon gasped. *Incredible. You're far too young to be able to see through them. Illusions?* Nikki's heart skipped a beat.

Avalon chuckled. *Of course. Why didn't I see it before?*

Nikki almost cracked a smile. "They hid it in plain sight!" she cried. It was almost genius. Of course someone would suspect the door to have a complicated code, not a lever. And a lever only seen by trained Ewyon.

"What is it?" Lincoln asked.

She didn't answer him. "Pick me up," she said.

Lincoln frowned.

"Pick me up," she repeated.

Within a moment, she was hoisted up onto Lincoln and Lawrence's shoulders. The boys wavered below her, and she almost crashed into the wall. She thrust her hands out, catching their weight against the wall. She breathed a sigh of relief.

"What the heck is she doing?" Giles said.

She narrowed her eyes to where she remembered the lever, and reached out. She groped around the stone but found nothing.

Avalon?

The Stone gave no instruction. Nikki sighed, then her hand hit something. Her heart sped. She grasped the air, feeling the rust crumble in her fingers. She almost laughed at the air she grasped. It looked impossible.

She pulled.

She held her breath. The wall remained the same. Lawrence shifted her weight to Lincoln, who swung her down to her feet. She couldn't take her eyes from the wall.

This wasn't right.

"Just give it up," Tabitha said. "We can try something else. Whatever the heck Nikki did proved not helpful."

No. This wasn't right.

Nikki balled her good hand, and struck the wall. The stone crumbled from beneath her feet. A scream was stolen from her throat as she fell into the darkness. She hit the ground, tumbling down, another ledge ramming into her chest, knocking the air from her chest. She scrambled for something to hold onto, but her attempts to hold onto the slippery steps were pathetic. She hit the ground with a thud.

She groaned, a painful shudder overcoming her. She sat up. Her entire body throbbed, both of her hands now sending painful strikes through her bones. She grit her teeth, a painful cry escaping as a horrible pain tore through her broken wrist. That could not be good. She gasped for air, rolling to her back.

She rubbed her eyes.

The room was dark.

She panicked. She'd fallen. Where were the stairs? Did they know where she was?

"Lincoln!" she screamed, scrambling up. She hit a wall, sending her falling back. "Lincoln! Where are you?"

Calm down, child! Avalon snapped.

Nikki shut her mouth, her heartbeat thundering in her ears. She slipped her trembling hand into her pocket and withdrew the Stone. Avalon glowed brighter.

Nikki took a deep breath. Everything was okay. It was fine.

Where are we? She asked.

Avalon didn't answer, but the light in the Stone began to swirl, sending an excited shiver down Nikki's spine. Did this mean Avalon did, in fact, know this place? She had guessed it was cursed.

She took another deep breath, and headed farther.

The cellar, as Nikki decided it, seemed to be completely empty. Every inch of darkness unveiled by Avalon's light was replaced with nothing but an empty stone floor, and another fresh coat of dust. The place smelled musty, the air cold, and sent goosebumps up her skin. She was about to declare it empty and turn around, when something glinted in the light. Nikki frowned. She held up Avalon, and her jaw dropped.

Piles and piles of jewels, coins, and polished possessions glittered in the light. She took another step. The treasure trove reached farther. She picked up her pace, then burst into a run. The cellar was full of riches. Chests, wood rotten from time, had ancient fabrics spilling from them. Tables, with melted candle sticks, were covered in thick books with golden binding. Nikki turned, something catching her foot.

She jumped back and clamped her hand over her mouth.

On the floor was a body.

Thousands of years old to where all that was left were the clean bones, left untouched by centuries. A jewel encrusted gown lay loosely over the bones.

What was this place?

She waited for Avalon to intrude her thoughts and answer, but the Stone's voice never came. "Nik!"

She whirled around, wincing at the bright light. Lincoln's face came into view, his features tense with worry. He heaved a sigh of relief. "You're okay."

The other clambered in after him.

Tabitha was the first one to catch sight of the skeleton. Her eyes grew wide and blinked as she opened her mouth, then froze.

"Just a skeleton, Delorous," Giles grumbled, stepping over it without an ounce of care. His shadowy figure picked up a golden plate, holding it up to his reflection. He frowned. "What's all this rich junk doing here?"

Cole rested a hand on Tabitha's shoulder. Her mouth shut, though her eyes didn't move from the body, like it might spring up at any moment and attack them. "This explains why the manor was mostly empty."

"They moved everything down here," Felicity breathed in realization. Her eyes glittered in awe, a small smile quirking at the corner of her mouth. "It's incredible. How long has it been here? Why? How has no one found it?"

"These woods are enchanted," Lincoln said. "It's a pretty established fact." "So the more it grows, the more it unveils,"

Felicity said.

"Then where has a whole freaking castle been hiding?" Ray said. His brow was furrowed, looking nothing but skeptical.

Crash!

Everyone whirled around to Giles, the plate he'd been holding rolling on the cobblestone floor. He flashed a toothy smile. "Ever heard of the Void Theory?"

"Didn't think you'd be much interested in theories, in all honesty," Felicity said.

Giles snorted, sorting again through the pile. "The Theory is that there are existence of other dimensions, and universes. Like time travel. Theoretically, you can't change what's already happened, so traveling back in time is just going to another dimension in which the events haven't occurred yet."

"And this has to do with the woods?" Felicity frowned.

"Well, there has to be a way to travel dimensions, Bentsworth," Giles said, like it was the most obvious thing ever. "That's where the Void comes in. The space between. How do you think Mathews can teleport? He slips between and wills to another location. Minor usage of the Void. Mere seconds."

Ray looked down at his hands with a wicked grin. "Wow. So I can travel dimensions?" "You can't even get down from a ceiling," Lawrence snorted.

"Oquelite get their illiah-essence from outside sources. So, no, Mathews. You can't travel dimensions. Even if you were a full-breed." Giles tossed a jeweled necklace aside, pulling out a leather satchel, which he opened, dumped out a spider, and swung over his shoulder. "Not even the most powerful Impure could. There were stories in ancient times about that."

"You sure know a lot about … that," Ray said, seeming a little disappointed about not being able to travel dimensions.

"Took a course after the Trials," Giles said. "Contrary to popular beliefs, Aviduous can retain information. Though I have nothing on shrimp and his mind."

Lincoln rolled his eyes.

"The woods contain all of what disappeared after the Ancient age, where the races were all full-blooded and roamed freely. No one really knows what happened, but it all had to go somewhere, eh? And now it's all coming back to rapidly?"

Nikki hated to admit it, but for once, Giles had a point. That sounded logical. "Nice lesson, but we should really be getting out of here," Cole said.

Giles patted his bag. "Already started. This stuff's too good not to bring back."

"Gather *supplies*," Cole said. "Whatever we can use to possibly get away from the Oquelite and out of the woods. Then we can go further and find an exit."

Nikki didn't need to be told twice. She tightened her grip on Avalon and timidly made her way around the skeleton and moved to search a pile of discarded furniture. Nikki knelt down and set Avalon down on the ground beside her, the Stone giving her a bit more light. Nikki crawled under the chair, batting away an abandoned cobweb. She grabbed a small box. She held her breath and opened it.

Nothing.

She set it aside. She crawled over to a knocked over table. Using her back, she pushed the table from the wall. Behind it lie a dozen woolen sacks, tossed carelessly on top of each other. Nikki reached for the Stone, jumping when someone stepped into the green glow. She looked up to meet Felicity's eyes.

Felicity knelt down beside her.

Nikki didn't acknowledge her, pulling at the string tied around the bag. It fell away easily, and she opened it.

Avalon gasped.

The bag was heavy with gold, and gems all beyond Nikki's belief. But something green glinted in Avalon's light. Nikki frowned, reaching in and drawing out a delicate golden bracelet adorned with a green crystal shard.

It looked almost identical to the Stone, but more preserved with time, and it lacked the powerful glow. Nikki didn't doubt for a moment *this* was the material Lincoln was talking about that the Ewyon had created the stone from and used the excess to adorn their royalty. *I thought it was all gone.*

Nikki swore the Stone choked up.

It's incredible. Nikki noted.

Avalon huffed. *Oh child, if a simple bracelet blows you away, you truly haven't seen anything the Ewyon had to offer.*

Nikki slipped the bracelet into her bag. *It might be useful in the future.*

How so?

I'm still figuring that out. She had a vague idea, but she had to test it first. Perhaps more research with the help of Lincoln—

"Are you okay, Nikki?" Nikki forgot Felicity was even there. "How're you doing?"

Nikki blinked. She had not been expecting that. Sympathy? What for? She was perfectly okay. Oh right.

"I'm fine," she said quickly. She turned back to sort through the sack.

"You don't need to lie."

Nikki frowned. "I'm not lying," she said, looking over her shoulder. Was she expecting her to break into fits over things she couldn't control right now?

"Well," Felicity said, with a shrug of her shoulders. "I'm sorry if we made you uncomfortable to where you thought you had to hide your identity."

They thought she was lying about not knowing her parents? Nikki was speechless. She hadn't *remembered.* Even if she had, how was she supposed to identify her parents as the infamous Aguirres? She almost understood now why Miriam got angry at the constant pointing out of her Curatrix family member.

"I mean. I should know!" Felicity laughed. "My father is *Bentsworth.* Richest man on Earth. Maybe I should-"

"No. I wasn't hiding anything," Nikki spat out a little too quickly. "Everything is fine."

Felicity jumped. Her eyes widened, with an uneasy smile. "Oh. Okay."

Nikki felt a pang in her stomach. She hadn't meant to be so direct. Great. "I-I-"

"No, no. It's okay," Felicity said, with a wave. "Just know I'm open for talking. I'll leave you be now."

With that, Felicity turned and crawled out of the pile of furniture and walked away. Nikki groaned quietly to herself. She needed to use her words better. She'd explain herself to Felicity once they were out of this mess.

After she emptied the sack, Nikki had found nothing of

importance. She had found a rat that definitely had some sort of supernatural in its red eyes that hissed at her before running away, long golden sticks with strange wax cylinders, and chests of delicate fabrics. She grabbed Avalon and crawled out. She rose and made her way farther into the darkness.

The cellar seemed to go on forever, full of more and more piles of treasure. Nikki peered only once over her shoulder. The faint light of Lincoln's device lingered behind her. She took a deep breath and ventured further into the darkness. It seemed to stretch on forever. Finally, light shed over a wall.

She had reached the end of the room. She turned to find a small corridor in the left wall. She frowned. She crept toward the narrow staircase, cobwebs decorating the hall, a light drip echoing through, and the smell of mold overwhelming.

Nikki looked to Avalon. She wasn't surprised when the Stone said nothing. Nikki took another deep breath and headed up. She hummed Tabitha's number song under her breath as she tested the first creaky step. *Four my friend. Two too much. Seven Eleven. Three we Two do.*

She crouched, running up the spiral steps quickly, batting at the web. It caught up against her hand, and she nearly slipped on a step, and she caught herself with the elbow of her bad hand up against the step. She grit her teeth and rose. The staircase went in a circle, rising higher and higher.

The higher they rose, the cleaner the stairway became. Mold no longer stained the wall. Moss didn't cling to the cracks in the stones. The air even felt cleaner.

A shiver went down Nikki's spine.

Finally, sunlight spewed out over the steps. Nikki's heart lurched. She burst into a run. She found a small wooden door, with a small square window, and splintered planks of wood. Nikki thrust it open.

She lost the ability to breathe.

It was untouched by time, holding a bed made in bright red fabrics, a lace canopy draped over the frame. A small desk was tucked in the corner, a quill still upright in the inkwell. Nikki hesitantly stepped onto the deep blue carpet. To her surprise, it was soft, and had a bounce under her feet.

She looked up to the window, where sunlight streamed in through the branches.

Nikki rushed to the window, sticking her head out, smiling with a twinge of childlike delight. She was so high up. She could breathe cool, fresh air

Then a realization struck her.

This is my tower, Avalon gasped.

Nikki jumped. It was? She remembered the flashback Avalon had shared with her distinctly, but the room in the flashback had been much grander, and the tower far less high up. *It doesn't look like the one you showed me.*

Because it's not, Avalon said, her voice low. *After I was found by the Ewyon troops, and after Orion—*Nikki shuddered at the mere mention of the man. She'd been face to face with the cold Oquelite Lord himself, once. He was safely locked away in the prisons of the Capitol North, on the top of the world, but it didn't give anyone any comfort. His two sons, Silas and Matthias Idicous, were still loose on the world—*abandoned me, they were horrified to the fact I was with child. Once conceived of Oquelite blood at that. The higher ups confined me to this place.*

Avalon rarely mentioned her daughter, who Nikki had only seen once in her flashback, as an infant. According to a record, the daughter had been killed. *Kathryn.* That had been the girl's name.

Do not think of Kathryn. Avalon snapped, reminding Nikki that when the link was open, her thoughts could sometimes be seen by Avalon.

I'm sorry that she died.

I barely knew the infant, Avalon said. *Only that life had mercy on her and killed her. How did you know she died?* Avalon had been confined in a Stone all that time. How had she been able to see what her daughter had been up to?

This is not important right now, child. The Stone made a sound that sounded close to a snarl. *Sorry.*

Avalon sighed. *This is not my castle, though.*

How's that possible? If this is your tower?

I don't know. These woods are full of strange essence. This tower seems untouched by time, yes? Nikki agreed.

Perhaps Fate had it be this way. Adding this peculiar tower to this Ewyon castle.

Nikki frowned. That sounded odd. *You said this must have*

been a result of some dark event. *What castle is this?*

My speculation of this castle is the only other possibility. Once my kind escaped across the sea, and created their own kingdom, Carastene had a place built. What happened here, I don't know much of. I can only guess the Shadow Soul.

Nikki frowned. *How did you know Carastene built a place at all? And what's a Shadow Soul?*

Avalon gave a long sigh. *The Shadow Soul is the reason for the Ewyon's dislike of the Oquelite. It was only a silly prophecy, but it always sent my people into hysterics at the thought of it being born. My body might have been dead, but my essence, my subconscious, went to The Stone. I learned from my surroundings.* Avalon snorted.

Oh. Right. And the Stone was with ... Her heart leapt. *Kathryn!*

Avalon sighed with annoyance. *Yes. Will you stay on topic? Your new fascination with my deceased daughter is underwhelming.*

Nikki shut out the Kathryn thoughts for now, though she couldn't promise she wouldn't bring it up again. *We can use the window to get out. We can get into the trees and climb down. And not fall out?*

I'm sure Ray can teleport some of us.

Ah yes. That boy. Avalon never liked Ray. Nikki wasn't sure if it was because of his tendency to talk too much or the fact he was an Oquelite hybrid. Probably both.

I think that's the best option.

I cannot argue with that. Use the window. Don't venture further. I can feel your rebellious thoughts. *I won't,* Nikki promised, and Avalon severed the connection.

Nikki's rebellious thoughts were indeed not about venturing further. Instead, they were focused on what Avalon's tiny room contained. There had to have been something useful here. Under the bed was empty, besides a half melted candle. The desk had a stack of blank paper, weighed down by the inkwell. One paper, thick and textured, indeed did have writing on it. The ink was smeared and hurried, and in a language Nikki didn't understand, all but the last words, signed *'Avalon Idicous'*.

She had signed with Orion's surname. Why had she done that?

Nikki finally moved to the chest. She opened the lid to find gowns. The material was rich and heavy, though nothing extravagant and large, like Nikki had seen in the portraits. How was Avalon treated after they found her? They left her to a tower and plain dresses, despite being the lawful heir to the throne. The sunlight glinted off of something at the bottom of the chest.

Nikki frowned.

She pushed the gowns aside. A shield. The shield was silver, though polished the best it could be, was still worn, the engraving weathered away, despite the symbols around the edge. Nikki reached to pick it up, but the side pricked her hand. It was sharp.

She found two sides of the circle were ragged and sharp, and two other sides were safe to touch. With her one hand, she pried it from the bottom of the chest, dropping it to the ground. She cringed as it clattered.

In the sun, she was able to see the many dents in its surface, and the shadows of the symbols. Letters.

Her heart skipped a beat.

The symbols were *letters*.

She guessed where the small diamond shape intersected the pattern indicated the end and beginning of the word.

S I L

She restarted. She was going backwards.

FIDELIS.

"Fidelis." Nikki smiled. She liked the sound of it.

On the back of the shield, was a leather strap tied through two loops in the back. Had Avalon used this? Nikki slung it over her shoulder. She was sure E could fix it up to be useful. She put the gowns back into the chest, and rose to leave.

She looked back at the room frozen in time, and tightened her grip on the leather strap. *I have questions, Avalon.*

"So this is what you do everyday?" Lawrence wasn't sure if he could get used to this.

Tabitha laughed, tossing her head back. "What? No, I *wish*. We never got to explore a magical, probably cursed, castle before. I mean the Glass Tower comes in second, but it still has nothing on this."

Ah, right. This was *the* group at Imperial. Couldn't have all their adventures too close together. "Everyone re-group!"

Cole shouted.

Lawrence and Tabitha perked up. It felt like they'd been searching for hours. All Lawrence managed to find were hundreds of coins and jewelry, and a snapped-in-half dagger, and after ten minutes of disappointment, deemed the pile full of nothing useful.

They all grouped around the light.

"Alright. Anything useful?" Cole asked.

Felicity found a canteen. Tabitha had collected about a dozen satchels, and also tried to convince Cole to let her take a portrait of a funny looking woman, but was turned down. Lincoln found nothing useful, besides scrap metal that only proved useful to him. Giles offered a bow and arrow, but almost instantly the string snapped, so it was deemed useless.

"Anything else?" Cole said. He looked around and frowned, and then began to count. "Where's Nikki?"

"Here! I'm right here!"

They all whirled around to see the small girl bounding toward them. Lawrence's nerves settled a bit. She looked unharmed.

She opened her sack and dumped the contents onto the floor. Lawrence's eyes widened. She'd found quite a lot. Two knives and a sheath. A torch and oil. And a bracelet. She also had something strapped onto her back, but it was hard to see in the faint light. Was it… a shield?

Nikki tentatively raised her voice again. "I found a way out."

"What did she say?" Giles shouted.

Lawrence's heart leapt. "She found a way out!"

"Why didn't you mention that first?" Giles said, unimpressed.

Lawrence glared at him, though he knew Giles would never see. He wasn't exactly loud or invited, but the guy was getting on his nerves.

"Well we know now," Lincoln said, rushing to her side. He winked at her. "Lead the way." They all followed Nikki down the dark cellar, and Lawrence purposely kept to the back. He was uninvited, he reminded himself again.

He didn't belong here.

He was only here because Isabel was convinced that Nikki was the Nik they had known as children. She should be dead…

They made their way up a crammed hallway that spiraled upward, until they reached a door. Nikki opened it, nearly blinding Lawrence with the unexpected stream of daylight. He squinted, his eyes adjusting to see a moderately sized window in the wall of the tiny room. A window.

In a tower.

"Ray, you feel okay enough to teleport?" Cole said.

Ray squeezed his eyes shut, and flexed his hands. His eyes burst back open, and he released a sigh. "I have enough for… maybe just myself."

"So that's a no," Cole said. "We go out the window manually. People with one working arm are going to need assistance."

Ray and Nikki exchanged glances.

Tabitha was eager to get out, though Cole appeared to not trust her in the slightest. Lawrence didn't blame him. The bubbly girl would fall out of the tree laughing, but there wasn't much of a choice. Felicity went after Tabitha.

Ray chose Lincoln over Giles to help him down.

Cole looked to Lawrence. "You and Nikki."

Lawrence hid his surprise, ignoring the beating of his heart in his ears. He and Nikki moved to the window sill. He took a cautious step out on the branch. It swayed slightly, but it maintained his weight. He grabbed hold of a branch above him, and held out an arm to Nikki. She without hesitation stepped up beside him, clasping the branch with her good hand, and Lawrence wrapped an arm around his waist, his face heating at having her so close. Her eyes were so near to his. He could barely breathe.

He knew the eyes.

They didn't belong to her face. The deep blue that stared back at him, with certainty, and such innocent trust. Her eyes reminded him painfully of his mother's.

He felt himself threatening to choke up. He looked away.

The descent was a painfully slow, tricky process.

Lawrence was astonished with the structure of the tree. It was thick and sturdy, despite being part of a rapidly growing forest. It seemed ages old. Other trees braided their branches, creating an intricately woven path downward. Once they reached a steady branch, Lawrence steadied himself without the support of a higher branch. Nikki didn't let go of him.

He almost pushed her away, but released her hand.

She must have been afraid to lose her balance again. Especially with one working hand. He scolded himself. "We won't fall," he assured her.

She nodded, though her face was still tense.

Finally, they dropped safely to the ground. Lawrence was quick to let go of Nikki and get control of his composure. Had Isabel been right? No. That was crazy.

Way too coincidental that he just so happened to stumble into her.

She was dead. Just like his aunt and his mother.

"Run!" Giles screamed.

The high pitched command caught everyone off guard.

"What?" Tabitha shouted.

"RUN!"

A howl met them with an answer.

"Are you kidding me?" Lawrence turned on his heel and ran. The others barrelled after him. How many times could someone be chased by wolves in less than twenty four hours? It was more than once, apparently.

A spray of water threw Lawrence off. He nearly stumbled right into Lincoln and off the short ledge. They all had stopped. Lawrence's heart beat painfully against his chest. What was going on? They stopped? Rain? Wolves!

"A river," Lincoln gasped.

He looked over his shoulder, Cole and Giles chasing after them, two shadowed figures of wolves picking up speed.

"Jump in! Go! Get in! Gosh darn it!" Giles sputtered, his face red in hysterics. No one waited another moment, leaping over the ledge. Lawrence hesitated. Someone grabbed his collar and sent him over the edge, plunging into the raging rapids. It wasn't until the wave crashed over his head, that he remembered how much he despised the water.

24

"WHERE'S MUM?"

Isabel sat on the green velvet sofa, her face buried in a tablet, ignoring her younger brother tugging at her sleeve. He scowled. "Bel!"

She looked up. "What, Cents?"

He cleared his throat. "Where's mum?"

Isabel shrugged, tucking a lock behind her ear, her eyes piercing, as she frowned. "Why are you wondering?"

Cents heaved a dramatic sigh. "She said she was going to take me to town while she did errands." "Well, where could she be?" Isabel said, her eyes bored, turning back to the tablet. Cents swatted it. "She went to the garden," Cents said. "I asked her to get some bashil."

"Basil," Isabel corrected, pushing his glasses up to his head. "She spoils you."

Before Cents could respond, Isabel laughed. "Go check the garden!"

Cents stuck his tongue out, though he couldn't help but laugh too. He pulled on his rubber boots and bounded out the front door. The air was cold, carrying the winter with it as it stung at his exposed skin. That air smelled of rain. A smell Cents found calming. He began his trek around the small, cozy house, set in the small farm lands of the *region, near the mountain. His mother always loved the view of the feared mountains.*

But she hadn't been the same recently. Not after the faces on the screens had told her about his aunt. Isabel told him she had died, but Cents was convinced she was playing a prank on him. He skipped to quicken his pace. "Mum? Mum, where are you?!"

He stopped in the garden. It was deathly quiet. His mother was nowhere to be seen. The basil plant was untouched. He frowned. A splash caught him off guard.

He jumped, looking to the small pond a few feet away. He hesitantly took a step closer. "Hello?"

No one answered. He took another step, the water now reflecting back, becoming clear—

The memory was thrust aside by a mouthful of waves.

Lawrence's head shot above the very different water, scrambling to keep afloat. Waves crashed into him, dragging him under. He gasped for air, inhaling the waves. He was thrown up, coughing and gasping for breath.

He was going to die.

He was going to *drown.*

His glasses bit into the back of his ears, hanging on for their dear life. He was pulled back underwater. Water weighed down on him. His mind flooded his sight with horrible faces. He wanted to scream, both out of pain and for air. His body slammed against something. He dug his fingers into it for his dear life and pushed his head over the crashing waves, gasping for air. The log in his grip turned, dunking him back into the water. He tried to get a grip, but the log kept turning and tossing in the water.

No! I can't lose it!

He grabbed it with his hands, feeling the wood slice into his palms, and heaved himself over, lying with his torso against the log, balancing himself.

A body clinging to a rock, jutting out from the river, caught his attention. "Nikki!" He got a mouthful of water in return, nearly losing his balance. His glasses slipped, clinging for their dear life on his ears, his vision completely blurred. He cursed. He tried to steer the log with all his might. He was going too fast. "Jump!" he screamed.

Nikki's eyes were wide in horror. He held an arm out to her.

And then a wave crashed against the rock, Nikki losing her balance and disappearing under the crashing river.

"No!" Lawrence cried out. "No! Nikki!"

He grew sick, his head growing light. The blurry world greeted him coldly with death. The water tore at his skin. And now she was gone. Dead—

"Lawrence!"

He whipped his head in the direction of the voice. All he saw were the blurred whipping waves.

Curse my eyes.

"Nikki!"

A hand grasped his extended wrist. He gasped, the weight nearly pulling him over. He wrapped his opposite arms around the log, pulled with all his might. Nikki wrapped her arms around him, her breath shaky on his neck, and he could feel her heart beating against his own chest. They barely had a moment to breathe before the log was thrown and dipped back under water. It was spit back up, and Lawrence's glasses slipped back over his eyes. Water droplets distorted his vision, but he could finally see.

"What do we do?" Nikki shouted, now holding onto the log, her arms clenched around it. Lawrence cringed for a split moment. Her hand was never going to heal at this rate. "Just don't let go!"

They needed to get off. They couldn't keep this up. Eventually they'd fall prey to waves. They would die. Another set of blue eyes would drown because of him.

They needed a ledge.

Perhaps he could steer the log and get caught and jump off.

Something hit him in the back of the head.

"Sorry!" Nikki, holding onto the log with her bad hand, lifted the shield from her back. "What are you doing? Are you crazy?"

She didn't answer him, her eyes focused on the shore. She had gone mad, Lawrence decided. He wrapped an arm around her waist, not trusting her bad hand to keep her on board. She paused for a moment, then threw the shield, her bad hand gripped tight around the leather strip. The shield flew like a frisbee. Well... a heavy, clunky, not-so-effective one. Lawrence's jaw dropped as the blade sank into the trunk of a tree.

He had to close it as he ended up swallowing a mouthful of river water and was thrown into a coughing fit.

Nikki cried out in pain.

The leather strip slipped from her finger. Lawrence jumped out and grabbed it. Nikki nearly slipped into the water, grabbing on with her good arm.

She wasn't crazy, he realized.

She was a *genius*.

A genius with a broken hand, and on the verge of falling into a roaring river. *Pull. Pull.* He pulled the strap, the water fighting against him, the water and blood on his hand threatening to slip any moment. They were reaching the surface.

Every inch was a victory.

Her plan had worked—

Lawrence's hands slipped, the strap falling, and he was pulled under the water. He clawed at the waves. Kicking, desperate for air. He needed to breathe. He needed to help her. His foot hit something. He looked down, terrified at the darkness.

He couldn't kick. His feet were hitting up against a surface.

A hand grabbed his collar and pulled him above water.

Nikki's blurry face met his.

Air pricked at his skin.

He could breathe.

Was he dreaming?

"You lost your glasses," she said. He felt her fingers gently pry his fist open, and press the familiar frame in the palm of this hand. He slipped the glasses onto his face, everything coming into view. Nikki sat straight across from him. She was drenched, her hair sticking to her face, her body shaking in the cold.

Lawrence's heart bounded in his chest, realizing his hands clenched the dirt below him. He relaxed his sore muscles, and took in a long, deep breath. They were safe.

"You saved us," Nikki said, her voice raspy.

"Me?" Lawrence said. "I didn't do anything."

"You pulled us in. And you came for me." She bit her lip.

Lawrence got to his feet, his boots heavy in the wet weight. "You're the one who came up with the plan," he said.

She smiled and turned away.

He tied the laces of his boots together and slung them over his shoulder. It was going to take forever for them to dry. He looked to the river. "Where do you think the others ended up?" Nikki rose beside him.

He could barely believe they had, only moments before, been fighting in those waters. The current rushed by, taking anything with it, waves violently crashing and dipping with no warning. The river was wide, the other side being a high rock ledge, perhaps cut through time by the rapids. He guessed they had jumped from a similar height. Nikki suddenly gasped. "The ear-comms!" Her hand flew to her ear only to draw away with disappointment. "It's gone."

Lawrence checked his own. Surely, the small piece of tech was tucked securely in his ear. He drew it out and inspected it. "How does it work?"

Nikki stared at it for a moment, and then sighed. "I have no idea," she said, quietly. She turned and met his eyes. His breath was caught in his throat at her eyes. They were young, and youthful, still full of childlike innocence, but he knew them nonetheless.

Then, she turned and ran.

"Wait!" he shouted, spinning around after. "Where are you going?"

She froze. Her shoulder slumped forward, standing still for a moment. Then she looked over her shoulder. "I got everyone into this mess. Now, I have to figure out how to get them out." She ran to the tree, where the shield's sharp edge had buried itself, and with one hand, threw herself down, pulling the weapon free. She strapped it to her back, and began to stride toward the woods.

Lawrence looked down to his bare feet and scowled. He followed her, struggling to pull on the heavy boots and tie them simultaneously, nearly tripping over a branch in the first minute. This portion of the woods wasn't as densely wooded as what he'd seen previously. The ground was mostly flat, despite some fallen debris, and was carpeted with a thick moss. The trees still held their enormous ancient trunks, soaring high above them, light dancing through the gaps in their leaves.

"It's not your fault," he said, rushing to Nikki's side,

matching her pace. "If anyone, it's the Sergeant's fault."

Nikki shook her head. "No. It's not Taryn's fault," she said. "She had every right." Oh, please. "She basically arrested you! By force!"

"I resisted."

Lawrence frowned. "How can you be so defensive of her? She's a Defending Sergeant." "Yes. She is." Nikki didn't seem to understand what he meant.

"She's not in it for you, personally. She's doing her job."

"Doing her job is good," Nikki agreed.

"But your private information isn't her business," he spat out. How could she be so ignorant?

Nikki's lips twisted. "It is her business."

"You really think that?"

Nikki nodded, her head heavy. "I do."

"Why?"

Nikki turned to meet his eyes, which caused his heart to jump, like she was studying him. Then she turned her eyes back on her path. She didn't answer.

Lawrence instantly felt bad. She had to have her reasons. Her parents were Defending Agents. But they also happened to be his aunt and uncle, and it didn't seem like any officials should be trying to pry at a sixteen year old girl for information.

He swallowed his swelling pride. "I'm sorry."

She stopped suddenly. "What for?"

"Lashing out," he said. "I-I just don't want you to think you owe everyone something." She nodded, looked away from him, and continued to walk.

Awkward.

He needed to calm down. She seemed capable enough. Who was he to be so concerned? She had no reason to trust him. Besides, he'd been nothing but cold since they'd arrived, despite his attempts.

Try harder, Lawrence.

They continued into the woods. The wind picked up, snipping their exposed skin. Being drenched didn't help. The woods itself seemed to grow more fantastical the farther they went. It was nothing like other parts they had been in, with their cobwebs and heavy debris, and a creepy aura to it.

The trees were full of bright colors, despite the cold,

twisted and curled peacefully toward the sun hidden behind the gray sky. Vines hung tastefully along the branches, the brush cleared almost conveniently for a path.

Lawrence wiped his wet, tangled curls from his face. The place was beautiful. Nikki's cry threw him back to reality.

"Nikki?" He whirled around in her direction.

She was on her knees on the ground, clenching her bad hand.

He ran and dropped to her side.

"I tripped," she said, frowning. She looked over her shoulder, like she was searching for one responsible, then looked to Lawrence. "I-I tripped."

Lawrence was less concerned about that fact. "Your hand?"

Nikki's gaze fell to her hand clutched to her chest. She held it out cautiously. He gently ran his fingers over her wrist. He was no Medic, but it wasn't twisted out of place. He sighed. "You're really going to need to have that checked out. Does it hurt?"

Nikki pursed her lips, then nodded. "A little."

"Try and lay off it. Don't use it and—"

"Your hand." Without warning, Nikki clasped her hand around his hand, which he had forgotten was pressed against her arm. She brought his hand up and pressed it against her cold, damp cheek. Her frown deepened. "It's so warm."

What did she mean, warm? They'd just fallen into a river, for crying out loud. She pressed the back of her hand against his forehead, and he nearly stumbled back. "Are you sick?" she asked.

Lawrence pushed her arm away. "No! Of course not. I'm fine."

Nikki studied him, before her shoulders relaxed and she said, "You were right. We need to take a break."

He nodded.

The two settled on a patch of moss next to the road. Lawrence did not trust, even though it seemed gentle, not to find themselves lost in the ever changing woods. The closer to the path, he decided, was better.

The two sat in silence.

Nikki played with the moss, with the utter most interest, occasionally shivering with the cold. Lawrence tried not to stare. That would come off the wrong way, not "Hey. Did you know we might be related? And this feels too much of a coincidence and a setup for my sanity?"

"Who are you?"

Lawrence's heart jumped in his chest, whirling around so hard, he collapsed from the rock he was sitting on. *Was she a mind reader too?*

Nikki stared, raising a brow.

"W-what do you mean? Who am I? I'm Law—"

"No. no. Who are you? I want to know more about you. If we are going to be friends." It was an innocent request.

"Friends?" Lawrence frowned. "We've known each other for at most four days."

Or possibly our entire lives.

"The foundation is trust," she said. "We need to learn to trust each other." That was fair enough. She had saved Isabel's life. He knew far more about her than she did.

"Fine," he sighed. "What do you want to know?"

"About you," she said, drawing her legs to her chest.

Lawrence thought for a moment. "I've lived here in North Cordell all my life. I have an older sister, Isabel, and a younger brother, Charles. Parents are dead."

"I'm sorry about that," Nikki said, quietly.

Lawrence shrugged, ignoring the build up in his throat. "My father didn't think clearly after my mother died."

"He didn't try and stop Cain from marrying Isabel," Nikki noted, quietly.

Lawrence shook his head. "She didn't have a choice."

Nikki's eyes were wide, her lip trembling with horror.

He guessed the idea was new to her. No one would present such a horrible concept to her. It must have been unthinkable to her mind.

Nikki snapped out of her shock. "I thought fathers protected—"

"Sometimes," Lawrence choked, his eyes burning. "They just don't."

He removed his glasses, turning his face away, cleaning them against his pants. A hand gently touched his shoulder. He tensed.

"Both of our fathers are dead," she said, her eyes bright and shining. "Both have different legacies, but right now it's up to us."

Lawrence stood up, putting his glasses back onto his face. "Up to us. Right. Together." She jumped up beside him.

"Together," she said, slowly, like trying out the feel of the word on her tongue. "Yes."

"Now," Lawrence said, with a deep breath. "Don't die. Don't use that hand of yours. And don't wander off."

She nodded. "Any other conditions?"

A small smirk rose on Lawrence's lips. "Take that shield."

25

COLE SPAT OUT A MOUTHFUL OF WATER, GASPING FOR AIR AS HE scrambled up onto the muddy bank of the river. He sat down, trying to scrub the mud from his face, but his contaminated hands only seemed to worsen it.

He was dirty and panicked. Where was he?

Were the others okay?

Had he just given them a command of suicide?

Why had they listened?

"Cole!" A familiar wet cough followed.

"Ray!"

Cole scrambled to his feet, his boots sinking in the mud. He caught sight of Ray, unharmed, but caked in dirt from head to toe, hugging himself, his golden gaze unmoving. Cole made a painfully long and awkward walk toward him, the mud clinging at his shoes, trying to pull him back. He crouched down beside Ray and placed a hand on his shoulder.

"Ow!"

"Sorry. Wrong shoulder."

Ray smiled, then took a long deep breath. "We're alive. Again."

"That's a great realization," Cole said, swallowing the relief bubbling in his chest, and burning at his eyes. He had to be firm. He offered Ray a hand. "Come on. Let's go find the others." Ray grabbed his arm, and Cole heaved him from the mud.

"Do you think any of the others could have gotten washed up in this swamp?" Ray said, pulling his foot up, leaving with suction *pop!*

"That's possible." The entire bank of the river was practically a mud bath. The river moved slower than Cole had remembered, and the woods cleared out of the way. It was only a short walk through the muck to the solid ground of the trees and forest.

He shook his head, mud flinging from his hair. "Did it work?" he asked, looking up hopefully.

Cole bit his lip. Mud still clung to Ray's head. "Not exactly."

Ray cursed. "Alright then. Let's get a move on and look for everyone else, shall we? LINCOLN! WHERE ARE YOU?"

The mud held Cole back from running. And it frustrated him. He still had the Illuminate buckled to his thigh, which seemed surprising, due to the fact the rushing rapids seemed to be more than capable of ripping it from its sheath. But the Blade couldn't do him much good with his mud situation.

"Felicity! Giles? Nikki! Where are you guys?"

No response.

"I found Lincoln!" Ray cried out. He had wandered off from Cole. The mud anchored him to the ground, but the rest of his body was still writhing with excitement.

"Where?" Cole called out to him.

Ray pointed down. "He's knocked out. Don't worry, I've got this all covered." Cole didn't trust him one bit, and the fight that broke out after Ray shocked Lincoln with his cube device proved it. While the two tumbled around in the mud, Cole continued to search. Three out of ... eight.

Had he really gotten *eight* people lost in this creepy wood? Great job, Cole. The others must have gotten washed farther downstream.

"You two! Stop fighting!" Cole snapped.

Lincoln and Ray stopped immediately.

"We need to get to the woods. That way we can travel faster. The others might have ended up downstream."

"Got it," Ray said.

Lincoln snatched his device from Ray's hand and shoved it into his pocket. They made their way through the mud, and after what seemed like an eternity, to the solid ground. Cole was never so relieved to be able to walk normally. Now to find the others.

He moved quickly through the trees, scanning the muddy banks for any signs of bodies. Ray and Lincoln lagged behind, but he barely cared for them as of the moment.

He saw nothing.

Did they drown?

He shook off the thought. No. They couldn't be dead.

Please, don't let them be dead.

And then he spotted them. Bright, red hair, pulled at by the wind. In the woods. A shorter, younger girl clung to her, stumbling at her side.

Tabitha. Was she hurt?

Cole broke out into a run toward them. "Is she okay?" he cried out.

Tabitha lifted her face, streaked with mud and dirt, with a drowsy smile, but completely healthy. "I'm fine. Just… tired. Very… tired."

"Can-can I help?"

Tabitha shook her head. "You don't always need to have my back, Cole. I've got myself." Felicity cleared her throat. The two looked to her. "We should find shelter."

"But the others!" Lincoln cried out from behind Cole. He looked over to see Ray and Lincoln running to them. "We have to find them!"

Felicity pointed up at the sky.

Cole looked up and gulped. The sky was dark, and the clouds twisted, smeared across the sky. A storm was brewing. "That doesn't look so good."

"But we can't just leave them here!"

"They're not here," Cole said.

"Yeah! Maybe they got knocked out, and are laying unconscious somewhere? We have to look!" Lincoln looked frantic, his eyes wide and darting. He tried to the ear-comm. "The signal's dead." He frantically tried to pace. He picked up the Cube. "Nikki's tracker!"

He shook the machine, but it only glowed dimly. Lincoln's face fell.

"Is it broken?" Ray said.

"I can fix it," Lincoln sighed. "But the longer I don't have it working, the longer they'll be lost."

Ray placed a hand on his shoulder. "They're more than capable of taking care of themselves."

"But—"

"Lawrence is tough, and Nikki is clever. And really no one is too worried about Giles." Lincoln clenched his jaw. If he had further objections, he didn't voice them. Five.

Five out of eight. That was a majority.

Cole felt horrible for thinking to actually leave the others behind, but this was in the majority's best interest. He couldn't screw up again.

There wasn't much of another choice.

Nikki tried to follow what Lawrence had said, and kept her arm still. But it seemed impossible. She couldn't touch or climb. She couldn't fidget. She couldn't run fast, in danger of tripping. Her arm *did* hurt, but her brain was far too excited.

She needed better binding. The temptations were far too strong.

Lawrence kept himself a few feet ahead, keeping reasonably quiet.

Nikki's mind was still recovering from its shock. How could people be so cruel? She knew how.

She'd seen it first hand. Or more like she knew she had, but the memories weren't placed or clear. But now it had a place. And it was wrong.

Fundamentally, she knew hurting other people was wrong. She knew other people did it regardless. But they were so convinced it was right, and would be worth it in the end. And your own family?

That was what stumped her. How could anyone convince themselves hurting their own family would be worth it?

Her new memories tried to resurface, but she forced them away. She couldn't break down in front of Lawrence.

"So how exactly do these woods work?" Lawrence looked over his shoulder. Nikki rushed to his side. "No idea. Giles said they came from the Void."

"When was the first time you saw them?"

"Six months ago. They came out from the ground right under me."

Lawrence smiled. It was small, but it was something. "Really?"

Nikki nodded.

Lawrence was about to respond where a growl cut him off. They both froze. Nikki balled a fist, and Lawrence's composure flew back to its stone cold glare.

Nikki's heart pounded against her chest.

The brush rustled.

She held her breath, itching to reach for the shield-weapon. If she pulled it out quickly, maybe she could shield them, or injure it—

The growl led to a sharp canine bark.

The creature stepped out of the shadows of the brush. A wolf... though considerably smaller than the giant ones they'd seen. Its coat was a striking black, its eyes a glowing orange. But the most startling part was the smoke flowing from its nostrils. It bared its shiny white, full set of teeth.

And then it lit on fire.

It bounded toward Nikki, as she struggled for the shield. Lawrence threw himself in front of her. All in a second, the wolf leapt onto Lawrence, knocking him to the ground. And then Lawrence started ... laughing?

The flames had gone out and the wolf began licking Lawrence's face, as the boy tried to swat the wolf away. The wolf jumped up, wagging its tail excitedly. As soon as Lawrence sat up, it bounded back at him, playfully tackling him to the ground. Lawrence tried to kick it away. "Oh, come on. Not now."

Nikki's mouth hung open in disbelief. "I-it likes you."

The wolf stopped and snarled at her.

"I don't think he likes you," Lawrence said from under the wolf, with a look of irritated defeat. Lawrence managed, after struggling for a minute, to get out from under the playful wolf. He brushed himself off, though it did nothing for the new grass stains, and muddy paw prints. Nikki took a step toward Lawrence, and the wolf barked at her.

The wolf was also protective of him? How?

Lawrence and Nikki exchanged glances. Lawrence began to frown.

"It's okay," Lawrence said. He slowly put his arm around Nikki's shoulders, the wolf watching with an intense stare. "Look. She's good. She won't hurt me."

The wolf turned its head, like trying to see them from another angle, then got up on its feet and made its way around them. Then it sat back down, right in front of Nikki, raising its paw. She knew this gesture.

A human gesture.

"Does it want me to—"

"Shake it," Lawrence said, his eyes wide. He ran his fingers through his curls, his eyes wide with bewilderment.

Nikki cautiously grasped the paw of the animal glowering at her and shook it. The wolf seemed satisfied, and then went to nuzzle Lawrence's hand for a pat on the head.

"Do-do you know each other?" Nikki said.

The wolf shot her a look.

"No," Lawrence said, simply.

"He *really* likes you."

The wolf nudged itself against Lawrence. Lawrence hesitantly scratched behind the wolf's ears, and looked to her. "I know. It's strange."

"And you're okay with a... fire wolf?"

Lawrence snorted. "This is the craziest thing to have ever happened."

The wolf yipped.

Nikki frowned, watching the wolf closely. "What is it?"

"I wouldn't know."

A wolf that could set itself on fire, and seemed to have an intelligent personality. A Lyntox? But the wolf didn't look anything like the mammal shifters that Officer Jack Sallow had been so thrilled about Felicity meeting all those months ago. Its animal instincts still seemed too strong. Would someone with a human soul jump upon a random boy and start licking their face?

Nikki decided against it.

"He should come with us," Lawrence said suddenly.

"What?" Nikki frowned. "You want to take the wolf?"

Lawrence shrugged. "He knows the woods better than us, and he seems to be oddly loyal to me." Too odd. The connection made no sense. But Nikki had never seen such sheer joy in the boy's face before. "Fine."

"Wait! Nikki," Lawrence jumped to his feet. "Do you have something of the others'?"

"What for?"

"So he can track it."

"Can he even do that?" Nikki said.

Lawrence shrugged. "It's worth a shot. It's that or continuing to mindlessly wander through the woods."

Nikki opened her bag. Everything had been drenched. She pulled out Giles's lantern doubtfully. "The scent is probably washed away."

"It's a supernatural wolf," Lawrence urged. "Let him try."

Nikki handed the lantern to Lawrence, who let the wolf sniff the handle.

"Can you find them?" Lawrence asked.

The wolf licked him.

"No." Lawrence shook his head firmly, speaking as he did to Charles. "Can you find the others? Please."

The wolf cocked its head, got up to its feet, and began to trot into the woods. It paused and looked back at them.

"It wants us to follow," Nikki said.

The two set off into the woods, with a wolf obsessed with Lawrence that could light itself on fire leading to them to what they could only hope was their friends.

Follow the weird wolf or wander pointlessly till they died?

Nikki didn't take too long to decide.

26

Darkness greeted her. The mud on her skin cracked as she squinted. *Mud?* She sat up, her eyes adjusting. They were in a shadowed hole of sorts, the walls looked like overgrown braided roots, and the ground below her was damp. The four others were out like rocks, their bodies still besides the slow rising and falling of their chests. The light outside was still dim.

Tabitha guessed it was at least six in the morning.

She slumped back against the wall of roots, quickly sitting back up as a branch stabbed her in the back. She must have passed out before they found shelter. That was pathetic. And it only unsettled her more to realize Cole was the only one capable, and willing, of carrying her. How much more of a burden could she be? She'd already broken down to him twice. How long was it till she started annoying him?

Then he'd ditch her. Who wanted to be around someone who couldn't take care of themselves? A small voice in the back of her head nagged at her. *Cole would never leave.* He was way too loyal for that. But she didn't completely believe it.

She had to prove herself independent and capable. She could manage a half decent loaf of bread and could write songs on her own—

Her heart leapt. Her binder. The river. She felt around desperately for the back, nearly kneeing Felicity in the stomach as she tugged it out from underneath her. She tore the zipper open, tearing her binder open.

She couldn't breathe. *No, no, no.*

She opened the binder, and hot tears pricked her eyes. Dozens of drenched muddy pages clumped together, some torn and ripped, their halves lost to the river. The writing was mostly washed away. Tabitha tried to tear two pages, but was left with a wet mesh of paper, and a shredded paper.

All of her writing since she was thirteen.

Five years.

It was all destroyed. She slammed the binder shut, thrusting it back into the pack. She squeezed her eyes shut, and curled up back in her place. She would not cry over a stupid binder. She would *not* cry. She would not—

"Tabs, are you okay?" The groggy, tired whisper belonged to Cole. Of course it did. "Another nightmare?"

"I'm fine."

"You're a terrible liar."

"Oh, shut up."

She heard him sit up, the few pine needles crunching as he moved closed. She tried to prod at him with her foot in his chest to keep him away. "I'm fine," she urged, careful to whisper.

"You only say that when you're upset. When you're okay, you complain about everything." Tabitha gaped, kicking him lightly in the chest. He stumped back against the wall of roots.

"I do not," she argued.

Cole frowned at her, and instantly a lump formed in her throat. She sighed, drawing her legs to her chest. "Fine."

He waited, not moving closer, staying right in the place she had shoved him. "It's stupid."

"Doubt it."

She rolled her eyes at him. "It's my binder."

"Why would—" His brows shot up. "Oh."

Tabitha clenched her wrist. "It's fine. It's gone. Destroyed."

"Tabitha."

She pressed her lips together, waiting in the daunting silence, not daring to look up into his eyes.

"I know how much that thing means to you. Really. You punched me for it," Cole said. She couldn't resist a small smile.

He scooted closer. "I know it's not ideal. It meant a lot. Got you through a lot." Tabitha heaved a heavy sigh. "But those times are over. I'm *never* going back to Liberty. Maybe this was just the final riddance. It needed to be done."

"Hold up. You're never going back to Liberty?" Cole twisted his lip.

Tabitha nodded. "I have a purpose now, right? We both do."

"Y-yeah, I guess."

Tabitha rose to her feet, hitting her head on the braided ceiling. Dirt sprayed down. She cringed and cleared her throat. "A purpose. So it's fine. I can just start over." *The bloody mountains would make a great song.* She cracked a smile at herself. *A horribly scary one.* Cole gave her a forced smile. "If you say so."

"I do."

He nodded, looking over to the others. "Should we wake them up?"

Tabitha smirked. "That would be an honor."

Felicity Bentsworth wasn't fond of mud. Or the dirt Tabitha had graciously thrown at her. She was horrified of the monster staring back in her reflection in the river. She desperately tried to clean her face and tear her fingers through her hair. She had let the others see her like that? Then she realized her concern was probably pointless.

The boys didn't care about her appearance in the slightest, nor theirs. And Tabitha didn't count. In fact, Ray had gotten muddier than he was when he left the river.

And his bandage wasn't looking good either, only growing bloodier.

He didn't complain, pretending the only thing that bothered him was Lincoln's navigating skills. Lincoln had spent the better half of the morning fixing the cube, and it finally picked up the weak signal of Nikki's tracker. But Felicity couldn't blame him. They didn't have any better ideas about how to get around in the hellish swamp.

She tried to ignore the green mud that sucked up to her ankles, and the gasps it gave as she walked through. She repeated Tabitha's song in her head. *Four my friend. Two too much. Seven Eleven. Three we Two do.*

Ray peered over Lincoln's shoulder. "Are you sure that thing works, Linc?"

"Of course, it works," Lincoln said. He held the device close to his face, half blinded by it as he walked.

In the light, the little device was even more curious. It was a perfect square with a smooth screen, yet the back was roughly melded with little screws and hinges, with the possibility to unfold into untold things.

"Can't you use your Aviduous senses or something?" Ray groaned.

Lincoln stopped in his tracks. "My Aviduous senses tell me we're lost."

Everyone went quiet.

Ray shifted his gaze back and forth from Lincoln to the ground. "You-you're joking, right?" "I sure hope so!"

"Just be straightforward with it, *genius!*"

"Stop fighting!" Tabitha jumped between them.

"We weren't fighting," Ray snapped.

Tabitha glowered at him. "You two are always fighting. Bickering and glaring at each other. We're not going to get anywhere!"

"You're the one fighting," Lincoln mumbled.

Tabitha elbowed him hard.

"Hey!"

"You deserved it!"

"You're not in charge of me!"

"The only person in charge of you is Nikki."

Lincoln's face flamed. "What?!"

"Break it up!" Felicity screamed, stomping her foot into the mud. It splashed, spraying her with mud. Not the desired effect, but it worked nonetheless.

The three stared at her. Even Cole seemed a bit shaken, his face paled.

"I get you're all tired, and frustrated, but this is how other

Councils got themselves killed!" Felicity shouted, blowing a fallen hair out of her face furiously. She began to move forward. "So if you don't want to die, get your act together and start being useful."

They all nodded silently, even Cole.

"Sorry," Tabitha grumbled, glancing to Lincoln.

Lincoln cleared his throat. "It's fine."

Felicity stepped aside to let him continue leading the way. He stepped ahead of her, his head kept low, the screen back up in his place. Ray retreated to the back.

They continued silently through the swamp. No one spoke. Cole glanced at Felicity occasionally, but she didn't speak up. She pulled a hanging, mossy vine from her path, careful not to trip on an eroding log, half submerged in the muck. She forced herself to swallow.

Sharp pain suddenly struck her side, feeling as though the bone might crack. She cried out, her knee buckling as heat flared and she began collapsing into the mud. She caught herself from going face first, her knees lost in the muck. Her side seared in pain. She grit her teeth, trying to breathe. She heard her name, but she couldn't respond. Breathe. She needed to breathe. But the pain held her back.

She is coming.

The world came rushing back, leaving Felicity gasping for air.

"Felicity!" Ray was on his knees beside her. His amber eyes were large and etched with worry, and… pain.

"Ray! Your shoulder."

"It's fine. Did you trip?" Ray said. "Show me your hands."

Felicity did so. Ray wiped away the mud and inspected them closely.

"I guess there was too much mud to scrape yourself," he said with a sigh of relief. "Can't imagine the infection rates of this place. What happened?"

Felicity took her hands back, rising to her feet, swaying back forth. "Nothing." "I'm a Medic," Ray said, getting up after her. "You can tell me."

Felicity took an unsteady step forward in the mud, gritting her teeth, bracing herself. Her leg ached, but it was unbearable. "I'm fine. Tripped."

"You didn't trip." Ray appeared in front of her.

Felicity looked him in the eyes, but nearly fell back. There was no glint of humor in his eyes, they were squinted, studying her. His jaw was tight, in what she could only guess was his own pain. His eyes were strained and serious, something she rarely ever saw in him. "Look," she said, taking in a deep breath. "It's okay now. If I fall again, we can try and figure it out." She forced out a tiny smile.

Ray pursed his lips, and then gave her a small, reluctant nod.

Felicity then cleared her throat. Now that that was avoided... "So where are we?" Lincoln jumped. "Right!" he said, tapping his finger against the screen. "I don't know." "Wha—" Ray stopped himself, as Cole shot him a glare.

"Well, it's not a *map*. It's a tracker!" Lincoln said, beginning to walk farther into the mud. He gathered a few mossy vines and held them back for the others to cross through. Pain weighed down on Felicity's legs. It was growing. It was getting worse. She couldn't say anything. Her friends were already on edge.

27

"Fire Wolf, stop that. Nikki, if you look at him like that, he's going to growl at you." Nikki stopped her attempt at a frown at the wolf, and the wolf stopped smoking. The wolf seemed intent on watching her every move, and the only thing between it and her was Lawrence. She clung to his hand. He hadn't seemed to mind, though she could never really tell.

The wolf turned its head back on their path, and continued to trot proudly down its self-proclaimed path.

"I wonder why he doesn't like you," Lawrence said.

"Maybe because I don't like him," she said.

Lawrence cracked a smile. "And why would that be?"

Nikki bit her lip. Why didn't she? Well, the wolf *had* tried to kill her. And it could light on fire, but fire never bothered her. Her mind pierced her. She used to be. Her house had burned down. She'd watched it. She'd tried to go back, and—

Nikki didn't have time for this. She mentally swatted the thoughts away, and shook her head. The wolf stopped in its tracks, crouching down, ready to pounce. A loud growl

215

vibrated from her throat. His hair stood up straight.

Lawrence and Nikki froze.

Nikki held her breath, staring straight at the shadowy woods ahead of them. A loud, careless crunching and rustling echoed through the woods.

Someone was coming.

Fire Wolf ignited and jumped into the brush.

A trail of familiar, frustrated, loud string of curses followed. "Get off of me, you stupid dog. Ow! Go!"

"Giles?" Lawrence said. He looked at Nikki with a frown, then called, "Fire Wolf! Off!" The wolf pranced happily from the brush, having no remorse.

Giles stumbled out of the woods, his face flushed red and angry. His hair was a mess, matted with mud, and his clothes scattered with little burns. He tried to kick Fire Wolf, but the supernatural wolf leapt gracefully out of the kick, and Giles stumbled backward. He caught himself, spat, and then wiped his hands off on his pants. He glared at Lawrence and Nikki. "Just my luck," he grumbled. "Where are the rest of you scrawny kids?" Fire Wolf barked at him.

"We got separated," Lawrence said, his face surprisingly calm, though his eyes still held their dangerous edge. "We think that the wolf is leading us to them."

Giles broke out laughing. "You think that stupid dog will lead you to them? I bet it's luring you to your deaths!" He wiped a tear from his eye, containing his laughter. "Look here, dog. I'm going to kill you, cut you up and roast you over a fire, and enjoy a nice meal stuck in these here cursed woods."

Fire Wolf whimpered and slunk behind Lawrence.

"There," Giles said, a sly smile on his thin lips, as he crossed his arms across his chest. "Now then, I'm leading."

"What?" Lawrence said.

"I'm not trusting a dumb dog."

"Well, we don't have to go with you."

"You're under my charge."

Lawrence scowled. "I'm not."

Giles rolled his eyes. "Right, sorry. Forgot about the stray farm boy. But little Miss Aguirre here is."

Nikki clenched her jaw. *Aguirre.* Right. That name was associated with her now.

"Now, you can run off on your own and I can take her."

Nikki opened her mouth to retaliate, but Lawrence beat her to it. "Fine, I'll come with you." Giles smiled. "Good boy. Now come along, children. Follow that wolf."

Lawrence stared at him, gaping. He shut his mouth and scowled.

Lawrence and Nikki reluctantly followed Armstance Giles, who puffed his chest out with pride as he led them up through the mossy terrain. Fire Wolf refused to be controlled, prancing ahead, though keeping a safe distance from Giles.

"He's so... unpleasant," Lawrence said, muttering a less pleasant word after. Nikki shrugged. Unpleasant was something she was used to. It was the reminder of being an Aguirre that threw her. It still felt like a hazy fever dream, not yet settled in her mind. They were heading back to the camp. There she would be forced to face Jessica Taryn, and tell her what she remembered.

And every part of her detested it. She did *not* want to tell Taryn. Why should she? The sound of rushing water cut off her thoughts.

She froze.

Water.

Rushing water.

The river.

She ran. "Giles, stop!"

She pushed the officer aside. Giles tripped and fell backward. He cursed. "What was that for?" Nikki tore at the matted tangle of vines, and tossed them aside. She now stood at the end of a ledge, where below ran the crashing, rapid river.

Lawrence's hand clamped around her arm, holding her steady. He whistled under his breath. They took a step back, Nikki's heart still racing in her chest.

"Oh, you have to be kidding me," Cole grumbled. He got to his feet and adjusted his holster. "We'll have to go around."

"I-I don't think we can," Nikki said.

Giles groaned. "Why are you all so *stubborn?*"

Fire Wolf sat on the ledge, whining. He looked down-ward, then back to them. Giles frowned, looking from Fire Wolf and back to them. "You want to jump off a cliff because a stupid dog wants you to?"

Lawrence cried out. "From what I can see, there isn't a crossing anywhere. Which means, if there is, it's way too far for us to see. There are dangerous creatures in these woods and it's only a matter of time before we're slaughtered! So yes! I'm going to cross that darn river!" They all fell silent.

Lawrence's face was tense and cold. His hands were clenched into fists.

Giles flinched, gritting his teeth, moving toward Lawrence. He stopped a foot away from him. Nikki could have sworn she saw the slightest hint of fear in his black eyes. Lawrence was thin, but in no way weak. He was about an inch taller than Giles, and his determination far more fierce.

"Fine!" Giles threw his arms up. "But if you all die, I'm saying it was the farm boy's fault." "Good!" Lawrence snapped back.

"So, what's your plan?" Giles grumbled. He tucked his hands in his coat pockets and kept his gaze hard on the wolf.

"Can anyone fly?"

Both Giles and Nikki gave him a quizzical look.

Lawrence sighed. "I guessed not. You're both weird magical races. I was just checking."

"Only Wingors can fly," Giles snorted. "And last I checked, we don't have an Outown or a Wingor Member present."

Lawrence ignored him. "Nikki, help me with that log."

Giles scoffed. "What?"

They traveled a bit down the slope, leaving Fire Wolf and Giles behind by the ledge. Nikki guided herself down, careful to not slip.

"There!" Lawrence said, pointing.

She caught sight of a large branch, freshy fallen from a tree, its leaves still green, with many smaller branches protruding from it.

The two of them ran for it. Nikki wrapped a good arm over the base of the branch, and Lawrence took the other side. The two of them heaved it off the ground.

"This is probably a bad idea," she heard Lawrence grumble. "But wood floats." They quickly made their way back up the stope. Nikki kept her mind focused. Up the hill, and over the ledge. Get across the river. Ignore the pain.

Working one armed was not a fantastic experience.

They finally dropped the branch at the ledge. Lawrence dusted off his hands and ran to check Nikki's wrists. Again, she noted the unusual heat of his hands.

His eyes were focused on her wrist, though they seemed fragile, and his shoulders were tense. His eyes were fascinating to her. How much they showed his vulnerability, even hidden behind the thick glass of his glasses.

"Are you okay?" she asked quietly.

Lawrence glanced up, frowning. "I'm fine."

"Are you afraid of water?"

"No." His face hardened, and he let go of her wrist.

"It's alright to be afraid." She touched his shoulder.

Lawrence looked away. "That's easy for you to say."

"Sometimes, the only way to conquer our fears is to face them."

He paused, then sighed. "Then, shall we face them?"

The small moment of acceptance made Nikki feel warm. She wanted to hug him, but she held herself back.

Giles helped pull the branch the rest of the way. Fire Wolf cowered away from the water but attempted to help them pull the branch by pulling at it with his teeth.

They set it at the ledge, and Lawrence turned to them. "Alright. This is a little spontaneous, and it might epically fail, but this is our best bet. Come on, Fire Wolf!"

Fire Wolf stayed planted a few feet away.

"Come on," Lawrence said, getting to his knees. "It's just a little water. We need you." The wolf didn't move.

"If you don't come, I'm going to get Lawrence!" Nikki jumped toward Lawrence, and Fire Wolf jumped to its feet growling at her, its fur smoking.

Good.

It worked.

"Everyone, grab on!" Lawrence said.

Nikki grabbed a sturdy branch with her good hand. She wrapped the leather strap of the shield around the branch, and tied the end around the elbow of her bad hand's arm, using the shield as an anchor. Her stomach flipped. She felt Avalon rustle in her mind.

Fire Wolf clamped down on a branch near Lawrence.

Nikki took a deep breath, tightening her grip. Curse her broken wrist.

"It's okay, Nikki." She met Lawrence's eyes. He must have noticed her anxiety. "You're strong. Just hold on."

She nodded, and took a deep inhale. She stared straight on.

"Ready?" Lawrence said.

Cole grumbled and nodded.

Lawrence took a deep breath. "On the count of—"

"GO!" Giles shouted.

In an instant, the ground disappeared below her, and the world was falling. Her mind whirled. She might have screamed. The leather strap tugged at her arm. And then they hit water. Waves crashed over her head, and then she was thrust back up.

The hardest part had just begun.

Nikki wasn't aware she was in pain. The only thought running through her head was: *Get out. Get out. Get out.*

Giles's head bobbed out of the water, as he held onto a branch, gasping for his dear life. "Lawrence!" she screamed. A wave crashed against her face.

Where was he? Was he alive? Dead?

No. No. No.

"Nikki!"

He was not directly behind her. His form was rigid with terror as he clung to the branch, his glasses half clinging to his ears.

The rapids began to slow.

Fire Wolf perked up. He leapt from his position on the base log of the branch, and without hesitation, jumped to a rocky ledge.

Giles followed. Nikki was surprised how athletic he moved as he, without a stumble, swung him onto the log, and sent himself flying to the ledge. He scrambled onto it and held his arms up. "Come on!" he shouted. "It's going to be too late!"

Nikki threw her weight and grabbed the trunk, and with a swift tug of the strap, pulled the shield free. She jumped, Giles grabbed her arms, and swung her up onto the ledge. She whirled around, catching her breath, seeing Lawrence still in the river. "Jump!" She got to her knees, reaching out for him.

He remained frozen.

Tears burned at her eyes. They only had moments. "Please!"

He suddenly blinked, his eyes thrown back into reality.

"Jump!" Giles shouted.

Lawrence struggled to get to the trunk and jumped. He slipped, missing the ledge. Nikki jumped for him, grabbing his arm. His weight pulled her off the ledge.

She was pulled back, her grip still hard on Lawrence. They made it safely to the ledge, and she tried to settle her mind. She brushed the burning tears from her eyes, and took a deep breath. Giles had saved them.

Nikki blinked. Giles?

She turned to see Giles now tending to Lawrence, who was on his feet, his entire body trembling. His face was pale, his eyes glazed over, not focused. "What got into you!" Giles shouted. "You could've died! You could've dragged her down with you!"

Lawrence opened his mouth, as to speak, but then coughed. "I—I'm sorry. I—I don't know... what happened."

Giles's face softened. "Are you feeling okay?"

Lawrence stumped back against a boulder for support. "I—I'm fine."

Giles's dark eyes widened. He glanced to Nikki. She came closer. "Lawrence…" "I'm fine!" he snapped.

Giles froze. "I've seen this before."

"Yeah! And it's nothing, I promise!" Lawrence's shuddering grew worse.

"Where did you get those marks only on your hands from?" Giles asked.

Lawrence clenched his hands into fists.

"They look like minor burns. Fire." Giles pushed forward.

"I don't know what you're talking about."

"You need to calm down—"

Lawrence shook his head, squeezing his eyes shut.

Giles reached out, but Lawrence kicked him.

Giles scowled. "You've been overexposed. In the water. Two near drowning experiences would do it. Your veins are made of fire. Your body can't handle it…"

Wait. Fire? Nikki's jaw fell slack. "A Ywondie?"
"A full-blood."
"I'M FINE." Lawrence shouted, and then passed out.

28

IMPURE.

No. No. That can't be right. No. No.

Let me wake up.

Please.

I'm sorry, young boy.

Who are you?

You are bold to ask.

Get out of my head.

I like you. Quite headstrong. Broken too. I can relate to your pain, young boy. You are ashamed of what people have done to you. The fact you let yourself live is because you care for others. It's noble.

GET OUT OF MY HEAD.

Tell me your name.

No.

I can heal you.

Leave me alone.

As you wish.

Lawrence's eyes flew open.

For a moment, he couldn't breathe, his vision was blurry, and his limbs stiff against the hard ground. Where was he?

What happened?

The voice. Where was the voice?

"Lawrence!"

His shoulders relaxed, allowing him to take a deep breath. He felt around his face, rubbing his eyes, only to come away blurry.

Oh, right.

Glasses.

He sat up, seeing a small blurry figure he assumed to be Nikki crouched a few feet away. The air was still. They were no longer out in the open. A blur of light stood not too far away and the walls pressed close.

For a moment, his heart jumped. They were back at the camp. But his senses quickly corrected him. There was dirt beneath his hands, and an earthy smell drafting about him. "Where are my glasses?" His throat was sore.

Nikki paused. "They got a little … broken when you were in the river."

Lawrence's heart skipped a beat. He couldn't blink, and for a moment, the only thought in his mind was "Miz is going to kill me. She's going to kill me."

But she's gone.

He didn't have to worry about her. Years of carefully caring for each rare pair of glasses, and now they were damaged.

He took another deep breath. "How-how bad?"

"Giles tried his best to bend the frame back in place. You have a cut on the back of your ear from it."

So that's what the stinging was.

"But one of the glass pieces is cracked."

A lump formed in his throat. "Oh."

"It's not that bad," Nikki said. Her voice sounded so innocently optimistic. "Here. Try them."

She moved closer, and he extended his hand. He felt the metal frame gently placed in his palm. He unfolded them, finding them to be as she said, bent, but they still fit over his ears, though a bit lopsided. The crack on his right lens distorted his sight on that eye a bit, but it was manageable.

Nikki sat on her knees, staring up at him, her eyes wide as she watched him. They were in a cave. A very small one at that. It only went a few feet deep and was maybe about six feet high. Outside he could see the crashing river across the sands, the storm clouds blocking out the sun, and the hard rainfall crashing across the green terrain.

He turned back to Nikki, still watching him. She was barefoot, and the ends of her jeans had been rolled up above her ankles, and were stained with mud. He spotted her boots and jacket against the wall behind them.

How could she not be scared? How could she still emit such childlike energy? And innocence? He caught himself growing angry and shook his head. "So?"

"Yes?" she said.

"Is it true?"

"What?"

He bit his lip. "I'm an Impure?"

"That's what Giles said."

Lawrence let out a groan. "Well, then, can I just say he's wrong? Where is he anyway?" "Collecting firewood... somehow," Nikki said. Fear flickered in her eyes as she sat back. "He was really worried about you."

Lawrence blinked. *Giles?* "Oh."

Nikki's eyes were glued on her hands, as she flexed her fingers. "He said your unusual heat is a sign. Being submerged in water too long can cause you to overload your senses. Those scorch marks on your hands, and the scars—"

"What scars?"

"On your back." Nikki glanced at him.

Lawrence's face went warm and shifted his gaze away. "They-they don't have anything to do with being Impure," he said, quietly.

"I know."

Silence.

He looked back up. He met her eyes, and instantly, feeling flooded over him, tears pricking at his eyes. No. No. No. He was safe now. He couldn't think about Cain now.

Her eyes were so much like his mother's it terrified him.

"Where are the scorch marks from?" she asked, softly, drawing him from his shock. His chest was still tight, but he felt he could breathe a little easier. No further questioning, just a simple "I know." He cleared his throat. "It's… complicated."

She leaned closer. "How so?"

Lawrence paused. He could hide the truth from her, but he already felt heavy inside enough. It would be nice for *someone* to know how weird he was. Even if it did make him an Impure. He opened his mouth to begin, when an idea struck him.

He turned to Fire Wolf, who sat at the mouth of the cave, watching Lawrence with their dark, beady eyes. Lawrence patted the ground beside him, and Fire Wolf seemed to understand, trotting proudly to sit beside Lawrence.

The strange bond with the wolf creature sent a shiver down Lawrence's spine. *It's because you're Impure.*

Shut up, he snapped at himself. He leaned closer to Fire Wolf, and whispered, "Ignite." The wolf looked at him curiously for a moment, then without warning, his fur went up in flames. Lawrence and Nikki jumped.

Fire Wolf just sat happily, his tongue hanging from his mouth, his eyes on Lawrence. Nikki had pressed herself against the wall, her eyes wide, her breathing short. She looked at Fire Wolf, and then back to Lawrence. "Alright," she said.

Lawrence *almost* laughed at the surprise on her face, but he contained himself. He looked at Fire Wolf, and began to extend his hand.

He froze.

Was he crazy? Touching *fire*? No. That was absurd. Ever since he was a small child, he knew the consequences of touching fire. It burned you.

But he'd done it before. He had marks to prove it.

But it was still fire.

He squeezed his eyes shut, and thrust his hand out before his mind could hold him back. For a moment, there was nothing, but Fire Wolf's fur in between his fingers. He probably looked like an idiot thrusting his hand out and—

"Your hand!"

Lawrence's eyes burst open. Fire Wolf was still in flames, and Lawrence's hand lay untouched amongst them. No pain like he'd experienced the first time. A small trickle of warmth went down his arm. His jaw slowly fell open.

He slowly focused on a wisp of a flame, and closed his hand over it. He withdrew his hand from Fire Wolf. He turned back to Nikki, who now leaned forward, her eyes wide and unblinking. Her lips trembled, struggling to form words.

Lawrence exhaled, and uncupped his hand. There was the little flame dancing in his palm. "That—that's incredible," Nikki gasped. She blinked twice before she crept closer. "How does it feel?"

He shrugged. "It stings... slightly. Besides that, it's really warm."

"And you deny being Impure?" Nikki looked up into his eyes.

Lawrence balled his fist, crushing out the flame, a small trail of smoke rising from the cracks between his fingers.

"This must be over... over... overwhelming?" Nikki said.

Lawrence shook his head. "Sure. I guess. Maybe. But I've always known I was a freak." "A freak?" Nikki's brow furrowed.

"A freak of nature ... not natural."

"Oh." Her eyes fell. "How long?"

"How long have I been able to hold fire?" Now that was a sentence he thought he would say. She nodded.

"Since the other night," Lawrence said, quickly. He was calm, composed. He was fine. "But I can't be Impure. I just can't," he whispered.

"Why?" Nikki huddled closer to the Fire Wolf.

"They attacked Imperial! They burned down acres of farmland. I'm sure they've done more." Nikki shook her head. "No. Those were Oquelite."

"Are Oquelite not Impure?" Lawrence frowned.

"Yes, but they're different. Their organization is bad," Nikki said. "The Oquelite aren't. They're people. Hurt people, yes, but they're ... still human. But they've been raised in an organization that wants to destroy the world for revenge."

"The fact they exist is wrong." Just like him.

Nikki flinched.

Lawrence wanted to slap himself. "Not you. You're fine. More than fine. You are good." She shook her head. "I've hurt people too."

Lawrence was silent. He waited for her to look up to him.

"I blew up a building when I found out I was an Ewyon." Her eyes glistened with tears, but her lips seemed to be trying to contain a smile.

"I-I'm sorry," Lawrence said.

She laughed, surprising him. She brushed the hair from her face, and the tears from her eyes. "It was a mostly empty building. It's funny to think about. And I'm illegal. And part of a Council. But that's what I am, and I get to choose what sort of things I want to do."

"And you chose to help rebuild the Inn?" Lawrence said.

"To be happy," Nikki corrected. "You should try it sometimes. No matter what, you're still Lawrence, and I think you're amazing."

"We've known each other for … three days?"

"Yes?" She shrugged.

Lawrence couldn't help but smile. For a moment, he felt a little bit lighter. "I think you're amazing too. Really. You confuse me. A lot."

Nikki smiled back, and shyly spoke up. "I can answer your questions... if you can answer some of mine."

Lawrence shrugged. "Why not? What do you want to know?"

"What's a cow?"

Giles returned not long after the sky had gone entirely dark.

Fire Wolf curled up in the center of the small cave, fast asleep, his body ignited, serving as a campfire. It had begun to storm even harder, thunder crashing and rumbling across the sky. Lighting would greet them with a shock, seeming brighter and closer than Lawrence remembered.

He didn't know how long he'd spent listening to Nikki's long explanations of their journey, occasionally helping her with her word choice, before Giles came stumbling in. His red hair stuck to his fa, his pale face now bright red from the cold, his uniform drenched to the core. From the look on his face, he had no luck.

"I couldn't find them. Nowhere near the shore of the river. No darn wood either," Giles grumbled, tossing his bag to the ground. He noticed Lawrence, and his face was flooded with relief and the tension in his shoulders fell away. "You're awake."

Lawrence couldn't think of anything intelligent to say, so he just nodded. Giles smiled, and nodded back. "That's a good sign. How do you feel?"

"Fine," Lawrence said.

"Aguirre, is he still warm?" Giles asked as he peeled off his coat.

Nikki frowned at the mention of her last name, and turned to Lawrence. He gave her a small nod of approval before she gently placed her hand on his cheek. "A little," she said.

Giles gave a sigh of relief. "Good. Being a Ywondie—"

"That fact is not confirmed," Lawrence grumbled. There was no way he was showing Giles the whole 'I can hold fire' thing.

"Well, I'm definitely having the Sergeant request tests from Imperial to prove you wrong," Giles said, with a flash of a grin. "As I was saying, *if* you are a Ywondie, and a full-blood at that, it's said they have abnormal body heat, especially under stress and intense situations. If Ywondie don't have enough exposure to sunlight, or aren't in great condition, being submerged under water too long can be extremely harmful, since they have no heat to keep them going."

Lawrence crossed his arms. "And you know this?"

"I might not look like it," Giles said. "But I specialized in Impure studies. We may not have any active full-bloods anymore, but I've made sure I can spot one if I ever do come in contact with one."

"Huh. I thought Defenders were all punch this and that, and 'protect the region' and 'order.'" Giles's shoulders sagged. "Most of them," he said. He immediately perked up and grabbed his bag. "Now who wants to eat?"

"You have food?" Nikki said, with a frown.

"Mostly from that Delorous girl." Giles dumped out the contents of his bag. The three sat around the fire, conversing quietly, though it was mostly Giles with extravagant and biased stories that managed to pull a smile from him.

Lawrence couldn't remember the last time he'd felt like this. He didn't try to recall it. He let the night mesh together, eating Tabitha's random supply of food by the light of a wolf, who could light itself on fire, while being stuck in an enchanted wood, with his long lost cousin, and a Defending Officer.

Giles constantly asked if Lawrence was okay, demanding Nikki check his temperature, and making Lawrence swear if he felt off, he was to tell Giles right away. Lawrence agreed, though mostly only to get Giles off his back.

By the time the food was gone, Giles already had new orders. "Sleep," he said. "We're going to need to get a move on tomorrow if we're going to find the others and get out of here." Lawrence thought that was a good call. Nikki looked just about ready to slump over, but she pushed it away.

"What about you?"

"Me too, of course," Giles said. "I, for one, quite enjoy sleeping. I'm going to scan the area, I'll be back in a few. Don't try anything stupid, Williams."

"Hey! Why me?"

Giles just glared at him, pulled on his half dried coat, and stalked out into the rain. Lawrence turned to Nikki, who turned to him at the same time.

"You're the youngest, so you have to sleep first," Lawrence said.

"That's not fair at all."

"Well, it's the law. So you have to listen."

Nikki sighed. "Fine," she said. She began to crawl to one of the shadowed corners, and Lawrence tossed her her jacket. She caught it, and looked back at him. "Uh... Lawrence?" He froze. "Yeah."

She paused, her eyes searching him frantically.

His heart began to beat against his chest. Did she know? Did she remember? "Thank you," she said simply.

Lawrence nodded, pretending to be unphased.

With that, Nikki curled up into a tight ball in the corner, and draped the jacket over herself, her back turned to him.

She didn't know what her past had been like. Did she? Did she remember him? The last time he'd seen 'Nik' was when he was seven. Five months before his mother died, and only one before Nikki's.

He knew what her past had been like. The good, happy part. "Nik?"

No response.

Lawrence looked back to her. She was totally still, except

for the small movement of her breathing. She really had been exhausted.

"It's all clear," Giles stormed back into the cave. He froze, seeing Nikki asleep in the corner. He quietly and slowly sat down next to Lawrence and removed his jacket, and tossed it next to Fire Wolf. The wolf growled at him. Giles growled back.

"You got to her to sleep quickly," Giles said, turning back to Nikki, an eyebrow raised. "Don't look at me like that."

"You two get along well."

"She's my cousin." The words slipped from his mouth before he could stop them. He spun around to be sure Nikki hadn't woken up, and turned to face Giles, who he was sure would be full of jeers.

But instead, Giles shrugged. "Right. you're Reyna Wents' nephew."

"Yeah, but I don't think she's really put that together," Lawrence said quickly. Giles frowned. "And you haven't told her?"

"I didn't want to make her even more stressed after she had to reveal and remember her family. Which you forced her to reveal, by straight up arresting her."

Giles gave an angry sigh. "You're making it worse by keeping it from her." He got to his feet and moved to the opposite side of the cave. "Get some rest, Ywondie boy. We have a lot of work to do tomorrow, and if you slack, I'm leaving you behind to die." Giles laid down and pulled his jacket up over his face, without another word, leaving Lawrence alone, feeling sick to his stomach. He needed to tell her.

He shivered, suddenly feeling cold. He grabbed his own coat, and slipped it over his shoulders. Fire Wolf dimmed his flames, and made his guard at the mouth of the cave.

Lawrence took off his glasses, letting the world become a dimly lit blur. He had no desire to sleep. He wanted the feeling of joy to return again. He wanted to make sure his siblings were safe. Then maybe, he'd feel better.

Was that the solution?

Nothing made sense. Everything hurt.

All he could do was hide his face in his hands, and whisper to himself, "Hey, Nik. We're cousins."

29

COLD.

Nikki opened an eye, met with a stone wall. Cold nipped at her face, a shiver suddenly rushing through her. She blinked a few times and sat up. Her covers fell from her shoulders to the floor of the cave, cold rushing to meet her exposed arms. She was going to need that jacket. She turned to grab it when she paused.

Two coats laid on the ground beside her.

Nikki's heart skipped a beat, and she looked to Lawrence, who curled up on the ground near Fire Wolf, who still glowed dimly of a soft orange. Lawrence had tucked his hands under his arms, his glasses beside him, and his arms bare of any covering.

Nikki smiled softly, picking up his coat. *Thank you.*

She brushed her hair from her face, and turned to the opening of the cave. She nearly cried out. The entire world was white.

She jumped to her feet. "It's white! The sky is white! The ground is white!" she shouted. She bounded out from the mouth of the cave, almost tripping on her own feet, out into the new bleached landscape. As soon as her feet touched the ground, it *bit* her. It was startlingly cold. "It hurts too!' she yelled back.

"What the—" Giles rubbed his eyes, his eyes going narrow, as his jaw fell. "Oh my mortals." Nikki stepped back into the cave, her feet stinging with the cold, feeling damp and wet. The white was wet?

"Snow." She turned back to see Lawrence, now upright and awake. He didn't even have his glasses on. The word came out barely as a whisper. He was frozen, his eyes unblinking. "Heck. It's snow."

Snow. This was snow? E had hyped up a bunch of cold wet white stuff? Nikki had to admit she was a bit disappointed. But it was beautiful. The sun was just beginning to rise, and every inch seemed to glimmer like its own tiny little fracture of a crystal. It clung to the branches of the fir trees. The entire ground was a smooth white blanket, despite the occasional jutting rocks and river that still crashed mercilessly in the terrain.

"What *is* snow?" Nikki finally asked.

Giles snapped out of his shock, gave her an annoyed look, and sighed. "Frozen water particles. It hasn't—"

"—snowed in a hundred years," Nikki finished for him.

Giles rolled his eyes, and nodded. "Yeah. They say when it last snowed in the region of North Cordell—"

"It brought death." Lawrence's voice quivered.

Giles scowled. "Two times in a row, you two. Yes. The EarthShaker."

"It's snow!" Lawrence jumped to his feet suddenly, hitting his head on the ceiling of the cave. He didn't seem to care. In less than half a minute, he'd laced his boots, put on his glasses, retrieved his coat and burst outside. "This is incredible. Look at—Ah. My boots are getting wet." Giles grumbled, grabbing his own boots. "North Cordellians don't have proper snow gear. It snowed in Manifest all the time. You're going to be soaked soon."

Lawrence didn't seem to care, despite the last time he'd been soaked in the past twenty-four hours, he'd passed out. He made his way through the snow, proving to be a significant struggle as it seemed to be pulling him back. Fire

Wolf was excited by this, and he ran out to join Lawrence. With every step, the snow melted around him.

Nikki grabbed her own boots, jacket, and her shield, and ran after them. It only took her about two steps to catch her foot, and send her falling flat into the snow. She sat up, shaking it from her face. A cushion for death? It was a cold, sad cushion. A coffin of punishment, more like it.

Lawrence and Fire Wolf got to her by the time she was on her feet, and freeing herself of snow before it had any more time to seep into her clothing. Lawrence's face was flushed pink, the tip of his nose nearly red. "I didn't expect snow to be layered," Lawrence said.

"Indeed it is," Giles grumbled, carrying the now empty bag, on his bag, trekking out into the snow. His boots stayed atop the snow, allowing him to move with much more grace than Lawrence and Nikki.

Nikki reminded herself to never underestimate the ability of a Defending Officer's uniform. Fire Wolf suddenly went still, the hair on his back standing on edge. He looked at Lawrence for a moment, let out a piercing howl, and broke out into a run, leaving a trail of melted snow behind him.

"Fire Wolf!" Nikki shouted, turning, breaking out into a run after him. He'd sensed something. What?

"Aguirre, get back here!"

"Nikki!"

She didn't slow down. Something pulled at the back of her mind. A familiar, unknown presence. Like when she'd fallen off the Inn.

What are you?

I'm Avalon, came the Stone's inhabitant's reply.

Not you, Nikki sighed. She trained her eyes on Fire Wolf. He took a harsh turn, and bounded up a slope. *I... feel something.*

You're a teenaged girl. You feel a lot. And being connected to your mind gives me far too much of it—Can we not talk about this now?

Ah. Yes. We're doing a life threatening thing because a new 'feeling' is in your head. Perhaps romance now.

What's ro—

Nikki nearly slipped, catching her balance by whirling around catching herself against a tree. Snow made the ground muddy, and therefore not the easiest to run uphill in.

She thrust Avalon from her mind, and made a note to inquire about it later. She found her footing, and made her way carefully after Fire Wolf, who sat up top, his tail wagging, looking back at her. Mocking her, almost.

She dug her heel deeper into the mud, grabbed another tree, and thrust herself forward into a sprint. She made it a few steps before she slipped, grabbing hold of another slim trunk, steadying herself, and thrusting forward again. She stumbled to the top, collapsing beside Fire Wolf. She looked down to see Giles and Lawrence making their way up toward them. Fire Wolf growled, getting to his feet, turning around, his tail swaying.

Nikki looked over her shoulder. A lake lay in the snowy terrain down a short gradual slope, a line of trees crowded by the shore. But the lake looked glossed over... frosted in a way. Frozen.

"The lake is frozen," she gasped, looking to Fire Wolf. The wolf either didn't understand her or didn't care. He kept his eyes trained downward, hard, fast, and steady.

A figure emerged from the trees. They paused, then took a tentative step onto the lake. They took another step forward, the frozen sheet of water holding them upright.

Another figure emerged. Then another. And then two more. One leaned on another. One dressed in dark clothes, almost like a Defender, and the other had fiery red hair that spilled over their shoulders, glimmering in stark contrast to the bland, icy landscape. Nikki's heart leapt. "They're here!" she shouted back to Giles and Lawrence.

She didn't wait for their response; she dashed down the slope. Fire Wolf ran after her. Her feet were weighed down, the cold nipping at her wet clothes and exposed face. Her feet and hands felt numb. But she didn't care in the slightest.

Her mind took full control of her body, letting her run down entirely on instinct. She stumbled, and with a turn caught her balance, taking advantage of every stone that jutted out from the deathly cold blanket of ice.

"Nikki!"

Her eyes flew back into focus, the ground beginning to level below her feet. Lincoln stood ahead of the group, mud still clinging to his cheek, hair damp and tangled, his coat was wet like hers, and his nose was also a bright red. His breathing was quick and harsh, bringing a cloud into the air with every exhale.

She stopped at the edge of the ice, and held his eyes. Lincoln moved toward her, slipping multiple times, but hardly seeming to care. As soon as he reached the edge, he tackled her into a hug, holding her so tight she almost couldn't breathe. "You're okay! Oh, mortals. You're okay. It worked. It really worked."

She hugged him back, feeling suddenly warm, despite the freezing temperatures around her. "Wolf!" The cry had come from Cole.

In an instant, Lincoln pushed Nikki behind him and withdrew an arrow as if it were a knife, pointing it straight at Fire Wolf, who sat casually a few feet away from them, scratching his ear. Nikki knew the arrow didn't need a bow to function. It exploded on impact. Lincoln loved his explosions. But it would hardly work for a wolf that literally had fire capabilities. "He's fine! Don't touch him!" Lawrence stood at the top of the slope, out of breath. "Don't!"

"What?" Cole reached Lincoln's side, the Illuminate Blade drawn and ready. Now Fire Wolf whimpered, cowering back.

"I said, leave him alone!" Lawrence shouted, and turned his attention to the wolf, who, on meeting Lawrence's eyes, bounded up the slope to greet him, standing beside him. "Oh look! Williams has an animal friend!" The only person who laughed was Tabitha, and she was the one who had delivered the line. Cole just rolled his eyes.

"What's wrong with Felicity?" Nikki asked, turning on her foot. Ray was helping Felicity across the lake. She didn't appear ill. Her face was more red and splattered in dirt than usual, but hardly anything else.

Lincoln sighed. "She says she's fine."

Nikki looked to Lincoln, his eyes were set on Ray and Felicity. His breaths were now long, and unsteady. He didn't believe the words he'd spoken. Something was wrong with Felicity. Nikki tightened her numb fists.

Lawrence had finally descended from the slope. Tabitha was immediately at her knees beside Fire Wolf, seeming to attempt a staring contest. "What's his name?"

"They keep calling him Fire Wolf."

Giles seemed to appear out of nowhere, jumping down gracefully from the branch of a tree, brushing himself off.

Cole groaned under his breath.

Tabitha wrinkled her nose. "That's a terrible name."

"Why are we discussing the name of a freaking supernatural wolf right now?" Cole said. "Supernatural wolf? Where?" Felicity pushed through the line, her face falling on seeing Fire Wolf. "Oh. Just a wolf."

Fire Wolf apparently took this as an insult, and to demonstrate he was not "just a wolf," lit himself fully ablaze, sending Lawrence and Tabitha scrambling back.

Felicity's eyes widened, though her face didn't brighten. No hint of fear, or a curl of an amazed smile.

"A work of the ancients," Lincoln muttered. "When the Ywondie and Aviduous still collaborated. Fire and Earth."

Nikki watched Lawrence flinch at the mention of the Impure race Ywondie. It suddenly made sense to her why Fire Wolf had such a quick connection to Lawrence. She felt stupid not realizing it as soon as Giles said Lawrence was. They shared blood... in a way. How long had it been since Fire Wolf has seen a full-blooded Ywondie? One of his creators? He'd been stuck in a Void for eons.

"We need to get moving," Giles said. "You. The weird Aviduous. How'd you find us?" Lincoln held up the small little black square device.

Giles groaned. "That thing *again*? It's also a GPS."

"Tracker," Lincoln corrected. "Nikki and Ray both have them... but yeah, I guess it can function as a GPS too. It's running off of trackers right now and landmarks."

"Trackers to what landmark that's *not* here?"

"The closest farm," Lincoln said. "North side one. We went there on our pick up with Cole. I made it a destination just for a test. If we can make our way there, we'll hopefully be out of the woods. If not, at least we'll have a landmark."

"I admit. A decent plan," Giles grumbled. "But I get to use the device."

"What?" Lincoln frowned. "No way."

"I'm the leader here."

"No you're not," Ray whistled under his breath. Cole elbowed him.

Lincoln held steadfast, his brows furrowing. "I *made* this."

"Impressive," Giles deadpanned. "Now hand it over. Come on. Hurry up." Lincoln scowled, and tossed the device into Giles's extended hand. A spark burst, and Giles jumped. Lincoln smirked, seeming slightly satisfied with himself.

Giles cleared his throat. "Now. Let's go. Everyone stay together. I'll leave you behind, and won't shed a tear at your funeral."

Everyone grumbled into submission. There wasn't much of a point to try defying Giles. Giles began to march forward, his eyes glued on the device, and the others followed shortly. Nikki began to follow when a shiver shot down her spine. She froze, her instincts instantly overcoming her, as her body naturally slipped into a stance.

Fire Wolf began to growl again.

Giles shouted for her to follow, but she blocked out his voice, and focused on the whistling of the wind whipping through the trees. The wind slowly began to pick up, the whistling began to run through the wind.

"A storm is coming," Tabitha said.

No. It wasn't a storm.

The earth trembled, birds flew cawing from the trees. The wind pulled at them faster. "Oh mortals, no." Lincoln had felt it too. He gripped his arrow, his eyes darting around. Fire Wolf ignited, and burst onto the icy lake.

Before Nikki had a chance to cry out, the lake exploded, water spraying, shards of glass flying. The sign of the Fire Wolf was nowhere to be seen.

Or maybe she just wasn't looking because she was now far more occupied with the dark, hooded figure across the lake.

The Oquelite were back. And this time, they looked ready.

30

The Oquelite were attacking, and this time Lincoln actually had nothing to do with it.

It was a strange revelation to be having when running for your life.

They didn't have time to sit around and process it. All he knew was that Cole shouted to run, and everyone, including Officer Armstance Giles, listened to him. Running was pointless. Running in snow proved to be increasingly difficult, but Lincoln blocked it out. If they slowed, they died.

The Oquelite were here to kill them. There couldn't be another reason.

"Draw you weapons!" The cry tore through the wind. Lincoln barely heard it, unable to even register who might've called it, but within an instant, pulled out his bow.

Someone shouted in the distance. Lincoln turned to run toward them, when he was thrust to the ground. He jumped back up in an instant, the wind beating harder at his face. He pulled back the string, letting go. The arrow fell forward into the snow, fizzing out like a candle.

The Oquelite, still invisible, tore the bow from his hands, flashing into sight in their full dark caped glory. With a quick fly of their fingers, Lincoln watched as the bow melted, the metal dripping into the snow before all that was left of it was a puddle of melted metal.

The Oquelite conjured a bright purple flame, and Lincoln took off running. Second bow he'd lost to these lunatics.

The terrain was thick and twisted. He dove through a gap in the tangled, giant roots of a towering tree. Within moments, it blasted to pieces behind him.

A positive was that this Oquelite couldn't teleport, otherwise Lincoln was sure he would be done with. His lungs began to burn in the cold. *Faster. Faster. Faster. Think, boy.*

He pulled a tiny knife from his boot, twirled around, jumped, and thrust it at the shimmering shape that bounded toward him.

He didn't even look back to see if he'd hit anything.

He just ran, tearing through the brush.

"Lincoln!"

Gray dust exploded, staining the snow. Lincoln dove out of the way. Nikki stood, with the curious shield in arm.

"Nik!" His relief vanished. "WATCH OUT!"

A cloaked figure dropped from the trees. Nikki reacted instantly, lunging as it reached out for her. She tumbled out of the way. The Oquelite vanished, and appeared behind her. Nikki whirled around, the shield in hand, and rammed it against the Oquelite's head.

For a moment they faltered, then crumpled down.

"You just knocked out an Oquelite?" Lincoln said, blinking.

Nikki stared at the shield for a moment, surprised, her lips slightly ajar, before swinging it over her shoulder, nodding, and taking off into a run. Lincoln ran after her.

It had been months since he'd seen her in combat. She was an entirely different person. The innocent ignorance was thrust aside for pure instinct.

His fascination only lasted a moment, and he quickened his pace to match hers. "That shield thing is proving to be useful."

She nodded. "It's a little out of shape," she said.

"I bet we could get E to help you fix it."

"If we get out," she called back.

The air shattered, the ground shook. Something had exploded. In the distance, a flame had appeared. Lincoln braced himself to fight, but the flame bound forward.

A walking flame, his mind registered before quickly correcting himself.

Fire Wolf.

"Come on!" Lawrence shouted, appearing from the brush and ushering him with the full expanse of his arms, waving them wildly. "This way! We have to go!"

A ringing sound shot through the air. A painful screaming that echoed and tore at his eardrums, pulling him to his knees, his palms pressed against his ears.

The ringing only grew worse. Lincoln grit his teeth.

"What's your name, kid?"

"His head, Kolt. It's bleeding. He can't hear you."

"He can hear me. Look, he's waking up now. What's your name, little guy?"

Lincoln's eyes burst open, tears burning as they trickled down his face, his head reared in pain. It felt as though a force pressed him down harder and harder, waiting for his skull to finally crack.

You don't have many memories, do you?

The new voice was one he did not recognize. It soothed the pain slightly, warm and refreshing, but cold and sharp all at the same time.

Your past left your mind when you were young... It is hard to breach your mind without your name.

Lincoln's eyes burst open. He forced himself to breathe. Keep breathing. He blocked out the voice. He rose to his feet trembling. The wind was picking up, catching snow in its path, the air becoming a flurry of white.

The pain in his head was too great to focus on the cold eating away at every inch of his body. "Nik!" he cried out, though the wind caught it away to barely a whisper. "Lawrence!"

No reply.

Not any that he could hear, at least. He fell to his knees, squinting, looking for anything. Anyone. The wind picked up harder.

Something burst to life in the corner of his eye.

Light. A small glow. Only a few feet away.

The wolf. He was with Lawrence

"Nikki!" Lincoln cried out, his heart beginning to beat harder against his chest. She'd been right next to him. Where could she have gone?

He pushed forward toward Fire Wolf's glow, controlling his panicked breathing. "Nik! Please!"

"She's here!" Lawrence's voice called out, barely audible through the storm. Lincoln broke out into a run, swaying and crumbling every other step. He couldn't stop.

He ran toward Fire Wolf's glow.

Young Aviduous. You will obey me.

Lincoln fell to his knees, his headache rearing. The voice was back.

He ignored it, crawling painfully forward. He was so close.

"Lincoln?!" Lawrence's voice was trembling.

What is your name?

He didn't have time for this. He cried out, forcing himself to his feet, and with one last push of energy, he burst forward, nearly collapsing atop Fire Wolf, who growled at him. Lincoln got to his knees quickly, registering Lawrence kneeling, his body swaying, his eyes looking dazed and tired, and Nikki passed out on the ground.

"I hear voices," Lawrence said, his eyelids beginning to droop.

"No!" Lincoln shouted. "Don't give in to them! Stay awake!"

Lawrence promptly collapsed.

Lincoln cursed under his breath. The voice was in Lawrence's head too? Had it infested Nikki too? Did the voice have connections with their memories? It had echoed voices of the past back to him. Who were they?

The unanswered questions pounded against his mind, but he forced them aside, crawling to Nikki's side. She was twitching, his face hardening in a pained form, her jaw clenched, like she was fighting to wake up. Lincoln shook her.

"Come on, Nik," he pleaded. "Come on. We don't have time. Fight it!"

Her eyes burst open. She went still.

"Nik!"

She looked up into his eyes, and he would've dropped down and hugged her if they weren't about to die. And the fact she shoved him away, quite forcefully, and gasped for air, most likely inhaling some snow, breaking out into a coughing fit. She caught a glimpse of Lawrence, and her face dissolved into panic. "Wake him up! He's fighting! The past! The past…it's haunting-" she broke out coughing again.

Her eyes began to roll back again, but she caught herself, shaking her head.

Fire Wolf was already at Lawrence's side, barking and howling. Lawrence, unlike Nikki, was deathly still. Lincoln shook him, tried to shout at him, and slapped him.

It didn't work.

"We don't have time!" Lincoln said, turning to Nikki. She was on her knees, her palms pressed against her eyes, taking in deep breaths. She dropped her arms, her eyes glossed over with the film of sleep.

"We can't leave him."

A voice echoed clear as day through the wind. "Over there! I see a light."

Fire Wolf immediately extinguished, and Lawrence suddenly shot up. The wolf was thrilled by this, licking the confused boy's face as he stared around in horrified bewilderment, his mouth slightly ajar, his eyes dilated.

"Where are we?"

Lincoln didn't answer his question, just grabbed his arm, jerked him to his feet, and screamed. "Run! Go! Now!"

Fire Wolf lit his fur, tearing ahead as a guide. Lawrence stumbled, his mind seemingly still not entirely grounded in reality, as he muttered inaudible words under his breath as Lincoln pulled him fumbling by his wrist.

Pain seared through Lincoln's mind. Dots lined his vision.

Feelings tore through him.

The feeling of overwhelming joy, and pressing his face into someone's sweater as they wrapped his arms around him.

The feeling of pushing through a crowd, scared and alone. Like he'd never find his way out.

Then a rush of relief as he found his way into those same arms.

He tried to pull himself into reality. Stay alert, he told himself. Focus on Fire Wolf.

The emotions pulled at him. Tears pricked at his eyes.

Now he felt the cut of ice, cold water enveloping over his head, tearing at his skin like a hundred knives. The feeling of acceptance, and hopelessness.

Then his heart was torn into feeling far more raw and recent.

Betrayal stung the most. The feeling of glass cutting through his skin. A similar feeling of acceptance and hopelessness.

And then… something else. A feeling that was far more warm, but pulled and pained him at the same time. Arms he wanted to be in, but this time they were different.

He feared them, and he feared for them.

"There!"

The headache subsided, leaving Lincoln gasping for air. Lawrence had torn from Lincoln's grip, running at Lincoln's pace, pointing ahead, where Fire Wolf was running. A faint, perfect, straight line of trees.

"We're almost there!" Lawrence shouted.

Lincoln's heart leapt, energy bursting through his limbs. Faster. Faster. They were nearly there.

"Lincoln!" Nikki's voice.

He looked over his shoulder.

She had slowed nearly to a stop. Her body swayed. She looked up to him, her eyes strained. She reached out her arm. He turned and ran, catching her before she could crash. He supported her on her feet.

"We're almost there, Nik," he said. "Just fight it. Just a little longer."

She looked him in the eyes again. He looked back to hers as they discerned him. Her pupils were dilated, her eyes cold and solemn. No longer wide and innocent.

She gave him a single nod.

And they ran.

A black cloak fluttered in the corner of Lincoln's eye. The Oquelite gracefully jumped tree to tree. He kept his grip tight under Nikki's strong arm and ran harder.

He was pulled to a stop by a figure looming in the distance. Lincoln braced himself, grabbing an arrow from his belt.

The figure turned, and Nikki strangled a gasp.

Glowing amber eyes.

A stature that held far much maturity that the teenaged boy would ever muster, the light glow of energy sitting at his fingertips.

Without a word, not-Ray tore toward him with a swiftness not in his skill set. Nikki dashed out of the way, and with a cry, tossed the shield, catching Ray off guard. He stumbled back, catching himself quickly.

"Ray! Snap out of it!" Lincoln cried.

Ray didn't say a word, willing an abundance of purple energy to swell in his palms. Lincoln hardly thought. He grabbed Nikki's shield. The energy hit it with a thud.

Ray flashed out of view, appearing right behind Lincoln, giving him moments to withdraw his sword, and Lincoln to turn with an arrow, crashing against the blade.

The sword shattered, Ray blown back.

Good thing Ray didn't have his *actual* sword or the outcome might've been worse. "Ray! Please!"

Begging with him, as expected, did nothing. He was on his feet, and already swelling a new attack of energy. Lincoln dodged each with the shield.

He glanced to Nikki, finding her tucked away behind a tree, fighting her own battle in her mind.

Lincoln tore out another arrow, careful to toss it feet away from Ray. It blew, thrusting them both back.

Too big, Linc. He scrambled to his feet, finding Ray groaning and slowly turning over. Lincoln held the shield and another arrow.

"What—what—" Ray's eyes widened, no longer glowing. "Ah! What the heck, Black Eyes!"

Lincoln narrowed his eyes. "You spasmed again. Unless you're still in one and you're…"

"No! Lincoln, it's me!" Ray's voice became panicked and breathless, his eyes glassy. "It's me, Raphael Mathews! I—I attacked you? Again?"

He stared at his trembling hands. He clenched them, and buried his face.

"We don't have much time," Lincoln said, tossing Nikki back the shield and tucking away the arrow. He offered Ray a hand, but Ray rejected it, getting to his wavering feet, his eyes hard on the ground.

"I'm sorry—"

There was no time for an apology as a blast echoed from behind. "Go! Run!" Lincoln shouted.

Ray gave a hesitant glance before dashing away. Lincoln ran to recollect Nikki, helping her to feet. Her eyes were still wild, and her breathing uneasy.

He could feel the overwhelming sensation of the Oquelite's essence. They were so close. They were so angry.

They broke out into a clearing. Only a dash for the treeline now.

"I—I can't…" Nikki cried out.

"Nik! Hold on!"

She slipped from his grip, crumbling onto the ground, gripping her head, crying out, and panting. "Leave me!" she screamed.

"I'll never leave you," he whispered.

"I… I… need to… fight!" She cried out again in pain, fingers entangling into her hair.

Lincoln didn't stall another moment. He barely had time to think. In a moment, he scooped Nikki up into his arms, and ran. An easier task than it sounds, taking into account the girl was fairly small for her age.

He ran for the trees, fighting against the storm and the time, while Nikki fought battles of her own, trapped in her mind.

Lawrence stopped at the border, waving his arms, shouting to them.

An Oquelite glittered into existence in Lincoln's side view.

Faster. Faster. He ran, tearing past Lawrence, jumping through the fog. The air around him exploded, snow went flying, the air rushing to a still state as Lincoln was drawn out into a world where the air was still, and warmer. Snow littered the ground of a dirt field that stretched onto the fields and houses of the nearby farms painted against the grey North Cordell sky, and the familiar four peaks.

He didn't stop running there.

Adrenaline pulled him forward, his mind still reeling, preparing an attack. He saw a few persons, their figures blurred by his tears, approach him. Every muscle in his body eased and he sank to his knees, closing his eyes, and holding Nikki tight, as he struggled to catch his breath.

"I dealt with a few," Giles's voice came up from behind him. "They didn't follow us out of the trees…"

"We can't trust they won't soon." Cole's voice.

"That's why we need to get to Sergeant Dow and Officer Hunter as soon as possible."

"Taryn's a Sergeant too," Ray grumbled.

Giles scoffed.

"Lincoln?" Felicity's voice. She was beside him, her voice gentle and soothing. Everyone's bickering went silent.

Lincoln opened his eyes slowly, looking to Felicity, who knelt beside him, a hand against his shoulder. Her red hair was thrown about her face, littered with snow. Her eyes looked tired as ever, dark circles underneath that seemed larger than normal. "Is she okay?"

Lincoln loosened his grip on Nikki. She was still out and struggling.

Ray dropped down to her side. His eyes were wide, and his pupils dashed frantically. "I'm sorry."

"It's not your fault this happened," Felicity said, placing a hand on Ray's good shoulder.

Ray shrugged her away. "I—I lost control again." He met Lincoln's eyes before letting his chin fall with shame.

Everyone was quiet.

"I—I saw memories," Ray said, his voice quivering. "I thought they were from the past... but they felt like they hadn't happened. It was horrifying. They called me things. Some sort of Soul with shadows?" Ray shuddered. "I don't know what they were. I don't know what's going on. I'm so sorry."

Lincoln couldn't believe he felt a pang of guilt in his gut. "Hey, look. I don't think you turned on us willingly."

"Does it matter?" Ray said, jumping to his feet. "I still tried to *kill* you."

"*You* didn't." Cole got up after him. "Whatever's using you did. Look, it hasn't happened in forever, so it might have just been a fluke?"

Weak reasoning, Lincoln thought, but it seemed to comfort Ray slightly coming from his brother.

"We won't tell Taryn," Cole said.

Ray nodded.

"Whatever this whole 'memory' thing is, it was probably just an Oquelite mind trick," Tabitha said, though her voice quivered with uncertainty of her own words. "They're just twisting your memories to make you scared."

"I've never seen anyone quite like what I saw," Ray said, turning to Tabitha. "It had to have been a girl—"

"Girls are so scary."

Ray glared at Tabitha. "It was dark. Her skin *glowed*, Tabitha. Her eyes glowed, and stared right at me. Then she chased me... and killed me. That's when I woke up from the spasm."

Everyone went quiet.

Lincoln watched Ray's face, his eyes staring hard into the frozen ground below their feet. His amber eyes flicked for a moment, then settled back to normal.

Lincoln's heart skipped a beat.

Nikki suddenly sat up, gasping for air. She looked around wildly, her pupils narrow, her shoulders tense.

"Give her some space!" Felicity demanded.

They all stepped back.

Nikki blinked a few times before her breathing settled back to normal. She got to her feet. "How did—" Her eyes fell on Lincoln.

Lincoln gave a weak smile, getting up after her. "You owe me one."

Her voice was hoarse and scratchy. "I saved you after a building collapsed on you."

"She has a point there," Tabitha laughed.

Lincoln sighed. "Then consider it payback."

Nikki's lip only quirked with a forced smile. Her face was tired and drawn. Perhaps fighting had taken it out of her.

A sudden grumbling in the distance brought Lincoln out his thoughts. Everyone else heard it too, turning around to see a vehicle, decked out in all green, with square-like shapes making up what seemed like a geometric auto on thick tires, racing toward them.

"Defenders!" Felicity cried out, breaking into a run after

the auto. Everyone else ran after her. They stopped at the road, and the auto pulled up. The door burst open, two male figures jumped out.

One was Dow, whose face had an unprofessional compassion etched in his brow.

Agent Lopez stumbled out after him, his entire scrunched face displaying displeasure, and every muscle in his body seemed flexed and tense.

"The Oquelite are here," Agent Lopez said, before anyone could say a word. "Get in. We're going back to the camp. We don't have much time."

Dow sighed. "Calm down, Lopez." He stepped forward, looking to Giles. "Are they all right?"

Giles stepped forward. "Physically, yes sir."

Lopez ushered them in. "Hurry! Get in! I do *not* have time for you kids and your shenanigans for another darn minute."

They all did as instructed. They had already experienced enough "getting-attacked-by-Oquelite" for one day.

Giles wasn't so happy about being instructed to squeeze in the back with them like a child. The eight of them were squished window to window. Lincoln found himself in between Ray and Giles. Ray was deathly quiet, his eyes closed the entire time, but Giles took the time to inform Sergeant Dow and Agent Lopez of everything that had happened... but to Lincoln's surprise, left out the whole Ray incident.

Agent Lopez took it as a chance to give them a long and hard lecture about how important being the Council was and how dangerous it could be if they got lost or hurt. It rivaled even Taryn's.

But Lincoln zoned it out, watching the woods.

What had they shown to Ray?

What were they doing to Nikki that had distressed her so much?

But most importantly, *who* was the voice?

31

"Cents!"

Charles bounded into his brother's arms, tripping over his own feet. He threw his arms around Lawrence's neck and squeezed him. Lawrence hugged Charles back, not wanting to let his little brother go.

"I missed you," Charles said.

He heard another call of "Cents," and looked up to see Isabel running toward him. Her hair was down from its usually weary, messy braid. It flowed down to her waist, and her eyes were bright with life.

She hugged him, smiling even. Charles suddenly let go, and ran for Nikki with a sudden embrace.

She was surprised, nearly falling off balance.

"You're safe!" Charles exclaimed.

Nikki gave a soft smile and patted the top of his head.

"Did you know you're my cousin, Nikki?" Charles said.

Lawrence's heart dropped.

Nikki frowned. "Cousin?"

"Cents told me. He said that your mom is my mom's

sister!”

Technically that wasn't true, since Charles's mother was Miz, and not Caroline, but Lawrence didn't have time for technicality. He ran over to his little brother and scooped him off his feet.

Nikki shifted her eyes to Lawrence. “We're related…”

Lawrence opened his mouth, struggling to get a word out. “Yes.”

Nikki's face seemed to search for an emotion to feel, stumbling back before settling on a frown. “Oh.”

Giles had been right. He should've told her. “I was going to mention it. I thought you would've put it together. But I just couldn't find the time. I—I'm sorry.”

“No… no. It's fine,” she said, seeming to be fighting against herself to keep her eyes on his. “I probably should've realized that sooner.”

“Right, because—”

“Our parents are…” she fumbled over herself, shaking her head.

“Siblings,” Lawrence finished for her, wanting to groan at the awkward tension. *Great going, genius.*

She forced a smile, and a nod before backing away. “Sorry,” she said.

She tugged on the strap of her shield, and without warning, turned on her heel and jogged off.

Lawrence stepped after her, but Isabel caught him by the shoulder.

Isabel's face was hard, staring into his eyes with demanding force. “Leave her be. She might just need some time alone to process… everything that's happened.”

Lawrence's heart burned to ignore Isabel, turn, and run away. His shoulders slumped. She was right. Nikki needed to be alone. It didn't mean it didn't bother him.

Charles tapped him lightly. “Are you okay, Cents?”

Lawrence nodded, putting his brother back onto the ground.

“Williams!”

Lawrence looked up.

Agent Lopez, if he remembered correctly, was stalking toward him. “Sergeant Hunter and I request your presence for a briefing.”

Right now? He'd just gotten back. And now he had to deal with growing anxiety that piled up in his throat over Nikki.

He forced himself to swallow and nod.

He gave Charles a quick pat on the head, gave a worried glance to Isabel, who just shrugged, and went off after the Agent.

"A Ywondie?"

Sergeant Taryn Hunter was smiling so big she seemed to have gotten stuck that way, her eyes unable to focus as she paced back and forth behind Agent Lopez, who sat in a chair in front of Lawrence.

Agent Lopez sighed. "Focus, Jess."

"A Ywondie, Nigel," Taryn said, laughing, putting a hand on the back of his chair. "Two full-bloods in one family. Is that even possible?"

Lawrence squirmed uncomfortably in his chair, hiding his hands in his pockets. Of course Giles told them about his theory.

It's hardly a theory, he told himself. You can hold fire.

But Giles didn't know that, and so neither did Agent Lopez and Sergeant Dow.

"That explains the Oquelite then," Agent Lopez sighed. "If you are indeed a full-blood. I'm sure we can run tests. Have you ever experienced anything recently... supernatural, Williams?"

"No," Lawrence lied.

"Well, let Sergeant Hunter know if you do," Agent Lopez said. He took a deep breath. "I've been in charge of the recent operations to keep track of the Oquelite groups that escaped from Imperial. They're nearly impossible to track, but recently we've found a loophole in our problem. You already know of the Curatrix machine."

"Thanks to Reyna Wents, and Lyell Aguirre, we do," Taryn said, with the quirk of a smile.

Lawrence kept his face blank, and nodded.

"They've given us a way to track the high essence rates, and pinpoint them exactly all over the entire globe," Taryn's face hardened. "Except it's incomplete."

"Why didn't you use it before?" Lawrence asked, leaning

forward in his chair.

"I didn't know what it was. I was instructed not to open it, until my uncle mentioned the Aguirre's still having a heir before he died," Taryn said, seeming not at all upset by the fact.

"That's disappointing," Lawrence said.

Taryn sighed. "Lawrence."

Lawrence's eyes fell away, his face suddenly heating at his name.

"I'm in charge of Council affairs, and the only surviving member of the Curatrix Team. If anything does happen, I would like you to tell me. Is that clear?"

Lawrence nodded, very subtly, his eyes still glued on his feet.

The two Defenders seemed to shift their attention from him for a moment.

"They're after full-bloods, Jess," Agent Lopez said. "It only makes sense if *he's* the new full-blood. Unless Armstance Giles is lying, which is highly plausible."

"Officer Giles has never been a reliable source. He's still a new recruit." Taryn heaved a heavy sigh. "You day they're moving toward Court Illegia?"

Court Illegia. The name registered itself in Lawrence's mind as the region directly south of Algery, the region right below North Cordell.

"You think there is another full-blood in Court Illegia, don't you?" Taryn whispered.

Lawrence didn't look up, but he assumed Nigel nodded, as an uncomfortable silence followed.

"Two locations. Court Illegia and North Cordell."

Lawrence could feel their stares.

"Anytime now, Mr. Williams," Agent Lopez said.

Lawrence's face burned with anger, but he kept himself composed. He wanted to get up and run and escape. He didn't trust these... adults. What would they do if they knew? Would they use him?

"My idea was to send out your full-bloods to search for the new Council members. You said the Ewyon and the Aviduous have strong senses for essence."

Taryn paused. "Yes. They do. And so does the Ray—Rapheal Mathews"

Agent Lopez took in a short breath, and tapped a tablet on the table. Lawrence stole a glance upward. Taryn was now leaning against the wall, her face contorted in thought. Agent Lopez stared at the table.

"I just don't think they're *ready*, Nigel."

"Not ready? They don't have time to prepare! They're needed now. The Oquelite won't wait. Whatever wakes in that growing woods won't wait for them to be ready!"

"They're teenagers, Nigel."

"Why teenagers? Of all people Fate could have chosen, it chose *teenagers*."

"I've been preparing them the most I can."

"Cadissa Dean is assuming lead of the Defending Department in four months, Jess. Once she's in charge, she won't take slack. The Council is a risky move. She won't hesitate to kill them. Teenagers or not."

Lawrence's heart lurched. *Kill?* Someone was out to kill the Members? The pressure tightened in his chest. Another reason he had to stay away.

A tiny voice in the back of his head pleaded otherwise. What if he could help them?

He thrust it away. No. He refused. He couldn't help anyone. Not even himself.

"We'll discuss this later. We still have the stubborn boy to deal with."

"Lawrence, if you don't want to talk, that's fine," Taryn said suddenly.

"What?" Nigel shouted.

Lawrence looked up.

Taryn's arms were crossed over her chest. Nigel took a heavy sigh and got up. He collected his tablets into his arms. "We *are* discussing this later."

"We don't have a choice. At the rate the Oquelite are travelling through the woods, I estimate they plan to attack at least by nightfall tomorrow."

Lawrence's breath was caught from his throat. Attack? He remembered the attack six months ago. He hadn't been in the actions, but smoke coated the air for weeks, and the mountains were still scarred by the flames.

And what if Agent Lopez was right? What if the Oquelite were here for him?

Agent Lopez left the tent, and Taryn stepped forward into the light. Her expression had softened. "How old are you, Lawrence?"

"I'm seventeen," he said awkwardly, fidgeting with his hands.

Tarn nodded, muttering something to herself under her breath. Her fingers tapped against the stable. "Seventeen is young. So young to be dragged into all of this. Three of them were only fifteen last year," she took a deep breath. "If you're hiding what you are from me, I wouldn't blame you. But there is a threat descending, and quickly. The Oquelite suddenly have a reason to pick up action. And they're going after Council Members we haven't discovered yet. It's not safe for you and your siblings here in North Cordell with that Council Member at camp."

Lawrence shot to his feet. "You can't send us back! We can't go back!"

Taryn froze, then shook her head. "No, no. I won't send you back there. Perhaps to another region. How does the Imperial City sound? We have some friends, the Outowns, there."

Lawrence took a deep shuddering breath. Leave North Cordell? He'd never left North Cordell before. He'd be leaving them behind... He'd be leaving Nikki behind.

He nodded. "That sounds good."

Taryn smiled, straightening herself, putting her hands to her hips. "I'll have tickets for you by noon."

Lawrence nodded again. This was his chance. Just tell Taryn, and she would know he was a Member and he could stay.

He forced himself to say, "Thank you."

"Of course," Taryn said. "Now, you must be tired. Get some rest."

Lawrence hesitated, holding his breath, Taryn watching and waiting for something to escape his lips.

Then he turned and left the tent.

Nikki didn't know a lot of words. But she knew the words for what she was feeling: angry.

She wasn't frequently angry, and she didn't even know why she was so. Lawrence had every right to not tell her about their relation. And it wasn't like he had all the time in the world to do it.

She should have put it together. His mother was technically *her* mother's sister.

Because now she had one of those, but it felt like it had such a hard time registering. Part of her felt like it was so right, and she'd always had one, but another part? It felt so lost and foreign. She had a mother?

Did it matter anyway? Her mother had been killed. Nikki would never really know what having one felt like. And it hurt.

Why did she have to act so awkwardly toward Lawrence? Was she that pathetic?

And she had run away.

But this time she had a clear destination.

E's workshop.

The snow had been cleared from the sidewalks, and her clothes were still damp from her countless falls. Her mind blurred her surroundings, focusing solely forward. *4. 2. 7. 1. 1. 3. 2.*

She could feel those looking at her, their muffled voices even greeting her. Her head rocked. The voices echoed against her skull. She tried to push them away.

She wasn't angry at Lawrence, but her chest still burned. She was angry at the thoughts in her mind tempting to haunt her. The voice was lying... It had to be.

She turned the corner, the tightness is her chest loosening a bit to allow her to breathe, seeing the rusted building tucked in the corner that housed E's curious workshop.

She broke out into a run. She burst into the workshop, which smelled freshly of gasoline. E looked up, his face covered in a metal mask, holding up two flaming metal bars. He shouted something, but she couldn't hear through the commotion. He dropped the bars into a tub of water, steam shooting up into the air. He tore his mask off, revealing his sweaty, oil stained face. His smile faltered on seeing her. "Surprise visits, I've learned, are not your thing, N. Is something bothering you?"

Nikki didn't answer him. She didn't want to think about the emotions swirling in the pit of her stomach. Instead, she thrust out the shield. "I found a weapon."

His face instantly lit right back up. He rushed over, jumping over a table, scattering an assortment of tools on the floor. He took the shield from her hands. "This thing is incredible. I've never seen a shield in real life before. And nothing I've ever seen on the net looks like this beauty."

Nikki decided it might be too much to tell him she had found it in the creepy woods, in a tower of a magic castle where a disgraced princess had secluded herself, and kept the shield in a chest, and now the maiden was trapped in a rock in her pocket.

He ran over to his work table, slammed the shield down, pulled up a holographic screen, and got to work. "I say we redesign the front. How does a little engraving of the Sergeant's face on the body of a bird sound?"

Nikki's eyes widened in horror.

E sighed. "It's *symbolism.*"

Nikki stepped up beside him at the table. "What if you just made the original design ... better?"

"Enhance it?" E said. His fingers were already dancing across the holographic screen, pulling the designs into place with a quick glance back and forth between it and the shield.

Nikki felt a little lighter. "Yes. Like that."

E offered her a stool, and she took it. The next hour flew by, and was exactly what Nikki needed to cool down. E suggested making the blade of the shield retractable, that way there was no way she could accidentally get cut. He asked her to bring Lincoln so he could help him with mechanics.

He also was pretty sure he had a way to make the shield lighter by reforming some of the electrons in words she couldn't dream of understanding. That way it would be easier for her to hold.

Another one of his ideas included re-coloring the shield a hot pink, which she also quickly rejected.

They finally finished, and E saved the file. "I guarantee I will be working on this all night. It's going to be *fantastic.* L will be impressed."

Lincoln had far more a tech minded genius, whereas E worked far better in creating things he could see and understand. If he did manage anything tech wise, the outcome would be more than amusing.

Nikki cracked a small smile. She watched him whistle to himself as he brought the shield over to his workspace. He looked back to her.

"Thank you," she said, quietly.

E smiled. "You're very welcome." He paused for a moment. "Is something bothering you, N? Be honest."

She tried to open her mouth to utter the words "I'm fine," but the horrible voices flooding her head pounded at her skull. Pain filled her chest. A chill swept over her body and images flashed before her eyes, finishing with the frozen, guilty face of Lawrence.

"I—I can't... think." She buried her face in her hands. Fight. Fight it, Nikki. FIGHT IT.

A hand pressed against her shoulder. "You know, I've noticed when you're usually distraught, you go to L."

Nikki balled her hands up into fists and rose to her feet. "I've already got him involved with enough," she said, her voice barely above a whisper.

"There is nothing shameful in asking for help."

Nikki's face burned. "What is shame, exactly?"

"You feel humiliated, embarrassed because you feel like something you did was foolish," E said. "L would have a better definition."

Shame. She didn't like that feeling. The things she saw haunted her. She would be their downfall. It would be her fault if she didn't do anything.

E patted her on the shoulder, drawing her back out of her thoughts. "People care about you. You care about them. There is no shame in that."

She forced her feelings down her throat. "Thank you, E."

The blacksmith nodded, giving her an exaggerated goofy grin. "Anytime, N. Now you better get back. It's getting dark, and it gets cold at night, especially with this... snow."

Nikki nodded. "Tomorrow?"

"Yep! See you then!" E opened the door for her. She thanked him again and left out into the bitter cold evening. She made her way through the down, taking deep breaths, trying not to draw any attention. Shop owners were closing shop early, it seemed. Snow had collected at window sills. Ice crusted the advertisement bots.

She made her way out of the town onto the familiar dirt road, catching sight of the flickering camp lights down the slope. She paused. She looked back at the four towering mountains.

The memory of the voice echoed in her mind.

Maybe she should go there now. Get it over with.

No. She couldn't go weak from a voice in her head. She would go back, and face her friends again. She would make things right with Lawrence, and she would talk to Taryn.

She had to put things right.

32

"YOU COULD'VE BEEN *KILLED*! I THOUGHT YOU WERE MORE reasonable than to run off!"

Nikki flinched at Felicity's words.

"I'm okay," she whispered. She sat on Felicity's bed, her knees drawn to her chest, a blanket draped over her. The world was still dark outside. Tabitha's curtain was closed, and somehow she was miraculously sleeping through Felicity's ranting. The tele on Felicity's dresser displayed the time as 4.00 AM.

Morning.

Nikki's chest felt tight. Today was the day. Perhaps the voice had been wrong.

"Are you listening to me?" Felicity snapped. She stood with her arms crossed over her chest, furious to the point her freckled face was flushed red. Felicity suddenly winced, taking a quick seat on the stool by the door, rubbing her knee.

Nikki nodded, forcing herself to look Felicity in her eyes. "I'm sorry, Felicity."

Felicity pressed her knuckle against her forehead and squeezed her eyes shut. "The Oquelite are out, and they've already almost nabbed us once!"

Nikki's face reddened, her face tingling as she once again diverted her eyes downward. "I am sorry."

Felicity let out a long, angry sigh. "Darn Oquelite," she muttered under her breath.

Nikki let the blanket slip away from her frame. "I want to talk to Taryn."

Felicity turned back to her, raising an eyebrow. "Speak up, Nikki."

Nikki got off the bed and brushed herself off, stared Felicity firmly in the eyes, and said, "I'm going to tell Taryn about my family."

Felicity's face instantly went from red to white. She blinked, then shook her head. "You-you are?"

Nikki nodded. She grabbed her boots from by the door, and began to buckle them.

Felicity frowned at her, but then shook her head again. "You better hurry, then." She grabbed Nikki's jacket from the stool at the end of Felicity's bed and tossed it to her.

Nikki caught it. "Thank you," she said, with a nod. She opened the door and slipped outside.

The camp was wide awake for it being four in the morning. Every Defender was on their feet. They were rushing in and out of camp. A truck had arrived and a group was helping unload crates. A few loaded into a van and headed off down the road toward the town.

A shiver ran down her spine. The voice's words echoed in her mind.

Defenders in full uniform stood guard at Taryn's cabin as Nikki approached. Neither of their faces were familiar, their eyes stared straight forward. She crept between them, and knocked on the door.

Taryn had been shocked to see her. Nikki was as terrified going in as she was going out an hour later. She had no other choice. Taryn was given the small bits of her childhood memories she knew. Taryn had been dead silent the entire time.

When Nikki had finished, Taryn sat up and cleared her throat. "I'm so sorry."

Nikki shrugged. "It doesn't hurt very much." It was unsettling, the empty void of feeling she had along with the forgotten memories.

"I remember that day vividly," Taryn said, leaning back in her chair. "The day they tried to kill *you*. It was a trial Executive, now Commander Dean had set up. Full-bloods are illegal, and she wanted to have you killed while your mother was still pregnant with... you." There was a pause. Taryn swallowed. "We lost the trial. I thought they'd killed the kid. I don't know how they did it, but now you're standing right in front of me."

A warmth filled Nikki's chest. A soft smile tugged at her lip.

Taryn laughed. "And mortals, your name even makes sense! Your grand-father, or more like your step-grand-father's name was Nikolas. Your father, Lyell, and my best friend, looked up to him so much."

A tear escaped from Taryn's eye, but she barely seemed to care.

Nikki never even knew she had a grand-father. Even the tiny bit of information made her feel light, and made her sit a little straighter.

Taryn studied Nikki a moment longer before getting to her feet, collecting the Curatrix machine in its case in her arms. Nikki stiffened.

This was it.

Taryn opened the case, the machine whirring to life. Taryn stepped aside, gesturing to the thumb pad amidst the holograms.

Nikki didn't take long to prick her thumb, but it felt like an eternity to force herself to press her thumb down, images and files all related to her... family surrounding her.

Taryn sucked in her breath. "Nothing's happ—"

The holograms suddenly went blank and glowed to a bright white light, before dimming a display of a grid, and terrain, a few sprinkled red dots across the screen.

Taryn gasped, before descending into a laugh.

Nikki stepped back, letting Taryn rush in front of her. "It worked. Oh mortals, it worked." She looked over her shoulder, her excitement stalling for a moment, meeting Nikki's eyes. "You really were the code."

How was she supposed to respond? She wasn't the mastermind to figure it out. Nikki just shrugged.

Taryn sat in silence, her lips parted, not a breath daring to pass. She suddenly laughed to herself and got to her feet. "Do you remember that ring I showed to you all those months ago?" Taryn said. "The one I asked if you recognized?"

Nikki remembered it. It had been a dark black ring, with a tiny little screen, that was dead black. She got up and followed Taryn behind another flap of the tent. It took Nikki a moment to register the place as Taryn's room. It was filled with tablets and crates, uniforms here and there. Taryn dug through a pile of bound newspapers, throwing them aside, littering the room even deeper in clutter.

She sighed. She stood up, putting her hands on her hips. "I can't seem—Oh! There!"

She turned back to Nikki, who kept herself half hidden in the doorway, a yellowed envelope in hand. "It rightfully belongs to you," Taryn said. "It either belonged to your mother or father. We'll never know for sure."

"You don't have to," Nikki said, quickly. "They were your friends."

"And they were your... family." Taryn laughed softly at the phrase, like she'd never thought she'd say them. "I have a decade of memories to remember them by. I think you deserve to know more about their legacy. And I need to give you a decent apology for dragging you in here."

Nikki took the envelope with thankful hands, peering inside to find the ring rolling against the paper, in its dead black surface. "What does the ring do?" Nikki asked suddenly.

Taryn shut the drawer. "It's usually worn by married couples," she said, her voice delicate with every word. "It's government issued, and is bonded with DNA and exchanged by each. Though it's also used by officials in need of opening doors and things like that."

Taryn's gaze fell to the floor for a moment, before glancing up with glassy eyes. "Well," she gasped, wiping her sweaty palms on her hands. "That will be all, won't it?

Nikki left Taryn in silence, unsure how to register it all. Why had Taryn grown so emotional about a ring? It wasn't her ring. Had she had one?

Regardless, Nikki felt like a great weight had been lifted from her, and she even forgot about the voice for a brief moment, almost skipping down the steps of the tent.

She found Lincoln pacing at the entrance. She froze. He'd been waiting for her.

He stopped midstep, catching her eye. "So, you finally decided to tell her."

Nikki nodded.

"I'm glad to see you're alright," he said.

Nikki nodded again, stepping off the last step and to Lincoln's side, moving a few feet further away from the guards. "I need to go to E's workshop."

Lincoln's eyebrows shot up. "You? Going to E's workshop... voluntarily?" He chuckled under his breath. "Are you sure this is Nik I'm talking to?"

Nikki crossed her arms, trying to hide a smile. She looked up at the sky. The sun was beginning to creep back, bringing the light back into the sky. Time was flying faster. "Yes. Now, I really have to—"

"Wait," Lincoln interrupted her. "You're not allowed to go alone. Agent Lopez said he doesn't want the Council Members going anywhere alone. Especially after what happened."

Nikki frowned, wrinkling her nose. "Really?"

"Yes, really," Lincoln said. "But lucky for you, it's a choice between me and one of the new Defenders."

"One of the new Defenders."

Lincoln frowned at her.

Nikki laughed. "Sarcasm," she said.

Lincoln's face relaxed, rolling his eyes. "Correct."

"You can come," Nikki said, already turning to walk. She ushered him after her. "We have to hurry."

Lincoln's mood immediately lightened as he dashed after her.

This time, Nikki made sure to go along the main road. It took longer, but it was safer, especially with the Defenders now patrolling it.

"What exactly are we going to E's workshop for?" Lincoln asked, as they hit the sidewalks of the town.

She looked over her shoulder for a moment back at him.

"You'll just have to see!"

They turned the corner, and ran quickly to the side door of E's shop. Lincoln knocked against the window, and Nikki heard a crash.

The door burst open, sending the two back a foot.

"The dynamic duo has arrived!" he shouted. "Great! Get inside. Both of you! Come on!"

Nikki and Lincoln did as E instructed, and ran through the door into the building. E shut the door quickly behind him. Nikki realized he hadn't been lying when he said he wasn't going to sleep. The shop was messier than usual. His scrap pile in the corner was scattered, holograms were up here and there. The furnace was on, making the room warm, which Nikki was grateful for, since the evil snow had decided to freeze the air. He had pulled his table out to the middle of the room, metal shavings decorated the floor beneath it.

"Oh my *mortals*." Lincoln dashed to the table, slamming his hands down on it, staring at the shiny silver shield that laid on it. "Man, it's incredible."

"Some of my best work," E said, crossing his arms. "N said no unicorns though. So, a bit disappointed." He winked at Nikki.

Nikki moved next to Lincoln and looked down at the shield.

Lincoln was right.

It *was* incredible.

The surface had been cleaned to perfection, the silver shimmering in the dim lights of the holograms flickering above. The engraving was further defined, and the sharp edge had been smoothed, the ends decorated with gold.

"Silver was the color for an Iso," Lincoln said. He tentatively brushed his fingers along the indents of the strange symbol. "Royalty in the ancient Impure times."

Goodness. What has he done to it? Avalon had appeared in Nikki's mind, her voice full of horror, and a tad amazement. *Wonders, I suppose. And I'd give that Aviduous boy of yours a talking to about Isos. They were only the rulers of each kingdom, not for anyone who was royalty. Of course he wouldn't know that, since the Ancient Times were wiped out and muddled in history texts.*

Nikki wanted to ask exactly *when* the Ancient Times were. Certainly if there'd been an era of supernatural beings roaming the earth, someone would have remembered it.

The Great Fall.

Right. Avalon could read her utmost thoughts when they were connected.

The mysteries of that time, I'm not not aware of. The entirety of six kingdoms were wiped out. The current reigning Council swore to not practice their abilities, and banish the Mythics to the Void till the time was proper.

Or at least that's what I heard.

Then who would this shield have belonged to? Nikki asked, leaning forward to examine it.

Avalon laughed. *It was intended for the queen, which was supposed to be myself, until I disgraced my name. Then it fell to Carastene. I hid it from her, and kept it as a secret.*

Avalon's act of rebellion.

Use it well, I suppose. It's not as if I can take it from you.

I will, Nikki said. It's not as though she could use it for long.

Avalon didn't hear the final thought as she severed the connection, falling back into the Stone.

"You zoned out for a second," Lincoln noted.

"The Stone," Nikki said. "She said Isos are not royalty, just the ruler."

Lincoln's eyes widened. "Why didn't I think of asking that thing? It's probably got a buttload of information no one else is capable of giving. A ruler over a certain race... brilliant, actually. Would that make Orion Idicous an Iso since he rules over the Oquelite without royal blood? Ask it."

Nikki smiled, and shook her head. "Maybe later."

"Definitely," Lincoln said. He picked up the shield and flipped it over, and frowned at E's attempt at mechanics.

E sighed, sitting on the table. "It isn't good enough for you, L?"

Lincoln grabbed a mechanical screwdriver from the table, pressed down on the center, and began to take it apart. "No way this thing would stay together."

"Yes it would," E argued. "I added extra supports and everything."

Lincoln deadpanned him. "You made it clunkier and heavier, and made the mechanics blocked from light. You used solar energy, which was smart, but doesn't work if you cover it up! That should be obvious. Also you connected a panel to the blade not the spring..."

E zoned out Lincoln, looked at Nikki, and rolled his eyes.

It took Lincoln approximately five minutes to fix E's mistakes. "Now to test it."

"The arm strap was designed to fit her arm," E said, smirking. "And she's much smaller than you."

"That is true," Lincoln sighed, turning to Nikki. The strap appeared to be leather, and it stretched across the shield, a leather like fingerless glove cleverly attached. Nikki slipped her arm inside. Like E had said, it fit perfectly. It fit comfortably, though had a cold metal feel to it.

"It's programmed to release the blade on the jerk of your wrist," Lincoln said. "E's simple like that."

E jumped off the table and joined them. "Well, sorry I didn't make her do a little dance before it activated the blade."

"Should I do it now?" Nikki asked.

E flipped the table over sideways, letting it fall with a bang. He jumped behind it. "Move a few feet out. Last time I tried, the blade went flying."

Nikki blinked. What?

"That's because it wasn't secured properly," Lincoln said, crossing his arms stubbornly. "I fixed that issue."

E grabbed him by the back of his jacket, and pulled him behind the table.

Nikki did as E instructed and moved back. E handed Lincoln a helmet and goggles, putting on some of his own.

"Ready?" Nikki asked, once she was at the opposite side of the workshop.

E gave her a thumbs up. "Ready!"

Nikki took a deep breath, flicked her wrist.

Nothing happened.

The room was still, before Lincoln let out a groan. "It doesn't work?"

"She's not doing it hard enough," E said. He jumped to his feet and waved his hands. "Don't be gentle, N! Go in for the kill!"

"How about go in for the punch?" Lincoln shouted, getting to his feet. "Keep it child-friendly, E."

"She's not a child."

Nikki didn't wait. She flicked her wrist as hard as she could trying to envision a wall in front of her that she could thrust through.

Both Linoln and E shouted and ducked.

The blade came out flawlessly along the edge.

"It worked!" Nikki shouted, her face lighting up. Just like before, half of the shield had a sharp edge, except now with the flick of a wrist, it coull retract back and become a normal shield. She flicked it again and again. And then again.

Lincoln and E emerged from their safe hold, taking off their helmets and goggles. E pumped his fist. "I knew it would work."

Lincoln ran to her side. Nikki turned to him, nearly slicing him with the blade, and he scrambled back.

"Sorry," she said, retracting it. "It's big."

"You'll get used to it," E said, practically skipping. "Extract the blade and take it off your arm."

Nikki did as he said.

"Now throw it!" E shouted.

Throw it? Nikki gripped it awkwardly with her good arm, and turned her body, sliding into a stance.

"What? Are you crazy?" Lincoln said. "That this is not a—Nik! Stop!"

It was too late. With a swift lunge and step forward, Nikki sent the shield flying. She expected it to go about a foot, then clatter loudly to the ground. But instead, it flew through the air, taking a small curve to the left. Lincoln dropped to the floor, covering his head, and E clamped his helmet back on.

The shield landed with a thud against the wooden pole in the corner, the blade sinking into the wood, holding its grip.

Nikki's eyes widened. Incredible.

E peered out from the helmet, his eyes sparkling seeing the shield lodged into the pole. He cheered, throwing his helmet to the ground. Lincoln scrambled to his feet, flustered, slapping himself in the forehead. He looked at the shield then to Nikki.

She tried to hide her smirk.

"Never do that again. Promise me."

"I promise." Nikki contained her laughter.

She hadn't been surprised it had worked so effortlessly.

The weight felt controlled in her hand, a bit wobbly at first, but with a quick step forward it was thrust with power, and shot straight off like that's exactly what it was intended to do.

She hadn't meant for the blade to get so close to Lincoln for a second time.

He recovered quickly though, as his curiosity always won over his fear. He and E were quick to run over to the pole. Lincoln clambered on top of one of E's dormant furnaces, which he used to store random scraps, and with a tug pulled the shield free, tossing it to the ground.

Nikki ran to it, slipped her arm into the glove, and retracted the blade.

"I had no idea it would be able to do that," E said, brushing his hair from his face, his eyes still wide in amazement.

"It seems it was designed to do it," Nikki said, holding it up to the light. "It's amazing. Thank you."

E gave a dramatic bow. "That's my job, N. It works pretty good."

"Better than good!"

She extracted and retracted the blade again. Amazing.

"Where did you find the material for the blade?" Lincoln asked.

E pointed to his pile of scraps piled high in the corner. "Found it in the far fields in southern North Cordell on a trip before the storm. I was able to collect quite a load."

"Could I take a look?"

"Take as much as you like," E said. He wiped his hands off on his apron. "I've got not many uses for it."

Lincoln thanked him and rushed for the pile, and immediately began sorting through.

"Oh!" E perked up, turning back to Nikki. "I still have that old piece of leather that you used to carry it with. I fixed it up a bit."

He pulled the drawer open to a dresser that looked to be used to paint random swatches whenever E felt like it. He pulled out a leather strap, fitted also as a belt. "It's a unique contraption. I didn't want the shield to be flopping all over the place while you walked."

Nikki's face burned. He'd done all of this?

He handed it to her, and waited for her to put it on and adjust it. Two clips fitted perfectly with rings on the shield, and it stayed snugly at her side.

"Wow, E." Nikki turned to see Lincoln, sitting in the pile of junk, his eyes wide. "I'm impressed. You really thought of everything."

"I'm impressed with myself too," the blacksmith said, putting his hands on his hips. "It was about time you had a proper weapon."

Lincoln went back to sifting through the pile. "She always insists on not needing one. I think the Sergeant will be pleased to hear you've convinced her otherwise." He gave her a teasing grin.

"How's your project going, L?" E said.

"Doing fine." Lincoln stood up, holding out a small piece of metal that looked like the end of a knife, without a handle. "Found a piece."

E opened another door, and tossed a cloth to Lincoln. Lincoln caught it and wrapped the scrap, pulling the ends tight before slipping it into his coat pocket.

Nikki's stomach suddenly revolted. She clenched her jaw. Her mind was flung back into reality. Today was the day. She had to focus. She didn't have much time for messing around.

Her sudden rigid stature must have caught E's eye.

"Don't let me stop the dynamic duo in their duties," E said, leaning into a deep bow.

"Thank you again," Nikki said, grabbing onto the strap across her chest. "Is there any way I could pay you back?"

E stood back up straight, putting a finger to his chin. "Hm. Nothing particular, though I'll let you know when you know when I find a situation I really need an N for."

Nikki forced a small smile. "Of course."

E tipped an invisible brim of a hat.

"I'll be back soon, if you have any more of those high def bolts in stock," Lincoln called from the door.

"They should be here about tomorrow," E said. "I'll see you then."

Lincoln nodded. He pulled the door open and a gust of wind burst through the shop. A shiver went down Nikki's spine, though she wasn't sure it was from the cold. She waved to E, and followed Lincoln outside.

The light of the town had grown brighter. A few shop's lights were on, Defenders patrolled the streets.

Nikki stayed close to Lincoln.

"So are you going to name it?" he asked suddenly.

She frowned. "Name what?"

"The shield."

That was strange. "Why would you name a shield?"

"It's sort of like a tradition," Lincoln shrugged. "Cole's sword's name is the Illuminate. Kind of like that."

Nikki looked down to shield at her side. Then she looked back to Lincoln. "It does say Fidelis. What is that?"

"It's an old word, I believe. I don't know, just one of the things in my head," Lincoln said with a shrug. "It means faithful. That shield has seemed to always have your back."

Whoever had chosen the name, chose well, Nikki decided. "Then you would also be a Fidelis."

"That's not how you use the word," Lincoln said, though he smiled anyway.

"I like it."

"You do?"

"Yes," Nikki said. "Fidelis it is."

When Nikki and Lincoln arrived, Taryn had emerged from her cabin, shouting orders right and left.

By observance, Nikki noticed Taryn tended to do the shouting, as Sergeant Dow took a more quiet, dominant stance, helping the Defenders move along. Agent Lopez could be seen nervously pacing with his hand on his pistol.

"You're back!" Taryn sounded, with a hint of tired relief. "Giles!"

Armstance Giles perked up from a nearby squad. He was decked out in full Defender attire, with a slick black chest plate, a pistol and knife at his side, full thick gloves, and metal plates on his thighs.

Lincoln groaned.

But Nikki had a bit of silent relief to see him again. That surprised her.

"Get these two some armor," Taryn snapped.

Giles frowned. "They're not going out, are they?"

"No." Taryn cut off Lincoln with a glare before he could protest. "But it's better to be safe than sorry. They can hold their ground back here at the camp. We're heading to the base of the far left peak near the north fields. That's where the biggest aggression has been spotted."

Giles's worried expression hardened. He gave a quick salute, and marched over to them. "Come on," he grumbled.

They did as they were told and followed him into a storage tent, where he threw two vests to the ground at their feet. "Go back to your appropriate cabins till you're called for, I guess," he said.

He left the tent in a hurry.

Lincoln picked up the vest and slipped it over his shoulders. "He doesn't seem to want us to go. Afraid we'll outshine him or something?"

The pit grew deeper in Nikki's stomach. Maybe he didn't want them to go because they would get hurt... or *killed*. She'd seen how he reacted to Lawrence getting overexposed to the water.

She simply shrugged and picked up the vest, which was heavy in her arms. She unbuckled Fidelis and slipped the vest over her head, feeling it weigh down against her shoulders.

Not exactly what she'd expected when Taryn said armor.

Nikki put Fidelis back in place, and followed Lincoln out the door into the bitter air of the outdoors. The air darkened. Dark clouds had begun to silently brew in the sky above.

"A storm must be coming," Lincoln said, stating the obvious. His face was tight as he looked upward. He swallowed and looked to Nikki. "We better get to the cabins. See you soon."

She nodded, wanting to stay a moment longer watching his dark eyes as they watched her, but she forced herself to tear away and head toward her cabin.

She walked up the steps, glanced up into the sky. She swallowed and took a deep breath. She grabbed the doorknob and pushed the door open.

She saw Felicity alone, sitting on the end of her bed, her arms wrapped around her legs, her face grimaced in pain. She looked up, seeing Nikki, and gasped for air and forced a smile. "You're back."

"Are you alright?" Nikki said.

Felicity nodded, pressing her lips together tightly. She rubbed her temples, mumbling the number song under her breath. "Four my friend. Two too much. Seven Eleven.

Three we Two do.”

Nikki didn't push her further. Tabitha's curtain was drawn, her corner empty. Nikki turned to her corner of the room, finding it tidied and empty. "Where's Isabel?"

"Taryn didn't tell you?"

Nikki looked back to Felicity. "Tell me what?"

"The Williams are heading to Imperial later today. To get out of the way of the commotion."

Nikki's heart plummeted. Leaving North Cordell? She hadn't even had the time to apologize to Lawrence for her outbreak. What about him being a full-blood? Had he not confessed it? They would be safe in Imperial. Right? She would see them again.

Felicity cried out in pain, gripping her leg again.

Nikki snapped back into reality. She rushed to Felicity's side. "Tell me what's wrong."

Felicity tossed her head back and gasped for air, taking a deep inhale. "Nothing. Nikki, it's nothing. Leave it be."

She slipped off the bed, steadying herself on her feet. One step forward, Felicity's body folded and she crumpled to the ground with a cry.

"Felicity!"

Hot tears began to stream down Felicity's face. She cried out for air, her breaths fast and rapid. "Oh mortals. It hurts!" she screamed.

"What hurts? Felicity!"

"My leg. Both of them—" Felicity cried out again.

Nikki quickly tore the end of Felicity's jeans, revealing the skin underneath.

The breath was stolen from her lungs.

The skin was bruised, an awful blackish-purple color crawling up her leg.

"What happened?" Nikki said, her heart beginning to beat against her chest, her mind scrambling. What could she do? What had Felicity done?

"I don't know." Felicity took a deep breath, trying to brush away the tears that wetted her face. She cried out again. "I don't know! It's just getting worse!"

"We need to get help." Nikki tried to stay calm. She slipped her arm under Felicity's, heaving her up. Felicity grabbed the edge of the dresser, heaving herself up to her feet. She screamed again. The sound of pain rang in Nikki's ear. Her throat began to close.

She pushed her feelings aside.

She burst through the door, barely keeping Felicity upright. "Help!" she screamed. "Please, someone help! She's hurt!"

Immediately, heads turned. She practically dragged Felicity to the steps. Felicity cried out again. Nikki sank to her knees. Felicity grabbed her arm, squeezing it so hard it hurt, but the pain was almost comforting.

"Someone get a Sergeant!"

"A Medic! Get a darn medic!"

Ray tore through the crowd. His face was pale as he dropped by Felicity's side. He took one look at her legs and cringed. "I—I don't know what this is."

"She can barely walk."

"Felicity. Try to bend your leg," Ray demanded.

Felicity squeezed her eyes shut, gritting her teeth. "I can't, it's numb." She held back a cry. "It hurts so much."

"Breathe," Ray said, pressing his hand against her forehead, then moved to press two fingers against her neck.

Nikki's heart pounded in her ears. It was freezing outside, but she was sweating. Small raindrops began to sprinkle from the air. No. No. Please not Felicity.

A Defender Medic dropped beside Ray, a Med Kit in hand. They scanned over her legs. "She's going into paralysis," they murmured. "Someone pick her up! Someone inform a Sergeant!"

"Paralysis?" Ray said.

A Defender scooped Felicity up. Felicity's hand was still clamped on Nikki's wrist, her eyes wide and her pupils trembling with panic. "I'm sorry," she muttered. "I'm sorry. I'm sorry."

I'm sorry too.

Felicity hands fell away from Nikki's as her eyelids fell shut.

"She's unconscious!"

Felicity was taken away, disappeared in a crowd of dark uniforms, questions and shouting; she zoned out to the white noise in the back of her mind. *Goodbye.*

Nikki hadn't said goodbye.

Ray's brows creased with concern. "Nikki? Are you alright?"

A tiny goodbye slipped from her lips, and she tore away. She tried to control her pace.

She needed to run.

She needed to scream.

She wanted to cry. A heaviness pulled at her chest.

She needed to get to Lawrence. They needed him. He was A Council Member. He denied it. They were going to need another one.

But he was leaving.

And she hadn't said goodbye.

She tore the envelope from her pocket, drawing out the ring as she ran. Her eyes burned. She burst into the cabin. She found Tabitha's stash of paper and tore a piece, scrambling to write the muddle of words on her mind, and crumpled the paper over the ring, slamming it down on her nightstand, ignoring her now bleeding thumb.

She ran to the boy's cabin, her feet uneasy under her body, her throat was closed up. The camp was growing empty. They had left. They were going the wrong way.

Her eyes were heavy. She tore up the steps and banged against the door.

No one answered.

She didn't wait a moment longer. She turned the handle and thrust it open. The inside was dark. The ground was littered with clothes, the cots left unmade. Empty.

She was too late.

She crumpled to her knees, pressing her hands against the ground, taking in deep breaths.

Don't lose control.

You have time.

You can catch them.

A Council Member.

If Lawrence was a Council Member, the Oquelite would be after him. A child in relation to the infamous Reyna Wents. The machine had said the Oquelite were heading for the mountains base, but the bus would be heading through the fields. It didn't add up.

She wouldn't let him be the one to die.

"Nik!"

Lincoln's voice shot through the air. She jumped to her feet, nearly stumbling over backward.

He stood in the doorway, his dark silhouette still. "Are you alright?"

Tears burned at her eyes. Couldn't he see it wasn't? "L— Linc—" She couldn't get his name up her throat. Tears rolled down her cheeks, her entire body trembling.

He rushed to her. She felt his hands gently clamp against her shoulders. She saw his height tower above her. "Nik, what's wrong?"

Her lip trembled. Her voice came out barely as a whisper. "I came to say goodbye."

He was silent for a moment. "No. Nik. Don't think like that—"

"I saw it!" she cried, a sob tearing at her throat. "The vision. The voice."

"Nikki." Her name.

His hands tightened on her shoulders.

For a moment, he was still, and then he hugged her. Nikki's heart stopped. Then she let herself go, breaking down into her best friend. He held her tight, and she didn't want him to ever let her go. She wanted to stay with his protective arms wrapped tightly around her forever. He would keep her safe. He always had.

But he couldn't.

"L-Lincoln. I'm going to die."

33

The words felt like someone had shattered her heart into a thousand tiny pieces.

She could feel it so heavily approaching.

She was scared.

Terrified.

"Please, Nik." Lincoln's voice faltered. "You won't die. I promise. I *swear*. You will not die."

She didn't say a word, just clung to him, listening to the quickening beat of his panicked heart, and the deep hum of his voice on the verge of breaking.

She looked up to him. He was looking down to her, his eyes glassy on the edge of tears. "Please," he gasped.

She'd never seen him like this. So vulnerable and fragile. She wanted to promise him she'd stay alive. That she'd make it through so he could be okay. But she couldn't. All she could do was rest her forehead against his chest. Her eyes felt dry and sore. Her face felt numb.

She gently grabbed his hand and uncurled his fingers, tucking the Ewyon bracelet in his hand. He'd need it.

He tightened his fist over it and wrapped his arms around her shoulders, and she heard the tears he tried to hold back fall. She engraved the moment in her mind, taking a painful swallow. The stillness of the room. The cold draft. The warmth of Lincoln's shuddering body holding hers. The weather worn material of his jacket in her fingers. His rapid breathing, and deep inhales.

"Lincoln," she whispered.

He squeezed her tighter.

"I have to go."

She felt him freeze and hesitate a moment, before slowly stepping back, hands still on her shoulders. In the dim light, she could see his face was wet.

She'd never seen him cry before.

"T-trust me," she said, quietly, burning tears falling freely as she held his eyes, trying not to break down. *Trust me, Lincoln.*

"I'm coming with you," he whispered, his voice hoarse. "I'm not going to let you go."

She pulled away from him gently. She nodded, her throat too sore to muster any words. She turned for the back door of the cabin, and opened it.

"We're coming too!"

Nikki jumped back, startled. Cole, Tabitha, and Ray stood at the steps.

Don't cry. Don't cry. "Thank you," she said.

Thank you for everything.

The first explosion went off ten minutes ago.

It was a earsplitting sound that shook the ground. Defenders were sent scrambling to find its source. And the five Council Members slipped out to chase down the real threat.

"Are we sure Lawrence is a Council Member?" Cole shouted as he clung to Tabitha, who really shouldn't be the one to be driving the high-tech Defender issued motorcycle.

"The test results came in this morning after the Sergeant left!" Officer Giles shouted back. "Little Aguirre here was right!"

He was the one who caught them leaving, and when he heard Lawrence had left, he took quick charge.

"He's a full-blood!" Giles shouted.

"And he's already reached his breaking point!" Nikki said, from behind him. She should've felt guilty for revealing Lawrence's secret of holding fire, but so far, she hadn't a surge of regret, only determination, and the fear they weren't going fast enough.

Giles had insisted Nikki ride with him, which meant Lincoln and Ray were stuck together. Surprisingly, neither of them bickered.

"Breaking point?" Tabitha said, turning her head. Cole shouted at her to keep looking forward.

"That means his essence has been activated," Giles said. "Which makes him the first non-Oquelite to do so in centuries. But it also makes him far more powerful and vulnerable."

Nikki's stomach was sick as she dug her fingers tighter on Giles's jacket. She should have told them sooner. She had known he was a full-blood the whole time. And now the Oquelite would be after him. And Isabel and Charles.

The Oquelite wouldn't spare them.

"How far do you think they've gone?" Cole asked.

"They're probably still on a bus to the SpeedRail!" Giles turned on the handle bars. "Aguirre! Hold on!" The vehicle burst a new force of speed.

The motorcycle ripped down the street. Nikki dared to peer over Giles's shoulder.

Trees were sprinkled around the empty terrain, beside the rolling hills at the base of the mountain. There were no autos in sight. They'd probably all left after hearing the explosion in the mountains.

"There!" Tabitha shouted. "A bus!"

There was a bus. A tiny blue dot in the distance. It wasn't moving.

Nikki strained her eyes. *Faster, Giles. Come on.*

Something flickered against the bus. A hologram?

The smell hit her before her mind even registered.

Fire.

Giles cursed under his breath.

They went higher and faster up the hill. The scene became closer and clearer. Nikki's breath was stolen from her.

"Alert!" Giles practically screamed into his wrist band.

"Alert! That Williams kid is a full-blood! A Council Member at that! The bus is broken down at the base of Peak One, on the western road. Immediate backup is required. Over."

Giles pulled the breaks. The cycle leveled itself. Giles tore off his helmet, his auburn hair frizzy and unorderly. He'd barely woken up by the time they'd left. He pulled out a pistol and ran for the scene.

Nikki's body froze. It told her not to go. It told her to run into the woods and hide till it was all over.

She was disgusted immediately with herself.

Her mother had died so she could have a chance to save others. *Run and don't ever look back.* Those had been her words.

Nikki would never look back. She unhooked Fidelis and ran.

These Oquelite did not acquire capes, their uniforms built primarily for combat as they circled the panicking passengers.

She scanned the scene. No sign of Lawrence.

And then an Oquelite burst into flames.

Lawrence stood on the top of the overturned bus, both of his hands in fists of flames. He had a cut on his cheek, the uncared-for blood dribbling down to his chin, which was the only wound Nikki saw so far.

A shot rang out. A Oquelite flashed from sight.

That wasn't good.

An Oquelite reappeared behind the cowering group of fire. A flaming ball of fire landed at their feet. They shouted in an unfamiliar tongue.

The people screamed.

The Oquelite charged forward.

Nikki flicked her wrist. The blade emerged. She dove in front of the Oquelite.

A flaming ball of purple essence formed in their wrist. They tossed it. She held up her shield.

To her astonishment, the energy bounced right off. Flying, it grazed the shoulder of the Oquelite.

The people screamed.

"Get them out of here!" Giles shouted.

Cole ran to them, his blade unsheathed. "Come on! We need to go!"

"What about Cents?"

Charles' tiny voice.

Nikki wanted to whirl around and tell him everything would be all right, but she had no time to consider it. The Oquelite was quickly back in commission, and back after her.

It disappeared.

She held her breath, feeling for the essence.

Above her. She scrambled out of the way. They landed in the snow.

Another appeared out of thin air. She almost thrust her shield at them, but her instincts caught Ray's eye. He swung his sword, which met the contesting Oquelite's.

Nikki didn't like the idea of abandoning her friend, but she needed to get the others out.

Then to Lawrence.

The group had made it halfway up the hill in Cole's guidance, Giles shooting after any Oquelite that dared follow. His accuracy was impressive.

An arrow shot past her. The Oquelite fighting Ray exploded into dust.

If they broke into dust, that meant these were older Oquelite. They were more expendable to the Oquelite. They were very easily destroyed. Why would they send their expendable soldiers here?

"Ray!" Lincoln yelled. "Teleport them away!"

"I don't have that kind of power!" Ray said.

"We don't have any time!"

Ray scowled, thrusting his sword back into his sheath. He disappeared, and reappeared next to Cole.

Nikki turned her full attention to the Oquelite now harassing Lawrence. He stood his guard atop the flaming bus.

So far, none of them seemed to be willing to get burned by getting close to him.

And none of them had been expecting him to have been able to withstand the flames *they* threw back at him.

That was to their advantage.

An Oquelite appeared before her. She thrust her shield out. Their blade met hers. She retracted. Their blade slipped. The Oquelite spun. Nikki ejected the blade, slashing out. The Oquelite burst into the dust.

The ground trembled. She held her balance.

"Another explosion!" Giles shouted from somewhere.

"Peak Two! Calling for backup at Peak One! Civilians are in danger!"

The ground trembled again. This time softer and slower. The snow began to shift. The Oquelite stopped fighting. A few disappeared.

Nikki held her breath and braced her shield.

Defenders. Please let it be Defenders.

The dark air glittered, the storm clouds grew thicker. A caped figure appeared out of thin air. Then another. And another. Then tens more.

Nikki's mouth gaped.

She'd been right. *This* was where the main Oquelite forces were heading.

The Curatrix machine had been wrong.

The hood fell off of the first Oquelite. His white hair had grown longer since the last time she'd seen him. He looked paler, and thinner. His eyes seemed to glow. Light blue veins ran from his eyes to down his cheeks and up his eyelids.

"She was correct." Silas laughed softly. His voice was jaded, sounding cold and distant. Nothing like what Nikki remembered. He raised his blade. A black substance dripped from the tip, hitting the snow, and it steamed. "They found a Ywondie."

Lawrence braced himself, his face only growing harder. If he was phased by it, he didn't show it.

Nikki glanced, without moving, to Cole and Ray, who were still teleporting the people away as quickly as possible. There were still six left, and Ray was growing slower every time.

"She will be pleased," Silas said. "Bring them—"

The end of his cape burst into flames. His dead eyes widened in surprise.

Lawrence shouted a word that Nikki knew Taryn would scold her for. "I don't understand why they hyped you up so much, but I'm not going anywhere. You're not going to touch *anyone*."

"She likes your spirit." Silas stamped out the flame with his heel. He swung his sword through the air. The wind picked up with a howl, whipping Nikki's hair against her face. She braced herself, shifting her feet into a stance.

She took a deep breath.

"Hah! Losers!" Ray was out of breath, his hands on his knees. Neither he or his brother were affected by the wind. "We got all those people out of there and you couldn't stop us!"

Silas smirked. "You thought that's what we came for?"

Ray's face fell.

"Attack!"

The world froze for a moment. Everything was perfectly still. The Oquelite leaning forward, either to teleport or to run. Lincoln had drawn his bow, Lawrence maintaining his stance on the bus, Ray unsheathing his unofficial blade, Cole with his hand on the Medallion, and Giles with his gun in hand.

And then the silence shattered, and the seconds sped up.

Nikki's senses overtook her, and the world became living chaos. One after another, an Oquelite appeared after her.

"Spread out!" She heard Cole shout.

She ran. She slashed at Oquelite after Oquelite that jumped at her. Their glowing eyes, their veins creeping down their faces. They looked far more dead than alive. Something had changed.

She didn't think about it.

She ducked a blow and, with the swing of her leg, knocked someone over. She thrust the shield out to a blade that came crashing down on her. She whirled out of the way of a flaming ball, deflecting a blow with the shield.

She ran with all of her might through the snow. Her heart beat against her chest, her breath burning against her lungs. She broke into the clear.

She wasn't even able to take a breath.

The prince appeared before her. He'd shed his cloak. His hair whipped against his face. "Do not try and escape her, little girl."

Who? Nikki didn't want to learn and find out. She turned and started to run back to the fight, but then her mind stopped her. In a second, her mind processed three things: A battalion of Oquelite were *here* at this spot, including an Oquelite Prince. The Defenders were distracted by explosions a whole range away from them. And Silas didn't want her to run away.

In the second, the very second she turned on her heel, thrust the blade from her shield, and ran toward Silas, she realized he was deliberately trapping them. Something down there, he wanted them to be there for.

The world threw itself back into action. She jumped, slashing her blade at him. He caught it against his own, as it appeared in his hand. She broke away, dodging his swipe. He mustered his own purple flame in his hand. He threw it. She lifted her shield, blocking its path.

That was her mistake.

His blade came crashing down. She barely had time to react. The tip of the blade hit her face, slicing down the right side of her face. The first thing she knew was blinding pain.

Then blood.

So much blood.

She squeezed her right eye shut, the blood stinging against it. She tried to brush it away, but the more she did, the more the red substance stained her own face.

Silas swung again, and she dropped herself to the ground into the snow. She bit her lip to keep from crying out as the pain reared as the wound met the snow.

She pulled herself up. The world was a blur. She barely kept up with Silas's attack. Blow after blow, she deflected. Her face began to grow numb. She felt a trickle fall to her lips. With a pain fueled cry, she twisted back, unhooked Fidelis, and let the shield fly. It hit Sila's shoulder, tearing the armor clean off. Red began to show.

For a moment, his eyes flickered, the glowing reducing. But then it flashed back and he growled, turning to her. "You will pay very dearly for that. They said to wait." He laughed. "But you can't run anywhere."

She tried to stumble back. She tried to cry out for help. But the world was chaotic around her. Her lips refused to move.

Then the pain tore at her face. It felt as though her very skin was being torn off. The blue mist flew from her wound to the palm of Silas's hand. The Oquelite's prime ability, taking the essence of others.

He smiled.

No. She refused to die like this.

"Bow, and perhaps she will spare you."

FIGHT. Avalon's voice finally burst through her mind. Nikki barely heard the voice in her own mind over the commotion and her own cries.

Her body was forced down to her knees.

FIGHT, CHILD.

She fought against the force, her body trembling as she pulled herself up, the pain in her face unbearable.

Silas frowned. The blue mist stopped coming. He stared at his hand, his mouth open in silent surprise. She steadied herself on her feet.

That tearing pain slightly subsided, but her head grew light, and her body felt like it had been hit by a truck.

Silas clenched his feet. He flicked his hand. A sword appeared. "Fine, then." He scowled. He raised the blade. Nikki braced herself to run.

And then an earsplitting siren tore through the air. Silas froze. He turned toward the noise. Nikki turned too, straining her good eye. An army of black.

More Oquelite?

Then she caught sight of a shorter figure, her short blonde hair whipping around in the wind. Next to Tabitha stood a woman, whose dark hair was tied back, dressed in a dark weathered uniform, her face cold as stone.

Tabitha brought back Taryn.

Nikki smiled. Pain shot up her face.

She could have cried with relief, but she didn't have time for little victories. In the moment of distraction she lunged forward, grabbing Fidelis from the ground. She jumped to her feet and bashed the front right of her shield into Silas's face. He stumbled back. A trickle of dark maroon dribbled down his nose.

And he shimmered out of existence. He had bigger things to worry about now that the Sergeant had arrived.

Nikki wanted to collapse. She ran into the commotion. Right where the Oquelite wanted her.

Something was waiting for them, and she needed to destroy it.

34

Sparring Taryn, a swordswoman who'd learned the trade by net searches an hour before sessions, was nothing like the whir of battle.

Cole's only advantage was the dulled effects of the blasts of power they sent his way, but in no way his weird magic-repellent self protected him from burns.

Tabitha was armed with a knife, which was almost more concerning than the charging Oquelite, but Cole knew far too well a knife against an Oquelite would do nothing. Tabitha was so small, and her agility wasn't something he knew much about.

An Oquelite burst to dust in front of him, and he ran, finding her small figure in the shadow of a hill, accompanied by Giles, engaged with a cloaked soldier. They raised a fist, batting off Giles's attacks, a burst of energy swelling.

Cole's heart dropped. "Tabitha!"

Whether she heard him or not, it didn't matter, she glided out of the way. She turned and caught sight of him, but didn't acknowledge him. She just ran.

Should he run after her? He'd surely get herself killed.

They were all going to get themselves killed.

A blast knocked him from his feet, slamming him against the wet ground, knocking the air from his lungs. His blade flew from his grasp. Cole gasped for air, grasping his side, struggling to his knees.

An Oquelite towered over him with a small chuckle. Cole watched helpless as they unsheathed a blade unlike any other he'd ever seen. The blade was black, though the middle was filled with a glowing red, the handle had no guard, and it was engraved with a marble design.

He scrambled back, catching sight of the Illuminate Blade a few feet away.

The attacker smiled, their hood miraculously staying put, shadowing their features... except for two red glowing eyes. Wait. Oquelite didn't have glowing eyes—

The blade came crashing down; Cole rolled out of the way. Again. He flipped to his feet, grabbed the Illuminate, and met the opposing blade with a crash.

He was thrust back, but he caught his balance quickly. The attacker took charge. Cole ducked, aiming for the side, but they evaded it, kicking Cole's feet from under him. He rolled back to his feet, his breath threatening to leave him.

The attacker lunged for him, Cole dodged. The attacker's blade hit the vest, tearing right through, cutting right through his side. Cole grit his teeth, his eyes burning. With a cry, he met the attacker's blade and pushed forward, letting the burn drive him.

He charged forward, his blade pulling out, thrusting for the folds of the attacker's cloak. He struck. For a split second, he thought it was over.

And then, a fist met his face, sending him back to the ground, coughing. He could feel blood drip down his lips. He tried to gasp for air, unable to take anything.

The attacker flashed a smile and fled.

Oh no.

"Ray!"

Cole tried to scramble to his feet, but his side punished his quick movement, and he fell to his knees with a cry.

His younger brother wavered on his feet, his sword broken, his eyelids drooping. He held the shaking sword hilt, stumbling back as the glowing-eyed attacker trekked for him.

Why had Cole let him teleport so many people?

His eyes burned, pushing himself to his feet. He struggled to push air to his lungs. *Faster. Come on.*

Ray helplessly thrust his hilt forward, nearly falling with it. The red-eyed attacker caught Ray by his face, holding him in his hands, as he struggled to tear away.

No!

Ray suddenly went still. Cole's heart dropped.

Ray collapsed. The attacker stepped away, and strode off.

"No!" Cole strangled a cry. What had they done? He hadn't been fast enough? Was Ray alright? Cole collapsed at Ray's side. Ray only suffered from minor cuts and burns, and his face looked as relaxed as if he were asleep.

Cole reached out to check his breath when Ray's eyes burst open, sitting up, gasping for air.

Cole's heart leapt. "Ray! You're—"

Ray turned his head, and Cole lost his words. Two eyes stared back at him, burning and glowing a gold that didn't belong to his brother at all.

She ran, her every movement tearing a breath from her chest.

A blade grazed her leg, she could feel a bruise forming on her side. Her broken hand was in pain.

Forward, she begged herself. Where in the world could the Oquelite have hidden something?

Just to her luck, it appeared itself.

She'd figured it out too late. Why was she always too late?

A blue bubble formed on the hill that broke out of the commotion. All it was was a stone that flickered with electric bolts. Its essence was overwhelming, beating on Nikki's senses like nothing she'd ever felt before.

"Nikki?" Lincoln broke out into a run beside her. He noticed her face, and she saw panic swell in his eyes. He quickly moved his attention to the rock.

"What is that thing?" she asked.

Lincoln froze, meeting her eyes. "I—It can't be." A crackle of energy snapped him from his daze. "Nik! It looks to be part of one of the relic stones!"

Nikki glared hard at it. "We need to destroy it!"

"What?"

"Trust me!"

Lincoln's face hardened. "I trust you with my life."

They burst up the hill toward the bubble. Lincoln shot an arrow, but it exploded harmlessly off the surface. Nikki's blade had a similar effect.

An Oquelite appeared beside them. Lincoln fought them off, his face soon covered in grey dust that he hurriedly brushed away.

"It's supernatural!" Lincoln cried. "We can't break it."

"But I know what can," Nikki said. "Get Cole!"

Lincoln's eyes widened. "You're a genius! Supernatural is repulsed by the Illuminate! Right! Cole!"

Lincoln bounded down the hill. Nikki watched him warily. His excitement and hope tore at her.

A figure appeared beside her. She whirled around, her shield crashing against a metal surface. Cole's face met hers. She stumbled back.

She forgot when the Medallion met the Illuminate Blade, Cole could go invisible. Cole's face was scattered with cuts. He'd suffered a wound to his side. He looked tired and upset. "Ray's gone mad, Nikki," he choked. "His eyes. He's back."

Nikki's heart dropped. *No.*

She pushed her feelings aside. "We need to break this! It's the only way we can keep them safe!"

Cole nodded, though he looked so solemn and cold. He raised his Blade, took a deep breath, and swung it. It met the force field and he bounced back.

It hadn't worked.

Nikki couldn't breathe. They'd failed.

And then it began to crack, sending out a force. Nikki slid back a few feet. The noise had her ears ringing. Cole groaned, picking himself up from the ground. He tripped on his own feet, reaching out for the Illuminate, straining himself with a cry.

Nikki scrambled for the sword, but it moved from her touch.

"I'm sorry," Cole whispered, looking up to her, his eyes shimmering with tears.

She nodded, taking in a shaky breath. "It's alright. It's okay."

She got up and ran to the force field. An Oquelite appeared on one side. And then another. They'd seen them try to break it. She tore toward it, unlatched Fidelis, and threw it. It hit the surface, falling harmlessly. She felt a force try to slow her, but she powered through. An Oquelite lunged at her, but she slid on her knees, then scrambled to her feet. She jumped, slamming her body into the force field.

All at once, it broke.

The explosion sent her flying backwards, crashing into the snow. An arm clamped down over her bad wrist, and pulled her to her feet. The Oquelite twisted it with no mercy. She felt a small snap, and a cry tore from her throat.

The Oquelite removed a blade.

Nikki squeezed her eyes shut. It was now, wasn't it? *Help!* She cried out. *Avalon! Anyone!*

Nikki?

She stumbled back, dust flying in her face. A voice in her head... that wasn't Avalon. She opened her eyes, seeing dust spread in the snow, and an arrow where the Oquelite once stood. She turned to see Lincoln, Tabitha, and Lawrence running up the hill, Lawrence looking none the pleased to be there.

You heard me?

Lincoln smiled, laughing under his breath. *I did.*

She smiled back. It was just like in Imperial when she and Felicity could hear voices from each other's heads. It was incredible.

Hey, I can hear you too. Tabitha's voice. *And I don't like it. What the heck?*

Can you read my thoughts? Lawrence's voice.

No, but if I could, I'm sure they'd be horrible. Tabitha smirked.

Lawrence sighed.

Ray's fighting down there, Lincoln said.

An Oquelite appeared out of thin air. Lawrence pulled a knife from his belt, and ambitiously attempted to take it on. Lincoln helped him out with an arrow. *He's going in and out of mind-control, it seems like.*

Nikki's head felt more level. *That's good.*

The ground rumbled underneath them. The three of them slipped in the snow. More Oquelite began to make their way up.

The rock began to glow brighter.

I'm going to destroy it! Nikki shouted mentally. *We don't have any time.*

Be careful! Ray's voice cut through.

Defenders ran up after the Oquelite and her three companions were swallowed once more by the chaos. She picked Fidelis up, then ran to the rock. She lifted the shield and sent the blade crashing down on it.

Nothing.

Wasn't it supposed to be an ancient shield? Powerful and all. Why wasn't it working?

Then it hit her.

She was using the blade. Not the shield. The Iso metal of the shield could destroy it.

"Nikki!" She caught Lincoln's scream too late.

The blade slid through her.

The sight was rebuking. Her entire body froze.

A blood-curdling chuckle followed from behind her.

A hand clamped down on her shoulder. Silas stared at her, the pupils completely white. This wasn't the sane Silas she once saw.

He smiled and, with a jerk, pulled the blade from her body.

She crumpled over to the ground.

She couldn't breathe. She clutched the wound, trying to stop the blood from escaping. Hot tears streamed down her face. She couldn't gasp for air.

Sulas muttered something, and then pulled her up the collar of her shirt. "She'll take you dead or alive."

Nikki choked. "No one will ever take me—" she coughed. A warmth began to overtake her. "—ever again."

She tore away, thrusting Fidelis with all her might against Silas. He fell back. She turned, raising the shield. Her body felt numb, her mind heavy.

I have to. She retracted the blade, and with a cry, thrust Fidelis down against the rock. The blast sent her sliding back a few feet. A blue light flicked in her blurry vision. She grasped the wound in her side. Her body went rigid.

"Nikki!" she saw a blurry figure tearing against the current of people toward her. Someone stopped them, holding them back.

They're going to be okay. You kept them safe.

The thought was comforting. *It's okay*, Avalon said. *I'll take care of you.*

Nikki's body crumbled to her knees. *Will I see them again?*

I will try.

Nikki smiled and fell back into the snow. She only caught a glimpse of the boy screaming her name, and the man dragging him away, before she welcomed the light that consumed her.

PART THREE

THE FAITHFUL

35

THE EARLY DAWN COLD NIPPED AT HIS FACE, HAND ACHING from the routine fiddling.

He thrust the sparking gadget to the ground and watched as it fell one step to the next till it hit the ground with a thump.

Lincoln sat outside the boy's cabin, alone. He'd been there since three in the morning, watching the central fire die out, and the Defenders switch their stations every hour. They barely regarded him.

He slipped his hood over his head and settled his chin on his knees as he drew them to his chest.

He looked to the Inn, sitting silently in the sunrise. The walls had started going up three days ago.

Two weeks ago, he'd stopped working on it.

Two weeks ago, Taryn said things would get better. They had Oquelite fugitives. More to send to the Capitol North for questioning. More Defenders had arrived, patrolling the towns and farms, keeping a close watch on the border of the woods.

She said things would get *better*.

Nothing was better.

He wasn't yelling at Taryn about leaving anymore, but nothing had changed inside. What in the world did they need him for anymore? They had *failed*. They hadn't been able to fight the Oquelite. They weren't an all powerful Council who could save the world.

They were a bunch of teenagers.

He leaned down and picked his gadget back up. So far, all he had was a dysfunctional handle. His brain was too scrambled to think on how to give an energy source.

He was too tired.

Lincoln tried putting on a brave face. Pretending he was alright.

But everything now felt … fake.

He remembered vividly how Dow dragged him away, his arms clamped tightly around him as Lincoln thrashed, kicked, and probably even tried to bite Dow in pure rage. He saw Silas thrust the blade. He saw her fall, the blood staining the snow.

She'd warned him.

It all hit him when Dow tried to restrain him. "We have to go!" Dow had shouted, practically dragging Lincoln. Lincoln had refused, fighting and shouting. "We have to go back!"

One they got to a safe distance, Dow let go. Lincoln collapsed to his knees as he watched smoke trail the sky. Tears fell freely. He refused to believe it. It couldn't be real.

His entire body had shuddered with sobs he'd never felt before. He was so utterly helpless.

She'd saved their lives.

"I'm sorry. I'm so sorry." Lincoln had kept muttering over and over to himself, to both Dow and her.

Dow had set a comforting hand on Lincoln's back. "Grief is natural. But we can't stay here."

Felicity took it the hardest. She'd eagerly been awaiting their return, sitting on the step unable to walk. She saw their pale, tired, and defeated faces and was destroyed seeing an absent member.

She was surprisingly strong, letting Lincoln sob until he could breathe again. She whispered to him questions about what had happened, which he answered simply with a nod or shake of his head. They'd fallen asleep by the fire. And Lincoln woke up to rain.

Taryn had tried to talk to him for two days, and finally she gave up, saying, "You can't let it consume you. You're still so young. Things will get better."

To which he'd responded with: "There's no point! We're bringing nothing but death! How many hours do we even have left? What even is death? It's us!"

And then Felicity had a panic attack, and the condition in her legs grew worse.

Lincoln didn't remember it getting better.

Cole was knocked out unconscious and kept in a Medic tent for five full days before he woke up.

Ray was under "cabin arrest" because of his sudden turning.

Felicity's legs hurt too much to walk, and there was no way to get a doctor to a random camp in North Cordell in less than a month.

Lawrence was *also* under cabin arrest, and Taryn and Dow tried to lecture him every moment they got, but Lawrence seemed to barely care, and left the cabin as much as he pleased.

His siblings were at Agent Lopez's new camp on the other side of the mountains. Sergeant Dow had deemed it too dangerous for them to be around Lawrence, and Lincoln swore that he'd almost seen Lawrence cry over it. Charles was there for the week, since no one besides Lawrence seemed to be able to control him.

Tabitha seemed to be the only one who was trying to be optimistic about the situation, trying to make a half-hearted joke here and there.

He sank his head into his arms. He squeezed his eyes shut, taking in a deep breath, letting the cold morning air fill his lungs. He heard the door creak open behind him. Someone paused, then walked forward and sat next to him.

"Hey, Lincoln." Lawrence's voice was quiet and tired. Fire Wolf followed after him, seeming the only one to be in high spirits.

Lincoln didn't respond.

Remember this? Lawrence's mind filled Lincoln's mind, and

Lincoln jumped. He'd nearly forgotten about it. The whole rush of the attack had overshadowed their new Council ability.

He nodded.

Look. You've been mourning for two weeks, which is okay, but you can't let it dictate your life. She was my cousin. I get it. My— Lawrence hesitated.

Lincoln peered up, watching the older boy stare hard at the ground, contemplating. Then he sighed and continued. *My mother drowned when I was seven.*

Lincoln's eyes widened, his stomach feeling sick. *I'm sorry.*

That was ten years ago now, Lawrence said, his features hardened, his brows furrowing. *She had the same eyes as... Nik did. We all called her Nik.*

As she'd told him. Lincoln clenched his fists. He tried to swallow, but it hurt. He finally forced himself to speak, even if it was just in his mind. *She was the first I ever remember knowing. Really knowing. But it'll be fine. I'm fine.*

Lawrence paused for a moment and watched him closely. *What's holding you back?*

Lincoln froze, blinked a few times before blurting it out before he regretted it: *I don't think she's dead.*

Lawrence sighed. "This is your battle to fight, I guess," he said out loud, getting to his feet. "But I've seen the way people regard you here. They need you. You can't give up yet."

But I haven't given up, Lincoln thought to himself. That was his problem.

The next hours passed a long, slow blur as they frequently did until Felicity was discharged from the Med Tent. She seemed to be trying to be in good spirits, despite the fact she'd been given crutches, and he could see the pain in her eyes as she moved.

She shouldn't stay here. She's only getting worse. She's losing her ability to use her *legs.*

But she was seeming to try to be optimistic about it, so Lincoln didn't voice his concerns.

They made their way to the central fire, where Felicity's face looked far too relieved for a chance just to sit down. "So, are you going to say something?" she asked.

Lincoln's face flamed. He rarely had the motivation to

speak.

He didn't have to disappoint her, because right away, Lawrence burst out from his cabin. "Do you know where Charles is?"

"He's been around for five days and you've already lost him?" Giles was supposed to be patrolling the road nearby, but he seemed to always disobey every order that wasn't stationed in the camp. Lincoln felt like they were constantly being babysat by the annoying Officer with the strong Manifest accent, which Giles flaunted mercilessly.

Lawrence shot him a glare. "He was here this morning!"

Lincoln was quickly on his feet. Felicity tried but she grimaced in pain, and sat back down in defeat. Lincoln ran over to where Giles and Lawrence were.

"Where'd you last see him?" Giles asked.

"In the cabin. I can't keep him cooped up in there all the time, but he hasn't come back."

"Aren't *you* supposed to be in that cabin all the time?" Giles raised an eyebrow.

Lawrence rolled his eyes. "Just try and make me. Right now, we need to find him!'

Giles's focus shifted to the woods. He sighed. "I'll form a team to search the border."

"I'm coming too."

"No. You're under hou—cabin arrest," Giles said. "We'll bring him back if we find him. You two search the camp."

Lawrence scowled. "Fine."

Giles nodded approvingly and dashed off to the Defenders on patrol nearby.

Lawrence turned to Lincoln. "Lincoln, you check the north cabins. I'll check the south cabins. And then if we don't find him, we'll meet up to search the Sergeant cabins."

The two separated. Most of the south cabins belonged to Defending Officers, most of which were gone for the day. Lincoln didn't bother taking too much time since he doubted the little boy felt comfortable hiding in a Defender's cabin. He was correct on all of his assumptions so far. Only one had been occupied, and when Lincoln knocked on the door, the poor woman looked so tired and angry for being woken up after being on guard all night.

She definitely grumbled something about teenagers and

slammed the door in his face.

Lincoln made his way down the steps, and stopped in front of a very specific door.

He'd checked every cabin on the south side to no avail. Well, that wasn't entirely true. He'd checked every cabin except for the girls'.

He was at his last resort.

He knocked on the door. No answer.

Of course not. Isabel was on the other side of the mountain, Tabitha was somewhere with Cole, and Felicity could barely move.

Lincoln reached for the door handle, and scolded himself. Was he insane? Walking into their cabin uninvited?

These were extreme circumstances.

He clenched his jaw and turned the knob. He very slowly pushed the door open, peering inside. The curtains to Felicity's room were drawn, and Tabitha's open. To his relief, Tabitha seemed to have *had* made an effort to clean it, though her drawers were stuffed and half open, and her bed seemed made in the rush of the moment.

The windows in their cabin were wider than the boys', and also were drawn, letting the entire room fill with a still light, dust dancing along the rays of sun that shone across the floor. He very quickly scanned Tabitha's room, deciding Charles was very unlikely to attempt to hide there. He peered into Felicity's room finding it to be superbly clean, and also there was much to hide in. He checked under her bed, and there was nothing. Not even a box.

He left her corner, closing the curtains behind him, and froze.

There was only one place left to check.

He immediately wanted to turn on his heel and run out the door. There was no way he could face it. But then again, it was just a room.

Just a room, he told himself over and over as he pulled back the thin curtain.

It indeed was just a room. A very empty, hardly used one. There was a tablet and stylus on the nightstand, a discarded dagger on the top of the dresser, probably something Taryn insisted on but the owner of the room refused to use, and a tiny little wooden lemon sat beside it.

One of her only personal belongings.

And maybe the only thing she'd ever used her knife to create.

Lincoln snapped at himself. He was looking for Charles, and *only* Charles.

Lincoln dropped to the floor, scanning under the bed. There were a few folded blankets and a few extra pillows, but nothing else.

Until one pillow sniffled.

Lincoln frowned.

The pillow moved, pushed away to reveal a tiny tear-stained face. Charles wiped his nose on his arm, croaking, "Hi."

Lincoln opened his mouth to speak for the first time in days, though the words refused to push through. "Is Cents mad I left without telling him?" Charles asked.

Lincoln shook his head.

Charles sniffled, burying his face into the pillow.

Lincoln blinked. He had no idea what to do. He couldn't just drag the boy out and deliver him to his brother like this. He sighed, and slipped under the bed as well.

Lincoln touched the boy's shoulder gently.

Charles yelled into his pillow. "It's not fair!"

Lincoln flinched. No. Don't do this to yourself, little guy.

"It's not fair!" he shouted again.

Lincoln wasn't sure what to do. All he could think of was to pat him on the shoulder. Charles looked up from his pillow, tears and sweat making his hair stick up straight from his forehead. "Why?" Charles sniffled.

The one word made Lincoln's heart ache more than anything he thought could.

"I-I miss her too." His voice was hoarse and dry, barely above a whisper.

"No one told me," Charles said, wiping his eyes, turning over to lay on his back and stare up at the bottom of the bed. "Cents didn't tell me. You think I'm too little."

He angrily stomped his foot against the bed.

Lincoln didn't remember being five, but he remembered being ten. A five year difference, but young nonetheless. Oftentimes, people underestimated the intelligence of a child's mind. Lincoln felt guilty. He hadn't even thought about Charles. In the short time they'd been together, Charles had attached to her so quickly.

"I'm sorry," Lincoln whispered.

"Why did she have to go away?" Charles said, looking to Lincoln, his eyes brimming with tears. "She really liked you. You have to know why."

Lincoln pushed down his tears. He had no time for that. He needed to be strong. For Charles. "I don't know," he said, swallowing. "But she told me to trust her, and I'm going to trust her and be okay."

Charles watched him closely. "She said that?"

Lincoln nodded, forcing a painful smile. It hurt to breathe. She couldn't be gone. She wasn't gone. That was all his mind was telling him. He'd tried to let go, but she'd told him. She'd be safe. Maybe just by some miracle…

Charles placed a tiny hand on top of his. "She is happy. She liked it when you were happy." Charles formed a small smile on his lips, his sore red eyes watching Lincoln closely.

Lincoln nodded.

Charles kicked the pillow out from between them. Lincoln noticed his fist was clenched to his chest. He slowly undid his fingers, revealing a crumpled ball of paper.

Lincoln frowned.

Charles handed it to him. "I found this. Can you read it to me?"

Lincoln was too speechless to try to tell the boy he couldn't even read. He unraveled the paper, a ring rolling out into the palm of his hand. He contained a gasp. A DNA ring. He held the ring up, finding the ring to be red through the small glass windows to its hollow interior.

It struck him suddenly. *Blood*. Nikki's blood.

He turned to the paper. A note. A ripped piece of Tabitha's beloved paper. Handwriting in blue ink. Handwriting that never bothered to dot the 'i's. Ink of one of Taryn's few paper writing pens.

A short message Lincoln couldn't make out.

But he could make out the final word. Four letters he'd engrained in his mind when she'd tried to teach him to spell:

-NIKKI

"What does it say?" Charles persisted.

Lincoln blinked out of his shock. "I—I don't know."

Charles opened his hand out for the note. Lincoln reluctantly placed it back in his hand. Charles held it out. "The first letter is a 'L'," he said proudly. He scrunched up his face, trying to make out the rest.

"How about we figure it out together?" Lincoln offered. Speaking felt a little less painful on his chest. "You'd have to come out from under the bed…"

Charles pursed his lips in thought. "But Cents will be mad at me."

The angriest Lincoln had seen Lawrence get at his younger brother was a smack of the hand when Charles tried to grab a knife off a table in the courtyard.

"I doubt it," Lincoln said. "He'll be really happy to see that you're safe."

Charles sighed. "Okay. I'm going to tell him Nikki is safe too! Then he'll be even happier."

A lump formed in Lincoln's throat as he nodded. "Yeah."

Charles seemed to notice Lincoln's mood change, and he grabbed Lincoln's hand. He opened it and placed the note in his palm. Lincoln blinked in surprise.

"We're going to figure it out," Charles said, wiping his red eyes.

Lincoln nodded, clenching his fist, keeping the little paper safe inside. "Now," he said. "Let's get you back to your brother."

They crawled out from under the bed. Lincoln picked Charles up from his feet. The boy's face was red in the light, the tip of his nose looked sore from being rubbed at. But the look on his face seemed content.

Something Lincoln desperately wanted. Just a small feeling of relief. Something to come and destroy the tiny spark of hope he had lingering in his soul.

He just wanted to breathe.

They left the cabin, and were met instantly with commotion.

Not over the fact the lost boy was found, but something on the road leading from the woods. A crowd of Defenders had formed. People were shouting and rushing to the scene. Taryn burst from her cabin.

A small group of people pushed through the ground, led

by a lanky, familiar figure.

Lincoln frowned, then his jaw fell, meeting the eye of the winged daughter of the Wingor Diones for the first time in six months.

Officer Miriam Outown had returned.

With one eye.

36

Miriam Outown was back.

That was the only thing Lincoln heard for the next two hours. Miriam had been leading a small group of refugees, and as soon as Taryn saw her, she ordered all of them to the Medic Tent before questioning.

Everyone had heard of the Outown Officer.

Lincoln didn't know why it came as such a surprise to him. She was the daughter of Wingor Diones, immortal guardians, and the younger sister of the infamous Aaron Outown, member of the Curatrix team. He only knew her as the aggressive, sarcastic officer who'd teamed up with them and helped them throughout their attack in Imperial. She had left to search for full-bloods six months ago, and now... she was back.

All of this Lincoln explained to Lawrence telepathically since he had no energy to speak anymore, and Lawrence was totally lost in why everyone was so hyped. They sat by the window in the boy's cabin, watching the Defenders assembled outside.

Charles was asleep against Lawrence's chest, and Lawrence held his little brother close, his face cold and determined as he stared out the window.

Lincoln had been correct. Lawrence hardly scolded his brother, especially when he learned the reason Charles had run off. Lincoln ran his fingers over the note, taking in deep breaths, constantly looking at her name to make sure he wasn't going crazy and seeing things.

The note was the last words unspoken he had.

The door to the cabin burst open.

Lincoln shoved the note into his pocket.

Lawrence glared at and shushed Cole who stood in the doorway and pointed to Charles.

"Sorry," Cole whispered. "Miriam's back."

Lincoln nodded.

"She's calling for a meeting tonight." Cole closed the door slowly behind him. "For Miriam to tell everyone what happened. Apparently she made some *big* revelations."

"Will Ray be there?" Lawrence asked.

Cole shrugged. "I have no idea. He hasn't gone psycho in two weeks."

Lincoln had to admit he kind of missed Ray's annoying presence constantly lingering. He'd only seen Ray at breakfast, where Felicity insisted Lincoln accompany her. He seemed tired and upset.

Lincoln couldn't blame him.

The time dragged onto the meeting. Lincoln tried to keep his mind busy, sitting cross-legged at his stool, and tried to figure out his problem on his device. If he sat still too long, he mind took too much freedom and tried to wander, then torture him.

He had no luck.

He leaned back, taking the blood ring and absentmindedly fiddled with it.

The cube project was a bust. He buried his face in his arms on his desk. The stupid cube was supposed to be revolutionary, but he couldn't even get an energy source to make the model run. What a great inventor he was.

He could just push it aside. Forget about it. Maybe he could try to just be normal. Actually participate in Taryn's training.

Just like she had. It wouldn't be the same without her.

Maybe he'd look up to find her right there. She'd burst through the door and tell him it was all a bad dream, and she was back. He'd hug her and this time he'd never let her go, ever.

You are madly in love with a dead girl.

Lincoln jolted up, falling backward, the stool tipping over and he crashed to the floor. His head felt groggy, and his body heavy. He'd fallen asleep.

That fact filled him with both panic and relief.

It had been far too long since he'd gotten sleep. But the voice trickled deep into his mind. It was achingly familiar. The one he'd heard in his mind in the words.

It was just a dream. It wasn't real.

He got to his feet, and checked the time on his square GPS device. *18.43 PM.*

He was going to be late.

He found his boots crammed under his cot, and didn't bother to tie them. He grabbed his green jacket, and an overcoat, and stumbled out the door.

You are madly in love with a dead girl, the voice had said. Lincoln wrinkled his nose. In love with? How cheesy. He tried to convince himself of that as he ran through the dying light to Taryn's cabin. A new snow began to fall, and the central fire was just being lit. More Defenders were set outside Taryn's cabin than usual.

They didn't give Lincoln a second glance as he bounded up the steps and tore through the door.

The entire room froze, all eyes glued on him.

Taryn face-palmed and pinched the bridge of her nose. Miriam stood in the center of the room, bandaging covering the right of her face. She smirked. "Good to see you again, Gears."

Lincoln closed the door behind him and nodded to her.

The room was packed with Defenders, some significant townspeople, and of course, the Council, though Lincoln technically didn't associate himself with the term. His heart skipped a beat on seeing Ray. The boy's face was solemn, and deathly pale from the lack of sunlight, and dark, purple circles had formed under his amber eyes. He was seated on the far side, and Lincoln noticed Cole was on the opposite side of the room.

He frowned, though he didn't take too much time to wonder. He came and stood next to Ray, who seemed surprised, raising an eyebrow.

"Continue, Officer Miriam Outown," Dow said. He sat up on the podium beside Taryn, who stood pacing. Agent Lopez had left a week earlier.

Again, Lincoln heard whispers echo the name 'Outown.'

"Thank you, Dow," Miriam said, crossing her arms. "But are all the Members here? I see Gold—I mean, Johnson over there, and I count six over there. I know you apparently got a new one. I'm guessing it's the guy with glasses glaring at me."

"Yes," Taryn sighed.

"Where's Squirt?"

Lincoln's mind left the room. Ringing blocked his ears and his vision blurred. He watched almost in slow-motion as Taryn informed Miriam of what had happened. All at once he flew back, out of breath. He grabbed the back of Ray's chair, trying to silently catch his breath.

"No. She can't be," Miriam snapped. She shook her head.

Dow sighed, his head hanging. "It was a loss also for the amount of research to be done on how full-bloods are born, especially concerning the fact she was the eldest Aguirre tchild."

Miriam's jaw dropped, as she practically screamed, "WHAT?"

She stared in total shock. "Squirt is an Aguirre?"

"Was," Dow corrected her.

"She can't be gone." Miriam shook her head. "That's impossible."

Yes. Exactly. Miriam got it!

"It is quicker to move on than live in denial," Taryn said, her glassy eyes seeming to show she spoke from experience.

Lincoln sank back in his seat.

"*She* wouldn't have let that happen," Miriam said, beginning to pace.

"Who is this she you keep talking about?" Taryn asked.

"You asked for a full report of my story, Sergeant," Miriam said, straightening herself, putting her arms to her side. "I will give it. I think it's going to change a lot."

37

It had been months of searching to no avail. She and her companion and fellow Defender, Officer and part-time Janitor Jack Sallow, were coming to a dead end. They'd practically explored every site of weird happenings they'd been able to research that occurred in the past year.

One of their leads turned out to be criminals who happened to have dealt with a black market dealer who sold him some insane grappling tech, and he indeed actually couldn't fly.

The only black market Miriam knew of that had such incredible tech was the Defender's pain in the side, the infamous Marketeers.

But Miriam had had a mission, and no time to try to track down the illegal dealers. Their next instances were also not productive in the slightest. They'd just arrived in Norris, one of the smallest, least interesting regions in the world. It was at the top of the west continent, and was bitterly cold. She and Jack had left the SpeedRail and were strolling the sidewalks that had frosted over. Miriam had counted two autos the entire thirty minutes she'd been in the tiny region town. And she'd thought North Cordell was boring.

"Cheer up!" Jack said, rubbing his cold nose. "This is our first lead in two weeks!"

"Our other forty eight leads have all been garbage," Miriam grumbled, getting to the sidewalk beside him. "I'm sure we'd have better luck on the East continent."

"You just want to go to Bōli."

"It would be more fruitful than this for sure."

Jack rolled his eyes, picking up his pace against the icy wind, blowing at his curls. "There's already been sightings here of an ability user," he said, spinning around and walking backward with ease to face her. "Which leaves two options…

"An Oquelite or a full-blooded member," Miriam sighed. He was onto something, but she wasn't exactly willing to give in just yet. "But the difference between them is there's—watch out for the light pole!—hundreds of Oquelite and only twelve Members."

Jack slowed his pace, seemingly unphased by his near crash, placing a thoughtful hand to his chin. "The Keyper legacy has always been amongst the northern cultures, right? Someone reported this incident had something to do with glowing?" His eyes lit up with pathetic hope. "That's pretty darn close."

"Oh wow," Miriam said, hiding the groan down in her throat. "Someone saw something glow, probably the super rare Keyper member... or a Bot activated by a rat at two in the morning."

"Look, that was a weird case."

"You're the one who wanted to take it!"

Jack shrugged, spinning back to walk forward, falling back next to Miriam. He flashed her a bright smile. "But hey, at least we learned about this place!"

"Okay, *if* it's a Council Member, where would they even be?" Miriam said. What could she say? Jack's optimism was contagious... even on a sleep-deprived, hungry mess as herself.

"Considering our current guess is Keyper, they're a hereditary Member." Jack nudged her.

"Are you trying to get me to say that means they'll

probably be with their family?" Miriam raised an eyebrow. "That's the second weakest lead I think you've had since the rat incident."

"Ah, you misinterpret me, my friend," Jack said, attempting to pat Miriam on the head as she shocked him away. "If there's a family around the Keyper, they're a bigger target. There's more people—"

"—so more people who can lead us to them," Miriam finished. *Not bad, Sallow. Not bad.* "That only works if this person happens to be a very specific Keyper Member."

Jack sighed. "You're such a downer, Outown."

"I'm hungry," Miriam corrected.

Jack ignored her, walking forward with almost a bounce in his step, his chin held up. Miriam couldn't help but hide a smirk. She didn't like admitting it, but she admired his positive attitude, though at times it seemed pointless.

But we've gotten this far. Three years ago, when Sergeant had asked them to work and communicate especially with her, due to her suspicion of an uprising, Miriam had been the one to think the idea of them ever finding a Council outrageous.

Jack said the fact Miriam's brother had been part of one proved it wasn't. That comment gave him a bruised nose.

It turned out Jack was right.

The town was eerily quiet. The sidewalks were mostly empty, except for the few scattering passerby, each of whom seemed sure to keep clear of the two young Defenders striding down the sidewalk.

Jack sidestepped a passing man quickly. "Sir, could you know where the—"

"Can't help you, Officer," the man said, quickly, trying to dance around Jack. "Not much time before sundown."

"Sundown?"

The man didn't answer, just shoved Jack out of the way and hurried across the street, disappearing quickly behind the side door of the two story shop.

Miriam frowned, looking to Jack. "Weird."

Jack shrugged. "I've dealt with weird before—"

"I don't need to hear another rendition about you and your twin friends chasing ghosts again."

"Hey! It's a great story!"

"Definitely," Miriam murmured, her eyes narrowing at the window of the shop, watching as the man's silhouette hurried to close the blinds. Something was off. "Good. This is very good."

"Did you just say this is *good?*"

Miriam chortled, hurrying past Jack. "Hurry, so we don't get eaten alive by your Keyper after sundown."

"Keypers don't—"

"I know!" Miriam groaned. "I was joking! Hurry up, nerd boy."

Jack rushed to her side.

"There!" Jack said suddenly. He looked up from his Comm, pointing across the street to a shabby little cabin that seemed out of place with the government issued steel-grey store buildings. "That's the motel."

Miriam frowned. "That place? Jack, the *Inn* was more capable than that thing."

Jack shrugged. He shoved his Comm into his pocket and dashed across the street. Miriam sighed and made her way slowly across. Not like there were any cars anyway.

Miriam chased after him, halting out of breath at his side as Jack knocked on the door of the motel.

"One minute!" a scratchy voice shouted. A crash followed, and then a various amount of banging before the door swung open to reveal an elderly woman, perhaps in her early 60s, her grey hair pulled up in a loose bun, wearing loose leggings, a T-shirt, and about three coats. "Whatcha want?"

Miriam groaned. Jack elbowed her.

"Um... this is the Norris motel, right?" Jack said.

"Oh, right!" the old woman said, stepping back and holding the door back wider. "Come in! Take off those boots. They're filthy."

They did as they were told, wiping off their boots on the mat and removing them. The motel was bitterly cold, and Miriam instantly wished she was wearing more layers.

The main lobby of the motel looked like the woman's house. She led them to the back, where she pushed open two foggy glass doors to a courtyard with doors to rooms lining the walls.

The woman smiled proudly and shut the door in their

faces. "Now how can I help you? None of you Defender folk come here just for a stay. Let me guess. You want a meal too."

"I'm Officer Sallow," Jack said, and then gestured to Miriam. "And my colleague, Officer Outown."

Miriam gave an uninterested wave.

"Out-a-town?" The woman frowned.

"Out. Town. It's simple," Miriam grumbled.

The woman smirked. "She definitely needs some food."

The woman led them to a living room. In the middle was a pit, with a fire lit and blazing. Miriam couldn't resist sitting beside it and warming her freezing limbs. For the first time that day, she felt like she could breathe a little.

The woman brought out soup, handing it to both of them. Miriam took it with a quick thank you. It smelled familiar. Almost sweet.

"Oranges?" Jack said with a frown.

The woman laughed, sitting back in a chair. "Norris is best known for its greenhouses where those things thrive."

So put it in soup. Why not? Miriam didn't think more on it. Jack finished quickly, and instantly started with the questioning, which probably was best, because Miriam was in no mood to deal with anyone.

"Have you seen anyone strange around these parts? We're here concerning an article published a little over a year ago, about a moving and glowing shadow?"

The woman leaned back in her chair in thought. "Don't be too hasty, lad. The only person I can think of would have to be... oh goodness, what does that guy call himself? Gorgon, is it? He's got the weirdest hair. Black and gold or something weird like that. He usually roams around the streets a few nights a week. Now, do I get paid for this?"

Jack handed her a bill.

The woman seemed satisfied, tucking it away in her apron and taking a seat in a chair across the brick fire pit.

"I am Nora, from Norris," Nora said, glancing back and forth from Miriam to Jack to see if either had a comment.

Miriam had one, but Jack would probably kick her for it.

"So," Nora said, leaning back and taking a loud sip of the stew. "Tell me your full names. Ages. Where you're from. And your division."

"Oddly specific." Miriam said, earning her a glare from Jack anyway.

"I'm trying to help ya out," Nora said, with a shrug. Jack sighed, putting on a cheery smile. "I'm Officer Jackson Sallow. Twenty Two. I'm from the region of Amana."

"Where's that?"

"Farthest south region on the continent."

"Ah. Don't get much of you folk way up north," Nora sighed, nodding. Her eyes darted to Miriam. "And you?"

"Officer Miriam Naomi Outown," Miriam grumbled. She glared at Jack when his eyebrows shot up in surprise. "Twenty Three. From Imperial."

Nora took another loud sip. "You coulda fooled me if it wasn't for your accent. I thought most Golden Regoiners had a bit more class, lassy."

Miriam rolled her eyes, though Nora's comment wasn't entirely false. Proper and Imperial went hand and hand.

Jack quickly jumped in. "We're both stationed in North Cordell usually though. It's a West Central region. We're under Sergeant Hunter."

There was a moment of silence as they watched each other, with suspicious eyes, eat.

"Sergeant Hunter," Nora mumbled to herself, before her eyebrows rose with sudden surprise. "I'll be darned if you mean Jessica Hunter."

"Yes," Jack said calmly. "The Curatrix Member."

Nora chuckled to herself. "Gracious, that woman is still alive?"

"Surprisingly," Miriam said.

"So when you say Outta-town, you mean the Outta-town? That one's still alive too?" Nora frowned, squinting her eyes at Miriam. "I thought the Curatrix Otta-town was a lad."

"I'm his younger sister," Miriam said quickly, feeling a cool rush overcome her. *Can we move on from the Curatrix, please?* "You mentioned a weird guy... Gorgon?"

"Oh, yes!" Nora tossed her head back and laughed. "Him, him. What a lad. Has he done something wrong?"

"Not that we know of," Jack said. "We'd like to speak with him."

"Tough luck," Nora said, slurping the last of the soup.

"He doesn't make appointments, and he's only out after dark."

Wait. After dark? Was *he* the one townspeople were fleeing from?

"Who is he?" Miriam said, leaning forward.

"A lad." Nora picked her stew back up. "Early twenties at most."

Miriam frowned, forcing herself to sit up. She leaned closer, watching Nora through the flames. "Why is everyone so afraid of him?"

Nora froze. "Who said that?"

"Is he terrorizing?" Miriam got up from her seat. Could they have found a rogue Oquelite?

Nora dropped her spoon into the bowl and gripped it with her hands. "He wouldn't want an Outown. It's been a long night."

Nora stood up.

Outown? What did an Outown have to do with any of this? Miriam tried to chase after her, but Jack leapt from his seat, trying to block her. "Miriam, no."

Miriam shoved Jack away. "Who is making your town so afraid?" she shouted.

Nora stopped at the doorway. She paused for a moment, then looked over her shoulder. "Things that were and things that are. Your keycards are on the table."

The two spun to see the keycards where Nora had said, and as quickly as they turned back, Nora was gone.

Miriam sighed, and Jack face palmed, taking up the key cards. "Great going, Mir."

"It *wasn't* going anywhere," Miriam retorted, taking her card.

"Don't act like it wasn't because of her mentioning Aaron." Jack cast Miriam a sad glance, pushing past her.

They headed out barefoot in the courtyard, the air bitter cold, nipping at Miriam's feet against the stone. She took a deep breath, following Jack up the steps to the second level. "Okay, fine. That was brash of me."

"At least you admitted it?"

Miriam smiled. *You're too merciful on me, Jackson Sallow.*

"Watch this 'Gorgon' guy be some sort of emo guy in a band," Miriam grumbled.

"Only one way to find out," Jack said with a smile. "Ready to go out?"

"Sleep first, then fight emo-band members," Miriam said.

Jack laughed. "Alright, fine. Have it your way."

38

MIRIAM'S COMM WENT OFF FOR THE FOURTH TIME AGAIN. Another message from Jack.

Miriam ignored it, rolling over. Jack was one of her closest friends, but he sure did manage to try and make her get up early. They'd been up too late for this.

She closed her eyes, hoping the dull lull of sleep would relieve her. The buzz of the Comm went off again.

Miriam sat up, groaning. "Fine, Jackson Sallow," she sighed, grabbing the Comm. "Have it your way."

She slid off the bed, pushing her sweaty hair from her face, as she stumbled into the small kitchen.

5.30 AM

Ready to go scouting for Gorgon/Keyper?? :D

As expected. How did that boy survive on so little sleep?

5.50 AM

I left w/o you, loser. I'll be back soon.

Of course he did. Ambitious as always. Maybe he'd find nothing and agree to leave.

6.20

I'm being followed.

Miriam froze. He what? She quickly scrolled.

JACKSON SALLOW HAS BEEN BLOCKED.

Jack. Her blood went cold.

She didn't have a moment to think further as the walls shook. Miriam crashed to the floor. She cursed.

"What the he-"

A gunshot echoed through the courtyard. Miriam's body went rigid.

"Jack!" she screamed.

Adrenaline took over. She scrambled to her feet, running to the door, slamming the keycard mercilessly against it. The door swung open, and Miriam burst out into the cold winter air.

She rammed herself against the railing, bending over to look into the courtyard. It was empty. Miriam's heart beat against her chest. She scrambled down the steps. Please don't be Jack. Please don't be Jack.

Her heel caught against the step, sending her crashing down the steel steps and hitting the ground with a thud.

She groaned, picking herself up, her legs swaying under her weight. She steadied herself, straining her eyes. Her breath was stolen from her.

The door to his room was torn clean off.

Jack. Jack. Jack.

She broke out into a run. Had Gorgon gotten to him? How could she have been such an idiot? Why had she ignored him?

She ran, bursting into the room. Three darkly dressed figures, blades hanging at their sides, masks covering their faces.

Jack was pressed up against a wall, his nose bent and bloody, his right eye swelling. He caught sight of her and she saw him pale. "Miriam! Get out! Run!"

A blonde Oquelite took notice in half a second. One sent a punch to her stomach. She reeled back, catching a flame in the corner of her eye. Miriam dove inside, letting the swirling ball of flames crash into the closet door behind her. She rolled over onto her back.

The Oquelite unsheathed his blade, stepping over her. Miriam scrambled back. She squeezed her eyes shut, gritting her teeth, trying with all her might to summon her wings to spring from her back.

Her body refused to muster the essence. She was too tired. Too drained.

"Miriam, no!"

Suddenly, there was a cry. Then, a thud. Two arms pulled Miriam from the ground, wrapping tightly around her, keeping her arms restrained to her side.

Her eyes burst open.

Jack lay on the floor where she had been, gripping his arm in pain. The blonde Oqurlite still held his poisoned blade, swinging it to Miriam.

For a moment, the world froze. Her vision fogged. Jack had taken the blade... for her. And she'd let him helplessly.

Her captor turned out of the way, taking Miriam with them.

To her horror, her captor had the tinted gold edge on his hair from the description that rocked her mind.

"I knew you were part of this!" she screamed, beginning to kick and squirm. She couldn't let him take her. No. She would only be failing Jack more. "Let me go!"

Gorgon ignored her, and sent a handful of sand in the Oquelite's direction. He burst out of the door, throwing Miriam easily over his shoulder, knocking the air from her lungs. She gasped, trying to stop the jostling world from trying to fade. She pounded against him, but she knew she was too weak to make any effect.

When Gorgon finally slowed, they were on the balcony. He had turned sideways, and she could see down into the courtyard. She watched as the Oquelite dragged out Jack's body, as he groaned and writhed in pain. His eyes began to grow bright red... that wasn't normal.

That wasn't Oquelite.

Hot tears pricked at Miriam's eyes.

He slammed his foot down on Jack's chest. "Bring a message back to your precious Council. They've had it easy. The real battle is only just beginning—"

Miriam didn't hear the rest, because the next moment she knew was Gorgon shoving a towel over her nose, and she was too weak to deny the sweet aroma, and let herself fall in the darkness.

39

MIRIAM WOKE TO DARKNESS, AND A BLANKET ON HER FACE, and something hard against her back. For a moment, she thought she had been buried alive. She shook her head furiously, the blanket fell away. She blinked a few times, her eyes adjusting to the light.

She woke in an unfamiliar room. The wall opposite of her held a window. The blinds were drawn. There was a small bed, the blanket ripped off and on the ground, and the sheet half peeled off. The floor was littered with trash, mostly take-out food containers. The side table had been over-turned, tablets sprawled on the floor. A Comm was cracked under a leg.

Miriam's arms were bound behind her to a dining table leg. Miriam's heart lurched.

She looked downward. She was no longer wearing her North Cordell uniform. She was wearing a sleek entirely black uniform, decked out with a hightech chestplate and leg pads. There was a holster buckled to her thigh, though it was empty of a gun.

"Oh look at that. She lives."

Gorgon stepped into view, dropping into a criss-cross position a few feet in front of her, perfectly safe from her flailing legs.

She cursed at him. "You killed him! You stupid, pathetic—" Pain flared in her side. She cried out. Tears picked her eyes. What the heck was going on? Was he torturing her?

She felt blood dampen her side. "Let me go," she gasped. Jack. Where was Jack? What had she done?

"I'm afraid I can't do that," her captor said, examining her from above, with a small dip of his brow.

"You're an Oquelite!" She jerked against her bonds, pain searing through her side.

"I'm not—"

"Oh shut up! I need to get out!" She thrashed furiously, but it was pointless. He reached out.

"No! Don't you—ah!"

Gorgon's eyes widened. "I cut you."

"Yes, stupid," she grumbled, taking in deep inhales.

"Calm down. I can help you." He got to his knees.

"No!" she screamed. "Stay away from me! You've already teamed up with Oquelite, kidnapped me, tied me up, and mortals knows what else!"

"I didn't touch you."

"My freaking *clothes* are changed, genius."

His face flamed. "You think I—NO! Not by me! And you're wearing an Agent Defender suit. Which should keep you much safer than those rags you were wearing."

"Why tie me up then if you're oh so gracious and kind?"

"Because you want to kill me."

"HECK YES I DO."

Gorgon massaged his temples. "You're only proving my point further, stupid Defender."

"I don't care! Let me go! My friend has been taken by glowing-Oquelite-eyes! Ugh, who knows what?" She struggled against the bonds. She could feel her side bloodying. Her head swayed.

"You're going to kill yourself! Let me help."

Miriam slumped back and glared at him. "How?"

Gorgon fidgeted with his hands. "Let me kiss you."

"WHAT?"

Gorgon laughed, causing Miriam's face to flame. "Sorry. I just wanted to see how'd you react. Your wound is caused by the power inside of me and is affected by me. The options are for me to kiss or bite you."

Miriam's stomach churned. She wasn't sure whether it was from her cut or the thought. "Why does it have to be your mouth?" she groaned. "What the *heck* are you?"

"Saliva," he said as if that explained *everything*.

"You're saliva?"

"What—No!" He pulled out a small jar from his layers of coats. "This will heal you. Since I caused the wound, I will heal it."

"Please don't tell me that balm contains your spit."

"It's this or—"

"Fine!" Miriam groaned. She almost preferred Oquelite. "But you are *not* applying it. Untie me."

"Good." Gorgon stood up and walked to the table and knelt down , quickly untying her bonds. Miriam pulled her arms free, and quickly snatched the balm from his hand, scrambling to the opposite wall. She turned away from him, ignoring the stare that burned into the back of her head. She carefully unzipped the underarm of her suit, exposing the bloodying bandages.

She swallowed hard, not letting her mind think too much as she applied the balm.

At first, nothing happened. Had he tricked her?

She almost turned and attacked him when suddenly, air was snatched from her lungs, the pain almost immediately evaporating.

Miriam pressed her hand against her side. No pain. No blood sticking to her fingers. She cried out. "It worked."

"I told you."

Miriam lightly tapped her side. Again, no pain. She smirked. She zipped up the uniform, turning to the warlock, chucking the jar at him, causing him to jolt in a panicked scramble-jump to catch it.

She laughed. "That's incredible... AND SO GROSS. Why does it work? Why in the *world* does it work like that? You *bite* people?"

He tore his hands through his hair. "I've never done *that* but—"

Miriam faked a gag. "I don't want to hear it." He wasn't the Keyper. That was obvious enough. But Oquelite? They didn't have weird sand abilities or saliva healthcare. She narrowed her eyes at him. "What are you?"

"Does it matter?"

"Stop dodging the question! People cower in the night from you. You use freaking sand and kiss people back to life. I'm owed an explanation." She huffed.

Gorgon scowled at her. "Honestly, Defender, you have a mouth for someone who I could kill in a matter of seconds."

When she fell silent, he laughed. "You are absolutely hilarious when you're terrified."

Miriam rolled her eyes. "Oh, I see now. You're no Oquelite, just a pathetic child."

"And you're going to listen to me," Gorgon said, bracing his hands behind his back with a charismatic smile.

"I don't want to hear it."

Gorgon glared at her. "But you might want to hear about the people who took your friend."

"I know you they are," Miriam spat. "They're Oquelite, and *you* work with them."

"I don't!" Gorgon groaned. "And they're not your typical Oquelite. I don't even think they are."

"How do you know what Oquelite are?"

"My aunt was a Defender on the island of Hai," Gorgon said, crossing his arms. With a huff, he blew a hair from his face.

Miriam knew her geography, thanks to her parents who'd loaded her with tablets during her private tutoring sessions, and she rarely heard of Hai. It had suffered during the EarthShaker, where it was more commonly known as Japan. Its reconstruction had been shaky and still incomplete, most of the island still deemed unsafe.

"Look. I'm sorry, but I don't know much about Hai and their Defenders, but why would she tell you about the Oquelite?"

Gorgon's face hardened. "It's not that important, Outown."

Miriam's eyes widened. "How do you—"

"Not important." He got to his feet. "What is important is that these people exist. They can't do Oquelite basics. You saw them."

Miriam scoffed. "Quit dodging my questions! One literally threw a fireball at my head! Only Oquelite have supernatural abilities."

"I thought you'd be smarter than this," Gorgon said, rolling his eyes. "They've taken over Norris. They've infested the place. They crawl from the shadows. Their eyes glow red, and they're a menace. That supernatural forest—" he pointed west "—is creeping closer to this town. The more of these creatures that show up, the faster it grows. It's connected."

"And you're telling me this because?"

A sly smile crept onto his lips. "Because you're connected to the Council."

Miriam's jaw dropped "How in the world do you know about that too?"

"I have a cool aunt," he said, quickly. "I have a feeling they're connected. Once *they* showed up, weird things have happened that weren't happening six months ago."

"You're blaming a couple teenagers now?' Miriam scoffed. "Please. I've met them. They're harmless."

Gorgon raised an eyebrow. "One of them crashed the Glass Tower."

"Okay. That was an accident, and he didn't technically—"

"Outown, I don't need specifics. I just need you out of Norris," Gorgon snapped. "Next I'm heading to Kennedy to get rid of the Council member there."

"In Kennedy?" Miriam gaped. The region below Norris?

"Yes," Gorgon's glare didn't give her much confidence to argue. "Please just leave. I don't want any more of the Northern Regions being destroyed."

Miriam snorted. That was a Defender's job. "I thought you were from Hai. What does it matter to you if any region is destroyed at all?"

Gorgon's face hardened. "When you're given abilities, you might as well use them well."

Given? What did he mean by given? She didn't dare ask. Given. People being given abilities... it wasn't possible. There was only one way, and it was very illegal. *No.*

"Then why help *me*?" Miriam shouted. She jumped to her feet, throwing her hands in the air. "Why give me this fancy suit?"

Gorgon's eyes narrowed. "So you can survive your ride home."

Miriam stopped midstep, whirling around on her heel. "What?"

Gorgon nodded, his eyes still glued on the window. "I bought you a ticket to Imperial. The faster we get someone connected to the Council out of here, the sooner these *things* leave."

Miriam scoffed. "Well, thank you for the generosity, *sir*, but I don't need it. I can go back to *North Cordell* on my own."

Gorgon's head suddenly jerked back to her, and he strode forward. "You don't have a choice."

"I'm a Defender. Don't even try to fight me!"

Gorgon slashed his hand through the air, and slammed his foot down on the ground. The room shook, dust flew from the ceiling and between the floorboards, flying up and whirling around, forming into glittering particles. His eyes narrowed.

Miriam staggered back. "You're a natural disgrace."

"Yeah," Gorgon sighed, tightening his fist. "I know."

Miriam was on a SpeedRail, and she was anything but happy about it.

She had a duffel bag of belongings that she sat on, crammed in the corner of the economy class car, near an old man with his reality-goggles on, laughing every other minute to whatever media feature he was playing, and didn't seem to notice Miriam beside him.

Miriam wasn't as lucky with the other passengers.

She wore a Defender's Sergeant uniform, and that meant as soon as she boarded the car, it had fallen entirely quiet, eyes glued on her like they were seeing an Oquelite. The stares had fallen away halfway through the first hour, though many crammed to be as far from her as possible.

And Miriam *never* rode economy.

That was a perk of having extremely wealthy parents. But Gorgon was obviously not extremely wealthy, and had taken money from his own pocket to get her out of Norris, because he apparently cared about it so much.

Miriam had put on an oversized jacket, draping the hood over her head, and tried to contact Taryn, but her Comm announced she was in a dire need of an update, but whenever she tried the system crashed. Something must have been damaged internally.

She wrapped her arms around her legs and her face, feeling tears begin to burn at her eyes.

"Leaving Norris border in fifty minutes," an automated message announced.

And going home. Like a little kid she had to go back home to her parents because she hadn't been strong enough to take them on her own. Jack was as good as dead now. Just like Aaron.

At the thought of her brother, she dug her fingernails into the fabric of the uniform. A lump formed in her throat. She had let down Eleazar, her nephew.

And now she might be too late to warn the Council kids of a dangerous force heading right for them.

Someone cleared their throat loudly.

Miriam peeked over her knees to see a man and woman now sitting directly opposite from her. The man had an olive complexion, his hair wavy and oiled, outfitted in a tropical print button up-short sleeves too. During the brutal Norris winter—cargo pants and sandals. A dark pair of sunglasses completed the look.

The woman beside him stared right at Miriam, her bright green eyes seeming to tear down into Miriam's soul. She wore a red suit, fitted to her well-defined curves, her neckline sweeping low. Her blonde hair was glossy, and hung down over her shoulders. Her lips were painted a vibrant red, outfitted with a smile.

"Where are you headed?" the woman said, sitting up inhumanely straight.

"None of your concern." She tugged on her hood.

The woman gave a shallow laugh. "Well, *Officer* Outown, you might be surprised to know you're actually our concern."

Miriam's head jerked up, her jaw agape. "What do you want?"

"The real question here, Outown—" The sunglasses guy leaned forward. "—is what do *you* want?"

His voice was deep, with an unfamiliar accent Miriam

couldn't place, yet it sent shivers down her spine like for some odd reason she knew exactly who he was. And she didn't like it.

The woman giggled. "We know where your friend is."

Miriam's head shot up, her knees pushed from her chest, as she nearly stood up, until she nearly fell over forward, quickly grabbing a pole for balance. She straightened herself, determined not to appear weak in the situation. She grit her teeth. "What do you know?"

"Oh my dear," the man said, leaning back in his seat, crossing his arms over his chest. "Very dramatic, isn't she? Maybe she'd like to know he's alive, but not for long."

Miriam's eyes darkened. "Give him to me."

The woman laughed again. "Oh no. I'm afraid that isn't possible, Outown. If you want your friend back, you must come under our terms."

Miriam paused. "How can I trust you?"

"This isn't a matter of trust. It's a matter of life and death." The man smiled. "For both of you."

"Your choice," the woman said.

Miriam sank back into her seat. *Say no*, was the first thought that came to mind. They could be tricking her. How did she know for certain they would bring her to Jack? But what if they made good on their threat to kill *her*? She should just get up and move. Ignore them entirely.

She took a deep breath, and looked up.

"Tell me what you want me to do."

40

MIRIAM STOOD ON THE PLATFORM BETWEEN THE MAN AND woman, watching her SpeedRail home zip by.

The man turned to her, though still examining his fingernails. "No turning back now."

Miriam sighed, balling up her fists. "What do you need from me?"

"Something simple, really," the man said. His head jerked up, and he snapped his fingers.

Miriam barely had time to process what was happening. The girl behind her shoved her forward, slamming into the man's chest. The world pixelated, not allowing her to scream. Her stomach dropped. The next moment she knew, she was crashing onto a cold marble floor.

She scrambled to her feet, her knees trembling. The man stood with his arms crossed opposite her.

"You-you're an Oquelite," she gasped in horror. Had Gorgon lied about Jack's attackers being non-Oquelite?

"You say it like it's a bad thing," the man chuckled.

"Where's Jack?!"

"Uh, uh." The man wagged his finger at her. "We had an agreement, remember?"

Miriam scowled. "What do you want?"

"Oh, just a simple interview. A few answers. Then we will let you go." He waved it off as if it was nothing.

"About what?" she said, hoping somehow she could still maintain dominance.

"That wasn't part of the deal. Now, your final chance to accept, Outown. Or I'll have to kill you."

She'd agreed to betray Taryn, and she doubted she could turn back.

Sorry, kids.

"Fine," she said.

The man gave a victorious chuckle. "I knew you would, Outown."

In a few moments, Miriam had a blindfold tied around her eyes, her hands bound behind her back.

"This is going to be so much fun," she heard the man say.

Again, his cheery voice sent a shiver down her spine. "Have we met before?"

"Me? I'm afraid not. I always heard about the little Outown. I encountered your brother once. His death was a shame, wasn't it? Funny you followed in his footsteps as a Defender."

Miriam's heart skipped a beat. She tried to whirl around in the direction of his voice, but the Oquelite hands kept her back. "You knew Aaron?"

"I doubt he ever mentioned a Rhun Ryynar."

No. Aaron hadn't. Miriam didn't bother replying. Aaron had never told her anything of what he did during the Trials, and his day to day job. For the most part he was just her brother, a fantastic Defender, and political wonder. And she was the "little Outown."

She shook the thought off. She was helping the Oquelite so she could help Jack.

But was it too great a price?

Miriam was jerked to a stop. She heard a knocking sound. And then she was thrust forward, her blindfold torn off. She stood in a doorway to a dimly lit room. Her eyes began to slowly adjust the small cell coming into view. Her heart jolted. The room was not empty.

She counted seven people, spanning from children to young adults with their arms chained up against the wall, staring at her with round, curious eyes. Miriam caught her jaw from dropping.

She turned around to the Oquelite, Rhun Ryynar. He stood in the light of a glowing purple flame in his palm that reflected off his sunglasses, a soft smirk on his lips.

"Where's Jack?" she demanded, refusing to let the look intimidate her.

Ryynar shook his finger. "Uh-uh. We had an agreement. You're playing by *my* rules." He turned to the Oquelite guards. "Lock her up. Don't think us cruel. We don't normally treat those we interrogate like this, but the Outowns have a dangerous track record. And have a stubborn streak."

Miriam tensed as the two Oquelite guards approached her. Her mind was screaming for her to jump out and pounce. Elbow the left on the face, grab the knife, and kill the other one before either have time to use their abilities.

But Jack. She needed Jack.

The gloved hands slipped over her wrists and harshly pulled her backwards, the dark room swallowing her hole. It smelled metallic, and cold pricked at her skin. She was thrust against the wall, in perfect view of Ryynar, who didn't move his head away from her. She could only imagine his eyes watching her as the chains were applied to her wrist.

After that, she expected them to walk away, but instead, they drew their swords. She heard a strangled gasp from the room, almost feeling the burn of the terrified stares.

"What's going on?" Miriam asked.

"This is the questioning."

Miriam frowned. "Around commoners?"

"They're traitors, anyway. Matthias is having them killed." The monotone of his voice horrified Miriam. "A shame, really. I quite liked them. But the Idicous brother is supreme."

Miriam took a deep breath. "What do you want to know?"

Ryynar laughed softly. "It's funny, really, after how long the Defenders controlled us, before we bred a more powerful generation, and now you're chained to a wall before me?"

"Enough taunting," Miriam scoffed. "The Oquelite hurt me more than you could ever know."

"A Defender killed your brother, Outown. Did you forget that?"

Miriam stiffened. She stared at Ryynar, and for a moment, she swore she saw the madman's face soften.

"You've killed more," she blurted out.

She heard someone groan in the room. "Your fighting is pathetic," a feminine voice scowled.

Miriam didn't dare look in the direction of the voice.

"Now. I don't want to fight you," Ryynar stepped into the room, his flame becoming brighter. "I have killed too many Defenders, but I've spared more. I'm willing to give you and your friend the same fate."

Miriam couldn't sense anything in his voice. Just the echo, bouncing from the wall, the crisp, harsh accent on the final vowel.

She gritted her teeth. "Get this over with."

"Where are the Council Members being kept?"

Everything in Miriam went cold. Her mind scrambled. The Council? Of course they were going to ask about the darn Council. The kids.

Her eyes darted to the side. She saw a young boy with thick, dark, curly hair shaking his head frantically toward her. She took a deep breath, turning to Ryynar.

"North Cordell Town #321, at the base of the third mountain, near the Defending Base—"

"No! Stop!" the same girl from before screamed out.

With one swing, the Oquelite brought the blade to her. Miriam shouted. The blade didn't pierce the girl, only shocking her, causing her to let out a horrible shriek.

"Very good," Ryynar said, a screen appearing above his wrist. "Which members have been located?"

"An Aviduous."

Ryynar scoffed. "We knew that already."

"A Humanic." She took a deep breath, feeling like one by one she was losing them through her fingers. "A Shadow Holder... the Oquelite Hybrid. The Illuminate Holder. A-and one is unknown to me."

"Which one?"

"Felicity Bentsworth."

The girl shouted out again. "Are you stupid—" She was cut off with another shock.

"And then that leaves the youngest female of your little group." Ryynar looked up.

Squirt. She was an Ewyon. The Oquelite didn't know that. If they knew she was an Ewyon, that would take away one of their few advantages—but Jack.

She scammed the room.

The shocked girl was glaring at her, her eyes reflecting heavy with tears. If she wasn't bound to the wall, it looked as if she would kill Miriam.

Miriam took another deep breath, and turned to Ryynar. "I don't know."

"You're lying."

"I'm not."

"I've been to the Void. I can feel it," Ryynar snapped. "You are lying."

Miriam's sweat went cold. "I—I can't tell you."

"The deal."

"I won't tell you!" Miriam shouted.

Ryynar scowled, turning to the guards. "Punish them. All of them."

Several horrified shouts echoed in the room as Ryynar left, the door closing behind him. And Miriam lost all ability to think.

Breathe, Miriam. Breathe.

Miriam Outown.

Miriam's eyes burst open. She looked around. No one was focused on her. They were all shouting amongst themselves. The voice felt direct, echoing in the crevices of Miriam's own mind.

I will save you. The voice was comforting, youthful yet... ancient? With a hint of an unfamiliar accent. Not from any of the regions Miriam could think of.

A shiver went down her spine. Oquelites couldn't mind read. That ability had been lost to time with the Ewyon and Sublinight.

The world around Miriam began to blur, her own heartbeat beating rhythmically in her mind.

Hold on. The voice sent a shiver down her spine.

Who are you? Miriam demanded, trying to push away the growing panic in her chest, counting her breaths.

There was a moment of silence.

I shall come for you and your friend soon.

Miriam waited.

She waited for what felt like days on end for the voice to come for her. She was sure she'd gone mad waiting for a *voice* that had spoken to her in her mind. The stress was growing on her, but that was her only string of hope.

It was either that, or give up and accept death like the girl, Dennis, had. The group was for the most part quiet, the only action being the routine checkups from Oquelite guards who would take a select few and return a few hours later.

The room was quiet, most of the group was asleep, except for Miriam, who stood anxiously, ignoring her anxious arms, staring hard at the door ahead of her, thinking of her nephew, Eleazar. She was going to get out of this for him.

The door opened with a bang.

Miriam jumped, her heart skipping a beat, her breath catching.

For a moment, Miriam thought this was the moment her savior had arrived.

But instead she was met with the spiteful eyes of the older Idicous brother, Matthias. Two Oquelite guards were stationed at his side.

The room was rustled from its sleep, full of shuffling of feet, caught breaths, and rustling of chains. The energy was poignant and still as Matthias's eyes lifted to Miriam.

She held her breath.

"Unchain her. Bring her to the Excenctial."

The guards nodded in unison, and stormed toward Miriam, unchaining her from the wall in a quick motion, harshly thrusting her backward, twisting her arms behind her back. She bit back a cry.

She stole a glance at Matthias. He was shorter than his younger brother, Silas, with rolling dark curls. His demeanor was far more conserved, his features rounded and aged, lacking what made University students swoon over Silas back in the day.

But watching Miriam grimace in pain brought a smile to his lips, and Miriam realized why he was far more feared.

With the flick of a wrist, her arms bound behind her, Miriam was flung from her feet, skidding across the floor, out the door, and hitting the hallway's wall.

Matthias chuckled. "Always wanted to do that to a Defender."

He grabbed her by the collar of her shirt and yanked her to her feet, thrusting her against the wall, his dark steel eyes bearing into her own.

She spat at him. He didn't flinch, promptly slapping her in her face. She watched as a purple flame flickered in his eyes. Something far different than Silas.

She heard the echoes of the cracking electric bolts and the cries of the prisoners in the room.

What made the Oquelite tremble before Matthais was far more terrifying than Silas ever had mustered before her. He was genuinely angry. He *hated* her.

So did Ryynar.

They were old enough to know what horrors were done to them.

Matthias grabbed a fistful of her hair and flung her forward, sending her cursing and stumbling into the bulky arms of the guards. A blindfold tied around her eyes, and a needle jabbed into her shoulder.

The world went into slow motion. Miriam could feel it moving around her, but she couldn't process it. Her mind was fogged and confused. She could hear deep voices, but no words.

And then all in a moment, her world flew back to normal, her blindfold was torn off, and she was thrust to her knees.

The room was huge. The floor was marble, columns aligned around a circle in the center. Matthias stood at a podium in the front, where it was illuminated with torches. A few masked and hooded Oquelite stood beside him. To the side of the podium, she saw two Oquelite, with their faces exposed. One was clearly Silas, though he looked thinner, his hair longer, his eyes bigger, veins crawling down his cheeks.

He hardly looked alive.

Beside him, half hidden by his shadow, stood a... woman. Her hair was nearly white, reaching to her calves, the tips greying, hiding most of her face. Her skin was deathly pale, and her fists were clenched to her chest. Her eyes stayed glued on Miriam, unblinking.

The two guards stayed by Miriam's side. She tore her eyes away from the woman and back to Matthias. No sign of Ryynar.

"We will give you one chance, Outown." Matthias took a step down from his podium. "I heard of your last stubborn outburst. But this time, there will be no second chances."

The door banged open.

Something thudded on the ground, followed by a human cry.

Miriam scrambled to look behind her on her knees, choking back a shout on seeing Jack on the ground, struggling to hold his head up. Dried blood stuck to his face, his exposed skin smeared in soot and dirt, filthy with cuts. His eyes looked paler. A small smile crept on his lips, seeing her. "Hey, Mir."

She wanted to punch him. Really hard. Right between his eyes. He was *alive*.

"Now, you see we have your companion in our possession. He's weak. Very easy to kill."

Jack laughed, then broke out into a coughing fit, blood lining his lips, but still maintained his smile. "Don't listen to them, Mir. I've been worse."

A foot came slamming down on Jack's back, pressing him against the ground.

Miriam grit her teeth, glaring hard at the guard's eyes, who were unfocused on her, staring straight ahead to Matthias. No, she wouldn't be responsible for someone else's death.

"Silas."

Silas jumped, looking around like he'd been woken up from a daze. He nodded and walked toward Miriam. His hands were shaking, and once again she was struck by how much sicker he looked when he walked into the light.

"What is the final member's bloodline?" Matthias demanded.

"I will not—"

Jack cried out behind her. "I'm fine!" he gasped. "Don't look! Miriam, just don't—" He cried out again.

Tears burned at Miriam's eyes. She clenched her fists. She

wanted nothing more than tear from the bonds and fight like a Defender should, not be at the knees of two stupid princes.

Tell him.

Miriam perked up. The voice. Then it clicked. Her eyes rested on the woman on the corner. She stood a bit taller now, her hands at her side. *Tell him of the Ewyon.*

I—I can't do that. They'll KILL her.

The smallest hint of a smile breached the woman's lips. She flexed her fingers, sparks flickering around them. *I will assure you I know what I am doing, young Wingor. Tell them.*

Who was this person?

"Tell me!" Matthias's words thundered throughout the room.

Miriam whirled her attention back to him, her heart racing. Tell *him*? Betray little Nik like that? She didn't have a choice.

"Three."

Silas unsheathed his knife. She heard Jack cry out again. She squeezed her eyes shut.

"Two."

I'm so sorry, Squirt. I'm *so* sorry.

"O—"

"An Ewyon!" Miriam shouted, her eyes bursting open. "The kid is an *Ewyon.* That's what you want, don't you?"

Jack's pain ceased. Matthias's lips lined with a smile. "You made a wise choice, Outown." He nodded to Silas.

"Do it."

Miriam frowned. And Silas slashed right through her left eye.

"HOW'D YOU GET OUT, THEN?" RAY LEANED FORWARD IN HIS chair.

He ignored the sudden shift of attention to him. He tried to appear unphased by it, holding his expression still, digging his fingernails into his knees.

Miriam turned her head, the eyepatch even more apparent as the final words rang loud in his mind, and sighed. "My memories afterward are hazy. Jack and I were brought back to the cell room. Hours later, the door opened, and the woman was there. She unlocked all of the cuffs, and left without a word."

"Gorgon was a warlock," Giles said, abruptly, all eyes turning to the young Officer. "A Modified, or whatever."

Miriam nodded solemnly. "I guess that's the term for it. I remember studying the Modification revolution, but I didn't think that was still a practice—"

"What is it?" Tabitha butted in. "You're talking all smartsy, and I don't understand a *thing* except for there's people other than Oquelite who want to kill us, which is flattering."

"We've discussed scientists modifying plants to have abilities, like the P9F file," Miriam said, her voice slowly becoming quieter. "And you've seen how it can be applied to humans."

Ray caught Lincoln flinching at the indirect mention of Nikki. Ray fought the urge to squirm.

"But that's not the same thing. Modified are the *highly illegal* result of people trying to give Unidentified Impure abilities through procedure and experimentation," Giles sighed. "That doesn't make any sense, why he'd be trying to keep trouble out of the Northern regions."

"Does it matter?" Miriam said, her gaze falling. "The fact that this attack happened was my fault and I should be held responsible."

Miriam had given the Oquelite their location. They knew Nikki was an Ewyon. They wanted her dead…

"We'll discuss later," Taryn said, her voice unsteady. "Your circumstances were no doubt unique."

"I didn't think they'd kill her," Miriam said, her head hanging low. "I thought that woman would spare her. Did they get the Stone?"

"That's what you're concerned about?" Lawrence shouted. "A stupid rock!"

Miriam glared at him. "It's not a stupid rock. It holds more power than you could ever know. If in the wrong hands, it could possibly lead to a total dismantlement of the Council, and possibly unlocking the Ewyon ancient abilities inside."

"I have no idea what you're talking about. But it's all stupid."

"Williams. Sit down," Sergeant Dow scowled.

Lawrence shot him a look and slunk back in his chair, with his arms crossed over his chest.

Miriam kept her attention on the Members, her hands on her hips as she scanned over them. "Did anyone directly witness Squirt's death?"

"Lincoln did." Felicity looked up, her shoulders shaking, a blanket draped over them.

Miriam's eyes widened, turning to Lincoln. "Gears. The Stone is *vital*. If there is any possibility Squirt dropped it, left it *anywhere,* we must find it."

"Agreed." That was the first word the Sergeant had since Miriam had begun her story. Taryn's eyes were trapped on the table, running her finger along the pin on her jacket.

Lincoln suddenly shoved his way through the crowd, and without a word, ran out the door, slamming it behind him. The room went still.

Felicity nudged Ray. He frowned at her. She sighed, and motioned her head in the direction of the door mouthing, "Go."

Ray reluctantly nodded, got up from his seat, and awkwardly made his way to the door, with the entire cabin watching. He gave a quick nod to Taryn, who waved him off. He stepped out into the cold, shutting the door behind him.

It had been a good two weeks since he could appreciate a deep breath of fresh air. The sky was still gray, streaked with storm clouds, the sun hidden from sight. The air smelled of smoke from the central fire, and was a bitter cold nipping at his skin.

To his surprise Lincoln hadn't wandered far. He sat beside the dying fire, his face in his hands, staring at the ground, clenching a piece of paper.

Ray sighed. He walked over to Lincoln, sitting down beside him. "Why'd you leave?" he asked, not entirely interested.

Lincoln sat up, not looking at Ray, moving his eyes to the fire, running his thumb over the paper methodically.

"Come on, Black Eyes. You can't stay quiet forever."

Lincoln shot him a glare.

"This is Silas's fault," Ray said, clenching his fists. "You can't be mad at Miriam. This is that... pathetic, piece of crud... person's fault."

Lincoln's face softened and he shook his head. "It's not."

"You talked."

Lincoln nodded again. "It's our fault."

"Linc, seriously. Come on, you don't think—"

Lincoln's hand clenched around the paper. "I do."

Ray was speechless. Words refused to form in his mind. All he could do was stare, with his jaw unhinged at Lincoln, who watched the fire somberly.

Lincoln suddenly tossed his head back, and took a deep

breath. He unclenched his fist, revealed the crumpled paper... and a ring. "But I think there's something we can do about it."

Ray's eyes grew wide.

He grabbed Lincoln's arms, and thrust him to his feet, trying not to be irritated with the fact that Lincoln now stood taller than him. "What?"

Lincoln pulled from Ray's grip, showing him the ring. "It's a DNA ring. I-It has their DNA."

"Look Linc," Ray sighed, his chest aching at having to tear down his friend's new found sliver of optimism. "The Curatrix machine is bugged. It didn't track the Oquelite right. DNA won't help."

"The machine isn't complete," Lincoln said quietly. "Remember?"

Ray's eyes widened. "You think you can... fix it?"

Lincoln's shoulder sagged. "I'll just wreck it."

Now he was doubting his abilities? "Lincoln, I *hate* stroking your ego, but believe me, you're stupid talented, and no matter what happens that'll always be the case."

Lincoln put on a forced smile.

It was something.

"I'll try to believe that."

"Oh, come on, Black Eyes. You can trust me." Ray cracked a smirk.

Lincoln chuckled. "I have a favor to ask."

Ray raised an eyebrow. "Yeah. Sure. What can I do?"

"Could you teach me to read?"

With the turn of a screw, the screen of the cube illuminated back to life, lighting up the space beneath the blanket. Lincoln quickly slammed his palm on top of it. He waited till he was sure he heard no one move from their bed, then slowly moved his palm from the screen.

It worked.

Maybe Super is a good name for it. He glanced at Ray's cot, which lay empty and abandoned ever since he'd been locked in a far cabin. Lincoln sighed.

He'd gotten the Square, which he'd begun to call it for lack of a better term, to work. A warm feeling swelled in his chest. It felt nice to accomplish two things in one day. First, a long discussion with his friends, and then Taryn, that left him craving time to be alone and break down from trying to hold it all in for so long. And then second, getting the cube to work.

He set the Square down, and gently unfolded Nikki's note.

Pain clawed at his mind, making his eyes burn, wanting to sink and fall away, but he couldn't give in. Not now. It wasn't over yet.

His hands tingled, as he glanced at the list of letters Ray had made. For the most part, Lincoln memorized sounds, but none of it really stuck. Looking back and forth between the list, and the note, made Lincoln realize this wasn't as easy as he anticipated.

First word. That's all he needed to figure out.

The letter struck him. "L."

Like in his own name. His name started with an "L."

He knew he could easily type in the letters into a Scroll, and it would read it to him, but he felt as though that wouldn't be as real.

It didn't stop him from looking up how the little letter with a dot on top was pronounced.

"Li," he pronounced, frowning.

Was she spelling his name? No, there were only two more left. His name had a lot more sounds than that. The next letter he did recognize, since it struck him odd when Ray was showing him at dinner.

"V."

"Liv," Lincoln said. Hey. That sounded like a word.

But there was still another letter. An… "e?"

"Liv-eh?" What could that possibly mean?

Sleep nagged at his eyelids. He couldn't sleep. Not now. But he had somewhat figured out a word, hadn't he? He'd figured out one of *her* words. Despite the fact it made no sense.

He tapped the screen of his Square, the light going out.

He shoved Ray's letter guide and his Square under his cot. He clutched the note to his chest, and took a deep breath, and the next moment he knew, Giles was banging on their door.

"The Sergeant's called an emergency meeting! Council

idiots only!"

Cole was already dressed, coffee in hand. He calmly took a tablet under his arm, and waited by the door for Lincoln and Lawrence to catch up. The "Council idiots only" comment apparently didn't phase Lawrence, who picked up his little brother, with no trust that Charles wouldn't wander off again.

Lincoln tucked Nikki's note into his boot, and strolled behind the two older boys to the main cabin.

The walk was becoming a usual.

They trailed into the cabin, and what first caught Lincoln off guard was the lack of Defenders. Or the fact there was none. Just Taryn, not dressed in a Sergeant uniform, her hair undone, sitting on her table, a gadget in hand.

She looked up as they entered. "Let the others in behind you."

They stepped back, seeing Tabitha, Felicity, and Ray there as well. They all stepped inside, the door swinging shut in the wind. They stood in a line, in awkward silence as Taryn scanned over them. She met Charles's eyes, who was in Lawrence's arms.

"Good morning, Charles."

"Morning," he returned with a sleepy smile.

Taryn smiled back, jumping off the table and grabbing the strange gadget. "The past few weeks haven't been ideal. Ever since Dow arrived, everything has been going wrong. And I fear I am to blame for it. I haven't trained you properly, but I fear I can't. You're teenagers. And now we have a new Member—" A nod to Lawrence. "—though he has not officially joined us. I think Nikki was right about something. You work very well together, and I think that's the only thing that we can use to give us one step ahead." Cole took a step forward. "Does this mean you've approved Lincoln's plan?"

Taryn took a deep breath, her shoulders heaving, a glint of pain in her eyes. "Yes. I checked the machine, and he was right. Nikki unlocking the Curatrix machine *did* unlock new files... and the location of an important chip that actually tracks the Oquelite."

The room went stiff.

Lincoln's heart leapt. He'd been *right*. He'd predicted

Aguirre tech. No. It was just a coincidence. It was basic knowledge. He needed to do better.

"I have *no* idea what it was tracking before," Taryn sighed. "But we now have confidence we can track Oquelite with this chip. We know the Oquelite are trying to kill new members... so we have to get to them before they do... and whatever new potential group Miriam mentioned."

The glowing eyes guys. Right. The ones who'd nearly beat Jack to death. Lincoln shivered.

Taryn cleared her throat. "Our one advantage is intel. They have three locations of interest, which you all volunteered to travel to yesterday with enthusiasm, but I made a few modifications to Lincoln's assignments."

Lincoln frowned. What?

With the stomp of a foot, a holographic screen burst to life above her desk, three regions popping into view.

"Court Illegia. Kennedy. Liberty."

Both Felicity and Tabitha perked up at the mention of their home region. That hadn't been in the original plan.

"The Curatrix machine revealed Liberty to be the location of the chip, and considering the Defender Base in Liberty is located in the Dome, it's most likely there." Taryn began to pace swiftly. "I could send battalions of Defenders to each of these locations to scout out the Member that the Oquelite are targeting, but as Members, you'll be able to find your fellow Council Members. You all have a connection." She looked up to see if they were still paying attention.

"Just get on with it already," Tabitha sighed, though Lincoln heard the slight tremor in her voice. "We went over this yesterday."

Taryn just gave an amused smile. She zoomed in on the biggest region of the group, Court Illegia. "I have organized a group of three to go to Court Illegia and meet with Agent Nigel Lopez at the Skyline City. Since this is the biggest operation, I'm sending Coleson Johnson, along with Tabitha Delorous—"

Lincoln frowned. Originally, they'd decided *he* would go to Court Illegia. That's where the *Mors Vis* were.

"Yes!" Tabitha cheered, punching Cole's in the shoulder. "Cole... bitha for the win!"

Taryn cleared her throat. "And Lawrence Williams."

Lawrence smirked. "And I come in to ruin the mood."

"Oh no. You'll make a fine third wheel," Ray laughed, before Tabitha elbowed him in the stomach.

"Now. For the other three, I have assigned Ray to Kennedy."

Ray quickly recovered from Tabitha's attack. "Just... Ray?"

Ray was supposed to go with Cole to Kennedy. Lincoln frowned. Taryn had really screwed with their assignments.

"After your mishap during the attack, I can't risk you going... mad on us again." Taryn didn't even look up to meet his eye from the hologram. "Defenders will be in the area for your assistance. I fear that these Members might be the reason for your outburst."

Ray's face fell, and he nodded solemnly.

Tabitha dropped her threatening elbow, to pat Ray on the shoulder. "It's fine, Mathews. I know a guy in Kennedy. Maybe you'll run into him, and you can make bad jokes together."

"You know someone in Kennedy?" Felicity butted in.

"And Felicity," Taryn said, catching the girl's attention quickly back to the Sergeant. "I would like it if you headed to Liberty with Armstance Giles. You stated your health was strong enough and I trust you were being truthful. You're not searching out a Council Member, but to find a chip the Aguirres have there. I was able to pin its location somewhere in the main city, and I'm sure you will be able to track it down in time."

Felicity paled. Lincoln saw her hands begin to shake. "M-me? Go-go back to—" she took a deep breath. "—Liberty?"

"Unless you can't handle it. I've arranged for you to stay with your family."

"My family..." Felicity blinked, shaking herself. "Yes. I can go."

Taryn gave an uneasy smile. "Alright then. I'll give the DNA ring to you to unlock the chip, which I suspect will have similar DNA locks to the machine, later." She rapped her knuckle against the table, and the hologram disappeared. "And your mental link is brand new in your minds. I have no idea how she was able to unlock it so early, but I imgine for those of you with unbroken essence, it might take a mental strain to communicate mentally over long distance, so don't be stupid. That will be all."

Lincoln raised his hand. "What about me?"

"You'll be staying behind. I need your tech skills to help me assemble the tracker."

Lincoln dropped his arm. So now he was the repair boy? This had been *his* idea. What an almighty Council Member he was. He didn't say anything, just nodded. At any moment, he could leave. Taryn wouldn't know, and she wouldn't be able to stop him once he ran far enough.

He'd run before, and the only person who'd been able to stop him was a curious girl with big blue eyes.

COLE WAS LEADING A MISSION. ON HIS OWN.

He stared at his hands, the scabs still healing from the attack two weeks ago. He'd collapsed in the snow, in pain and totally helpless. He had been so close.

He squeezed his hands shut and closed his eyes. He took a deep breath in.

His father always told him about a curse.

Was he the reason Ray had gone mad?

Cole's eyes burst open, and he jumped to his feet. He shook his head. "I don't have time for this," he scowled, muttering under his breath to no one specifically. The cabin shook with thunder. Rain pounded outside.

He was supposed to be packing.

He, Tabitha, and Lawrence were supposed to leave that morning, but with the storm, he anticipated a delay. Rain poured outside, drumming against the window panes.

The cabin was empty, except for Lincoln, who was asleep in his cot as of ten minutes ago. He'd been busy studying a tablet, and a piece of paper, but Cole was too concerned with packing to bother to ask about it.

He glanced at the Illuminate, which he'd tossed into the shadowed corner two weeks ago.

He glared at the sword. Not like it was its fault. It was his. It was just a stupid sword after all.

Cole shoved the intrusive thoughts away, grabbed the sword, and shoved it to the bottom of his pack. He zipped it up and tossed it over his shoulder. He grabbed the starting card for the truck off their dresser, and with a snap of his finger, turned off the lamp.

It was just Court Illegia. It was practically a big tourist region. Nothing could go wrong. He'd be sure of it. He wouldn't let things get out of control again.

The only light that was left on in the little lamp that hung awkwardly on the frame of Lincoln's cot.

Cole took another deep breath. He gently knelt down beside Lincoln's cot, and reached out for the lamp.

"I can do it," Lincoln grumbled.

Cole jumped.

Lincoln didn't open his eyes, his hand searching for the switch. He flicked it and the cabin fell into darkness.

"Sleep well," Cole said, getting back to his feet.

"Drive better," Lincoln said, before shifting and going quiet.

Cole smiled, though his chest hurt. He left the cabin, making sure to close the door gently behind him, and pulled his hood over his head, making his way out into the stormy courtyard of the camp.

The central fire wasn't lit, but officers were still stationed outside, holding bright swinging lanterns on the ends of poles. The lights to the girl's cabin were on, and he caught sight of a fidgety silhouette waiting on the steps.

He ran across the courtyard, through the mud, and rain till he hopped onto the safe ground of the porch of the cabin.

"Took you long enough," Tabitha said. She turned around, nearly hitting Cole clean in the face with a pole. Cole scrambled back. "Tabitha!"

"What?" she shouted. "I need help! They gave me one of those pole light things, and I don't know how to turn it on!"

"Give it to me."

She stuck her tongue out at him, and he rolled his eyes. He took the pole, finding the lantern on top. There was no button, or sensor.

"I don't know," he sighed, looking back to her. "We can do without it."

He caught Tabitha mimicking him under her breath. "No we can't. Your truck is a piece of garbage, and we'll be—"

"You bang it on the ground two times."

Cole and Tabitha swiveled to the new voice.

Lawrence Williams stood in the rain, a new pair of glasses sitting firmly on the bridge of his nose. They fit his face better than the circular ones. His side was noticeably empty from both a five-year-old boy and Fire Wolf, whom Taryn had forbidden them from bringing. He wore the same trench coat that reached to his boots, and a bag was slung over his shoulder, his arms crossed, and his eyes switching back and forth between Tabitha and Cole in a nervous anticipation.

Cole banged the pole twice, and just as Lawrence had said, the lantern burst to life.

"Nice glasses," Tabitha said.

"You just noticed I'm blind?" Lawrence raised an eyebrow, with a deadpan expression.

Tabitha rolled her eyes. "Of course not. They're new. You fixed them."

"That Sergeant of yours," Lawrence said, his brows dropping to a frown. "She got them for me."

"Yeah. She's pretty cool like that," Tabitha laughed. "I like it."

Lawrence's face softened, and he gave a small nod.

"Welcome to Team Cabitha!" Tabitha spread out her arms and jazzed her hands in the air.

Cabitha? Cole contained a smile and swatted her hand. "Yes. And I can kick you off."

Tabitha winked. "You wouldn't."

Lawrence groaned. "Can we get moving?"

Tabitha dropped her arms, grabbing the strap to her bag, and bounded down the steps laughing. "Come on! Meet you at the truck!"

Cole forced a smile, though his stomach churned watching Lawrence and Tabitha make their way toward the truck, parked near the autos behind Taryn's cabin. Taryn trusted him, even after all his failures, to find and protect whatever Council member was in Court Illegia.

He wouldn't let her down.

And he wouldn't let Lawrence or Tabitha down either. He looked up to the lantern, tucked his Medallion back into his shirt, and ran after them.

His heart dropped on seeing a light was already perched near the truck. Sergeant Taryn Hunter stood talking with Tabitha and Lawrence as Cole joined them. She shifted her attention, and gave him an acknowledging nod.

"I was just telling them once you read the Skyline to find Agent Nigel Lopez. He said they have a station set up near the entrance to a theater where you can find an Agent, or find his residence," she said.

Cole nodded, afraid if he said anything, he might hurl. Don't mess this up again. Not again.

"These have been a hard few weeks, and I would like for you to try not to get too hard on yourselves." Taryn's gaze was now set on Cole. "And please, behave. Your behavior gets blamed on me, so try to be nice. Especially you, Williams. Think of this as a way of proving yourself."

Lawrence just held a steadfast glare. "Alright."

"I'll be sure that your siblings are taken care of," Taryn said, and then looked from Cole to Tabitha. "And don't do anything stupid."

"Oh, Cole won't let me," Tabitha grumbled.

Taryn sighed. "I have weapons supplied in the trunk. Williams grabbed your food. You should be set. We'll be in contact."

Cole nodded. "Thanks."

Taryn nodded, attempting a smile, before it faltered. She wrinkled her brow, and gave another nod. "Goodbye then. Call me once you arrive."

"Will do," Cole said.

Taryn's face seemed to relax a bit, and she walked off back to her cabin. Tabitha claimed the opposite seat of the truck, and Lawrence settled silently for the back.

It took longer than Cole had liked for them to trek through the mud stricken road to the main street into town. Tabitha was practically bouncing in her seat.

"Any of you ever been to Court Illegia?"

Cole gripped the wheel, keeping his eyes on the road, trying to ignore the growing volume of his heartbeat in his ears. "No."

He guessed Lawrence either didn't reply or shook his head as Tabitha rattled off: "Well, I have. Once. When I was five. And I can tell you, it's fantastic. The Skyline, at least. There's plenty of people there, and while we search for a Council Member, we can totally hang out among the attractions. You're going to love it. I bet Ray ten pounds that we'd find a Member first. I would've bet more, but he only has eleven pounds since he and Lincoln bought all those potatoes to try exploding two months ago."

"Ten pounds, you say?" Cole chuckled. A bet sounded like a very Ray and Tabitha ordeal.

"A ten pounds I intend to spend well, sir."

"How will we know if we found the Member?"

"Maybe some flashing lights? An explosion? That's what happened when we figured out N—" Tabitha stopped herself, and the atmosphere fell cold.

"A weird person. Got it," Lawrence said quickly.

"Exactly," Tabitha said, clearing her throat. "And preferably someone with a good sense of humor. No offense to you boys, but for one thing, there are *plenty* of you, and none of you are very funny."

"I am funny," Cole said.

Tabitha laughed. "No you're not."

"You laughed!" Cole felt the tension in his chest loosen.

"I laugh a lot, Goldfish." Tabitha banged her feet up on the dashboard. "And I guarantee you this new Member will bring a lot of it. And I'm going to be the one to find them."

"Really? What about Lawrence? You don't think Lawrence will?"

"No offense to you, Lawrence, but I can't see you erm— becoming friends with anyone all too quickly."

"No offense taken," Lawrence sighed, his voice becoming quieter. "And I don't intend on it."

"Great!" Tabitha said, with a laugh. "That leaves just me."

Felicity wasn't panicking.

That's what she told herself. She was simply hiding under her covers, ignoring the throbbing pain in her legs, and trying to think happy thoughts, and repeating the number song over and over. *Four my friend. Two too much. Seven Eleven. Three we Two do.*

That proved to be hard when nothing happy seemed to be happening. She was alone in her cabin. Tabitha hadn't even woken her up to tell Felicity she was leaving.

And Felicity was going to Liberty.

Back home. Of all places.

A banging echoed from the door. Felicity wiped her nose and peered out from the blankets. "Who is it?" she called.

"It's me!" Lincoln's voice.

Felicity sat up, a smile breaching her lips. "Come in!"

The door creaked open, Lincoln peered inside. Once he caught sight of her, he stepped inside, and closed the door behind him. He had a bag slung around his shoulder, making a clanging sound when it was jostled.

Lincoln looked as if he'd just woken up, his hair untamed, and his jacket wrinkled. He rubbed his eyes.

"Okay, Liz. I know you're leaving soon, so I stayed up last night making you something."

Felicity's eyes widened. "What? Me?"

Lincoln nodded hesitantly. "But you'll need to change first."

Felicity's face flushed, and she frowned. "Why?"

Lincoln must have realized his words as his eyebrows shot up and he shook his head. "L-let me show you." He ran to the end of her bed, opening up his bag, and removed a metal cord, with three hinges placed along it, and buckles connected securely to the hinges.

"What are those?" Felicity leaned forward.

"I made them to … help you walk." He looked up to her, his dark eyes searching her face, chewing on his lower lip. "I just need contact with your skin."

Felicity's stomach dropped. "You're not going to put that in my sk—"

Lincoln laughed hoarsely. "Just put on shorts."

Walk. She tackled him into a hug the best she could. It was worth the pain it gave her to move. He hugged her back, and tears pricked her eyes.

She pulled away and slid off the bed. Her knees nearly collapsed under her weight, and she toppled forward. She cried out, grabbing the dresser. Lincoln grabbed her arm. She balanced herself on her feet and took a deep breath. "Thank you."

He nodded.

She closed her curtain. "Don't you dare try putting that thing *in* me!"

He laughed again. Softly, but it was something. And it made Felicity smile. She quickly changed into shorts. She already had two bags packed on the side of her bed. She had no intention of staying in Liberty long. And there was no way she would be revealing to her family whatever was going on with her body.

She flopped back on the bed, her legs giving in from being under pressure so long. "Okay. Come in!"

Lincoln stepped through the curtain. She caught the slightest cringe of his shoulders as his eyes passed her legs.

She laughed. "They're not pretty, are they?"

"No—I mean, no off—Ah." He shook his head, starting over. "What do you want me to say? It looks... painful."

He wasn't wrong about that. Felicity looked down, biting the inside of her mouth. Patches of black and purple had infected her skin, looking like horrible blotchy bruises growing larger and larger. So far, none had dared creep higher than her upper thigh.

"I'm useless," she whispered.

"Felicity. That is *not* true." Lincoln rushed to her side, grabbing his bag. He dropped to his knees in front of her. "I know you're not in the same physical condition as the woman who escaped a direct attack from an Oquelite Prince, but you're still in there. I'm going to help you."

"You really think you can?"

"Of course." He forced a pained smile. "I promise."

She gave him a weak smile. She took a deep breath, trying to control the fluttering in her stomach.

Lincoln removed a belt from his bag, and handed it to her. "Put this on."

She did as she said, and buckled the belt around her waist. It looked like a normal belt, which she wouldn't have been surprised if that's what it originally was, but instead it had two clips on the opposite sides, and a small metal box sewn in.

"Okay. I'm going to figure out how much I have to adjust the attachments. Is that alright?" He looked up to her.

She nodded.

He gently felt around her knee, and she flinched. He pulled away quickly. "No. It's fine. Please."

Lincoln bit his lip, and nodded hesitantly. He adjusted the straps on the attachments, and then sat down beside her, showing her how to attach them to the belt, by sliding the small metal tub into a cube, and they would click in place.

He then helped her fasten the straps around her knees and ankles. She held her breath, and grit her teeth, willing herself not to cry out as tiny waves of pain ran up her leg at every touch.

Finally, Lincoln stepped away, crossing his arms, and scanned over her. "Everything seems to be in place."

She let out a long sigh of relief.

"One more thing."

Felicity froze. She'd celebrated too soon.

Lincoln chuckled. "No other attachments. I promise." He reached into his bag, and pulled out what looked like a metallic headband. "I haven't exactly mastered neural technology, but I've been learning to be able to make my Square take mental commands. But I decided this was a better use of it."

Felicity's jaw dropped. "No way. Lincoln. You did that for me?"

Lincoln shrugged. "You're my friend." He held out the headband. "Come on. Put it on."

She took it gently into her hands, and slipped it into her hair. It was a bit tight, and the metal cold against her head, but besides that, it was comfortable. "It feels good."

Lincoln let out a whistle under his breath. "And now, we power up. Don't freak out." He looked up, meeting her eyes. "Are you ready?"

She gave a single nod, and Lincoln tapped the metal plates against her knees and ankle. She heard them begin to whir to life, the rims glowing a bright blue. Her headband felt warm. It sent a vibration up and through her legs, which made her shiver. She laughed nervously.

Lincoln's face was pinched. "Are you okay? Does it hurt? Do I need to turn it off? I'll turn it off ri—"

"No. It's great, Linc," she laughed again. "It doesn't hurt. It just feels numb... Oh. It feels so relieving."

His face softened, and he took a shaky breath. "Now try to stand."

Felicity took in a deep breath till she couldn't take in any more air, and then exhaled. She pushed herself up from the bed, feeling the pressure against her feet. She clung awkwardly to the bed post, looking to Lincoln for help.

"Here." He offered his arm, but she ended up grabbing him in an awkward hug around his chest for her life. He steadied her. "Calm down, Liz. Breathe."

She did as he said, taking in deep shaky breaths. *Breathe.* She balanced herself.

"You can do this," he said. She loosened her grip from his chest, grabbing onto his arms, and he grabbed hold of her elbows.

She took a small step forward. A small shock went up her leg. She cringed. She took another step. No pain. She looked down to her feet, then back up to Lincoln.

"I'm going to let go now," he said.

Her heart did a flip as he pulled away, and she teetered. She cried out, grabbing his hand. They both froze. He gave her a reassuring squeeze, and slowly let go.

She held her breath, sure any moment she'd lose control of gravity and topple over, but no. She was standing. Standing.

And then she took a step. And another. She was walking. She cried out, laughing uncontrollably, looking to Lincoln, who sat on the end of her bed, his jaw dropped, astonished.

"You did it! It works!" Tears welled in her eyes.

She ran to him, nearly stumbling over her own feet, and she crashed into him with a hug. She could feel him freeze before giving in and hugging her back. She stepped back, shaky on her feet, brushing away the burning tears. "You work miracles, Linc."

Lincoln smiled. A sad half-smile, but it was something. "Is something bothering you about Liberty, Liz?"

The question came out of nowhere, seeming to slam into her chest, making her stumble a step back. She opened her mouth to protest, but her eyes fell to the machinery he'd made around her legs, and she sighed. "I can't do it. I can't face them."

Lincoln frowned. "Who? Your family? Do you not have the DNA ring?"

"No, I have it." Felicity flashed the ring for Lincoln to see, controlling the sickening feeling in her stomach, seeing the crimson it contained.

"So it's family, then."

Felicity nodded, rubbing her shoulder. If she told him about the voices, would he think she was crazy? "Mostly. I haven't really spoken to them since I was sixteen. Besides formal messages from my dad. Ever since the accident, I've been too afraid... angry too. Oh, gosh, Lincoln. It's going to be so awkward."

She brushed away a tear, balling her hands into fists, feeling her chest burn. "You know me. I always need people to lean on. I can't do anything on my own. And now that she's not here, I have to stand on my own."

She saw hurt flash across Lincoln's face, and for a moment, she thought he was going to get up and leave, but instead, he picked her tele off the dresser, and held it out to her.

Felicity eyed it suspiciously, before taking a shaky step forward, and taking the glass device from his hand.

"You know my Comm ID," he said, shoving his hands into his jacket pockets, keeping his eyes set on hers. "If you need anything, just call me. Don't be afraid."

Felicity brought her lips to a small smile and nodded. "You sure you'll be okay all alone?"

He hesitated for a moment, his eyes quickly glancing to the empty room to the left. "I—I'm sure." He zoned out for a moment, before jumping and shaking his head. "The braces won't stay active forever. I made a charger for them. I'll get it out of my bag. So far with my tests, they can stay active for up to two hours."

"Thank you, Lincoln. Really. For everything." Felicity held herself back from hugging him again. She already felt on the edge of tears. She wanted to hug him and tell him things were going to be okay. But she didn't. She just watched him quietly as he removed a package from his bag and handed it to her.

"Do you need help getting to Giles?" he asked.

"Yes," Felicity lied. Technically, she could carry both bags fine, especially now that she could walk somewhat, but she wanted Lincoln to feel needed. She could tell by the longing in his eyes that the fact he would be alone was killing him. He'd been lonely for the past two weeks like nothing Felicity could imagine. The most she could give him was a feeling of fulfillment.

She changed into sweatpants to cover the braces, and followed Lincoln outside into the courtyard.

"Felicity!" Ray's mouth gaped, dropping his backpack as he stood in the center of the courtyard. Felicity caught the golden glint of the Key Ring on his thumb, but she didn't mention it. How'd he gotten away with that? "You're walking!"

Felicity laughed, taking careful steps down the stairs, tapping her headband. "Thanks to his genius."

"What? No way. *Lincoln* did that?" Ray turned to Lincoln, who just shrugged, dropping Felicity's bag near a bench.

"Dude, if you can make her walk, imagine the things you could make us as a team!" Ray grabbed Lincoln's shoulders and dramatically shook him. "Like—like jetpacks! Imagine that! Jetpacks! Or motorcycles! Or—or get this, brain implants that allow you to search the net!"

Lincoln shoved Ray away, brushing himself off. "I'm not the team tinker boy."

"But you'll have plenty of time on your hands here, won't you?" Ray gave a teasing raise of the brow.

Lincoln scoffed. "We'll see."

Ray pumped his fist. "You won't regret it, Black Eyes."

"Are you all done yet?" Giles grumbled, making his way across the courtyard, decked out in his Defender gear, a pair of goggles on top of his hair. "I want to make this a quick trip. Why does that darn Sergeant keep assigning me to deal with you stupid kids?"

"We're not real thrilled either," Ray said. Felicity contained a laugh.

Giles shot him a glare, then looked to Felicity. "You got everything?"

"Yep," she said, grabbing both her bags from the ground.

She looked back over her shoulder to Lincoln, who stood with his hands in his pockets, watching them with dull eyes. He caught her gaze, and put on a quivering smile.

She sighed, dropping her bags, and hugged him. To her surprise, another pair of arms joined her.

"We'll be back, Linc," Ray said. "I promise you that. You won't lose us."

They stepped back, and she saw Lincoln's eyes shimmer. He nodded. "Goodbye, then."

Felicity picked up her bags once more, and followed Giles, who seemed bored by the whole display anyway. She looked back over her shoulder to Lincoln, who wiped his eyes and waved.

43

IT HAD BEEN SEVEN HOURS, AND THE RAIN SHOWED NO SIGN OF stopping.

Tabitha's tele informed them initially the trip would take about four hours, but it kept adding on more and more time, accounting for the storm, and icy roads, and an unpleasant auto accident that caused a detour.

Tabitha had talked almost the entire time too. Mostly about whatever came to her mind at the current time, which helped relieve the unspoken tension in the air, but she ended up falling asleep, and Lawrence remained quiet in the back, staring out the window, without contributing so much as a word every once and a while to prove he was indeed still alive.

At least, she wasn't being terrified about the child's death, though he was sure it still contributed to her nightmare. And Cole was still nervous, which wasn't great considering he was driving through a storm, but it was better to be nervous now stuck in traffic, than out on an open road.

This time his mind kept drifting back to the last time they

were in these seats, and the most awkward conversation that ensued. Tabitha, the daughter of two very wealthy people, and younger sister to one of the most renowned actors of the media, herself being a talented musician, was worried about children?

Of course she was, he told himself. Because she doesn't think she had a place in Liberty.

The stupid two child thing. It was no longer law in the main five regions, but the prejudice and scorn still existed. The fact Tabitha was the third Delorous sibling made her unfit for that society. But she wouldn't end up like Isabel, arranged into a marriage to a crazy guy.

Tabitha didn't seem like the type to let that stand. Then what was she thinking?

Why not just branch away from the Delorous's and be rebellious like she always was, and pursue what she wanted to?

Not like you ever did that, genius. He had a knack for music as well, but never really considered that a path in life. Why was he worrying about the future when it was likely he could die at any given moment now?

His Comm went off, vibrating in the cup holder, tearing him from his thoughts. Ray's Comm ID flashed on the screen.

Cole accepted.

"Hello bro—" Cole quickly turned off the speaker.

"Where are you now?"

Cole checked Tabitha's tele map. "We're nearing the Skyline, Court Illegia. Shouldn't be longer than an hour now. You?"

"Well, my SpeedRail stopped an hour ago, and I got this guy to let me hitchhike—"

"You what?"

"Look. I'm fine. I lived!"

Cole scowled. "Be safe."

"Don't worry about me. I'm perfectly responsible."

"You're only fifteen."

"Sixteen, actually."

Cole frowned. "When?"

Ray went quiet. "Two weeks ago today," he said, sheepishly.

Cole's voice caught in his throat. Two weeks ago they'd been recovering from the attack. Ray had been locked up in a cabin after some Officers had tried to take the blame out on him. He'd been alone, and locked up. How had Cole not remembered?

"Happy late birthday then, *little* brother."

"Hey. Sixteen is one step closer to eighteen. You now have to teach me to drive."

Cole smiled. "If you stay safe, sure."

"YES!" the speaker blared. "Well, I have to go now. Talk later. Don't die!"

With that, Ray ended the call, and Cole was thrust back into the degrading void of his mind. They really had a thing for missing birthdays, didn't they? Nikki had kept the fact her unofficial date of birth was the last day of the year a secret till a good few weeks later when, like Ray, her age was brought up. Felicity had been extremely bummed out about it.

Thinking of it mixed many emotions, making him unsure how to feel. He just dug his fingernails into the wheel, and slowly moved forward.

It wasn't long before the horizon began to glow. At first, Cole thought it was the rising sun, but the closer they got, he realized that wasn't the case. They were lights. Towering buildings, a huge stadium, a ferris wheel even, all decorated in vibrant glowing lights of every color imaginable. Some changed colors. Some seemed to dance on their own, stretching across the sky... The Skyline.

It clicked. Cole almost laughed at it.

This was the Skyline. They'd made it to Court Illegia.

"Names. Ages. And registered regions. Please."

They'd stopped in line at a checkpoint, where a Defending Officer sat, struggling to keep his hood up in the wind, with a Scroll in hand.

"Coleson Johnson. Eighteen. Sulfur," he said. He looked to Tabitha, who was still asleep against the window pane. "Tabitha Delorous. Seventeen. Liberty."

Lawrence peeked his head from between the seats. "Lawrence Williams. Seventeen. North Cordell."

The Officer scribbled something down. His hood

flapped off, and he scowled, pulling it back over his head. "Where you kids heading from?"

"North Cordell," Cole said.

The Officer nodded. "Well, that clears you."

"Thanks." The window pulled itself back in place, and Cole slowly pulled through the checkpoint. They were now officially in the Skyline.

"I don't think we'll be able to park in that mess of light," Lawrence said, now perched between Tabitha and Cole.

"Neither do I." Cole caught sight of a packed lot of autos, with a hologram signaling "No Fee Parking." It was a decent walk away, but they didn't have too much money to spare. Cole pulled in, parked, and let go of the wheel, finding his arms trembling.

"I'll get the stuff out of the back," Lawrence said, hesitating to burst out from the back. A draft of cold air slipped in the warmth of the cab.

Cole turned to Tabitha, taking a deep breath. The most dangerous task of all. He shook her shoulder gently. "Wake up, Tabs. We're here."

She was still. Almost too still.

"Tabitha!"

Cole jumped from the truck. The air was chilly, and damp, but was bearable compared to the harsh, chill-in-your-bones that North Cordell's weather had been pushing. He walked to Tabitha's side and slightly opened the door. She screamed, nearly tumbling out.

She blinked a few times, and then tried to kick him. "You're a monster."

"You weren't waking up."

Cole saw the fear hitch in her eyes as they looked away. Something had happened in her dreams again.

She jumped out from her seat, shoving him, and then she froze. Her eyes widened, glittering in the reflecting of the dancing lights. "Oh my gosh!" she screamed. "It's even cooler than I remember! Look at it! Oh mortals! LOOK AT IT."

"It's a little over the top if you ask me," Lawrence said, appearing from behind the truck.

"Oh. You'll learn to appreciate it," Tabitha said. She took her bag from Lawrence, and then grabbed Cole's hand before he had time to fully put on his backpack, and took off running.

Cole was both out of breath and partially blinded by the lights screaming in his eyes as they burst into the SkyLine. The crowds at the entrance were insane, and Tabitha had no problem with shoving through, dragging Cole shouting "Sorry!" behind her. They burst out into a path sorting in between stands and shops. The air was full of food that made Cole hungry. The sound of sizzling meat, the clash of music, and hundreds of voices and cheers filled the air. Stringed lights were drawn above them.

Tabitha's hand tightened on his and he didn't mind. This would certainly not be a fun place to lose her.

"So your Sergeant said the Defenders have a checkpoint set up near a theater," Lawrence said.

"The real question is: Which theater?" Tabitha sighed, pointing out a building down the path to a building, decorated with mask holograms along the roof. "There's one there, and another there, two stands down."

Well. That proved a problem.

"Maybe we could ask around?" Lawrence suggested.

"Sounds like our only option," Cole sighed. With a place like this, there had to be some law enforcement lingering around somewhere. They wandered through the crowds, who didn't seem to bat an eye. Most people seemed to be tourists, from the clash of accents, and wealthy ones at that. There was too much to look at for anyone to take a moment and pick out the three teenagers who were out of place.

Tabitha was hardly focused on finding the theater, leading them down whatever path interested her. Each turn provided a new display. One man even had a stand set up claiming to be selling magic feathers, which a couple from Liberty seemed to be nearly convinced into buying.

"Get out!" A shrill scream from a space between tents and buildings caused Cole to halt. "I've had enough of you Lopez kids!"

"Lopez?" Lawrence's brows shot up.

He didn't hesitate, and ran after the voice. Tabitha let go of Cole's hand and bounded after him. Why couldn't they just go to the theater like safe and normal people?

He sighed, and ran after them.

They came out into a small dirt lot wedged between stalls and buildings to find a plump woman, with pale skin and purple paint decorating her features, standing at the top of the steps of a backstage entrance. A muscular man stood at her side, with a cocky grin on his features.

At her feet was a boy, with a mop of brown hair and a striking green T-shirt, a long sleeved shirt underneath, and a pair of outdated headphones on the ground at his side. That was as much as Cole could collect before Lawrence started yelling. "What are you doing?"

"Oh. Tourists," the woman scoffed. "Scram. I'll give you a free ticket or something."

The boy on the ground looked from Lawrence to the woman, beginning to get to his feet when the woman snapped. "Don't you think about it. I've been cheated by you people for the last time."

The man grabbed the back of the boy's shirt and yanked him back, kicking the headphones farther. The boy tried to kick the man's ankle, but instead, was kicked off his own feet.

"We need to know where Nigel Lopez is!" Tabitha said. "You have to let him go."

The woman laughed. "He's not who you're looking for then. Now please go."

The boy shot her a dark look, muttering something under his breath. The man smacked him in the back of his head.

Cole was fed up. This was taking too long. He reached into his backpack, grabbing the familiar hilt into his grip, and swung out the Illuminate. Both him and the woman cried out when the silver blade burst out into flames.

He caught himself far faster than he usually did, ignoring the pounding of his heart in ears as he pointed it forward at the screaming woman. "Let him go. Just keep things easy."

Lawrence smirked, the flames reflecting in his glasses.

Cole sent him a warning glare not to do anything stupid.

"Witches!" the woman shouted. The boy flinched at her screech. "I'll report you to the authorities. Grab the boy. Run, Richmond."

Lawrence cursed. He caught a flame in his hand, and threw it at the woman's foot who jumped back and shouted. "Fine! Take him then! And don't you, your family, or your witch friends think of coming back! I'll report you."

The man, Richmond, shoved the boy forward, and he lost his balance, sprawling into the dirt. Lawrence knelt down to offer him his hand, a gesture that surprised Cole, but the boy ignored it. He grabbed the headphones from the dirt, put them around his neck, got to his feet, and brushed himself off.

He wasn't exactly very tall. Maybe slightly shorter than Ray.

"You okay?" Tabitha said.

The boy jumped, like he hadn't expected to be spoken to. He nodded. "Thank you," he said, quickly, before putting on a forced smile. Cole noted an accent that reminded him of Nikki's, but stronger.

The boy cleared his throat, shoving his hands into his pockets.

"Do you know Nigel Lopez?" Tabitha asked

The boy nodded, eyeing Cole's flaming sword. "I do."

Cole wasn't sure exactly how to put it out. He settled for dropping it and stomping in it. It did the trick.

"Can you take us to him?" Cole said.

The boy narrowed his eyes.

"You owe us," Tabitha said, with a shrug.

"Technically, I could've handled it," he said. His face seemed to relax, his hint of a smile becoming genuine. "I do appreciate the help, though."

Tabitha laughed. "You looked like you were handling it real well."

The boy blushed.

Lawrence scowled. "What was she after you about any-way?"

"Speaking of, I'm in a rush," the boy said. "And before the guy with the fire sword yells at me, I can take you to Nigel Lopez."

Tabitha playfully put her arm around the boy's shoulder. "I like this one."

The boy tugged away from her grip. "Thanks?"

Cole sheathed the sword, tucking it away in his backpack. Tabitha continued to crack jokes, with the boy seeming entirely uninterested by her, despite her obvious attention. Lawrence stood, staring at the back door of the theater. Cole spotted a black mark where Lawrence had thrown the flame.

"You good?"

Lawrence blinked, shaking himself. "Yeah. I'm fine. We ready?"

Cole nodded, and turned back to Tabitha and the boy. The boy caught Cole's eyes, though they almost instantly fell away, and he eagerly turned on his heel leading them out, back into the street. He moved quickly, naturally weaving through the crowds.

How could they be sure he was taking them to Nigel? They'd heard the woman call him "Lopez" once. Didn't mean he was related to the Agent. Lopez was a popular last name, right? They should've gone to the checkpoint.

"Hurry up!" the boy called.

Cole picked up his pace, Lawrence right beside him. They exited the main SkyLine attraction abruptly, bursting out into a cobblestone street, where the buildings were lit in neon lights reflecting off the glass of the dark windows.

"Hurry and jump on!" the boy cried out, who without hesitation jumped onto a hovering, open car, grabbing onto a pole. Cole ran and jumped, nearly slipped, but grabbed hold of the pole, and Tabitha the back of his jacket.

"This is so cool," he said, her voice giddy with excitement.

"You're tourists, right?" the boy asked.

"Hardly," Lawrence grumbled.

The boy looked at him quizzically, before his attention snapped. "Jump off!"

Cole leapt, his feet hitting the safety of the ground. He looked up and what met him was a huge building. Hundreds of windows, and dazzling displays of light intertwining in between them. There was a front gate with men in green suits taking cards. The boy slipped past them without them batting an eye.

They stepped into a huge courtyard, decked up with trees, hanging jars with lights, and fountains. There were tables and dozens of people talking, laughing, and dancing to the blaring music. Even the serving bots were decorated in lights and they zoomed in between people and tables.

The boy ushered them after him as he made his way through the courtyard. They caught a few eyes, but no one said a thing. They made their way out of the courtyard, and followed the boy into a dark space between a wall and the gate.

Cole tightened his grip on the strap of his bag. This didn't feel right.

The boy typed in a passcode on a door, and it burst open. Almost as soon as the door opened, a girl jumped out, slamming into the boy with a hug, then grabbed his ear, and began shouting out at him in a language Cole had never heard.

He responded, pointing to them. The girl froze, her jaw dropping. She cleared her throat. "I'm sorry," she said, quickly glaring at the boy. "Come inside."

The four trailed in behind her. They entered a kitchen that was mostly empty besides two other girls. One looked about ten, and the other maybe about Lawrence and Tabitha's age.

Both of them froze as they entered.

The girl who had ushered them in sighed, rubbing her temples. She had wavy dark brown hair that was brought up with a bandana, a light brown complexion, and golden hoop earrings. Her eyes were bright, and alive, and currently very annoyed. "I am Iracema Lopez. Nineteen. Court Illegia. I'm sorry for however you ran in with my brother. From the looks of it, he was cutting ties with one of the wealthiest sponsors."

"Good riddance then."

All eyes turned to Lawrence.

Cole wished he could sew that boy's lips shut.

Lawrence shrugged. "She seemed like a jerk."

"A jerk with a lot of money. It was *your* fault, Iracema. You're the one who paid her back half. You just sent 'Teo to do the hard work." The second eldest girl rubbed her fingers together and tossed back her long dark curls, ignoring her older sister's glare. "I'm Calynda. And you?"

"Lawrence."

The girl laughed. "How'd you find this one, Matteo?"

The boy, Matteo, shrugged. "I'm going to bed. They're here for Nigel."

He left the room in a hurry, and Cole heard a door slam shut a few moments later.

"Don't mind him," Iracema sighed. "He's usually like this at this time. Usually, he's quite up and about. Now, you're looking for Nigel?"

"We are," Cole said. "I'm guessing you're related to him?"

Calynda yawned, leaning back in her chair. "Oh yes. He's our father's brother. You caught him at the right time. He's rarely here."

Iracema sighed at her sister's remark. "Yes. And I can take him to you. You can leave your bags here. I assure you nothing will happen to them."

There was an awkward silence of them shuffling off their bags to the ground.

Iracema smiled. "Good. Now, if you'll follow me—"

"Does the Lawrence one want to stay here? It's *so* boring out there."

Lawrence raised an eyebrow. "I'm good."

"I think that's a great idea," Tabitha said, shoving Lawrence forward. She whispered something Cole didn't hear before locking arms with Cole and waving Lawrence, who looked bewildered out of his mind, behind in the kitchen.

They left the kitchen out into a bright lobby, rich with color and the smell of leather. Iracema wiped her hands on her skirt, walking down the steps. Cole realized she was barefoot.

"I'm guessing you're not tourists," she said, turning. Her entire mood had changed, her face now outfitted with a mischievous smile, her arms crossed over her chest. "No one comes searching for a Defender without their reasons."

"And we have reasons," Tabitha assured her.

"I don't doubt that," Iracema said. She grabbed the handle of the glass door that led back outside. "But if your reasons interfere with anything, or harm anyone, I promise you, I will be the one you're going to fear."

44

Tabitha knew her face looked astonished. It wasn't that the sight of the courtyard when Iracema thrust the glass doors open *wasn't* one of the most glorious things she'd ever seen. Inside, she wanted to turn on her heel and run back outside.

That was pathetic, she told herself. Keep your chin up.

Iracema walked down the steps, with a bounce of confidence in her step, tossing her bouncing waves over her shoulder to peer back at them with a slight frown.

Tabitha pretended not to take notice of her. Iracema had every right to be suspicious. Court Illegia, especially the Skyline, was practically as developed at the Golden Regions. People were dressed richly, and spoke with clear, educated dialects, and they sipped on sparkling drinks from crystal glasses. Their clothes consisted of bright colors, full of suits, flowing skirts, and shawls.

Tabitha and Cole were out of place, by a lot. Tabitha preferred the lesser regions, like North Cordell, where she didn't feel the invisible pressure against her every breath.

"*Tio!*" Iracema called out, quickening her pace toward a table in a far shadowed corner. A man looked up from a glowing Scroll in front of him. He barely had a moment to see who'd called his name, when his niece collided into him with a quick hug, turned on her heel, and threw her arm out to present Cole and Tabitha.

Tabitha couldn't help but admire Iracema's quick and collected actions.

"I'm sorry. I've already forgotten their names," Iracema chuckled. "Do you know them, *Tio?* They came looking for you."

Agent Nigel Lopez rose to his feet, patting Iracema on the shoulder. He frowned, his eyes keen on Cole. "I thought Hunter said she was sending three of you."

Cole nodded. "She did. Lawrence is—Lawrence Williams, I mean—is back in the kitchen of this place."

Nigel let out a long sigh. "She sent that brat here? He's going to make a mess of things."

"He'll be fine," Cole said quickly. Tabitha noticed a small line crease on his forehead. "I—I'll personally be sure of it."

Nigel rubbed the bridge of his nose. "How can I be sure? I'm not the greatest fan of kids—"

Iracema promptly elbowed him.

Nigel glared at his niece. "Teenagers specifically, then!"

Iracema spoke a string of words Tabitha didn't understand, the words weaving, rich and quick. She crossed her arms, her lips teasing a smile, before her words fell back to what Tabitha understood. "I didn't know you now concerned teenagers in your job. Are you two Defenders too?"

"No," Cole said, simply.

Iracema raised an eyebrow. "Alright then."

Nigel sat in thought for a moment before snapping at Iracema quickly. Iracema's face slowly slipped into a frown, responding to him slowly.

Cole glanced at Tabitha. She shrugged.

"Fine," Iracema said. She turned to them again. "Good *Tio* said you'll be needing room and board for a bit, and since my mother is out—" she glared at her uncle. "—he is in charge, and will let you stay for free. Not in the hotel?"

She gave Agent Lopez a quizzical look.

"No. That's too vulnerable."

The thought of the *Mors Vis* crept into Tabitha's mind. Visions of the deadly feather force from her nightmare flashed in mind. She shuddered. They were close now.

"Oh," Iracema stole a glance at Cole and Tabitha again. "I see. I'll see what I can do."

She took out her tele, one of the latest editions, and began typing something. Nigel turned back to them and began rattling off to Cole about protocols or something. Tabitha didn't exactly know what, because she was soon distracted by the light jar sitting on Nigel's table. It looked like little insects were flying around, their bodies lit up, slowly changing colors. Incredible little robots.

She looked to Iracema again, who was busy on her tele. She wore a flowy white blouse that hugged her shoulders, and exposed her midriff. She had a blue skirt that flowed down to a little below her knees, and above her bare feet. She wore two golden hoop earrings, a rapidly growing trend thanks to the media star "Viv" for featuring them in her last film.

Was Clarence in that? Her brother seemed to be in everything. She hadn't seen him in years—

"Delorous? Are you paying attention?"

Tabitha jumped. She snapped her attention back to Nigel Lopez, and cleared her throat, putting on a smile. "Sure I was. Something about protocols."

Nigel glared at Tabitha, and if looks could kill, Tabitha would have been dead a long time ago.

"Mama said it's fine," Iracema cut in before Nigel could snap at Tabitha. "But it wasn't easy to convince her to let some kids from your *work* hang here."

"Johnson, you understand what I told you, right?" Nigel said.

Cole nodded. "Yes, sir."

Nigel glanced at Tabitha. "Stay in line, kid."

"I'll meet you tomorrow morning to begin," Nigel said, taking a seat.

Iracema took her cue, slipped between Cole and Tabitha, locking her arms with theirs and strode from Nigel back into the hotel.

FELICITY BENTSWORTH KNEW SHE WAS AN ANXIOUS PERSON. IT was no mystery to anyone. A therapist back in Liberty had told her repeatedly. Tabitha reminded her. Sergeant Taryn did whenever they had drills.

Four my friend. Two too much. Seven Eleven. Three we Two do.
Felicity thought she'd improved.

She thought she'd conquered a few fears, and look, she could ride in an auto without breaking down, and she could run without being too worried about tripping and breaking her neck. But here she was, her arms wrapped around her legs, her face buried in her knees, trying to count her breaths.

She was going back to Liberty.

Home didn't sound like the word. Her last memories there haunted her. The crash, the hospital ceilings, and the panic attacks.

Four my friend. Two too much. Seven Eleven. Three we Two do.

No. She couldn't go back. She was too weak. What was she thinking? She should've said no. She could hardly walk, for a reason they didn't understand. And she had no idea what she was doing.

She began to choke up, but she clenched her jaw, forcing herself to take in a deep breath.

Four my friend. Two too much. Seven Eleven. Three—

"Uh, you good?"

Felicity didn't respond to Giles. Her chest began to squeeze. *Breathe.*

A hand clamped down on her shoulder. Felicity shot up, her body unravelling, and she scrambled back. She hit her head on the wall behind her, the headband sliding over her eyes.

She heard Giles chuckle. "Gosh."

She flushed red, pushing the headband back up in its place. She pulled her bag to her chest, and forced herself to peer at Giles.

His hair was a disaster due to the storm in North Cordell, his mullet sticking to his neck, and his freckled face redder than usual, a scarf tied up to his chin. He raised a suspicious eyebrow.

"Leave me alone," she grumbled, pulling up the collar of her jacket to hide her flushed cheeks.

Giles huffed. "I'm supposed to be making sure you're safe, you little scrawny mole rat."

Felicity turned away from him to look out the window in the tunnel. "I'm safe, thank you."

"You're scared to go back to Liberty and face your family."

Felicity's heart leapt into her throat, her entire body cringing. She might as well have just said, "Yes. That's it," right to Giles's face.

Giles chuckled. "Think of this as a way to help your 'Council.'"

"I'm no help," Felicity blurted out, refusing to face Giles. She leaned forward, pressing her forehead against the cool window, taking a deep breath. "All I do is freak out, and stay on the sidelines. I'm going to screw this up like I usually do."

"Yeah. You probably will."

Felicity's face burned. "Thanks."

"Well, I mean you don't *have* to. You're the only one holding yourself back. If you say you can't do it, you can't. Simple as that."

Felicity whirled around in her seat to face Giles, who sat with a Comm in hand. He glanced to her.

"It's not all my fault!" she shouted, slamming her hands over her mouth. A few eyes turned. Come on, Liz.

"Nah. It's not." Giles shrugged. "But it's your fault that you let it control you. You can't let one failure that wasn't your fault control you."

Tears burned at her eyes, and she balled her fists, her mind burning to punch him in the face. "I can't help what I'm scared of. My brain just… does it. I can't—augh!"

"Woah. Calm down," Giles said, with a snort.

"Stop laughing at me."

"You're making me."

She kicked him, which quickly came back to shoot pain up her leg, and she groaned, grasping her heel. She grit her jaw. The throbbing seared up her leg, splicing into her hip. Deep breaths, Liz. Deep breaths.

Within a few moments, the pain released its grasp, and she settled back shivering in her seat, and remembered she was supposed to be mad. But why was she mad? Because Giles said her own doubt and anxieties were holding her back? It wasn't her fault she had anxiety… but could she control it? It always seemed to control her.

She took another deep breath and grumbled, "Sorry."

"S'okay," Giles said, with a broad smirk, that made Felicity immediately want to take back the apology. "Emotions get the best of us."

"When'd you become a therapist? I thought you were a Defending Officer."

Giles glared at her. "Why does *everyone* think being an Officer means we can't have studied anything intellectual?"

Now it was Felicity's turn to laugh. She felt her chest lighten. "Well, I mean, you of all people don't look to be interested in that stuff…"

"What's that supposed to mean?" Giles narrowed his eyes.

Felicity bit her lip, holding back a smile, and shrugged. "Nice mullet, Armstance Giles."

"Oh har har, very funny."

Felicity pulled her legs back up on her seat, and held them to her chest, resting her chin on her knees.

Giles held a glare, before it broke, and he laughed. "Look! See, once you started thinking differently, you got better."

"Tabitha said I do better when I'm angry."

"I wouldn't say cover anxiety with anger." Giles wrinkled his nose. "But I wouldn't cross you when you are, mole rat."

"Don't call me that."

"Fine, how does fuzzy worm sound?"

Felicity opened her mouth to reprimand him, but the speaker blared over her.

"APPROACHING ENTRANCE TO CENTRAL LIBERTY DOME STATION."

Felicity's body went cold, thrust back into reality, as quickly as the Rail shot out of the tunnel onto the bridge soaring and twisting through the skyscrapers of the city. The breath was stolen from her. The glitter of the dome sparkled in the blue sky, the skyscrapers' spotless windows shone the Rail's reflection back. Government organized trees grew between them, vines aesthetically grew in between stories, nothing out of place. A brightly dressed couple watched the Rail pass from an apartment balcony. Sparkling white manors shone in the distance, their lawns sprinkled with bright white grass, and bright blue Joined World Democratic-Republic banners, hung from walls, and windows of nearly every other building she passed.

She was back in Liberty.

The SpeedRail dipped back into a tunnel, submerging them back into the darkness. Felicity peered over Giles's shoulder. He still sat, his eyes glued on the window, his jaw unhinged, like a small child.

Felicity cracked a small smile. "Never been to Liberty."

He shook his head.

The smallest spark of pride bloomed in Felicity's chest. "You've seen nothing yet."

"I hear guys wear suits and stuff here. All the time."

Felicity laughed. "In professions, yes. Not typically for casual wear. But the bright red bloomer shorts are probably going to be really unnerving after years of cargo shorts and jeans."

"Bloomer shorts?"

"You'll see."

"Please tell me I'm exempt from this."

She didn't tell him he was a Defender on a job, meaning technically he was required to be wearing his uniform the entire time. Instead, she let him suffer in the silence. The Rail pulled into the Emerald Station, a place Felicity visited frequently as a child. It was an enormous building, fueled entirely by sunlight filtering through the emerald glass panels. Dozens of SpeedRail tracks ran through the center, huge crowds jam packed into lines.

The last time Felicity had been here, she had been in a disguise by order of her father, and she and Tabitha crammed into an overloaded car to North Cordell.

"Ms. Bentsworth?" The door to the cabin car opened. Two Officers stepped inside. Giles jumped to his feet, his hand on the gun in the holster strapped to his thigh. He gave a two-fingered salute.

"And who might you be?" one Defender scoffed.

"Officer Armstance Giles, under Sergeant Rayder Dow, sent by Sergeant Taryn Hunter to protect Felicity Bentsworth on her visit home." The recitation was impeccable.

A Defender raised an eyebrow. "So you're Dow's new assistant? He's that kid who majored in history, Carlyle. Didn't think you'd make it this far, Giles."

"Do I know you?" Giles said.

"No. But everyone knows anyone who associates with Curatrix team affairs."

Carlyle sighed, annoyance in his brow. "We'll escort you home, Ms. Bentsworth. We will also remain a silent professional stance, and not pester with politics."

The two Defenders turned, and stepped aside, letting Giles and Felicity pass.

Felicity stayed close to Giles as they moved from the car and down the steps out onto the platform of the station, the air around her cold. The crowd had been parted with security. The crowd around her had dropped silent, and she could feel their stares burning into her. She heard whispers of "Bentsworth," "North Cordell," and "Crazy" all in the mix, making sure she didn't move her gaze from the floor until she heard a door open, and Giles ushered her inside.

They entered a private hallway that led to a backstreet where she guessed an auto would be waiting for them. That way it was much harder to get swamped with a crowd. She shivered, her vision blurred for a moment, nausea rose from the stomach. Her knee buckled, and a cry refused to fall from her mouth. She stumbled forward, Giles catching her. He dropped to the ground, cradling her gently.

"What happened?" Carylle shouted. The two Defenders rushed to her side, their blurry faces appearing above her.

"Give her space!" Giles snapped. The two back away. "You good, Bentsworth?"

"My-my knee," she stammered.

"What's wrong with her knee?"

"Shut up," Giles growled. "Can you walk?"

Felicity willed herself to sit up, closing her eyes, taking in deep breaths. What was going on with her?

She adjusted her headband and opened her eyes, the world coming back into focus. Giles sat beside her, his eyes narrowed with concern.

"I'm okay," she said, her voice shaky.

Giles raised an eyebrow. "Alright, Bentsworth."

She used his shoulder to help push herself up to her feet. Pain seared in her legs. She grit her teeth. Giles jumped to his feet and slipped a supportive arm under hers, allowing her to remove the weight.

"Hey! Don't touch her!" the Defender shouted.

"He's fine," Felicity said. "Can we just hurry?"

"Yes miss," Carlyle grumbled, passing them, his partner following, shooting a glare at Giles.

They followed them down the twisting hall, Felicity trying hard to ignore the growing panic in her stomach. Wasn't Lincoln's device supposed to let her walk? Was it malfunctioning? Was she getting worse? She couldn't do this if it got worse.

No, she snapped. I can't think like that. It's going to be fine. It has to be.

They finally reached the back door. Carlyle pressed his hand against the door, a light flashing green, and the door swung open to a concrete staircase to a long black auto. Giles helped her slowly down the steps, and to the door, which opened automatically. Inside, the smell of leather filled her senses. It was spacious, and well lit. And her entire stomach rocked, her entire body tensing.

"You good, Bentsworth?"

She looked up to Giles, her lips trembling. Words fumbled each other, her throat too tight to try and speak.

Giles let out a sigh. "It'll be alright, Bentsworth."

She tried to trust him. The problem was: She didn't trust Giles. She didn't even like him very much. He was insufferable most of the time, but here he was helping her into a seat, in an auto, in the city where, four years ago, she'd been victim to an auto crash.

"So, plans for finding the Aguirre chip?" Giles sat down across from her.

Felicity tore herself from her mind. She frowned, playing with the fray of her sweater. "The what?"

Giles leaned back in his seat. "What we're here for, genius."

Felicity swallowed hard. "Oh, right."

"Any ideas where it could be?"

"I don't know," Felicity mumbled. "I didn't pay a lot of attention to politics."

"The Aguirres weren't all politics, you know?" Giles said.

Felicity saw his eyes glimmer, like on command, he would burst into a history lecture. "I know," she said, simply. "They had... kids."

"Technically, they could be considered political."

Felicity clenched her fists, her chest burning. Right. "Then where do we even start?"

"You're the daughter of one of the biggest businessmen in the country," Giles said, leaning forward with a mischievous smirk.

Felicity blushed. "Yeah. I guess."

"Then you have to know some other kids of important people too."

Felicity clamped a hand over her stomach. "Giles. That won't work. I haven't talked to any of my old friends in ages—"

"Bentsworth," Giles said, sternly. "That's our *only* lead right now."

Felicity took a deep breath, scrambling through her memories, trying to remember the faces of her old classmates. None of whom she'd been particularly close to. There was a reason she chose Tabitha to go with her to North Cordell. Tabitha was in a level below her, a third child, though no one knew it, and a notorious trouble maker, but she was brutally loyal.

Something none of the others were.

"Yaeda Spade," Felicity finally said. "Daughter of Caesar Spade, a Liberty representative."

"Just because she's the daughter of a politician doesn't mean she'd know much of it," Giles sighed.

"From what I remember, she was interested in politics herself. I didn't really talk to her much. She was very loud." Felicity cringed, remembering a specific occurrence of the girl screaming Felicity's name in a class hall. To say the least, "Bentsworth" turned a few heads. "Like you said. Our *only* lead."

Giles sat back, running his fingers through his hair. "Better than nothing. You'll contact this kid once you get there. Right away. Right, Bentsworth?"

Felicity nodded. "Sure of it."

"Good," Giles said. "Now. Don't be too direct about it. We just need to know the location of anything Aguirre. That'll be good."

"Sounds easy enough."

"Good, because—" Giles cracked a smile. "—we're here. Congrats on not freaking out the entire ride, Bentsworth."

Felicity's jaw dropped. Giles had been keeping her distracted. She hadn't panicked about a crash... at all.

She scowled at him. "I hate you," she grumbled.

Giles shrugged.

Felicity was scared to look out the window. Like maybe if she just waited long enough, it would just disappear. The door opened.

A familiar voice greeted her. "Welcome back, Felicity."

Felicity snapped her head in the direction of the voice. A woman stood in the door, wearing a fitted black suit, her arms behind her back, sunglasses sitting neatly on her head. Her dark purple hair was pulled up in a tight bun.

"Renee," Felicity breathed. A smile crept onto her lips as she stepped out of the auto. "It's been a while."

"Years," Renee Kitts said, giving a small bow. "It's an honor to serve you again."

Felicity rolled her eyes. "Still the same formal Renee."

Giles stumbled awkwardly out of the auto, slamming the

door shut behind him. He wiped his hands off on his shirt and cleared his throat.

Renee lifted a thin, plucked eyebrow to him.

"Officer Armstance Giles." Giles held out his hand.

Renee glanced at it and turned on her heel. "Follow me, Felicity. Your sister is expecting you."

Felicity groaned internernally. "Veronica? Why not Mother and Father?"

"They'll greet you later."

"I see not much has changed."

The huge metal gates swung open. Felicity heard Giles gasp, and curse under his breath. A smile quirked at Felicity's lip.

The towering marble building shone in the sun with a powerful dominance. Weathered statues decorated the pillars, gold trim decorating the base. Glass domes made up the ceiling, full of exotic trees and plants. Vines crawled down in between the huge windows of blue trim, and metal wire balconies overlooked the giant courtyard decorated with cobblestone, and a huge fountain, a driveway leading to the steps that ended with two large doors, guarded by security.

"Welcome to the Bentsworth Manor." Felicity looked to Giles, who was still staring.

"I don't know how you could ever choose a crummy cabin over this," he laughed.

Felicity shrugged. She felt spoiled saying anything to disagree with him. He had a point. The Bentsworth Manor was incredible. A work of art. The inside was even more glorious than its exterior, but she much rather preferred her crammed cabin, where she could fall asleep to Tabitha's obnoxious snoring, and watch the central fire flicker outside, knowing the next day she'd be eating breakfast with the people closest to her.

Not anymore.

The closer she got, the taller it became. She could feel her breath becoming short. Don't freak out, Liz. Don't freak out. Think of the song. You're okay. *Four my friend. Two too much. Seven Eleven. Three we Two do*

The guards saw them coming, quickly rushing to their station, pulling the doors open the old fashioned way. With a handle.

The history nerd in Giles must've been exploding as they rose up the steps, the main room coming into view, adored in pre-earthshaker era portraits along walls. A large room, with a tree in the center decorated in lights, towered upward, a grand staircase branching off into multiple, floor to ceiling windows sending rainbows across the marble floor.

And a small redheaded girl in a short yellow dress and socks, sitting at the base of a tree, drawing on a Scroll.

The girl looked up, his face brightening. She threw her Scroll and Stylus down, and ran screaming "Felicity!" through the doors. She threw her arms over her older sister's neck. Felicity nearly toppled over, catching herself on the base of the door. She gave Veronica a pat on the back.

Her sister let go, practically bouncing. "You're back!"

Felicity forced a smile. "Yeah. I am."

Her sister played with a necklace around her neck. It was a silver chain that held a purple "53" on the end. She grinned, tucking a long hair away from her face. "I missed you so much. So did Mom and Dad. They'll be excited to see you."

"So excited," Felicity lied, with the little enthusiasm she could muster.

"Now Veronica," Renee said, saving Felicity by stepping between the sisters. "Felicity is tired from her journey and will require at least twelve hours of sleep before you can plan further activity with her."

Veronica rolled her eyes. "That's like forever, Renee." She turned back to Felicity. "I'll be waiting for you! I can't wait."

She ran to collect her Scroll and Stylus, when she stopped, turning around on her heel. "Hey! Renee, I have a great idea. How about *I* take Felicity to her room?"

Renee looked to Felicity.

Felicity shrugged.

Renee sighed. "Alright. I'll take this Defender to his quarters."

"I'll be staying here?" Giles's jaw dropped.

"Yes," Renee said simply. She clapped her hands. "Go along now."

Felicity took a step away from Giles. He gave her a reas-suring nod, and turned to follow Renee through a doorway.

Veronica slid on her socks to Felicity's side. She grabbed her hand and took off. Felicity nearly tripped over, trying to gain her balance as Veronica practically dragged her behind. They raced up the steps, taking a left turn, and about four steps up, Veronica let go, out of breath. She laughed. "I don't run much. Mostly working on becoming an artist."

"An artist, you say?" Felicity took hold of the rail.

"Yeah," Veronica said. "Remember *you* used to draw these characters, and you told me this super cool story about them all the time when I was little."

"Yes," Felicity lied again. She felt bad saying that she actually didn't remember. She didn't even remember when Veronica was little. How old was Veronica?

Thirteen? Fourteen?

"I heard you dropped out of Uni though," Veronica said, her voice becoming more sober as they ascended the steps. "Because of what happened in Imperial. So you probably don't draw anymore."

"I still draw," Felicity retorted, feeling suddenly defensive over the old hobby.

Veronica perked up. "You do?"

They approached the elevator. A golden cage powered by hover tech. Having been stuck in a rural region for four years, Felicity was a bit taken aback by the idea of trusting it. Veronica skipped inside happily, and Felicity followed her hesitantly. The cage doors slammed shut, and it began to rise.

"You wanna do something tomorrow?"

"I'm actually seeing a friend."

Veronica's face fell. "Oh. Who?"

"Yaeda," Felicity said. She searched her sister's face for a reaction, but nothing.

"Well, I'll be here." Veronica clutched her Scroll against her chest, with a smile.

Felicity tried to smile back.

The elevator stopped and the gate opened. They stepped out onto a balcony leading down a hallway into a parlor. Felicity's parlor. Her corridor. She swallowed hard. It was untouched. A few palm trees grew by the windows, beaded strings hung from the ceiling. Bean bags were scattered about, a hologram projector on a coffee table. The walls were decorated in artwork. Most Felicity recognized as her own. There were doors along the wall. One led to a hallway that broke out into the family parlor. One to her private room. And the others she'd forgotten.

"Your bags will probably be up in a few minutes," Veronica said. "I'll go to my room now. I'll see you later, Lizzy!"

Veronica turned on her heel and rushed from the room. Felicity collapsed on a sofa and curled up in a ball. She was back home. And Veronica, her little sister, was so happy to see her.

Felicity hadn't even said goodbye to Veronica.

She'd shoved her family from her mind for her first year away to prevent herself from breaking down. They shouldn't have given her anxiety. They'd done nothing wrong. But she couldn't help feeling angry.

Felicity turned and stared at the ceiling far above her.

She missed North Cordell already.

She took her Tele out of her pocket, bringing up the contacts. She scrolled through the abundance of numbers and names, and she stopped on Lincoln. Her thumb hovered for a moment before scrolling past, and selecting "Yaeda."

"LOOK UP, LITTLE GAZELLE."

Tabitha groaned. It felt like her brain was pounding against her skull. Her wrists were sore, and rubbed against a cool metal surface that dug into skin. Bile coated her tongue. The air around was thick and humid, and smelled of... smoke.

She slowly opened her eyes. Her eyes stung from the heat. Her heart dropped as her vision cleared.

The world around her was molten rock, cracks upheaving the rocks, molten lava spilling from it, glowing a bright orange. A van was up in flames, crashed against a jagged rock. A sword was plunged into the ground, a battered flag swung weakly in a draft. Where was she?

Tabitha tried to scream, but her throat was raw, and blood coated her lips.

The air shimmered in front of her, then seemed to tear before her eyes, revealing a black abyss, and then a figure... a man stepped out, the gaping hole sealing itself behind him.

He had moderate brown skin, and flowing brown waves

that fell uncared for across the thick pair of sunglasses that rested on his nose. He wore a flower print button up, cargo shorts, and flip-flops.

Flip-flops? Tabitha craned her neck up to meet the lenses that shaded his eyes. She squinted, ignoring the pain that seared through her head. "Who are you?"

The man chuckled. "I suppose there's no use keeping secrets. I'm Ruhn Ryynar."

The name was familiar. Miriam... Miriam had seen him. The Oquelite who'd taken her and tortured Jack and the room of refugees. Tabitha's breath hitched.

"That is correct," Ryynar smiled. "I am of Oquelite blood."

A weak gasp escaped Tabitha's lips. "How—"

"I can read your mind, little gazelle." Ryynar knelt down in front of her. With one touch, the shackles around her wrists fell away.

Her stomach revolted at the sign of the burned flesh. "Where am I?"

"In a future reality." Ryynar stood up, and held out a hand to her.

Tabitha foolishly clasped it. He pulled her to her feet. She looked around her, seeing four familiar jagged peaks in the distance. One top had been blown off, lava spilling from the crater like a volcano. A building sat at its base, blackened with flames, the roof completely crumbled.

A cry escaped her. She spun around to Ryynar. "This is North Cordell!"

Ryynar only smiled. "Yes. It is."

"You said a future possibility," Tabitha said, stumbling backwards. "Where am I?!"

"In the future, little gazelle."

"Where am I?" she screamed. "Who are you?"

Ryynar just laughed softly, reaching out to pat her on the top of her head, but Tabitha tore away, stumbling. "They used to call me Protector. Now?" He shook his head. "Now, little gazelle, I'm far more dangerous than that. We've been in touch. Remember the Hall of Heroes? A particular serpent that sought out your demise?" His voice switched to a horrible, familiar raspy tone, and he laughed. "Well, times have changed. I have an enemy. One that will soon become yours as well."

"Who?" Tabitha said, clenching her fists. If this guy made one move, she'd punch him square in the face and then find Cole. She was going crazy. Cole was here. Right? He had to be.

"Oh, she is far more powerful than I could ever dream of," Ryynar sighed. "I am not permitted to tell you, but I can request your assistance."

"Why would you do that?"

"Because, little gazelle, I'm the only one who can make your nightmares stop. I know all that haunts you. Such as the Core Force? Oh, sorry. You think of it as the *Mor Vis*." He laughed and blew a hair casually from his face, clasping his hands behind his back, looking to the mountains. "You fear of your future, little gazelle. You fear death above all else. And above your own death?" He looked at her. "The death of someone you love."

"Everyone's scared of death," Tabitha snapped, though she was trembling.

"Oh?" Ryynar laughed again. "But how many are scared of killing?"

Tabitha froze.

"Blood scared you, little gazelle. The thought of your own hand bringing the demise of another is beyond you. Funny, seeing how you're supposed to be a Council Member? The twelve warriors of power beyond what mortals know? And you're scared of death. The Shadow Soul knows no concept. How weak you will be in comparison."

Tears burned at Tabitha's eyes. "No," she sputtered. But she knew the lie lay thick on her tongue, and anyone could see it.

Ryynar smiled. "And, little gazelle. The death of that little child? It was your fault."

And then, he vanished. "He can't save you from your nightmare now."

Over and over, the bloody memory spun around her. *Your fault. Didn't act fact enough. Died because of you. Can't be trusted. Impulsive.* The child is dead because of you.

Tabitha screamed. "No! Get me out of here!"

The ground began to tremble below her, throwing her off balance. She clung to the chalky ground.

Your fault.

She sank through the earth, falling through the darkness, her voice stolen from her. She landed hard with a thud on a forest floor, a fire burning in the distance. A boy, a man, stood a few feet in front of her, a sword at his hilt. His blonde hair was pressed against his forehead with sweat, and his cheek smeared with blood.

Tabitha's heart leapt. "Cole!"

Cole whipped out his blade, not saying a word, slashing at her, catching her torso. Tabitha cried back in pain, crumpling to the ground. "No! Please, Cole! It's me! Tabitha!"

Cole froze, frowning. He knelt down in front of her. He lifted her chin with his hand to meet his eyes. But instead of the familiar green, a blood red stared back.

Tabitha tore away, grabbed the fallen hilt of the Illuminate. Not-Cole jumped at her, slamming her shoulders down against the ground. Her shoulders began to burn, the smell of burning flesh filling her nose. She screamed, holding the sword.

She couldn't do it. She loved him. She couldn't hurt him. No. Please no.

She couldn't kill anyone else. "Cole. Please *STOP!*"

He didn't. His red eyes just continued to stare down into hers. A sob choked her. She fastened her hold on the hilt and with a scream, thrust it through her best friend.

Tabitha woke up crying.

As soon as her eyes burst open to the darkness, feeling the cool covers pressed over her, her body shook with sobs of relief, muffled with the pillow. She was tempted to flick on the light to make sure she wasn't still asleep, but she wasn't sure she wanted to risk waking up the Lopez girl, Calynda, who snored across the room.

It was just a bad dream, she told herself. It's not real. You didn't actually hurt Cole. Cole's okay.

But she didn't believe it. She slipped out from under the cover, unzipped her bag quietly, changing quickly into a T-shirt and shorts, grabbing her shoes. She peered back at Calynda. Still asleep.

The child's unbreathing blue face haunted her. She tried to breathe. *No, leave me alone.*

Tabitha forced herself to take a deep breath. She crept across the room, pressing her hand against the handle. The door swung open with a bang. Tabitha froze. She heard Calynda groan, blankets rustled, and then the room went quiet.

Tabitha let out a sigh of relief.

She closed the door slowly behind her, and took in a deep breath of the cool fresh air.

The shaking in her arms had gotten better, and the pain in her head had lessened. It was just a nightmare.

But the child dying of your impulses wasn't.

She walked down the hallway, hopping on one foot, pulling on her shoe. She met the staircase, leading down into the Lopez's large living and dining area. A dim light was on downstairs.

She frowned.

It was nearly five in the morning. She sat down on the top step, peering down through the railing. Pacing on the living room floor was the boy, Matteo.

Tabitha's face brightened. She jumped up, racing down the stairs. "Matteo!"

The boy jumping, tripping backwards, landing with a clatter against the coffee table, sending a pile of audio chips all over the place, cursing. Tabitha cringed, rushing to help him, falling to her knees, scooping up chips from the ground into the palm of her hand.

"I'm so sorry," she said, dumping a handful into the jar. "I didn't mean to scare you. I had no idea anyone else would even be awake, considering—"

"No, it's fine." To Tabitha's surprise, the boy laughed softly, getting up from the ground, dusting himself off. He smiled, his back straighter and more confident than yesterday, though fiddling with the headphones around his neck.

Tabitha couldn't help but frown. "Oh-kay. So whatcha doing up so early?"

She watched as his eyes scrambled around the room. "Er. School work."

"Nice try, buddy," Tabitha laughed, jumping back on a sofa behind her. "I used that one all the time when I was a wee lass."

"A what?"

"A little girl," Tabitha said, with a sigh. "It was a joke."

Matteo forced a laugh. "Oh. And you aren't little now?"

"Hey, you're not a tall human being yourself, sir!" She couldn't help but smile. He laughed *and* joked with her? Maybe she'd been onto something about making a friend here in Court Illegia.

Matteo shrugged. "I just haven't hit a growth spurt yet."

"How old are you?" Tabitha asked.

"Sixteen... as of three weeks ago."

Tabitha smirked. "Well, I'm seventeen."

"As of?" Matteo raised an eyebrow.

Tabitha scowled. "Almost two months ago." How had this conversation started again? Her eyes widened. He'd totally changed the subject. Smoothly too.

"Now, what were you doing up so late?" she said.

"I said school," Matteo insisted, with a shrug.

"Whenever I said that to my older brothers, I was *always* working on music." The binder always worked as a perfect disguise too. No one suspected much from a binder and real paper.

"You write music?" Matteo's eyes went wide.

"Yep." Tabitha couldn't help but sit a little straighter.

"Music's great," Matteo said, before he quickly shook his head and tugged the ends of his long sleeves. "I mean, I don't write it, but our family... performs?"

"You what?"

"It's a family thing!" Matteo said, quickly. "We do a little show for the Skyline."

She could tell he was subtly blushing, and she grinned. "So that's why you were at the theater yesterday?"

"More or less. That was a business call," he said. He shrugged, putting his hands in two of the various pockets of his shorts.

"That's amazing!" Tabitha laughed, jumping from her seat. "A show? Where do you all perform?"

"It's usually just here... and I don't do it often," Matteo said. "Sometimes the casino sponsors various rising theaters, and then us Lopez kids do something."

Tabitha piqued with a hundred questions. Why were casinos willing to let specifically the Lopez siblings perform? Was a sponsorship expensive? What exactly did they perform? How did one sponsor a theater? Did you need to be a big company or just an ex-Liberty teen who lived under a Defender camp?

Matteo barely had a moment to answer before seats of footsteps clattered down the steps, and a clear ring of laughter echoed through the room.

Iracema tied her hair up, as she called to Cole, who followed behind her. "You've really not gotten out much!"

Cole looked worse than Tabitha had ever seen him. His hair was a mess, wet from a shower, faint circles had begun to form under his eyes, and his Medallion hung loosely from the collar of his untucked shirt.

But he was alive.

Tabitha, in one swift motion, swung herself over the couch, ran to him, and threw her arms around his neck. Cole stumbled back, surprised, cautiously wrapping his arms around her.

"You good, Tabs?" He said, frowning.

She pressed her ear against his chest. His heart was beating fast, but beating. "Just glad you're alive."

"Did Calynda try to kill ya last night or something?" Iracema laughed, walking to the miniature kitchen, opening the refrigerator door with her heel.

Tabitha's face burned, pushing away from Cole. "No. She was fine."

"I swear she was up till midnight trying to flirt with that friend of yours." Iracema slammed a mug on the counter, offering to get a cup for either of them too. Cole rejected at the same time Tabitha accepted. "The one with wire and glass on his face. I think I've seen them in media films."

Matteo plopped down on the sofa, before he slipped his headphones on. "Glasses, Ira."

"Right," Iracema said. "I apologize for them. Calynda, I mean. Matteo isn't much to apologize for. Though if he is bothering you, I'll punch him in the nose."

Tabitha moved to the island, sitting crossed legged on a stool. "I think I can handle him."

A machine began to beep from the back counter.

"You sure you don't want coffee, Coleson?" Iracema said, taking up the pot.

"I'm good, thanks." Cole ran his fingers through his hair,

taking a shaky breath as Iracema chattered on. Tabitha tuned her out, watching her friend as he sat down on the bottom step, his tired eyes staring blankly at the floor.

Her stomach churned. Something was off about him. Did it have to do with her nightmare? That's all it was right. A *nightmare.*

A splash of burning liquid was enough to distract her thoughts. Tabitha stumbled back with a cry, which didn't help but to make it a bigger mess.

Nor did it help that Agent Nigel Lopez walked through the door as his niece was climbing up onto the table either.

Everyone froze.

Nigel looked from Iracema to Tabitha, then to Cole, who just groaned.

"Iracema, what are you doing on the table?" he scowled.

Iracema shrugged, turned on her heel, and threw her body backward, catching the edge of the counter with her hands, and flipping over, landing flawlessly on her feet with a thud. She again spoke to him in the language Tabitha couldn't place.

Nigel snapped at her, and Iracema shrunk back, yelling at her uncle louder now. The two began to bicker back and forth. Matteo weaved between them, opened a drawer, carried out a towel, and presented one to Tabitha, then began to clean the floor.

"Thanks," Tabitha said, scrubbing the front of her shirt. It was hopelessly stained. Not that it mattered much to her personally, but presentation wise, she already was starting out miserably representing a Council.

The arguing calmed down, leaving Iracema in a corner, her arms crossed, and a death glare on her uncle.

Nigel blew a hair from his face in an angry huff. "Johnson?"

"Yes, sir."

Matteo took the dirty towel from Tabitha, gave her a small smile, and ran past Cole on the steps and disappeared.

"Plan of action, boy," Nigel said.

"Explore Court Illegia," Cole said. He got to his feet, straightening himself. "Look for essence surges on our own."

"So we're relying on teenagers' feelings to save the day?"

Nigel raised a suspicious brow.

Cole looked to Tabitha.

Tabitha shrugged. "Yeah, basically."

Cole facepalmed. "Sir, if I can propose an alternative idea, maybe we can learn more about Court Illegia. With more knowledge of its history, we can more easily begin to narrow down how we can find the Council Member here. A wise woman once told me coincidence is fate. Things *must* be connected."

"And," Iracema butted in, "what's a better way to learn, than the last *Mor Virs* sighting, eh?"

"That's not open today, Iracema," Nigel sighed. "You know they locked that place up."

Iracema pushed past her uncle, giving them a wink. "I tour there on weekends. I'm sure I can get us a pass. We'd be all alone."

"I don't like that idea," Nigel said. "You? All alone."

"I'm eighteen," Iracema scowled, her hands on her hips. "Old enough to enter the Trials."

"Sir," Cole said. He stepped forward. "This might be our only lead."

Nigel pursed his lips, looked at Iracema, and sighed. "Fine. But beware of the *Mors Vis.*"

Iracema chuckled, with a smirk.

Ryynar's words echoed in Tabitha's mind. *Core Force... or as you call it, Mor Vis.* It didn't make any sense. *Mor Vis* meant Death Wish... not that.

"You have two hours, and if you don't return by then, I'll send a squad after you."

Iracema cheered in a word Tabitha couldn't comprehend. "I'll prove myself to you."

Nigel groaned. "Please. Don't try."

"Wake up your glasses friend," Iracema shouted, bounding up the steps. "We leave in ten!"

Cole sighed, pinching the bridge of his nose. "Hey Tabs?"

"Yeah?"

"You gonna drink that coffee?"

47

COLE HAD SLEPT A HOPEFUL TOTAL OF TWO HOURS. HE WAS glad the drive was a short one. He should've let Iracema drive.

The roads were crowded. People crossed whenever they felt like it. There was an auto jam on every other street. Iracema sat opposite of him, rambling on about the exhibits. Lawrence, Tabitha, Matteo, and Calynda were crammed in the back.

Lawrence hadn't been thrilled about being woken so early, and was shamelessly asleep in the back, with an order not to wake him till they got there. Iracema selected Calynda out of her siblings to join them, but a small request from Matteo got him squished in the back as well.

Five others whose lives were in his hands. What if they got attacked? He couldn't bring the Illuminate. They'd be defenseless.

They—

"Coleson, turn!" Iracema shouted.

Cole turned the truck, his eye catching the glint of a

domed building decorated in golden glass. The closer they got, he saw a beige building laid underneath, pillars circling around it, with a well trimmed lawn of grass, marked off by a small laser fence. A bright hologram sign indicated the exhibit house to be a monument dedicated to the EarthShaker.

The street was free of auto jams, only a few bouncing tourists made their way through the sidewalks. Cole parked by the side of the road.

"Alright! Unload, everyone!" Iracema ordered, slamming her door open, fixing her knit bag over her shoulder. Her authority was not denied, and the truck creaked and groaned under the shuffling of the unloading of the back.

Cole waited a moment to catch his breath. He pulled the chain around his neck, the Medallion slipping out of the collar of his shirt. He ran his thumb over the lines engraved into the face of the Medallion, trying to clear his mind.

It was just a research mission. No battles. No death. Hopefully no death wish *Mors Vis*. It was fine.

He pulled at the stubborn handle of the door and thrust the door open, hopping out into the surprisingly warm Court Illegian road.

"We cross after that red auto passes," Iracema instructed the group of tired teens. She seemed the only enthusiastic one among them. She held her head high with determination, her shoulders rolled back with an inspiring determination.

Cole couldn't help but quirk a smile.

The red auto hovered past them, and Iracema ordered them across like a Sergeant. They approached the exhibit house with hesitation. It was clearly closed, a thin red laser blocking the path inside, but Iracema whipped a card from her pack and swiped it in front of the sensor. The laser flickered for a moment and then disappeared.

They followed her down the path, and Cole's eyes couldn't seem to stay in one place. The yard acquired artifacts scattered about, including a polished bombshell case, a tire preserved in a glass case, and a peculiar pink bird on a metal wire stuck into the grass.

They turned the corner to the side of the building. Iracema unlocked the door, holding it open for everyone else to enter. Cole waited to enter last, checking over his shoulder.

Nothing.

He was just being paranoid. They'd been last sighted weeks ago.

Iracema smiled at him as he walked in, and she shut the door behind them. "You look awful tired, Coleson," she said.

He shrugged. If they slipped up, it was his fault. "I'm alright."

Iracema patted him on the shoulder, leading him down the dark hall behind the others. "Just let me know. I am in charge here."

"Proving yourself to Nigel?" Cole asked.

Iracema shrugged. "He's practically convinced I'm a good for nothing besides paperwork management."

"Why does he think that?" Cole frowned. "You seem very authoritative and in control."

Iracema sighed. "I—I messed up," she said, quickly. "But I'm not dumping my life story on 'Nigel', as you call him's partner."

"We're not partners," Cole said. "I'm not a Defender." Iracema's eyebrow rose. "You—you're not?"

Cole chuckled. "Nope. Never wanted to be. Sounds stressful."

"The stress must be worth it though, don't you think?" Iracema said. Her voice hinged with annoyance. "Anyone can apply for the Trials. Anyone can win them and become a Defender. It comes with a reputation, and you get to do things that can make *actual* change. An ordinary person. Even someone who had a rough past. You know about the Curatrix team, right?"

Cole's heart skipped a beat. *Better than I'd like to.* "Who hasn't?"

"Fair point." She laughed heartlessly. "Reyna Wents was apparently from the Algery slums, with a bad track record. She talked about it in an interview once. And *everyone* knows how much the Curatrix team was able to do! They made the Trial system less selective to allow those of all backgrounds a fair shot at acceptance, and established a stronger system for the recovering regions—"

"She *loves* the Defenders," Calynda laughed, pushing open a door to a room flooded with light. "A little too much.

Gets her hopes up. Agent Wents was a one-in-a-million chance, Ira.”

Iracema shoved past her sister. “Her title is Agent *Aguirre* 35, genius.”

The name ‘Aguirre’ caused Cole to cringe. Little did they know, they had someone standing in this very room related to the infamous Reyna Wents. And he was currently wiping his glasses, sitting on a bench, entirely unamused.

“Now stop telling everyone your big wide dreams, and let’s get this moving!” Calynda laughed, tossing back a loose bouncing curl.

Iracema cast her sister a scowl, but held her chin up and glided across the marble floor. “Fine. Come along.”

The exhibit house was incredible and nothing like Cole had ever seen. A plane replica hung from the domed ceiling, casting shadows along the floors from the sunlight pouring in around it. Holograms floated in the air playing scratchy videos of soldiers in bulky uniforms standing on podium giving speeches, trenching through lands, and replays of the clip Cole had only seen about a million times.

The first bomb that went off and sent a third of the population underground.

The second one was never recorded.

No one knew what happened, besides the death and devastation they saw when they began to rebuild decades later. The world before then had been lost, only fragments remaining.

And those fragments seemed to have made their way into the exhibit house of Court Illegia.

“A lot of this stuff is from the EarthShaker,” Tabitha said, stopping in front of a display of military medals protected by a grid of lasers.

“There’s not much left from before that,” Iracema said. But a smile twitching at the end on her lip said otherwise. “But there’s some.”

“Some?”

“The Defenders make it their priority to find ancient artifacts, right? And that’s kinda what you’re looking for,” Iracema stopped at two dark wooden doors, carved and decorated with an intricate design of the map of Earth, and the 95 regions.

Cole expected Iracema to stick out her hand for a grid to show up and scan it. Perhaps a DNA scan at least, but nope. She grabbed the brass handles and thrust her weight forward. The doors scraped against the floor with a groan, opening up into a whole new room. It smelled of old pages, and dust scattered in the sunlight of the windows above.

Paintings hung from frames on one wall, and on another, thousands of tiny creatures were pinned in glass cases. Another held a book shelf... of real books.

Cole didn't even have time to process the rest of the room before it felt like he took a blow to his face. He stumbled back, crashing into the door behind him. He grabbed the door handle, catching his balance. The room rocked around him. Energy coursed through him.

"Cole, you good?" He heard Lawrence say.

"Something's here," Cole gasped, steadying himself on his feet. His eyesight cleared. "I can feel it. Oh gosh. I can feel it."

"*You* can feel it?" Tabitha said. Worry creased her brows. "Usually the supernatural avoids you."

"I—I'm a Council Member. I'm not immune to Council stuff... I guess." His lungs decided to let him take in a steady string of breaths. He straightened himself.

Tabitha stepped toward him, but Iracema tore past her. "You sure you're good? I'm trained in the Health Care Systems."

"From net videos!" Calynda called out.

Iracema rolled her eyes.

"I'm fine," Cole insisted.

Iracama still grasped his shoulder like he would fall over. "Search the room," she instructed. She turned to Cole, her eyes studying him carefully. "Cole. Maybe you should sit—"

"No. I'm good," he said, gently nudging her hand off. "I'm the one who felt something. So I should be one of the ones looking."

Iracema nodded, squeezing his hand before letting go, and moving to step between an annoyed Lawrence and chattery Calynda. Cole walked to one of the large tables, piled in unorganized artifacts. The room seemed to be still in the process of being put up for display. So why was the door unlocked?

He found a funny looking device that opened and closed, with a flat broken screen and a tiny … keyboard? Lawrence sorted through opposite of him. The boy was for the most part quiet, his face still holding its hard composure. Guilt twisted in Cole's gut. He'd had six months to let the idea of being a Council Member settle in his mind, but Lawrence?

Two weeks.

Anxiety grew inside Cole's throat. Could he have helped the boy more? He looked so miserable. And angry. Why was he always angry?

"Cole!" Tabitha's shrill voice caused Cole's to jerk up.

He whirled in the direction of Tabitha's voice, only to be met with a wall. He scrambled around the wall, to a snug corner lit by a lamp, and a fallen tarp at Tabitha's feet. She stood, her eyes unblinking, her jaw was trembling, her lips struggling to make a sound.

Cole stepped back. A tapestry was painted with four mountains, a dark moonless sky behind it, grasses scattered around it, and towering pines.

And the mountains bled.

Red seeped from their peaks and down the rocky terrain, smoke rising from the base. Cole's stomach rocked. Feathers of gold danced around the border, obviously representing the *Mor Vis*. But as Cole's eyes trailed down the words lining the tapestry they met... *Cors Vis?*

"The Hall of Heroes," Tabitha said. "It was there."

Cole swallowed. And her nightmares. "Yeah."

She paused over an odd depiction of what looked like a black smudge. Cole frowned at it. It seemed out of place.

"Shadow Soul?" Tabitha muttered.

Cole raised a brow. "What did you say?"

"Nothing," Tabitha said, quickly. "Just-just something from a dream."

Tabitha knelt down and ran her fingers over the symbols on the bottom of the tapestry, pointing to an odd green letter. "This looks like the engraving on the Ewyon Stone," Tabitha breathed, her hand moving along till it met a familiar shape. "And the Oquelite Key Ring."

Tabitha's eyes drifted upward, no doubt thinking the same he was.

They were all artifacts, created to assist the Council. The

Ewyon Stone, the Key Ring, no doubt the odd symbols that followed too.

"What do you think it—"

"Probably nothing," Cole said, nearly tripping backward on the end of the tarp as he backed away. "Nothing, Tabitha."

Tabitha frowned. "Alright, then."

"Yeah," Cole turned on his heel, and mentally scolded himself. His intention was to *not* make her worry, and now she looked more distressed than before. He was screwing this whole operation up right and left.

They continued their search, and Cole found nothing more useful than a book of definitions and pronunciations. Iracema was busy scaling bookshelves and rattling off titles to see if they caught interest, and Calynda lay on a bench, obviously with no interest in being there. Matteo, again with his headphones over his ears, had sorted through a drawer without so much as a word, so Cole assumed failure there too.

He closed the book, reaching for his Medallion.

"I found something!" Lawrence shouted.

The entire room turned their attention. Calynda gasped, and kicked her brother, who removed his headphones. Lawrence held up a bright white feather, shimmering in the sunlight.

"Is that a—?" Iracema snorted.

Lawrence held it lower, glaring it at. "I felt something."

"Well, maybe feel harder on something else," Calynda laughed.

"It's a cool feather," Matteo grumbled.

His sister playfully punched him in the shoulder.

The angry resting face returned, and Lawrence brought down the feather and began inspecting it in his hands. Cole sighed internally, and walked over to Lawrence's side, looking over his shoulder to the curious feather. It didn't look dangerous. It looked quite... ordinary. There was no way this was the *Mors Vis* Agent Nigel Lopez spoke about.

Something crashed.

Calynda stood beside a broken case. She laughed nervously. "Sorry."

"Lynda!" Iracema shouted.

Suddenly sirens began to wail. The floating holograms shifted to red.

"Oops."

"Okay! No one panic!" Iracema shouted. "It looks like our visit has been cut short. Everyone move out!"

A metal covering began to crawl over the window above them, casting the door in shadows. Cole rushed to the door, pulling the handle.

It didn't budge.

"We're locked in!"

Iracema shouted in her language.

Calynda ran to the door, beginning to try and pull. "Come on! There's six of us!"

Cole scowled. Six of them against a lock to prevent thieves sounded like an unlikely battle. No one denied it. They rushed to the door, grabbing hold and pulling.

The wood creaked under their weight.

Suddenly, the handles disconnected, sending them collapsing backward on top of each other.

"The feather!" Lawrence cried, jumping up from on top of Cole. The feather had shot up from the mass of bodies and began to dance in the air. Upward.

Calynda screamed.

Cole's heart dropped. *No.*

Lawrence didn't seem to care about the impending danger, jumping up on the table, and in a desperate leap, tried to grab the feather. It darted away from his touch, almost mocking him.

"Leave it, Williams! It's dangerous!" Iracema shouted. She was up and off the ground, her body tense, fists clenched. "There's an emergency exit for employees. It can't be deactivated yet!"

"I touched it without freaking dying!!" Lawrence said atop another table. "It has to be *something!*"

Screw the Council. Currently, Cole's priorities lie with getting them out safely. "Get to the exit!" he ordered.

Lawrence scowled, jumping off the table, the feather slipping through his fingers, dashing to the ground. The others scrambled toward the door Iracema had propped open. Cole waited for Lawrence to reluctantly follow.

Cole jumped into the hallway, helping Iracema heave the

heavy door shut, and they were submerged into the darkness of the hall. Cole could see the faint outlines of those running in front of him, though he could hear Iracema's strong voice echo without a tremble. "Hurry! Come on! Ahead!"

Her resilience settled his nerves a bit.

Faster. Faster. The sirens echoed. Why couldn't they run faster? They'd be locked in. Some officer would find them, and he'd fail them once again.

"There!" Iracema's cry ran through the walls. "The door!"

He heard a bang, light spilled into the hall. They'd made it. One by one, they burst out. Matteo. Calynda. Tabitha. And then, there was just him and Lawrence left. Iracema held the door open, gritting her teeth. "It's closing!" she shouted. Her heels began to dig into the ground.

"We don't have time!" Cole shouted. "Iracema, move out of the way!"

Iracema frowned at him, but jumped out of the way. Cole thrust Lawrence with all his might to the door, Lawrence cried out in a string of curses, and he fell toward the door. Iracema caught him and the others rushed to pull him out.

"Coleson!" Iracema cried.

Cole slowed down, watching the door slowly close, the crack growing smaller and smaller. Their shouts became white noise, his heart skipped a beat.

The door clicked, locked.

And he was trapped.

Meet me at the Plaza 8.30 AM! Can't wait to see you Lizzy!

That was the last message Felicity had received, and Felicity's stomach churned too bad to try and even reply with a message longer than "*Okay.*"

She sat in the back of the long auto, wearing a collared shirt, a pencil skirt to her knees, and a bright red, fitting jacket, and her hair done in a painfully tight bun, to hide her hair that had far overgrown the typical Liberty bob. It had taken a bit to convince Renee to accept the headband, and for Felicity to hide the subtle bulge of machinery under the tights.

Renee wouldn't let Felicity be seen in public in a T-shirt

and jeans, and Felicity secretly didn't want to be either. She didn't need any extra attention, and fitting in was just what she needed.

"Hey, are you listening to me or are you being insecure about your hair again?" Giles raised a brow at her from the opposite seat. As Felicity expected, he'd been issued to wear his normal Defender uniform, and he seemed quite happy about it.

"I'm not," she spat back.

"Yes, you are," Giles said. "You keep reaching for it around your shoulders." He mimicked her, and she kicked him.

"Look. Am I not allowed to be nervous?" She crossed her arms over her chest, and settled a glare on him.

"You're allowed to be nervous, kid, but you gotta stop being unreasonably nervous about your hair, or that's going to make your friend lady think you're insecure or something."

"I am insecure," Felicity said, her cheeks flaming.

"Bentsworth," Giles said, sternly. He leaned forward, his hard, dark eyes staring her down, making her feel frozen against her seat. "You *need* to be the dominant one. You're getting vital information from this girl to lead us to the Aguirre chip. Felicity, you *are* the only person who can get this plan into motion. Cole and Tabitha are basically the backup. If they can't find the full-blood in time before the Oquelite do, then it's up to us to do it."

Felicity tried to force herself to swallow, but her throat had closed up. "O-okay."

Giles leaned back. "Chill out, Bentsworth."

"How-how can I chill out?" she murmured. "You just told me if this fails, it's my fault."

"It will be."

She glared at him. She felt tears pricking at her eyes, but she refused to let them fall. She wouldn't start crying in front of Giles. Definitely not Giles.

"And it's just two girls doing fun things like eating food and looking at jackets or something. Nothing can go wrong. And I'll be just a block away at all times if you need me." Giles winked.

Felicity rolled her eyes, though truthfully his reminder

settled the ramming of her heart just a little bit. Giles would be there if anything went wrong. She could rely on Giles at least to keep her safe, right?

She didn't really have time to come to an answer as the auto came to a stop.

The door opened.

Felicity stared at the empty sidewalk. They probably cleared the area, knowing the stupid security team. Giles tapped her shoulder. She jumped.

He chuckled, handing her two rubber dots, with tiny blue chips stuck in the center. She knew the devices all too well.

Face distorters.

She took them and stuck them below her jawline, hidden by the shadow of her chin. She'd activate them once she had to interact with the public. She didn't need people recognizing her and causing a fuss about her return.

She was surprised Yaeda hadn't spilled the whole ordeal to everyone yet. She took a deep breath, and stepped out of the auto.

"You got me in your contacts, right, Bentsworth?" Giles called from his seat.

Felicity didn't turn and look back at him. She'd be too tempted to turn and run back in. She nodded. "Yeah. I got it."

"Good." The door slammed shut. "Try and have fun, got it, Bentsworth?"

"Got it, Giles."

"Good lass."

She heard the whir of the engine, and screeching of the closing window. And then, the auto was gone. And she was alone.

In Liberty.

She could turn around now. If she called Renee, she would send for her. A nod to the guard behind a tree would. Even if she begged Giles hard enough. She didn't have to do this.

No.

She did have to do this.

This is for her.

She held her chin up, her hands trembling, facing the creamy pink building in front of her. She walked up the wooden white steps and through the shimmering holographic door.

The waiter, dressed in a blue striped dress and a paper cap, stopped dead in her tracks.

Giles told her not to activate the distorters till she got to Yaeda. That was going wrong fast.

Don't freak out, Felicity. She tried to remember her friends' faces. *Four my friend. Two too much. Seven Eleven. Three we Two do.*

Felicity forced a trembling smile, and nodded to the waiter.

The waiter blinked.

"She's here!" Another woman, this time in a suit, stepped out from an employee door. "Stop staring."

The waiter did as she was told.

The woman, who had a polished pin on her collar labeling her as the "manager," rushed to Felicity, grabbing her hand and shaking it.

Shock rippled through Felicity's body at the sudden touch, her palms wet with sweat, but the manager obviously hadn't noticed. She let go and turned on her heel. "Your friend awaits you."

Felicity wiped her hands on her skirt. "T-thank-thank you."

She talked, at least.

She followed the manager through two automatic wooden doors into the snug little diner Felicity hardly remembered. It smelled of disinfectant, and the booths shined like they'd never been touched. A hologram played a casual news station, and a serving bot was parked by the serving counter.

"Liz! You're here!" The shrill voice caught Felicity off guard. She whirled around to see a bright yellow haired girl, with huge blue wire decorative glasses, sitting up in a booth, a tele in hand, waving her hand in the air.

Felicity clenched her jaw and gave a wave. She turned to the manager. "Thank you," she said harshly.

"I'll be with you in a moment," the manager said, with a small bow, and disappeared behind a door.

Felicity made her way uneasily to the seat opposite of Yaeda.

"Goodness, aren't you skinny?" Yaeda laughed, looking to her tele before setting it down, clasping her hands. "It's been years, girl."

Felicity held herself straight, brushing off the comment. She wouldn't let Yaeda see her crack. She wouldn't be insane like they all thought she was. "It has. Four years."

Yaeda snorted. "Four years? Really? Four years ago we were best friends, and here I am looking at practically a stranger." She laughed to herself.

Yaeda Spade was and never had been even a close friend of Felicity's, but of course, everyone who maintained a conversation longer than an hour with her wanted to claim a Bentsworth as a good friend of theirs.

Felicity cracked a smile, and laughed softly.

"You gonna cut that hair, Lizzy?" Yaeda said, fingering her own cropped hair. "How long is it now?"

"Long," Felicity said simply. She took a quick breath. "I think I'll keep it. I won't be here long."

Yaeda pouted. "You're going to back to that dirt—"

A beeping of a serving bot cut Yaeda short and was Felicity's saving grace. Felicity ordered something simply to have an excuse not to talk to Yaeda. She wasn't hungry at all, her stomach churning with anxiety. The food was rich, and had a sweet aftertaste Felicity wasn't used to after her years in North Cordell, but she shoved it down anyway.

Yaeda didn't seem to mind Felicity's silence, as she filled the space all on her own throughout the meal. Most of it was petty school drama about classmates Felicity had practically forgotten, but Felicity's attention was caught when Yaeda mentioned Imperial. They'd recognized her on the holograms... and she'd become a net sensation. Yaeda thought it was hilarious, but Felicity was disappointed.

People had died in Imperial. It was horrifying, and haunted her nightmares. She'd watched one of her friends nearly die there, and Yaeda laughed it off as a joke.

Keep cool, Liz.

They left the diner, and Felicity activated the distorters, and followed Yaeda along the moving sidewalks to the shop central, where little shops of every color sprinkled in an organized maze around her. A few groups of people were scattered in the bright streets at the little cafe tables under the street lamps.

"So, I told you about Liberty," Yaeda said, elbowing her. "And now, you have to tell me about … East Mordell was it?"

"North Cordell."

"Right!" Yaeda said. She typed away at her tele. "Anyone cute there?"

Felicity's face flamed. "What?"

"What what?" Yaeda said, looking up. "I heard rough and gruff people are cute. And you have friends, right?"

"Yeah," Felicity said. How was she supposed to turn *this* around to politics about the Aguirres? She tried to play it off casual, striding beside Yaeda, keeping her face unchanged. "But they're my friends. And that's all. We had far more important things to worry about."

Yaeda pouted, but didn't look from her tele. "Sounds boring."

Felicity clenched her fist, picking up her pace. "Far from it."

'Well, can you tell me?"

"Confidential." A genuine smirk spread across Felicity's lips.

Yaeda sighed, tucking the tele into her pocket. "Oh. So you're up big now, Lizzy. That's great," Yaeda said, adding a skip to her step.

They turned a corner.

Felicity could feel herself breathe, as they weaved through a patch of people waiting in line. She could do this. Just get Yaeda to the topic. For her friends.

"So, how's your dad?" Felicity asked, once they were out of earshot, and beside Yaeda

Yaeda groaned. "My dad, Lizzy? He's boring."

She caught the golden handle of a shop, the door opening on Yaeda's touch. The shop smelled strongly of a suffocating perfume. The shop was lit with a soft pink light, and the employees wore similar short striped dresses, with tied sashes around their waists, and buckled black shoes. They didn't even look up from the counter where they pored over one of the employee's teles.

The shop was packed with candles, and little glass bottles. The smell was overwhelming, making Felicity's stomach churned. Maybe she should've avoided the rich Liberty food…

It didn't matter.

She was on a mission.

Felicity rushed to Yaeda's side, where she stood at a table, examining charms. "I thought you were pursuing a career in politics."

"And I thought you were becoming an artist," Yaeda shrugged. She moved to the next table of tiny tune players.

"Why drop politics? It's a very fruitful career," Felicity said. "In a world like this, wouldn't you want that?"

"I dunno." Yaeda pressed the button on the tune player, playing a familiar theme song Felicity was too angry to place. "I think I had a reckoning, Lizzy. I don't *need* to go into politics, because the world doesn't want me to do something I don't want to. I want to enjoy my life."

Scenes of buildings shattering, citizens fleeing with bloodstained faces, flashed in Felicity's red vision. "E-enjoy your life?"

"I live in Liberty, Liz. The only thing I want to change is to get to top society. A partner. Two kids. The name 'Spade' gets me anywhere, anyway."

"You just want to play into the system?"

Yarda laughed. "I'm a *rebel*, Liz. No one dyes their hair yellow, and like sure, maybe the system is messed up. I think everyone in Liberty should get top-class living spaces. Not those lower layers, like myself."

"Not the two kid prejudice thing? You wouldn't want to change that?" Yaeda couldn't be so heartless that she was completely okay with the system that had caused Tabitha scorn and torment every waking hour of her life.

But apparently, the universe was all for proving Felicity wrong today.

"Uh. No. What's wrong with it?" Yaeda raised an eyebrow. "You good, Lizzy? You look really pale."

Pale? Felicity felt like her face was burning. She nodded, taking a deep breath. "I'm fine."

"I think East Mordell did something to you. You didn't used to be so… concerned about what I did," Yaeda said. She plucked up a tune player, and a bot strode to her. She paid the bot a few chips, and it ejected a bag. She took it.

Not everything is about you, Yaeda Spade. Felicity bit her lip, keeping the words to herself. She and Yaeda left the shop.

"You thinking of becoming a politician? Or a Defender?" Yaeda burst out into hysterical laughter. "Imagine you being a Defender. Really. Picture it."

Felicity laughed mockingly, but Yaeda didn't notice. "No, I'm not," Felicity said.

"Good," Yaeda said. "I'm sorry, but it would be a disaster."

They walked along in silence for a while. Felicity's stomach tried to revolt against her, but she pushed it down. Not now.

Yaeda finally looked up from her tele, and asked suddenly, "You like surprises, right Lizzy?"

Felicity slowed. "What?"

Yaeda smirked. "Surprises."

"Wh-what surprise?" Felicity stammered.

"I know my dad doesn't like me going out too long, but I told him you'd come back into town, right? So I figured if I told my dad, why not everyone else? We're having a 'get together.'"

Yaeda jazzed her hands.

But Felicity was frozen. Everything came crashing down at once. Yaeda wasn't going to help her. It didn't matter how long Felicity followed her. The girl knew nothing except for parties and pleasure. And now she'd told a huge group of people that she'd returned and her cover was blown.

Felicity had failed.

Again.

She couldn't think. She turned and took off running. She heard Yaeda shouting after her. She saw blurry figures staring at her. Hot tears streamed down her face. She didn't care. She clenched her jaw in fear her stomach would revolt. Her legs screamed in pain.

She wasn't safe here.

Her breath refused to go through her nose.

Pain flashed through her body, memories of fire, a bloody figure beside her. Shambles of a crashed auto.

"Giles!" she cried out.

Where was he? Had he ditched her too? Was everything just a cruel joke? *Why did she need everyone to save her?*

She tripped over her shoes, one torn straight off her foot. She tried to scramble up, but slipped, slamming forward onto the concrete. She felt blood trickle from her nose.

They would find her. They'd laugh and call her insane.

She grabbed a chair, heaving herself to her feet. People around her backed away. "Giles!"

She ran, her missing shoe slowing her down.

It was pointless. She was lost. She was—

She slammed into someone. She screamed, scrambling back. Two sturdy hands caught her shoulders, and held her close.

"Back away!" Gile's voice thundered.

Felicity clung to him.

He led her gently away, and in a few short moments, they were back inside a leather auto. Her hair had fallen out of its bun, scattered around her face and shoulders. Giles tried to treat her nose, but she refused to show her face, just shaking in the seat beside him. Her stomach rose to her throat.

She felt a gentle hand on her shoulder, and she tore away from it.

Memories of hospital ceilings taunted her. A slow methodical beeping ringing in her ear.

Then a tear stained face of a black-eyed boy, who'd crumbled from his feet in defeat in front of her. A wave crashed into her and she gasped for air. She felt like she was drowning.

Before she knew it she was being led up the steps to the golden elevator.

"Liz!" Veronica's blurry face appeared at the base of the steps.

"Don't call me that!" Felicity shouted. "Just stop!"

Veronica stumbled back. "I'm sorry. It-it's just that you promised—"

Felicity's tongue took over before her mind could even rationalize. "I didn't promise anything! I don't want to see you! Get out! *Leave me alone!*"

"Felicity?" A soft feminine voice ran cold shivers down Felicity's spine. An elegant woman with a delicate scarf draped experly over her head and shoulder, her short hair framing her face from underneath, and a shimmering silver dress that dropped to her ankles, and elegant jeweled band around her head, rushed into the room. "Is that you?"

Veronica burst out into tears, and ran into her mother's arms. Felicity looked away, slamming the doors of the elevator shut before Giles could protest. It seemed like an eternity before the opposite door opened, letting her free into the hallway.

Renee looked up from the desk carved out from the wall, startled. She jumped to her feet, reaching out for Felicity. "Miss—"

Felicity shoved her out of the way, running through the parlor, grabbed the golden handles of her room, thrust them open with a bang, and closed them just as quickly. She entered a quick code, the doors locking as soon as Renee came to pull on the handles.

Felicity wanted to sink to the floor and cry, but every other instinct told her to run to the bathroom.

It was a good instinct.

Felicity laid on the floor, having vomited thrice, catching her breaths, her every bone shaking. She shouldn't have eaten.

Her mind was reeling, her body throbbing. How long had she panicked for? She felt sick.

She'd screwed everything up bigger than she could ever have imagined.

Why didn't she just tell Yaeda no, and that she had to leave instead of full on panicking? Giles must have thought her a fool. Just when she thought she was getting the hang of it.

She was nowhere closer to finding the Aguirre chip her friends needed, and was about fifty steps back from proving to her family she was okay.

She *wasn't* the same Felicity from when she left Liberty, but it sure seemed like it.

She sat up, nausea rolling through her. She ignored it, grabbing the edge of the counter, pulling herself up. She met her bloody, tear-stained face, staring at her in the mirror. She glared at it.

And then her pupils thinned upward in a feral fashion.

Felicity's jaw fell, and her legs gave out. She crashed to the floor. Pain swept through her legs. She tore the headband from her head. It was no longer glowing.

Lincoln's machine was dead.

Great.

After what felt like an eternity, she had dragged herself across the floor to her bag sprawled on the floor. She removed the charger, removed the braces, and placed them on top of the station. She transported herself awkwardly across the floor, changed into her appropriate comfortable wear from North Cordell, and only had enough energy to collapse at the base of the sofa in front of the projector.

Curse her huge room.

She pulled the blankets from the sofa, and wrapped herself up, hiding her face in the soft blue fabric. She let herself sob.

Not because she was sad, or because she was angry, but because it felt good.

She wanted to breathe. She wanted a distraction from the cruel purple marks crawling up her legs. She wanted to feel.

Finally, her eyes were sore, and it hurt to blink.

She peered out of her cocoon and breathed. The weight on her chest had lessened. She was okay. She was going to be safe. Giles was here. He could take her back—

She'd yelled at Veronica.

Felicity wanted to slap herself. She'd yelled at her baby sister in front of her mother, no less. Great first impression. What were they going to tell her father?

Guess what, honey? Felicity's still a lunatic.

"But I'm not," she choked. "I'm not a lunatic."

She wanted to go back to North Cordell. There things were stable, Taryn was getting her help, and she seemed to be on a good path, but now?

What did Giles say? *You're the only one holding yourself back. If you say you can't do it, you can't. Don't let a failure that wasn't your fault hold you back.*

She wasn't going to be in a stable environment forever. She needed to stop relying on it. Maybe take people's advice. She wasn't going to squash all the progress she'd made.

Felicity sat up. Her body ached, her face felt raw exposed to the air. She pulled the blanket back to expose her foot. She swallowed hard, seeing the purple skin staring back at her. She let the blanket fall back over it.

Another deep breath.

She grabbed her tele from the table. It flashed the time. 20.00 PM. She cringed. That long?

She deleted the few notifications from Yaeda, hoping to never look back at that name again. She'd yelled at everyone else. What was she even supposed to say once she left the room?

She broke down, and everyone knew it.

She needed their trust to be able to continue her investigation. She needed to talk to someone... *anyone.*

Felicity opened her contacts. She laid back down on the floor, holding a pillow to her chest, and tapped the screen.

There was a pause.

It was nearly 1.00 AM in North Cordell, surely—

"Hey, Felicity?"

Felicity's heart leapt. "Lincoln, you're awake?"

He laughed hoarsely. "What'd you expect?"

She cracked a smile as her heart hurt. She shouldn't be keeping him up. "You need sleep, Linc."

"Well, so do you, but I'm not going to nag you about it." The clanging of metal came from the other side. "You need something? Did your leg braces break?"

"No. They're fine." Felicity sighed. "I—I just needed to talk to someone."

The sound stopped. "Did something happen?"

Felicity swallowed hard. "Yeah."

"Oh."

She waited for him to ask to spill the story, but instead he followed up with: "I'm sorry. Can-can I do anything?"

"No. It's my issue," she said. "I'll figure it out. How's everything going there?"

"It's only been two days. Not much has changed."

It hadn't been longer? "It feels like an eternity."

A moment of silence. "Yeah."

"Do you maybe have any theories where the Aguirres would have hidden the chip?"

A bang of metal. "Not really. I hardly know anything about... them."

Felicity bit her lip. "You did in a way."

"What do you—Oh. She never told me anything." He continued to work quietly.

"Sorry." Felicity said, pulling her pillow closer. Why did she even try to do that?

"It's fine." Another bang. "Liz, do you know what f-i-n-d spells? When I sound it out, it doesn't sound like a word."

"Find?" Felicity said, with a frown.

"Yes!" Lincoln said. "Thanks."

"You learning to read, Linc?"

"It's not going well."

"You're a genius, though."

Lincoln snorted. "I'm not a genius. Just an overthinker with priorities."

"Says the boy who created a Cube that fascinated even Taryn. One that could solve our problems," Felicity laughed. Her chest ached. If only she could…

"You give me too much credit." Another loud bang, and then a crash. Lincoln cursed. "And I broke it anyway."

Felicity sat up so fast, her legs cried out in pain. "You what?!"

"I smashed it." His voice was flat.

"Lincoln!"

"I'm remaking it. Don't worry. You should hear yourself," he said, with a laugh. It was a small, short laugh, but it had a spark. It had a small echo of life, and it set Felicity's nerves at peace.

"Why are you remaking it?"

"Because I got an idea from a bracelet."

A bracelet? That was new. "Where'd you pick this one up?" She smirked.

A small pause. "Felicity, you'd call me crazy."

"It's about … Nik."

"Oh." Felicity didn't press further.

"You don't need to sound sad about it," he said, with another lively laugh. "Felicity, Nik had an idea. I can't tell you now, because that would make you tell me to get help or something."

Felicity chuckled, and shook her head. "Linc, just don't get yourself hurt."

"I'll do anything," Lincoln said.

Of course he'd do anything if that girl was anyway remotely involved.

Felicity yawned, holding the tele close.

"You should get some sleep, Felicity."

Felicity shuddered. "I—I can't sleep."

"Would it help if I stayed up with you? If you start to panic, I'll be right here."

Tears brimmed Felicity's eyes. "R-really?"

"Of course."

"You have to promise to get sleep too, Linc." She commanded the lights to dim.

"I will. Soon, Liz. I just need to finish this."

She didn't believe him. She wouldn't be surprised if he pulled yet another all nighter, but she couldn't stop him. His heart was set on something.

"Tomorrow, I'm going to get closer to the location of that chip," Felicity said, closing her eyes, pulling the thin blanket over her shoulders.

"Well then, sleep. 'Night, Felicity."

For the first time since she arrived in Liberty, she felt like herself. She felt... okay. She wasn't scared. She was determined to muster the confidence she had for a split second today tomorrow. This time... with no messes.

First priority. Veronica.

"Goodnight, Lincoln."

48

LAWRENCE DIDN'T SIGN UP TO ONCE AGAIN BE LECTURED BY A Defender with an ego.

Actually. Correction. He didn't sign up for *any* of this. The sole reason he was here was honor, and the protection of his siblings. Of course he didn't care about what Agent Nigel Lopez was rambling on about.

And he *really* didn't care about Calynda who tried to stand beside him.

She was the one who triggered the alarm, and the reason they were in so much trouble. It had been hours before they were able to get Cole back from the local Defender station, and Agent Lopez had to explain their situation, and Cole still had a penalty on his File.

So yeah. Lawrence was not in the pleasing Calynda mood with any sort of word of comfort.

Instead he couldn't seem to focus on anything but the rhythmic habit of the boy cowering in the shadow of his uncle. While Iracema argued, Matteo sat with his eyes on the floor, his fingers entangled in his sleeve, tugging on it.

For a moment, the kind, upbeat cheerfulness seemed to falter, and something deathly familiar filled the hollow eyes that struck Lawrence. But almost as quickly as it came, Matteo noticed, let go of his sleeve, and slunk out of sight.

"Right, Lorenzo?" Iracema said, turning harshly, her braid whipping around with her harsh jerk of her body.

She shook Lawrence without giving him a moment to speak.

"You saw that—that *malidito* feather!" Iracema said, dancing her hands in the air. "It flew. It lived."

"It didn't seem dangerous," Tabitha said. "I saw—"

"It's dangerous," Nigel said. "It destroyed a building only a few blocks from here. The whole force together literally means 'death wish.' It's searching for the Wingor to kill it no doubt."

"What do you think it's doing?" Tabitha said. "Maybe it can lead us to the Wingor."

Nigel scoffed. "It's a *killer*, Delorous."

Lawrence scoffed. So the big Defender man was scared of flying feathers? What could this *Mors Vis* really do?

"And it's a lead! One far less dangerous. We can take a full force. We're members!" Tabitha boldly stepped forward. "I think we should go back and find it. I read—"

"Delorous, *no*."

"The fate of this stupid world isn't in your hands. It's in ours!" Tabitha clenched her fists, staring up at Nigel, who stood a good foot above her. "Let me talk! It's—"

"You're on thin ice with the Department right now." Nigel growled.

"Well then, screw the Department! They haven't done anything to help us! They didn't help Taryn! They left her alone! To go insane!"

"Delorous, I command—"

"No!" Tabitha shouted. Lawrence jumped.

"Get down from your high and mighty pedestal! Defenders murdered the Curatrix team! They let one of my friends *die!* I'm sick of people dy—"

"Tabitha!"

Tabitha froze.

Lawrence felt nervous. He'd never seen such a dark shadow over Cole's eyes. He was tired, the light in his eyes had dimmed. He was angry.

"Stop," Cole said.

Tabitha glanced around, her pupils trembling.

He rose from his seat, and looked to Nigel. "We'll leave you alone."

"Thank you," Nigel growled. "Take Delorous with you. Williams, I need to speak to you about your experience."

Lawrence groaned internally, but followed Nigel from the room. He caught sight of Matteo. The boy smiled, but Lawrence could see it trembling.

Calynda quickly grabbed Matteo's arm and jerked him upward, and the door slammed shut in Lawrence's face.

"What were you thinking?" Cole said, leading Tabitha out into the cobblestone courtyard tucked away in the Lopez's private quarters, cut off from the casino.

That meant it was empty. Cole's voice echoed. And Tabitha had never seen him so angry, but she shouldn't be surprised. She'd seen the unease ever since the crash.

"Why do you let him boss you around?" Tabitha yelled back, stalking away to the opposite side of the fountain. Why wouldn't he listen? She needed to tell him about the tapestry. "I found something in there that could change this whole situation!"

"Agent Lopez's trying to do the right thing."

Tabitha wanted to punch something, but settled for kicking the fountain. Why was he so easy to follow? "Yeah, well. It's not working!"

"He's trying to keep us safe, Tabitha," Cole growled. "I'm trying to keep you safe."

"I don't need your darn protection!" Tabitha's face flamed. Why wasn't he listening to her? "Stop controlling me!"

"I'm not controlling you!"

"Yes, you are! I'm capable of doing things on my own!"

"How could you be so blind to your own ignorance?"

Tabitha snorted, whirling around to face him across the fountain. "Me? Ignorant? Look who's talking!"

"You're too impulsive!"

"You're too freaking cautious!"

"This isn't a game, Tabitha." His volume lowered. He

walked across the fountain to meet her, but she refused to look at him. "People die."

Tears boiled at the brim of her eyes. She knew that. Her mind reminded her all the time. That tiny... blue... face... "Well, maybe that's the cost! What are you so darn afraid of?"

"You don't even hear yourself."

She whirled around. "I do! And you call me impulsive, but that's coming from the boy who can't even stop his own brother from going crazy!"

As soon as words left her mouth, she regretted them. She didn't mean them. No no no.

Cole's face hardened. Any mercy he'd had in his features had vanished. "People are going to get killed, Tabitha Delorous. And you won't even care. Apparently, you still haven't learned anything!"

Tears streamed down her face, but she refused to back down from his eyes. "And apparently, neither have you!"

"Taryn should've never let you come. You should go home, back to Liberty." She could see the glass of his eyes reflecting back at her, but anger burned too painfully in her chest to care. He knew she hated Liberty. He knew how she was treated. She had trusted him with that.

"Why are you doing this?" she stammered, her voice cracking, clenching her jaw holding back the dam. *You should go back home to Liberty.*

She needed to fix her mistakes. She couldn't let someone die because of her foolishness.

No matter what he said.

He hesitated for a moment, his face softening, before hardening again. He turned and walked away, slamming the door hard.

Tabitha turned and ran. Her tears were furious. Everything in her mind was confused. She thought she could trust Cole.

She trusted him more than anyone in the world, but suddenly he turned on her like this? Why did his words matter more than anyone's ever had? Why did it make her want to punch him?

She ran up the wooden spiral steps, choking on her tears. Maybe it was better that way, to keep Cole out of this anyway.

She didn't want to risk him dying. Life was so delicate. Death was so real.

She burst through the door up into the living room.

"You okay?" One of the younger Lopez sisters Tabitha didn't know of looked up from the counter.

At the counter, a large array of fabrics, feathers, and sequins were spread out. Another little girl sat beside her. Maybe eight or nine year old. Her hair was done up in curls, and she stood atop a stool.

Matteo sat crossed-legged on the counter, fidgeting with a hem of a skirt, a needle between his teeth.

"I'm fine," Tabitha said, scrubbing away at the wet on her cheek.

Matteo took the needle from his mouth, his large dark eyes shifting to her, wide with compassion. "Do you want me to get someone?"

Tabitha forced a smile. "I'm fine."

Matteo narrowed his eyes, but didn't push her further.

"Do you know where Lawrence is by chance?" Tabitha said, trying to act casual as she headed to the counter with them. She crossed her arms, hoping to hide the shaking of her body. Thoughts ran in the back of her head: *Cole's mad at you. Cole thinks you're impulsive and stupid. Cole is—*

"Is that the one with the glasses on his face, 'Teo?" the youngest girl whispered to Matteo. Her eyes were glued to her brother's lap, not daring to look to Tabitha.

Matteo nodded.

"Cielo wouldn't know where he is," the other said, jumping down from her stool. "Iracema said that *tío* was asking him stuff."

Right. Agent Lopez did seem keen on Lawrence. And that also meant that *tío* meant uncle. Her muddled mind found some clarity to latch onto there.

"You are crying," the girl insisted.

"Jadie," the youngest, Cielo, whispered, her tone worried, glancing quickly to Tabitha then away.

Jadie shrugged. "Do you want a tissue?"

"I'm okay," Tabitha said, trying to force a smile. Her eyes watered. *QUIT THAT!* "I just need to find Lawrence."

Jadie nodded affirmatively, crossing her arms. "*Estupido,*

'Teo, might know."

Matteo shook his head. "I don't. I'm sorry."

"It's alright." But it wasn't. She needed to talk to Lawrence before Cole tried to stop her. As much as her blood boiled at the thought of Cole's face, she knew she couldn't defy him face to face when she knew he was right.

She was impulsive.

But doing the right thing wasn't getting them anywhere. People would die if they didn't find the Council Member.

Jadie got her a glass of water, which Tabitha drank, only to show the girl that her hands were in fact not shaking, though everything on the inside was trembling.

She watched Matteo expertly mend the hem of a shimmering blue skirt of Cielo's, seeming to block out the rest of the world, besides a few raised brows at Jadie who rambled to him in words that Tabitha didn't understand. Cielo hid behind her brother, besides trying to steal a few nervous glances to Tabitha.

Tabitha didn't have time to sit around. The Oquelites could attack any day now... or maybe they wouldn't at all. But they would. She needed to do *something*.

How could Cole be such a fool to ignore the signs?

The creaking of the steps sent her to her feet. She bit back a cry of relief seeing Lawrence trudge down the steps.

Instead she ran to him and grabbed him by the shoulders, which caused him to freeze and stare at her, horrified. At least she had his attention.

"Lawrence, we *have* to get back to the exhibit house and track down that feather! It's our only chance to find the Member! We're running out of time! It has to be a sign which means—"

Lawrence pushed Tabitha away from him, waving his hands in the air. "Whoa. Whoa. Hold up. You want to *break* into the exhibit house?"

"Yes!"

The room dropped silent. Tabitha cursed internally, slowly turning her head to their audience. Cielo and Jadie stared at them with blank stares. At least Matteo continued on like he didn't care.

"We don't have much time," Tabitha said, ignoring their burning stares. "If the feathers are here, a Council Member has to be. You saw what happened when *they* found a Council Member... when they found you."

Lawrence's face hardened. "You're trying to pull at my emotions."

"Well, duh!" Tabitha brushed her hair out of her face, tugging on the ends. "This should be emotional."

"Calm down. Something happened." Lawrence's brows knit together, his dark eyes studying her through the thick lenses.

Tabitha laughed nervously. "I can't go through that again, Lawrence. We need to find the member. And that's our only lead."

She heard Jadie whisper: "'Teo, I think she's going crazy."

Tabitha clenched her fists, keeping herself from turning and lashing out at the child.

"Tabitha, that's insane," Lawrence said. "Way too impulsive."

There was that darn word again. *Impulsive.*

"You too?" Now she was really feeling like punching someone.

Lawrence grabbed her wrist, and before she could lash out, pulled her up the stairs as she struggled to keep up after him. She had to admit. She was impressed by his grip.

But that didn't mean the first thing she tried to do when he let go in the middle of the upstairs hallway was slap him. He dodged it effortlessly.

"I'll do it."

She froze. He what?

"I'll do it," he repeated. "I'll go into the exhibit house with you."

"But you just—"

"Well, I didn't want them telling anyone."

Oh. Right. Tabitha's adrenaline suddenly drained. How could she have been so stupid? She unclenched her sweaty fists and took a deep breath, looking to Lawrence in the dark hall. "Thank you. But why? You don't have to."

"Because—" Lawrence paused "—I think I know who the member is."

Tabitha's heart dropped with her jaw. "*What?* Who?"

"I can't say."

Oh, come on. "Sure you can. It's just me."

Lawrence closed his eyes and shook his head. "We just need to get that feather."

Tabitha tried to not sound annoyed when he agreed. Why wouldn't he tell her?

"What suddenly makes you trusting of the *Mors Vis?*" Lawrence asked, with a frown.

"It's not *Mors Vis.* Nigel got it wrong," Tabitha said, balling her fists. If only Calynda hadn't set off the stupid alarm, and someone would have listened to her, maybe she could've shown them. "It's *Cors Vis.*"

Lawrence raised an eyebrow. "And?"

"*Mors Vis* means death wish, and *Cors Vis* means core force. Lawrence, the *Cors Vis* is supposed to help the Wingor. They're an artifact," Tabitha said, beginning to pace. Cole really hadn't been paying attention to the tapestry, hadn't he? "Without it, I don't think the Wingor can manifest its wings. That had to be why they are *feathers.*"

"Why don't you think they can?" Lawrence didn't look convinced.

He had a point, but the tapestry couldn't lie. Her dreams couldn't lie. "I—I think it might be because the Wingor's power is *all* in their 'wings.' Unlike you, who can slowly grow into using your abilities, the Wingor gets it all at once." Tabitha's eyes widened. "So something would *have* to help the Wingor control that."

Lawrence stood straighter. "So like Member training wheels?"

"Exactly!" It all made so much sense. Lawrence might know the Council Member, Tabitha knew the *Cors Vis*, and they had the combined efforts of being Council Members to their advantage.

"Well, when do we go?"

"How does tonight sound?" she asked.

"Great." He nodded, turning on his heel. "I'll meet you at 22.00 PM."

"Fantastic," Tabitha sighed. "Oh! And avoid Cole!"

Lawrence stopped, looked over his shoulder, and raised a brow. "Alright then."

Tabitha rolled her eyes, turned, and left, deciding against going back after Lawrence downstairs. She turned the corner of the hall, slipping into Calynda's room, closing the door behind her, and sank down into her mattress on the floor.

Lawrence thought he knew who the member was. Who? They hadn't been there long. There weren't too many options.

She turned on her back, staring up at the popcorn ceiling.

Who had really stuck out? Someone who had potential. Someone whose voice was brash and fought against. Agent Lopez was protective of all his nieces and nephews, but there was one he seemed to always be fighting. One with an ambition that was beyond their reach.

Tabitha sat up.

That couldn't be right... but there was no other option.

Could the Council member be Iracema?

PART FOUR

THE CODE

49

FELICITY CAME TO THE CONCLUSION THAT VERONICA HAD been wrong about one thing: Felicity was horrible at art.

At least now.

She sat on the floor, her braces still charging beside her, dressed in leggings and a sweatshirt that she'd packed from North Cordell, fidgeting with the paintbrush in her hand, and the spear on her lap.

The bright yellow and purple lines wrapping around the end of the shaft were shaky... and all over Felicity's hands.

She vaguely remembered the days where she could just plop down on a seat after a long school day and whip up a portrait. She'd really neglected the hobby since North Cordell.

Not that painting was going to save the world anytime soon.

Four my friend. Two too much. Seven Eleven. Three we Two do. She hummed under her breath. Saving the world felt far too great a task to even think about.

Painting was just a distraction, but she needed one of

those right now.

"Felicity Alexandria, open this door." Renee's stern voice carried volume that should've sent a shiver down Felicity's spine, but she was too tired to care.

She simply dipped the brush into the white, and attempted to fix the lines in her design.

"I will override the lock in thirty seconds if you don't open the door, Miss Bentsworth."

That got Felicity's attention.

Renee was not one to lie for a simple intimidation.

And Felicity had a full on spear in her lap, and paint all around her. Great. She grabbed the spear with her paint stained hands, thrust it under the bed, and pulled the ends of her legging down over her bruised ankles... but her feet. They were purple.

"Fifteen... fourteen."

"Give me more time!" Felicity cried. She pushed the paints out of the way. She laid down on the floor, and pushed herself to roll over to her bag. She unzipped it.

"One! I'm coming in."

Felicity grabbed a pair of mismatched socks.

The double door opened with a beep and the female butler, whose face usually carried an indifferent disposition, looked the slightest hint angry.

Felicity swallowed, hiding one foot under her bag, and pulled on a sock over the other. "H-hey Renee."

"It's 9.30 AM, Miss Bentsworth."

Did she have plans? She would've thought that no one was really seeking her after her episode yesterday. "Yeah?"

"You've delayed your family's breakfast."

"Ah, yes," Felicity said. "The all important breakfast. The Renee Kitts I knew must have changed a lot to be concerned about breakfast."

"I am also concerned about your well being, Miss Bentsworth," Renee said, with an annoyed snort. "Like your bruised foot."

Felicity winced. "W-what bruised foot?"

"Remove the bag."

"Oh Ren—"

"Felicity Bentsworth." Renee stormed over to Felicity, and Felicity kicked the bag aside before Renee could do it herself.

"I—er—hurt it. In North Cordell." Felicity said, quickly, praying Renee wouldn't take another step forward.

"And Miss Delorous wasn't able to stop you?" Renee's eyes widened.

"Tabitha wasn't my bodyguard," Felicity said. Great. Now she had gotten her friend in trouble with the most intimidating staff member of the Bentsworth manor, but also Felicity's favorite, and her cheeks burned with shame at the idea of lying to her.

But to Renee, it probably looked like she was embarrassed at being hurt... hopefully.

"Stand up."

Felicity opened her mouth to protest, but Renee held up her hand. "Really, Miss Bentsworth. You ought to realize the fact you ever tried to argue that is considered a concern."

Felicity forced a smile, and laughed. "I was just gonna kid you, Renee."

Renne raised an eyebrow. "Jokes never tended to be your thing, Ms. Bentsworth, and from that remark, you're still quite terrible at them."

Felicity's face fell and rolled her eyes. "Alright, Renee."

"Stand," Renee growled, balling her fists, a hand hovering above the Comm in her belt.

Felicity's heart skipped a beat. "Okay! I will!"

But could she?

She grabbed the blanket in her bed, thanking whatever power lived in the heavens that the house servers had tucked it in so securely. She pulled herself up, applying pressure to her foot. Pain crept up her femur.

Come on, Liz. Come on.

She pushed her leg up straight. Pain roared, shooting up her spine. Her stomach revolted, bile crawling up her throat. She placed her second foot down firmly. Her body swayed, but she plastered a painful smile on her lips, ignoring the sting in her eyes.

She let go of the blanket, her palms sweating. White flashed across her vision. "See?" she croaked.

"Alright then—"

Felicity didn't even wait for Renee to finish before collapsing on the bed. Renee froze.

Felicity burst out laughing. "I'm fine!"

Renee cleared her throat. "I'll be requesting your presence outside your door in five minutes to escort you to breakfast."

What? "Five minutes?" Felicity gaped at Renee.

Renee didn't respond, flying to the door, closing it behind her.

When Renee said five minutes, she meant it. And that meant Felicity had to face her family.

She swallowed hard.

In ten minutes, after Felicity had struggled her way out the door, adjusting her headband and the braces under her baggy pants, they arrived promptly at the glass spiral steps leading to the dining room. Well, a room didn't quite cover it. It was a suspended platform over the family common area, directly below the garden dome, meaning it was adorned in the beauty of natural light.

Felicity heard a cheerful, high-pitched feminine laugh as she ascended the steps after Renee.

The table rose into her view, as she stepped off onto the platform, raising her eyes to meet the suddenly quiet faces staring at her.

"Oh dear, Alla, you look dreadful." A woman sat on the right side of the table, with a signature Liberty bob and closely cropped brown curls, which were plastered with gel to immaculately frame her heart shaped face. Her eyes were a bright hazel, and her face brushed with freckles. She wore a stylish loose red blouse, a short skirt, and a pearled hat.

"My name is Felicity, Olivia," Felicity growled, plopping in the seat farthest away from any of the members of the table.

"It's Auntie Liv to you, Alla," Olivia Bentsworth said with a chortle.

Felicity glanced to Renee. Renee only smirked as if to say, "Hey. Your problem, not mine," and promptly left down the stairs.

"Now, when are you getting Alla a haircut, Hannah?"

Felicity could hardly face her mother, who sat the closest opposite Felicity. The temptation was too strong for Felicity not to steal the tiniest glance of her. The woman sat straight, her eyes on Olivia with a stern look of annoyance. A beige scarf was secured over her head, covering the sides of her face, her neck, and draped over her shoulders; her short strawberry-blonde hair hung free in the back. She wore a long sleeved blouse with buttoned sleeves, and Felicity had no doubt her skirt was long as well.

At least her mother hadn't changed much. And apparently neither had her relationship with Olivia.

"The hair is fine," Hannah Bentsworth said, her voice gentle, yet stern as she took a small sip from her steaming cup.

Olivia scoffed. "Alla, you will be changing. There is no way that the press can see you like this."

Felicity almost smiled seeing her mother silently fume over her plate at Olivia's remarks. Never had her aunt and mother gotten along. Olivia had always told Felicity that her mother was far too conservative and shameful to the public eye.

Felicity never saw what Olivia found wrong with her mother's dress, though she'd never asked either.

Felicity spotted Veronica staring quietly at her untouched plate in front of her.

Guilt struck her gut.

"How was the lower region, Alla?" Olivia said. She picked up a bell from the center plate and rang it, quickly motioning to Felicity that the question was purely to fill the space.

"I loved it," Felicity said, raising her voice. She held herself back from snapping about the whole "Alla" thing. Alexandria was her middle name, and Olivia's preference.

Olivia laughed. "But you are glad to be back, aren't you, Alla? Whose idea was it to send her? Mine? I do think so, right Hannah?"

Felicity's mother took a reserved breath. "The doctor's, Olivia."

"I'm sure I had some influence. I knew a trip away would make you all better." A server came quickly up the steps, taking Olivia's attention away before Felicity accidentally said something out of place.

Right. All it took to "fix" her was a trip. She scoffed under breath.

"It didn't work, did it?"

Felicity jumped, realizing the gentle voice came from her mother, whose curious green eyes stared into Felicity's soul.

"I-it was good."

Hannah sighed. "I saw your display yesterday, Felicity."

"It was an accident," Felicity said, her voice hardly a whisper.

Her mother shook her head in defeat.

Tears pricked Felicity's eyes. She had a million words swimming in her mind. But which were the right ones? What was she supposed to say? *Mom, I'm actually fine. Please, Mom. It's not that simple.*

Olivia leaned back in her seat. "Where were we?"

"You were telling us about Felicity's arranged courtship!" Veronica said.

Felicity's heart stopped. "What?"

Veronica burst out laughing.

Olivia looked, stunned, between Veronica and Felicity. "Oh," she said, her face softening. "That was a joke, I see."

Veronica sent Felicity a goofy grin, and Felicity held back a glare.

At least this made her job a little easier.

Someone tapped her shoulder. Felicity jumped, whirling around to see a suited waiter behind her. "Food, miss?"

Her mind flashed back to the hours of vomiting the night before, and had to force a smile and politely decline.

So far the breakfast was a trash fire. And Felicity needed to heal some relationships, not tear them apart, if she wanted a second chance at finding the chip.

That meant doing something she *desperately* didn't want to do, but if she did it now, her mother would see, and she could score two in one.

"Hey Veronica," Felicity said. She kept her voice level and loud.

Her younger sister perked up at the mention of the name.

"Are you free in an hour?" She asked, forcing as much emotion into every word as the lump in her throat would allow. She could feel Olivia and her mother's stares burning into her. Keep your cool, Liz. Keep your cool.

Veronica's face lit up, and she jumped out her chair, her

short curls bouncing. "Yes! Really?"

"Veronica," Olivia said. "Sit down!"

Veronica plopped down in her seat, and a server pushed her back in. Felicity saw the smile still plastered to her lips. "My room. One hour."

Felicity smiled, but her chest ached. How could her little sister be so forgiving after all the horrible things Felicity had said yesterday?

"Where is that little friend of yours?" Olivia asked, her voice lowering to a whisper. "The third born."

"Tabitha is doing well actually," Felicity said, sitting straight, tucking a frizzy piece of hair behind her ear. "They don't have that ridiculous social expectation in most regions."

"Of course," Olivia laughed. "I've heard rumors of as many as nine children. Can you believe that, Veronica?"

"No, auntie." Veronica obediently agreed. She poked at an egg on her plate, seeming anxious to leave. "May I be excused?"

"No, Veronica." Olivia turned back to Felicity. "Perhaps it's best for your little friend there. I never liked her influence on you much, though she did seem to calm your tantrums." Tantrums? Felicity grit her teeth, and nodded.

"It would be better if she didn't return," Olivia said. "Her poor parents would be blessed. Settle down on a farm, and do what... farmer's wives do."

"Auntie, can I be excused?" Veronica said again, stabbing her fork through her food.

"You can go," her mother said.

"Thank you, Mum." Veronica leapt from her seat and ran down the stairs before Olivia could call out after her.

Felicity took that as her cue to stand up. "It was an honor speaking with you, Olivia."

Olivia puffed her chest out in pride at the statement. "As with you, Alla."

Felicity turned and walked to the stairs, and paused stepping down the first step. She looked over her shoulder to her mother, who was watching her.

She opened her mouth, but no words came out.

Her mother simply just nodded, and Felicity nodded back.

It wasn't much, but it was something. Felicity would prove herself to her mother soon.

Just wait, Mom. I'm doing something you're going to be proud of. I promise.

"What was that yesterday?"

"It's called a panic attack. Can you zip this up?"

Felicity held her hair up from her back.

Giles sighed, zipping up the back of her blouse. "How weird is Liberty? You all get dressed up to see your sister who lives in your house?"

"I wasn't going to wear sweats and look like I just woke up." Felicity grabbed a gravity band, and bound her hair up in a ponytail. "Besides, if I can get on Veronica's good side, she can get me back on my parents' good side and then maybe I can learn something from them."

Giles sighed, shaking his head. "Sounds a bit far-fetched to me, Bentsworth. And how do you know you're not going to have another attack?"

"Like you said—" Felicity checked herself in the mirror, before turning around to Giles. "—It's just my sister who lives in my house. How do I look?"

"I dunno. Fine?" Giles frowned.

Felicity let out an exasperated sigh. "You're pointless."

"Fine then. You look like you got two hours of sleep maximum, you have rumply legs due to your braces, and oh, your eyes are still swollen."

"Hey!"

"What?"

Felicity rolled her eyes. "It shouldn't be too long."

"I'll be downstairs," Giles sighed. "Please message me if something goes haywire, and do *not* go screaming my name in public."

Felicity's face burned. "Sorry."

"Most anyone's talked about Armstance Giles since I passed the Trial," Giles snorted.

Felicity and Giles left her room, heading down the empty hall of her corridor to the elevator.

"You know," Felicity said, as they stepped inside the golden cage. "I've never heard anyone call you Armstance."

"Well, yeah. That's cause you've only ever known me on

a job." He paused. "Well, I guess that's all I ever do."

"Armstance is a funny name anyway. Giles suits you."

Giles elbowed her. "Well, my trial team mates would only ever call me 'Army,' so maybe you're onto the funny name thing. And no, you *cannot* call me that and that will be all the personal information you'll be getting."

The elevator came to a stop, greeted with a hall strung with purple fairy lights.

"We've arrived at your sister's corridor," Giles said. He held the door open for her. Felicity stepped out, and Giles back in.

He pressed the button and saluted her. "Message me."

"I will," she said, waving. "Bye, Army."

"Shut up, *Liz*."

She stuck her tongue out at him, and he gave her a rude hand gesture that caused her to snort as he disappeared. Who knew she would end up enjoying time with Giles?

"Liz, is that you?" At the end of the hall stood Veronica.

Felicity was taken aback by her sister's startling appearance. She wore jeans and an oversized T-shirt with a new media film series logo printed on it. She wore purple socks, and her '53' necklace around her neck, her red hair up in a tiny ponytail.

Felicity suddenly felt overdressed. "Yeah-yeah. It's me."

She walked out of the hall and into the light of the parlor room of Veronica's corridor, which was built in a similar fashion to Felicity's with huge windows, a wide marble space, and tall ceilings, but with more purple than Felicity even could think existed.

Levitating lampshades were decorated in glass purple shards. Couches and bean bags scattered amongst the red and blue flowers vines were also a deep violet, and practically anything Felicity couldn't think of.

Veronica plopped down in a beanbag by the window, offering Felicity one directly beside it. A plate of fruit and carbonated beverage cans were set out.

She'd been preparing.

Felicity held back a smile.

She sat down beside Veronica, looking past her out the window, in the Liberty noon skyline, full of glittering buildings and the artificial blue sky of the dome.

"I'm surprised you're not mad at me," Veronica said.

Felicity jerked her head to her sister. Veronica sat criss-cross in her seat, her hands clasped together, her eyes glued on them.

"I'm surprised you're not mad at *me*."

"I could never be mad at you," Veronica huffed. "I mean, I was a little bit. Auntie said that if I was really nice to you, that would make you not … freak out." Veronica looked up.

Felicity stumbled over her words. "I—I didn't mean to. Olivia doesn't know anything, Veronica."

"She does," Veronica said defiantly. Then her shoulders slumped. "Except about you, I guess."

"I have a... disorder of sorts," Felicity said, feeling suddenly embarrassed as heat flooded her cheeks. "But I'm working on getting better."

"Good," Veronica said. "I missed the old you."

"Onica, I don't think the 'old me' can ever come back."

Veronica looked away, and out the window. "Oh. Right. Because of the crash."

Felicity wanted to explain it was more complicated than that, but all she could manage was a nod.

"The crash ruined everything, Liz," Veronica said, quietly. "First it was you, and your freak outs—" Felicity cringed. "—and having to watch Renee try to calm you down, and hear Auntie say you had gone mental. Then, I lost my sister to a SpeedRail to North Cordell. And then the media goes crazy."

The childish, bubbly Veronica had melted away before Felicity's eyes. Maturity filled every pain stricken word as Veronica held her knees close to her chest and hid her face. "I'm sorry."

"Veronica, you-you have nothing to be sorry for." Felicity hesitated, then reached out a hand to her sister's shoulder.

"You've changed," Veronica coughed. "So much."

"Onica, please don't cry. I'm still Felicity."

"Then prove it," Veronica looked up, with watery eyes and a smile.

How in the world could she smile through the pain so flawlessly?

Veronica wiped a tear, and grasped Felicity's hand from her shoulder. "Let's play a game."

Felicity frowned. "A-a game?"

"Three questions. We both get three questions, and we have to answer in total truth."

Felicity sighed. "Alright."

"You first!" Veronica said, jumping up from her seat, and leaping on top of her coffee table. Through a command on her tele, she turned on music that Felicity didn't recognize.

"Alright then," Felicity bit her lip. "What's your favorite color?"

Veronica frowned. "Really?" She groaned, gesturing to the room around them. "You're going to throw away your first question on that?"

Felicity laughed. "Yes. Now tell me."

Veronica rolled her eyes. "Purple."

Felicity gasped dramatically. "That's incredible."

Veronica snorted a laugh. "You're *hilarious*."

"Well," Felicity said, leaning back in her seat. "It's your turn."

Veronica jumped down from the table. "What's *your* favorite color, Liz?"

"Red," Felicity said simply.

Veronica grinned. "So not everything has changed."

She took a seat beside Felicity and grabbed an apple. "Alright, your turn."

Felicity looked around the room. The walls were decorated in holo-posters of the latest MEDIA films, all starring "Viv," the breakout star and performer that had been the greatest hit since Felicity could remember.

There was a desk buried in canvases and styluses, and a cleaning bot charging beneath a shelf that held school tablets.

Felicity turned back to Veronica, who was fidgeting with her "53" necklace.

"What does the 53 stand for? A Viv thing?" Felicity asked.

Veronica's face brightened, clasping her hand over it. "53 stands for this brand new Media conspiracy."

"A conspiracy?" When had Veronica been into that?

Her sister smirked. "Six months ago in Imperial, after the attacks, a search warrant leaked through the web linked to the MEDIA management looking for someone... or something specified as '53.' They took down the evidence after it got public traction, but I being myself had access to download the files to my own server."

Felicity blinked. "You what—"

"Look, Liz," Veronica said, getting to her feet. "It's kinda huge. There's a huge net community online trying to figure out what '53' means, thanks to Bentsworth tech."

"Thanks to you," Felicity said, getting up after Veronica, who waltzed proudly to a dark purple closet door.

Veronica shrugged. "I'm just doing what intrigues me. And this really does."

She entered a code into the handle and the door opened. The door burst open, revealing a... closet. Veronica had gutted the place out of clothes, and replaced it with full on hologram projectors, key boards, and Scrolls, and holograms displaying documents and images, all bursting to life around them.

"How do you mention this so casually?" Felicity gasped, twirling around to grab her sister by the shoulders. "Veronica, this is amazing. You're in charge of an operation."

Veronica blushed, wiggling out of Felicity's hold. "Hardly an operation."

"So what have you found out?"

Veronica pulled out a metal board with glowing keys from a drawer, a hologram screen bursting to life. "That 53 is connected to the Curatrix team."

Felicity's heart did a backflip. "Did-did you just say the Curatrix team?"

Veronica turned with a prideful grin and nodded. "Yeah, I did."

Veronica had insider info on the infamous Curatrix team. Felicity couldn't even think of the right word, just stared dumbly at Veronica.

Veronica blushed. "And not just the Curatrix team, specifically the Aguirres, Reyna and Lyell."

Now, Felicity's head began to spin. This couldn't be happening. The Aguirres. "How so?" she stammered out, moving to Veronica's side, hiding her shaking hands in her pockets.

Veronica drew up a file on her screen. It was a public Defending Department file, and the site views towered at a hefty 985 million. That was no surprise considering it was titled "AGENT REYNA WENTS AGUIRRE."

Felicity's eyes grew misty seeing the photo of the dead woman. The date labeled it only fourteen years ago. She was young, full of life. She stood tall, defining her toned physique, with a mischievous smirk, her long dark hair drawn up, her skin a light brown without a single blemish. Her eyes were the only thing that threw it off. They were a dark violet, and looked ancient, full of unknown pain Felicity was only beginning to know.

And she looked so much like her daughter.

Don't cry, Felicity scolded herself, quickly dabbing the tears from her eye with her sleeve.

"Reyna's Defender Identification was 350," Veronica said. "Switched around is 053."

"Isn't that a bit far fetched?" Felicity said, clearing her throat.

"Yeah, it seems that way," Veronica laughed. "But we were able to track the call to action to a research organization searching for a cure of 'Bunker Syndrome,' a genetic disorder passed from the nuclear waste of the EarthShaker, from which Reyna suffered."

"Okay, so they were looking for a cure?" Felicity couldn't see how this all clicked together.

"Which led us to be linked through that organization to DNA harvesting," Veronica brought up an encrypted document. "And everyone knows Lyell Aguirre was into DNA technology."

Taryn had mentioned it, hence the DNA lock on the initial machine core. Felicity's heart began to race. Was this really happening? "So you think 53 is linked to the Aguirre's technology?"

"Exactly!" Veronica said. "Maybe they've left more than we thought, Liz. Maybe the Curatrix team isn't done changing the world just yet."

If only she knew... "And is there anywhere that the Aguirre tech is being held?" Felicity asked, trying to seem casual about it, and not show the sweat trickling down her face, and the nervous growl of her sick stomach.

"Plenty of it. They left it everywhere they did missions. Only problem is, we don't know how to enter most of it,"

Veronica sighed. "Dad caught a piece a few years ago."

"*Dad?!*" Felicity choked out her spit. "Here?"

Veronica frowned. "Yeah?"

"There's a piece of Aguirre tech here in the Bentsworth Manor."

Veronica shrugged. "Only one in Liberty."

No. Freaking. Way. "Where is it? Can I see it?"

"In his private office bridge. We're not allowed to go there, remember, Liz?" Veronica arched a brow. "I want to see it too, you know. It could confirm some of our 53 research."

Gordon Bentsworth's bridge was the most guarded place in probably all of Liberty, and Felicity had only been there once when she was seven years old for her birthday when her father wanted to show her the view. She'd always dreamed of painting the glittering landscape of the perfect world of Liberty, but she never did her memories justice.

But she had to get back in there. It was her only chance. She felt queasy at the idea. Break into her Dad's office?

She just needed some of Nik's DNA, which she had, and she would have the chip. The chip was in Liberty and this was it.

Felicity didn't need to pretend too hard to look disappointed. She shrugged. "Ah well," she said. "I guess it's for the best."

"The mystery of 53 isn't over yet," Veronica said, closing the drawer, the lights shutting off, the holograms disappearing with them. "I'm going to be a journalist like Mom. This could be my big hit."

The sisters got up and left the closet. Veronica locked it behind them.

"I thought you wanted to be an artist?" Felicity said.

"Why not both?" Veronica plopped down on her bean bag, sipping on her pink sparkling drink like she hadn't just revealed the information that could save the lives of millions.

Guilt hit Felicity in a heat wave. She'd been so wrapped up in her mind and being anxious over how much her family would reject her, she had actually been the one to reject Veronica. She'd underestimated her, thought she acted too childish, when in reality, Veronica Bentsworth had loved her all along.

And not to mention a casual detective on the side.

"You good, Liz?" Veronica said. "You're all red."

Felicity laughed. "I love you, Onica."

"Wow," Veronica said. "I didn't know the key to your heart was the Aguirres."

Felicity rolled her eyes, sitting back down beside her. She couldn't stop smiling, her hands shaking. But it was okay. If she started crying, they would be at least tears of relief and joy. "Second question?"

Veronica chewed on her straw for a moment, before her eyes shimmered, and a smirk lined her lips. "Tell me about your friends."

"My what? Like Yaeda?"

Veronica rolled her eyes. "Like the ones you have in North Cordell. We all saw the projections in Imperial."

"Oh," Felicity said. Her sister had given her more than Felicity could even ask for. The least she could do was share something about her friends in North Cordell. She put on a painful smile, got to her feet, pushed Veronica aside, and squished herself into a seat beside her and took out her tele.

"How about I show you?"

Veronica's lips parted in surprise, and then it melted into a smile. She curled up by Felicity's side, completely engrossed in the images on Felicity's tele. At first, Felicity hated it. She was sure any moment she would crack, but she found herself growing... lighter. Every photo had a story, and one that brought a laugh to Veronica and a smile to Felicity's lips.

A photo of Tabitha's messy bedroom, Tabitha and Cole drenched in mud after an incident in a creek, Ray hanging dangerously from the frame on the Inn while shouting it was fine since he could teleport.

And then there were photos of Nikki, which tore into Felicity like fresh wounds she couldn't bandage up.

It was rare the girl even allowed a camera on her, but one in particular had been taken when she fell asleep against Lincoln's shoulder as he was engrossed in their plans for the Inn.

Felicity's eyes pricked with hot tears.

She needed to get that chip. For them.

Felicity found herself explaining the entire ordeal ever

since Tabitha dragged her into the woods that one fateful afternoon, leaving out too much of the violence and the one event that still haunted her. She was sure a few loose tears had broken, but she hardly cared. She could breathe with every word, like weights were lifted from her chest. That pain she'd been harboring and hiding came all crashing out to Veronica, who sat with wide eyes and a pillow clutched to her chest, hanging on every word.

When Felicity finished, there was a moment of silence between them.

"I want to go back with you," Veronica said.

Felicity dried her damp cheeks. "You can't, Onica. You have to stay here."

"You get to go on huge adventures, and change the world. I just sit here," Veronica sighed. Her tele went off and she picked it up with a small smile, and then set it down.

"You're working on that huge 53 project of yours," Felicity said. "I imagine you could change something with that."

Veronica sighed, resting her chin on the palm of her hand. "I guess, but you have to admit, you're way cooler."

Felicity laughed. "Not at all, Onica. I'm the most boring out of all of them, trust me."

"Maybe that's because you haven't figured yourself out yet, Liz." Veronica shrugged. "Maybe you're waiting for someone else to do it, when really you're the only person who can find it."

"Real intelligent words for a 14-year-old."

"I do my best," Veronica said. She sat up. "So, your question, and I know there's *one* that you're dying to know the answer to. Don't deny it, Liz."

Veronica lifted a brow, with a big smirk, glancing around the room, then back to Felicity.

Felicity laughed shallowly. She closed her eyes and massaged her temples. She knew her sister was right. Her fear always held her back from asking and reaching out. The possibility of a bad answer was in itself too horrifying for her to handle. But she had to know.

She opened her eyes. "How-how's Falcon?"

"Why don't you ask me yourself?"

Felicity nearly screamed, whirling around. There stood a

tall, broad boy, hands in his pocket, a small, kind smile on his lips. She didn't waste a moment, jumping from her seat, and launched herself on him, tackling him with a hug, knocking him off his feet.

He laughed, hugging her back.

He was stronger than she remembered. No longer the feeble boy with wire glasses. She hugged him tighter. "You're okay! Falcon, you're okay." She let him go and looked down at his face.

Four years had done wonders to her friend, his light red-blond hair had lost its curl, and his freckles had become more ferocious. His jaw was sharp and formed, and his green eyes were bright, and fixed.

Then her eyes caught the light scars along his neck.

He sat up, pushing her off him, pulling her into a reassuring side hug. "I'm okay, Felicity. I'm okay."

Her eyes were tearing up. "I thought you were gone. Falcon, I—"

"It's okay, Felicity," he said, laughing. "Look. There's nothing even left. They fixed me up real good. Almost too good. I don't need glasses, and it's just a few scars."

"A few scars?"

His face darkened for a moment. "Some mental, some physical, but alive."

"I just can't—" Felicity hugged him again, tempted to sob, but held her back. He held her trembling body. He was alive. He'd survived the crash. They'd both survived the crash.

Someone who knew what tormented her every waking hour.

"You two are adorable," Veronica yawned. "You're welcome, Liz."

Felicity looked up to Falcon. "You planned this?"

"I came yesterday to surprise you, but apparently, you chose Yaeda Spade." Falcon shrugged.

Felicity laughed through the hot tears. "Oh mortals, I prefer you."

"How're you doing, Felicity?" Falcon asked, his face softening, his eyes searching her face. "You're definitely grown up. Not the little Level 10 girl I knew. More like a woman now."

Felicity blushed, and elbowed him. "I could say the same about you."

"Falcon is the envy of his class," Veronica said. "Who woulda known?"

"She lies." Falcon snorted.

Felicity couldn't help, but let her eyes wander. Falcon was right about the scars. They stuck out on his exposed skin, but they were only thin white lines now, much in contrast to the bloody nightmare that had been a gruesome reality. "You're okay," she murmured.

"And so are you," Falcon quietly replied.

She couldn't stop staring, like any moment he'd disappear before her eyes.

"If you guys didn't swear never to court each other, I'd say this would be a good time for a kiss."

"Shut up, Veronica."

That didn't stop either of them from looking away, blushing furiously. "How much longer are you staying?" Felicity asked, getting to her feet and brushing herself off.

Falcon got up after her. "Well, Renee invited me to lunch."

"Is Olivia still detested by even the name 'Falcon Armstrong' being said?" Felicity said.

"Falcon's her pity project," Veronica laughed, jumping from her seat. "You should see how she tried to coo over him when he was in that wheelchair."

A wheelchair? How bad had it been? Felicity's chest tightened. She hadn't been there for him either.

Falcon placed a firm hand on her shoulder. "Should we be off?"

"Wait," Felicity said. "Veronica still hasn't asked her third question."

"I'm saving it," Veronica said, skipping across the room to the hall to the elevator. She winked. "Till when I really need it."

With that, she ran down the hall, calling for them to follow.

Felicity looked up to Falcon. "I missed you," she stammered.

"I miss you too, Felicity," he sighed. "You have no idea."

"I think I do," she said, starting toward the hall. "I had to endure four years of no irritating dietary facts from a nerd."

Falcon chuckled, squeezing her shoulder. "It's good to have you back."

50

How could he have said those things? Why had they even breached his mind? Almost as soon as Cole had left the courtyard, he wanted to turn on his heel, run after Tabitha, and beg for her forgiveness, but he couldn't.

Not if he wanted to keep her safe and out of trouble.

At this rate, the predicted Oquelite attack could be any day, and knowing Tabitha, she would be more than willing to throw herself in harm's way. He couldn't let that happen.

No one else needed to die.

It didn't make it hurt any less. He'd apologize as soon as this was over, and he didn't expect her to forgive him. Maybe he'd even go to the Outown Diones and beg them to revoke their patronage. He stumbled through the empty balcony that overlooked the Skyline.

Why did he care so much? Why didn't he just let them all go? No wonder he'd steered clear of friends all his life. Love and compassion was painful. It coiled around your chest, not allowing you to breathe, taunting your mind. But wasn't it all worth it? Being able to call someone your own?

What would he know?

He grabbed hold of the handle of the door. He paused and looked over his shoulder to the morning sky behind him, as the sun rose into the gray sky over the magnificent city, sending rays of sunlight scattered across the buildings, seeping through the cracks, sending a brush of warmth across his skin.

That's why he'd said those things, wasn't it? He loved Tabitha.

He snorted. What twisted world did his mind live in where shouting at her till she cried equated to loving for her? She deserved someone who could do so much better than that. Someone who could actually save her, and not put her in danger. What could he even say to her?

He shook it off and opened the door, slipping into the hallway, a shudder overcoming him. The dark hall was unreasonably cold.

"We just need to get that feather."

Cole froze. Someone was in the hall....*Tabitha?* The feather? Cole crept quietly to the wall, before the turn in the hall.

"How does tonight sound?"

Tonight? The feather? Cole paled. She wasn't going after the feather. She couldn't be.

"Great." Undeniably the rough voice of Lawrence. "I'll meet you at 22.00."

What?!

"Fantastic," Tabitha said, her footsteps running off. "Oh! And avoid Cole!"

Cole's face burned at the comment. If she'd really wanted to avoid him, she wouldn't have discussed her illegal plan in the main hallway of the Lopez's home where they were all staying.

Cole's mouth was dry, his body tense. How could she throw herself in danger like this? Right after he'd told her not to?

Then it hit him. That's *why* she was. He'd known Tabitha long enough that he should've expected her rebellion in some way. He knew the times before this when she'd been scolded the same way, yet the girl's stubborn conscience took over anyway.

If she gets hurt, it's your fault. You made her do it.

Footsteps ascending toward him, snapped him out of his trance. His mind panicked. Where would he go? He hadn't meant to spy. If someone found out, that would screw up. Room—his room.

He grabbed the door handle of the closest door and slammed it closed, pressing his back against it, taking in shaky, shallow breaths. To his luck, the room was empty... not just of persons, but of character too. A simple made bed. A single mirror on the wall. A chair with a neat stack of laundry.

A knock came from the door.

Cole's body went cold.

"Is anyone in there?" Lawrence.

Cole frowned. What was he doing?

Cole didn't dare answer and find out.

"I heard you close the door," Lawrence said. "Look, Lopez. I think we need to talk."

This was the brother's room? Cole had to admit he was underwhelmed.

Cole waited in silence, and finally his silent prayer was answered when Lawrence gave a sigh of defeat. "Fine. Whatever. Later, then."

And with that, the clicking of his boots pattered out down the hall.

Cole frowned. Why had Lawrence been asking after the Lopez boy? It didn't seem like something Lawrence was inclined to do. Cole slowly eased his weight from the door, the boards creaking beneath his feet. He cringed.

Matteo's room was simple. A stark contrast to Court Illegia's need to be in every way extraordinary. A guitar was neatly collecting dust on a shelf above the headboard of the bed, and an authentic paper photo was pinned near the window.

Cole strained his eyes, unable to grasp the full photo. He was tempted to move forward, but then he really would be purposefully snooping around in Matteo's room, and he had no reason to be.

Cole took a few steps closer. He'd already made plenty of bad decisions today, what was another? He scolded himself.

The photo was worn with time, wrinkled and browned at

the edges, but seemed to have been handled with gentle care. In the photo stood a man, who looked like Nigel, but perhaps younger, sitting beside a woman on the verge of laughter, who seemed to be trying very hard to look annoyed. She had frizzy short curls and was dressed in bright red in a retired Court Illegia fashion, and the man, who must have been Nigel, Cole decided, since they looked so oddly similar, was clean shaven and confident, with a shoulder slung over the woman's shoulders.

Perhaps it was Matteo's uncle and aunt. It seemed relatively normal, right? Nothing concerning about that.

Cole took a deep breath and turned to leave.

There in the doorway, frozen, was Matteo Lopez himself.

They both stood frozen staring at each other, Cole cursing himself over and over in his head. If he'd just left right away, this wouldn't have happened. He was an *idiot*.

"I—I'm sorry," Cole stammered, clearing his throat. "I got lost."

Matteo pursed his lips and nodded. "Lost?" He didn't sound convinced. His eyes were darting around the room.

"I'll go now," Cole said, moving to the door.

Matteo stepped aside, letting him through, his eyes glued on Cole. "You didn't—"

"I didn't touch anything," Cole said, holding his hands up.

Matteo's face softened a little, tugging hard on his long sleeve. He nodded again, with a small, seemingly forced, smile. He slipped into his room and shut the door.

Cole stood again in the dark hallway and took a deep breath. He shook his head. He had too much on his plate right now to add Matteo to the list of things to be suspicious of.

Right now his priorities were clear.

Save Tabitha and Lawrence from being complete idiots.

Fourteen hours later, and Cole had to give Tabitha some credit.

He would've never guessed she would've climbed out of Calynda's window, and walked with full confidence along the horizontal grates along the windows. She had a light bag on her back, dressed in dark colors. He didn't even know

Tabitha was capable of wearing tightly fitted, black clothing. Apparently when the time called for it.

She reached the end of the sill, grabbing the pull of the patio cover, her body light enough to slide down. She hit the ground feet first. Without her usual baggy attire, he could clearly see the light muscled tone she was developing, as she subconsciously flexed her arms grabbing the straps of her bag, scanning the courtyard.

Little did she know, he stood in the center.

The Medallion was snug in the hilt of his sword, altering his body invisible.

She walked forward, her footsteps silent against the cobblestone, and stopped dead in front of him.

He held his breath.

Could she see him?

She let out a shaky sigh, biting her lip and turning on her heel.

Cole's heart faltered. Of course she couldn't see him. Why had he hoped she could? How many feelings were getting to his head?

"Tabitha!" A hushed shout came from behind them.

Both Tabitha and Cole turned around to see Lawrence hiding in the shadow of the moonlight in his trench coat, his glasses glinting in the light, giving his location away. He stepped out, flexing his hands. "Ready?"

"As I'll as ever be," she smirked, but the usual glint in her eye didn't follow. "You didn't see Cole today?"

"No," Lawrence said. He raised a brow.

Tabitha shook herself out. "I guess I'm just nervous. I've never done anything of this sort without him."

Cole itched to remove the Medallion and reveal himself, but he could only imagine how angry she would be. He couldn't risk that.

"Well, we could go back for him—" Lawrence started.

"No!" Tabitha said a little too loud. She cringed. "No. I'm good."

With that, she stormed off through the path between the two main buildings. Lawrence followed her with a small groan.

Cole's throat felt dry, his stomach burning with guilt. He readjusted his grip on the Illuminate's hilt and followed them. They went down the gravel path till they reached the coil gate. Tabitha lifted the latch, pulling the gate back with a creaking screech. She froze.

Lawrence slipped out into the alley.

Tabitha shook off her anxiety and followed him.

Cole made a break for it, squeezing past her as soon as she shut the gate. Tabitha cried out. Lawrence shushed her.

"Did you feel that?" Tabitha said. "Something touched me."

Cole cursed. Great job.

"You're really on edge," Lawrence said, starting down the alleyway out toward the glittering, never sleeping streets of the city. "You sure you don't need Cole?"

Tabitha snorted, running to catch up with him. "I don't need him to babysit me all the time."

Cole's cheeks burned.

They broke out into the glittering streets of Court Illegia. Cole decided to keep his distance, deciding against eavesdropping even further. Tabitha's words stung more than he liked to admit. He removed the Medallion from the hilt, clipping it back around his neck, sheathing the Illuminate at his belt. He pulled his hood over his head and disappeared into a crowd, keeping an eye on the curly haired boy in glasses, and the bouncing girl with an uneven bob.

The crowd molded around him with uncaring eyes, set on destinations and wonders. Cole gripped the hilt of the sword. Dread twisted his gut. Something was off.

He looked around the crowd. In moments, he had scanned over nearly a hundred bustling faces. None looking too suspicious. He was overreacting. Being paranoid, and then his eyes stopped on a pair of glowing red staring straight at him under a hooded jacket.

Oquelite didn't have glowing eyes, Cole had to remind himself. It was probably just a cool party trick, or whatever.

He suppressed a shiver. Energy ran through his veins, tingling his fingertips. Something strong was close. It was the same feeling he'd had entering the museum room.

He found the turn in the street and slipped out of the crowd, looking back over his shoulder. The glowing-eyed person was gone.

He breathed an uneasy sigh of relief. Lawrence and

Tabitha disappeared around the street corner. The street leading to the museum was mostly empty, and Cole couldn't exactly go invisible in the street without some major risks.

So how did he follow them?

His eye caught on a scrawny little ladder bolted into a brick apartment complex in the nearby alley. Better than nothing. He ran into the alley, and pulled himself up the rungs of the ladder, which creaked and groaned under his weight. He was halfway up when he heard something clatter below him.

Cole looked down, and was met with the glowing eyes... several feet below him.

His body went cold with panic. He turned and climbed faster. He was being followed. *Followed.*

He tried to keep his breathing even to keep his hands from growing sweaty and loose on the rungs. He grasped the brick end of the building and heaved himself up onto the rooftop.

He didn't even look back, scrambling away from the ladder and to the edge of the roof.

His feet suddenly caught on thin air, sending him falling face down.

Cole turned around on his back, scrambling backward as the glowing-eyes stalked toward him, their hand reaching into their long coat, drawing out a curved sword. "You're only a child," they rasped, in both surprise and laughter.

Cole bounced himself back to his feet, drawing the Illuminate from its sheath. He knew full well he wasn't experienced in the art of swordsmanship, but he didn't exactly have much of a choice. After this, he swore he'd find a better teacher than Taryn and her net videos.

"A child?" he said, coolly.

"Makes it easier." Glowing-eyes threw a blow at Cole. Instinct took over and he ducked backwards, grabbing on the railing of the roof. He raised his sword, blocking a blow to his face, dropping down and rolling, jumping on top of an air conditioning unit.

Glowing-eyes snickered, dashing toward him. They were having too much fun with this.

Cole jumped down, finding his best bet to be jumping to the next roof over. Deep breath.

Watch out! He whirled around, his sword meeting the blade racing toward him. Glowing-eyes forced harder, pushing Cole back.

He pulled out, dashing to the side. No more running.

He thrust about the Illuminate, but Glowing-eyes blocked easily, twisting around and slashing at Cole's middle. He stumbled back, air escaping his lungs.

A chuckle escaped from under Glowing-eyes's hood. They jumped, spinning mid-air, throwing a foot to Cole's face, and landed impeccably on their feet.

Cole's head reeled in pain, stumbling back, crashing against the fence. He could taste blood, his vision watered.

Glowing-eyes sheathed their blade, stalking confidently toward him. Cole sagged for a moment longer, tightening his grip on the Illuminate.

"Come easy, little Mem—"

Cole swung the Illuminate with a cry. This time, Glowing-eyes was caught off guard, stumbling back. Cole didn't stop for a second, clenching his jaw, taking swing after swing.

Glowing eyes dove under, a foot hitting Cole's. Cole fell, catching himself to his knees. He spun on his knee, and hit Glowing-eyes in the hood.

Glowing-eyes released a cry of pain.

Cole took the moment of distraction. He jumped to his feet and ran. He reached the end of the roof, and with no hesitation, jumped.

His heart hammered against his chest, his mind was screaming, but his feet planted firmly on the opposite roof. He looked over his shoulder as he ran, seeing Glowing-eyes holding their face, watching him.

They just stood there.

An unnerving shiver went down Cole's spine. He turned and ran harder. Who were they?

They'd called him a Member. They *knew* about the Council, but they weren't Oquelite. The ever-growing pit in his stomach sank thinking of the warning the warlock had given Miriam. Had he been right? Was there another force they didn't know about yet coming for them?

Another leap.

This time it was less flawless, giving Cole a near heart

attack as his foot slipped on the ledge and he grabbed a smoke-pipe jutting out of the roof just in time. He pulled himself up and kept going.

If that person was truly after the Council, then Tabitha and Lawrence were in more danger than he thought.

He reached the end of the neighborhood of apartments, his hands on his knees, catching his breath. The exhibit house stood in the dark below, only a few security lights on in the lawn. He unclipped the Medallion from his neck, which sent a shiver down his neck.

He rarely removed the Medallion from his person. Even if it was going to the hilt in his hand, it always made him feel more vulnerable. It was a weak feeling, he scolded himself.

He twisted it into the hilt, holding up his transparent hand just to check before crawling down the ladder to the ground. Lawrence and Tabitha jogged past him. He followed after them.

They approached the gate.

Lawrence pulled. It was locked.

Tabitha whipped out her tele, and in a few moments, a new set of footsteps joined them... from the inside. "You're late." Iracema flashed a smile.

Tabitha shrugged. "Hardly."

Cole's jaw fell. Why was he surprised Iracema was defying the law again?

Didn't she want to be a Defender? This wasn't the way to go about it.

Iracema guiltlessly opened the gate, letting them through. Cole squeezed his way past and followed them as they ran to the employee door on the side.

"So why'd we bring Iracema again?" Lawrence said.

"Well, for one, she got us in," Tabitha said.

"And, Delorous here thinks I can help you guys with your mission... in a big way." Iracema beamed, and winked. The door handle blinked green. The door unlocked.

What had Tabitha told Iracema? How could she help besides breaking in? If anything, they were doing Iracema's track record a disservice.

They wandered through the dark hall, the harsh air conditioning pricking at Cole's exposed face. They walked out into the main room, lit by the dim moonlight. The shadows along the marble floor were no longer astonishing, but terrifying.

"Now what?" Iracema said, her voice echoing off the empty walls. "I managed to turn off the cameras for forty-five minutes max. So we better work quickly."

"This is all Tabitha's idea," Lawrence shrugged.

Tabitha puffed her chest in pride as she led them to the side exhibit. Cole rolled his eyes.

"According to our theory of the tapestry, the feathers are caused by a Wingor presence in Court Illegia, also established by Agent Lopez weeks ago." She pushed the heavy door open with a grunt.

"Right," Lawrence said, still frowning. "And?"

"You found the feather when *Iracema* was with us. Cole felt an energy when they were in the same room together. And Nigel is so protective of her... "

Tabitha didn't even need to finish, Cole's mind was already spinning. Was she saying *Iracema Lopez* was the Wingor? The Council Member they'd been searching for?

He hated to admit it was plausible.

Iracema seemed to be unable to wipe the smile from her face. "Isn't that crazy? All these years of sitting here, and it turns out I was born with an opportunity."

Lawrence was frozen, his eyes wide, and his lips parted. "You-you're serious?"

Tabitha frowned. "Yeah? You don't think so."

Lawrence closed his eyes and swallowed. "Sure. I guess it makes sense. I—I was just being stupid thinking—yeah. It doesn't matter. Let's find this feather thing."

They began their search, with no intention of keeping quiet. Cole just had to stand, watch, and keep himself from cringing. Iracema was light on her feet, searching in the clutter under the desk, and Tabitha through the boxes piled by the escape hallway.

Lawrence just stood, staring at his scorched hands.

The Iracema reveal really seemed to have shaken him.

After a while of an unsuccessful search, Tabitha's morale seemed to falter. She bit her lip, searching the room with her glance. "Iracema, can—can you try feeling for it?"

Iracema hit her head under the table. She slid out. "*Que?*"

"If you feel, uh, something powerful I guess."

Cole snorted. Genius idea, Tabs.

"I guess so," Iracema said, getting to her feet. She shook out her hands, closed her eyes, took a deep breath, and held out her arms. Cole could've melted to the floor with shame for her, instead he settled for a biting of his lip to conceal a smile.

What had he been worried about? These three were harmless... if you ignored the fact they broke into government property. As long as the *Mors Vis* actually didn't show up, it was fine.

"Feel anything?" Tabitha asked.

Iracema peeked out of an eye. "No?"

"This is pointless, Tabitha." Lawrence sighed. "Let's just have the Serg test Iracema, and we can leave."

"But her essence might not be activated." Tabitha brought up a valid point. "As far as we know, you're the only Member here whose essence has been activated."

"Right." Lawrence's face fell.

Iracema continued to try and strain herself to feel.

Cole watched as Lawrence looked away, closing his own eyes. For the first time, Cole watched the boy's face relax. He unclenched his hands.

A light grew brighter below Cole. He frowned, looking down to see the Blade of the Illuminate glowing brightly. He prayed they couldn't see it.

Lawrence suddenly cried out in pain and crumpled to the ground, clutching his side.

"Lawrence!" Tabitha shouted, running to him. Iracema dropped her arms and jumped over the table.

The wind in the room began to pick up.

"Get away!" Lawrence shouted as Tabitha reached out. He cried out again, grasping his arm.

"What's happening?" Iracema stepped back, her eyes turning upward. Wind thrashed harder and harder. Where was it coming from?

A small glow appeared from the glass ceiling, peeking through the glass. And then another... and another.

The feathers. Not just one. But dozens... no hundreds.

Cole tore the Medallion from his hilt.

Tabitha screamed. "Cole?" She cursed.

He clipped the Medallion back on, gripping the

Illuminate and promptly ignoring her, even though he was sure her face was as red as a beet, and she had enough anger in her little over five feet to murder him.

"You have to get out!" he cried.

"No!" Tabitha retorted, storming up to him. "They're part of the Council essence. They're here to guide the Wingor!"

"They're going to kill you, Tabs... Tabitha!"

"And what—"

"Stop fighting!" Lawrence roared, collapsing to the floor.

Tabitha snorted, turning and punching Cole square in the jaw. It was weak, but enough to cause him to stumble, mostly from shock. "Get to them, Iracema!"

Iracema didn't hesitate. She jumped up on the table.

"No!" Cole shoved Tabitha out of the way, but she caught quick hold of his arm, wrestling with the hilt of the Illuminate. One well-placed blow and he could knock her down. But he couldn't do that.

Why couldn't his mind make up a way to feel?

The feathers spiraled closer.

He thrust his elbow to Tabitha's face. She ducked and twisted his wrist, ramming her heel against his ankle. He tripped forward, grabbing hold of a chair. She tore away the Illuminate. "Tabitha, no!"

It was too late. She cried out in pain, the smell of burned flesh already filling the space. She dropped the Illuminate, looking down to her bloody hands. She glared at him, clenching them, standing guard of his sword. "Fight me, Johnson."

"Tabitha, you're going to get Iracema hurt!" Cole scowled. How could she be so stupid?

"You're going to destroy the Council! More people will die, like you said."

No. Tabs that's not what I meant. I'm sorry.

I don't want *you* to die.

He jumped toward Tabitha, skidding to his knees for the Illuminate. Tabitha kicked in further, stepping on his arm to keep him down. Foolish choice, since in one pull, he sent her to the ground. He cringed.

He scrambled to his feet and grabbed the Illuminate. The force had begun to glow brighter with its slow spiral descent.

Iracema stood nervously on the table. The "feathers" began to spark into tiny glowing fragments.

He ran toward it, the blade igniting.

Tabitha threw herself in front of him, her body trembling. Her lips were bleeding, holding out her charred, bloodstained hands in front of her.

The wind whipped around faster, the ground trembling.

Tears streamed down her face. "Don't do it, Cole," she whispered.

He couldn't look at her. He held the flaming sword in a frozen back stance, feathers beginning to dance all around them in the air. He looked to the glowing forces spiraling toward Iracema, but then it stopped. It parted, taking a turn away from her... and toward the doors.

Tabitha gasped.

Iracema looked around, confused. "W-wasn't it supposed to come?"

"She's not the Member." Tabitha looked away, unblinking, pressing her hand against her face.

It didn't kill her. Tabitha had been right.

"Cole, your sword! It's touching—"

In one fell swoop, the air caught fire.

Everything around him exploded. The Illuminate flew from his hands, and he was slammed against the ground. His head seared with pain, his eyes unfocusing.

He heard a crash. Smoke took over the air.

And a pillar of fire came for its revenge.

51

For a moment, Felicity remembered what it was like to be normal.

Surrounded by her best friend and sister, joking over lunch, driving her aunt insane, and then spending the rest of the afternoon in the greenhouse roofs.

Before Falcon left, he wrapped Felicity in a hug. "You promise to call me if you ever need anything, right Felicity?"

She rolled her eyes. "Sure."

"I'm serious," Falcon laughed. "I don't care if you're basically a superhero now."—She cringed—"Call me up. I've learned a few things over the years."

"Fine," Felicity said. "I'll take you up on it."

Falcon smiled, his eyes glinting in the light with a familiar childlike shine before he departed into the darkness.

That was hours ago. Now, Felicity sat in her room, adjusting her braces and reviewing the map to her father's office on the screen projected on the far wall. She had the Aguirre DNA sample sealed in a pouch in her bag, a map downloaded to her tele, and most important of all, the most powerful override lock of all. That was her ticket in and out of there.

Giles was waiting in the parlor, and he was the only Defender Felicity had dared tell of her venture. Surely, someone else would try to stop her.

She folded her pants down over her braces. She'd used them all day, and only had a chance to charge them for two hours. It should be enough to get her through. She stood up, taking a deep breath through her stomach.

Something crashed behind her. A window slammed against the wall, glass shattered, and wind howled.

Felicity dropped to the ground, her heart ramming against her chest.

A heavy thud hit the ground.

Someone was in her room. Giles was outside. All she had to do was scream, and Giles would rush in. But what if they were armed? Or worse—her breathing caught—an Oquelite?

She gathered her courage, and acted. She crawled slowly to her bed, reaching underneath till her hand met the smooth shaft of her spear. She drew it out carefully from under the bed in her shaking hands. She moved up to a squat, tightening her grip. A set of heavy footsteps moved forward.

Felicity held her breath.

On the count of three, she'd make a break for it and call for Giles.

Three. The stranger's breathing was heavy and out of breath, their feet dragged on the floor.

Two. A small shock went down Felicity's spine, her hand on edge, leaning forward.

"One!" she cried out, springing to her feet, throwing her spear toward the lanking stranger and dashing for the door. "Gi—"

A hand slammed over her mouth, a strong arm wrapping around her. Felicity screamed and kicked. She was being kidnapped. She spit and dropped her weight, but her attacker caught her swiftly.

She whipped around, and her entire body froze.

Oquelite Prince Silas Idicous looked back at her with hollow eyes, a ghostly face. He looked like he should have been dead.

Suddenly, Felicity wasn't scared anymore. She sent an elbow to his face. He dropped her, and she hit the ground with a thud.

She scrambled to her feet and made a run for the door. Silas teleported, appearing in front of the door, his hands aflame in crackling purple energy. "Don't run," he said, his voice ragged and tired.

His hair was wet, his entire body shaking with every breath. He looked frail and uneasy, in contrast to his once familiar confidence and charisma.

What happened to him?

Whatever it was, she didn't care. She ran back, grabbing the spear discarded on the floor, slid into an informal stance, and held it with the point toward him.

A cracked laugh fell from him. "If that makes you more comfortable."

She glared at him. "Get out, or I'll call the Defender out in the parlor."

Silas was unphased. "You think a pathetic Defender could really make it past me?"

He had a point. All Silas had to do was wave his hands around and he could probably drop Giles dead on the ground. Felicity's sweat went cold. "What are you waiting for?" she sneered. "Why are you here, you filthy murdering piece of—" she was too angry to finish, her body burning with rage, wanting to run the spearhead right through his face.

He stared at her unblinking, looking on the verge of falling asleep. "I came to warn you."

"You what?"

Silas flinched, clenching his jaw, staggering back. "Warn you," he gasped. He head snapped back toward her. His eyes had rolled back, leaving only white. He cracked a smile that didn't belong to him. "Just on time. Another Member, right in front of me." He laughed. "You're pathetic, quaking there. Just like your friend."

"Shut up!" Felicity screamed, praying Giles would hear her.

Silas stumbled forward, his head shaking, his eyes returning. "No, Felicity, please listen—ah!" He grasped his head. "You realize the Council is hiding your true identity from you."

"That's for a reason." Felicity leveled her spear.

"They don't trust you."

Felicity took in deep breaths. Anger and anxiety *wouldn't* control her. Think about the truth, Liz. Just remember Silas can't hurt you because you can fight him. You can hit him square in the face. "I know who I am. Now, get out."

Silas head jerked backward, his pupils rolling back. He stumbled forward awkwardly over the couch, onto the floor. He tore his fingers through his hair. He cried out.

Felicity's heart skipped a beat.

"Felicity!" Silas said, sitting up. "Listen to me. You don't—" His eyes tried to roll back, but Silas hit himself. He scrambled to his feet, reaching for her, but she thrust the spear out, backing away.

His eyes were glassy. "She's coming for you," his voice whispered, cracking. "She's coming to kill you, Liz."

"Who?" Felicity demanded. "Who is *she?*"

"She is—" Silas cried out, left gasping for air. "I-I can't. You have to trust me. She-she's coming for you, *tonight.*"

A cry caught in Felicity's throat. Someone was coming for... her? She couldn't trust Silas. She couldn't; he had to be lying to her. But from the looks of his shaking, exhausted condition, she couldn't help but believe him.

"I begged her not to," Silas rambled. "She said she wouldn't. She promised. She said she'd keep you safe. She said—"

His eyes rolled back. "A fool," he spat.

Felicity's eyes widened. Silas was mad, out of his mind. Could he literally not be in his own head? The ways his eyes switched. The way he fought with himself.

She tightened her grip. Even if it was true, she held no sympathy for either.

His pupils rolled back. "It's almost time. I—I have to go." He stumbled backwards, catching himself on a sofa behind himself, crashing toward the window. He was so uncoordinated compared to the last time she saw him. She guided him at spear point to the window.

Why didn't she just kill him and get it over with now?

He crawled up to the window, one foot on the sill, and another on the frame. "Watch out for the dark, Felicity."

With that, he slipped out the window. Felicity ran to the window, looking out, but he was gone.

Giles burst through the doors. "What the heck did you do to that window, Bentsworth? Are you trying to run?"

Felicity whirled around, trying to form a coherent sentence, but she couldn't. Silas, a heartless murderer, had come to warn her... or trick her. She tried to convince herself it was a trick. She was the useless Council Member after all. The spare part, until she found out for herself who she was.

She turned back to the window and the dark night sky. *Watch out for the dark.*

Felicity slammed the window shut, pulling a heavy curtain over the broken glass. She turned back to Giles, picking her spear up off the floor. "It-it was an accident. Let's go."

Giles raised a suspicious brow, but just shrugged. "Alright. I suggest you put the hood on, Bentsworth. I've given you only 45 minutes' worth of stealth training, and that gives a pretty high percentage of failure."

Felicity pulled on the hood of the Defender Uniform coat. "I can try at least."

"Just, please, don't get caught," Giles said, leading her out of the room. "I don't need Dow angry at me."

"Well, he's the one who assigned you to this," Felicity shrugged. "So, his fault?"

"See how well that holds up in court, Bentsworth. I dare you."

Felicity rolled her eyes, as she stepped into the elevator after Giles. Her father's office occupied one of the top levels in the manos, and it required the elevator to go horizontal through a dimly lit hall. No stairs, no second elevator. One entrance.

"You said you got an override key?" Giles said, raising a brow to Felicity.

Felicity fidgeted. "Yep."

"And the stuff you need to unlock whatever case is keeping the chip?"

She patted her bag. "Got it."

"You seemed spooked, Bentsworth."

"We're breaking into my *father's* office, for crying out loud," Felicity lied. Silas's warning now had become the forefront of her fears. Silas. She didn't think they'd ever speak again. It wasn't a very good conversation, and she still hated him more than anyone on the planet, but there was a time when she'd loved him more than anyone. She'd *trusted* him.

Had that all been a lie, or had he genuinely felt for her?

He'd come to warn her, hadn't he? Or was that just another way to pull her into his twisted game?

They entered the hallway, the elevator grunting as it moved onto a new horizontal track. Giles and Felicity grasped the railing. She glanced downward into a black abyss. How deep it went, she didn't know, but she wasn't ready to find out. Or have her parents do the finding either.

A door stood at the end of the suspended hall, framed in glowing fluorescent lights. A digital pad was in the center of the door. The elevator stopped, and a small elevator ejected from under the door. Felicity took a hesitant step out onto the podium. She took a deep breath.

"Hey, Bentsworth?"

"Yeah?"

"Is the spear the override key or did you forget your bag by my foot?"

Felicity cringed and smiled. "Neither."

Giles's brows furrowed, but his jaw dropped as Felicity pricked her thumb with the tip of the spear.

"You're kidding me," Giles breathed.

Felicity pressed her bloody thumb against the key-pad. It glowed green.

"That's disgusting," Giles said, as Felicity jumped back in the elevator beside him, the door opening out into the hall. "Blood? The override key is *blood*?"

"Bentsworth blood," Felicity clarified.

Giles stared at her, speechless. She shrugged. She never thought she'd see the day where it would come in handy. Her father had told her it as a fun fact in case something dangerous ever happened, and it always stuck with her as absurd.

Absurd, but apparently very true. The elevator stopped, and lights across a marble path lit up.

Giles and Felicity exited the elevator. Giles handed her her bag. "You remember the self-defense Sergeant Hunter taught you?"

"Hardly," Felicity admitted, with a sigh. "But Nikki

taught me more than the Sergeant ever could."

Giles groaned. "You're hopeless."

Felicity gripped her spear, pulling the hood more snugly over her head, making sure no stray red hairs were peeking out. They reached another door, guarded by a half asleep Defender with chrome red hair. She jumped up as they approached. She strained her eyes. "This is a restricted area."

"I know that," Giles scowled, crossing his arms. "How do you think we got in? It's not a walk through the park."

The Defender thought about it for a moment. "I haven't seen you around before."

"I'm a new recruit."

The Defender whipped out a Scroll device. "Name?"

Giles paused, glancing to Felicity. She gave him a reassuring nod.

"Armstance Giles."

They typed the name into the Scroll, and waited for a moment until a harsh alarm rang from the device.

Felicity's heart stopped.

"There's no Armstance Miles in the system."

"*Giles*. G-I-L-E-S. It's not that hard," Giles groaned.

The defender re-entered the name. "Oh! You are here. Sorry about that. Been on this shift for almost twenty-fours. They heightened security after *another* stupid attack in North Cordell."

Felicity was too horrified to laugh. That was too close.

The Defender stepped aside, and Felicity and Giles passed through the hallway. As soon as the door closed behind them, Giles turned to Felicity. "We split up from here, Bentsworth," Giles whispered. "I'll keep as many Officers out of the artifact hall as I can while you get the chip."

Felicity nodded. "Good luck."

Giles snorted. "No. You're going to need all the luck you can get."

They stopped at another door. Felicity opened the forming scab on her thumb, and unlocked it. The door to the infamous Bentsworth artifact hall.

She took a deep breath and looked over to Giles. He winked. "You got this, Bentsworth."

"That's probably one of the nicest things you've said to

me."

"Don't make me take it back."

She suppressed a smile, turned on her heel, and allowed herself to be enveloped by the darkness of the hall. The door shut behind her. Dim red lights turned on above her. She shivered. That really set the creepy mood. Her father was all for restoring the environment, so no wonder he probably didn't use light on things he didn't think necessary.

She crept down the hall. Artifacts stood under their own little limelights in glass cases spread evenly apart along the wide hall. The original Joined World Treatise hung proudly on the wall. Among the hundreds of signatures of the surviving world leaders, the prominent "Patrick Bentsworth" was among them.

Felicity tracked further, keeping her mind focused on the path ahead. The Aguirres would be closer to the end of the hall since their prominence was hardly two decades ago.

But her mind couldn't help but stare at the original Defender uniform design pinned in a frame, or the map of the European Underground Bunker System. Europe was apparently a group of 'countries.'

An echo caught Felicity's senses. Her ears twitched. A soft footstep approached. Her senses sharpened. The footsteps were coming from above... how did she know that?

Wait, *above?*

She whirled around just in time to meet her opponent dropping from the ceiling, two knives expertly gripped in their fists. White hair spilled from a ponytail, red paint adorned a young face, and two glowing eyes seared into Felicity's soul.

The attacker didn't even give Felicity a moment to breathe or process the glowing eyes, running at her. Felicity evaded the attack, slamming herself against the wall. Her legs revolted with pain, but her mind suddenly took over. *Attack from the left. Just like with Nikki.*

She rolled, a knife landing in the wall to her left. She spun her spear, smacking the end in the attacker's face, and ran down the hallway. She heard the knife fly through the air; she scrambled to the side. The knife buried itself in a pillar. Felicity's heart leapt to her throat. She took a quick turn.

The exhibit to her left was the Manifest Treatise replica.

Still a hundred years off from the Aguirres and Curatrix team. The assassin turned the corner, one knife in hand. They ran toward Felicity, then took a quick turn, jumping against the wall, and running wickedly fast along it, then dropped. Felicity skidded out of the way, her mind once again surprising her.

She looked around, finding the glowing blue wall of exotic fish swimming happily despite the attempted murder happening beside them.

Do what the assassin did! Felicity's mind excitedly encouraged.

Now way. Too late, she was already running. Her instincts took over, her conscience was screaming, but everything felt right. A foot hit the wall, and her body flipped a spin, her spear poised to the glass, letting her aim and throw all in under a second before hitting the ground on her feet.

The glass exploded, water spilled out onto the floor. The assassin was knocked off their feet. Felicity grabbed a heavy metal case from a nearby display, and hit the assassin upward on the head in one quick distracted swoop, leaving them collapsed in the puddle of dancing fish and broken glass.

Felicity was out of breath, but any second wasted on breathing was another moment for the assassin to wake up. She grabbed her spear and ran down the hall.

Little bolts of electricity ran up her legs. She cursed. The braces must not have been waterproof.

Now she was really running on borrowed time.

Relief rushed through her, seeing familiar artifacts now. A video of Executive Defender Cadissa Dean's acceptance speech, and James R. Kordin's original Officer uniform.

Then she burst into the section she'd been waiting for. Despite having a custom engraving of *"The Curatrix Team,"* their little room was pretty empty.

There was a revolver of Aaron Outown's and a lock of hair of Zita Klirkpatrick's, but nothing much else. Felicity noticed not a single thing here was from Jessica Hunter, more commonly known as Sergeant Taryn Hunter now. When Taryn said the Defending Department had tried to erase her existence, she really meant it.

And then her eyes settled on a black case that made her want to sink to her knees and sob with relief. It was simply labeled *"Aguirre Tech, found in ruins of the Aguirre home in Algery."*

She felt a twinge of guilt. Her father had gone to the ruins of the Aguirre home? Or had he had someone search for him? Either way, it made her feel sick. It was common knowledge, Lyell and Reyna Aguirre, along with their two children, hardly out of their babyhood, had died in the burning house.

And now Felicity knew the Aguirre couple had probably been murdered... and she couldn't bear to even finish the thought about the children. It felt disrespectful to be searching through the ashes and ruins for something to put on display.

One good thing that had come out of it was the fact that the Aguirres' work was about to help another generation. Felicity walked carefully to the case. She reached her hand into her back to extract the DNA ring of Nikki's, and then she froze.

Panic overcame her adrenaline, suddenly shattering. She'd made it this far. She'd kept her head up. She'd made it, alone. But now...

She clamped her hand over her mouth to suppress a cry.

There was no DNA lock. It was a code pad.

Everything she'd fought for. All the courage she'd mustered, for *this?* It couldn't be happening. She'd failed them. She didn't know the code. How would she know the code?

"Calm down, Liz," she said, tearing her fingers through her hair. She sat on the ground, cradling her legs to her chest and rocked herself slowly. She hummed to herself.

A code.

Nikki's birthday was the 31st of the last month, but that wasn't her official birthday. That wouldn't work.

The number 53 popped in Felicity's head, but she thrust it aside. 53 had nothing to do with this.

"Four my friend, Two too much," she tapped her foot. *"Seven Eleven, Three we Two do."*

Four my friend.

Two too much

Seven

Eleven

Three we

Two do

Felicity's head shot up, her breath caught in her throat. "Nikki and Tabitha's song," she gasped. It was based on numbers from Nikki's memory.

No way.

Hot tears poured down her cheeks, as she scrambled to her feet to the podium, entering the code with shaking fingers, singing to herself slowly. *4.2.7.1.1.3.2*

The case clicked open. Felicity broke down in sobs. It worked. She gasped for air to her constricted lungs. She'd done it. All by herself. She'd done it. She thanked whatever power above allowed this. The song. Tabitha's stupid little song.

She opened the case, and the first thing she noticed was the strong, sweet, rose scent with a hint of smoke. The case must have been airtight. Inside was a crystal chip, with tiny silver wire running in lines inside of it wrapped in a foil tip. She removed a pouch from her bag, and carefully removed the chip from its safehold and into the pouch. She slipped it into her bag and clamped the case shut.

She took a deep breath, wiping her face wet from tears and fish water. Pain seared up her thigh. She bit back a cry. She didn't have much time. She needed to get the chip to Giles, and he needed to get it to North Cordell.

She burst out from the room and down the hall. She could smell the stench of fish as she crept into the soaked hall. Her heart did a flip, seeing the assassin's body gone... and her knee buckled on her and she crumpled forward.

Not now! She pushed herself up to her feet, gritting her teeth, and ran. She ran through the halls, away from the artifacts, and down the dark hall. She could make it. Just keep breathing. You have the chip. Just keep breathing. She burst in the final stretch of the hall. She pulled her hood over her face.

The door opened for her, and she burst out, her legs giving out, sending an electric shock through her body. She cried out.

"There!" a gruff looking Defender came running toward her, pulling out his pistol. "Bring your hands up!"

Felicity ignored him, pulling the headband from her hair,

the electric pain subsiding. She collapsed on the floor.

"Bents—Benny!" Giles's voice saved her. "She's a new recruit." He said quickly.

"New recruits in this high level security?"

"There-there was a break in," Felicity stammered. "Someone with knives."

"What?" both Giles and the Defender shouted.

"Get on it!" Giles shouted.

The Defender ran past Felicity into the hall, calling for backup. Giles knelt beside Felicity, his usually gruff black eyes now round with concern. "Are you okay, Bentsworth?"

"I got the chip," Felicity said, with a weak smile.

Giles cheered, scooping her up, and hugged her. "That's it, Bentsworth!"

Hot tears streamed down Felicity's cold, wet face, smiling. "I—I can't walk, Giles."

Giles's face immediately hardened. "Not even a little?"

He hooked his arm under her armpits, raising her to her feet, letting them rest firmly against the ground. He slowly let go. Felicity's legs didn't respond, pain searing up her spine, and she fell forward, crying out.

Giles grabbed her, his eyes wide. For a moment, she swore they were glassy. "Bentsworth, you're para—"

"It's fine," she said. "I got the chip."

"But you can't—"

"It's fine," she insisted.

Giles pressed his lips firmly together, and nodded. He picked her off her feet, and cradled her helpless body in his arms.

Her entire route was in Giles's hands now... literally.

She clutched the bag to her chest, closing her eyes, drowning out the noise before she had to face the inevitable.

She'd have to face the undeniable paralysis affecting her body, the crazy instincts awakening in her mind, and coming clean about herself to her family.

But for now, she was at peace.

52

"FELICITY FOUND THE AGUIRRE CHIP!" MIRIAM CRASHED INTO Lincoln's cabin.

He nearly toppled over in his chair, grabbing the edge of the desk. "What?"

Miriam grinned. "Giles's on his way!"

"It's almost midnight!"

"Yeah and?" Miriam raised a brow. "You're still awake working on…" She frowned and inspected the dissected cube on the desk. "… that."

"I'm almost done," Lincoln chided. "If the Aguirres made a machine that can track Oquelite, I can make a machine that can track full-bloods. "

Miriam leaned in the doorway. "And why would you need that?"

Lincoln blushed. "Because. It's just short distance." He clicked two of the cube sides together. The process was delicate, but if the stones on the bracelet Nikki had given him *were* the Ewyon stone material, it would all be worth it. It had to be just right, so the sensors could be adjusted properly.

"Well, Sergeant is going to need your help inserting the chip into the system with that mind of yours."

"Is that all I'm good for now?" Lincoln scowled, screwing a small bolt into the rounded corner over the cube. "I refuse to sit here, and just make stuff so that everyone else can run off and be useful."

He stood up, lifting the cube holding it to the light. With a small tap of the side of the cube, the little blue lines underneath the surface glowed. A small smile lined his lips.

"You do plenty of field work, Gears," Miriam said.

"Then why didn't you assign me to go somewhere?" Lincoln grabbed a satchel from his cot, taking Nikki's note from the desk, and placing it gently at the bottom, then tucked away the cube. He was just stalling. He didn't care. If his plan didn't work, it wouldn't matter what Taryn had planned for him next.

He wouldn't be coming back.

"Gears, have you seen yourself recently?"

Lincoln shrugged. "I'm sorry my mental state seems *unreasonable* lately."

"You went from non-verbal to a cheery little rainbow in the span of twenty-four hours, and that's suspicious."

Lincoln slung his bag on his shoulder, eyeing his bow that made itself home on Ray's bed. He'd be back for it.

"Giles's here!" the voice of Officer Jackson Sallow shouted through the courtyard. The usually stagnant night shift roused. The camp burst to life. Miriam and Jack ran out into the center. A truck tore down the road. Taryn appeared out of nowhere. "Lincoln, with me!"

Lincoln burst after her. Miriam took it upon herself to follow. "Dennie! Stay behind!"

"You are *not* the boss of me, Defender!"

The young woman, Dennie he guessed from Miriam's story, burst out into a run beside them. Her form was impressive, her body lean, and her sprints effective. She had a jacket tied around her waist, bare arms flexing scars.

Guilt tugged at Lincoln's gut. Another victim of the Oquelite's rage. The Council could stop them, and whatever other force was brewing.

Or the Council would hurt them more.

He wasn't going to be the one to find out. The truck came to a hard stop, skidding in the mud. Giles basically fell from the driver's seat, nearly ramming into Taryn.

"Do you have it, Officer?" Taryn demanded.

Giles ripped a pouch from his pocket. "She got it, Serg'."

Taryn grabbed the pouch, staring at in sweet disbelief, before she shook it off. Her brows furrowed into a determined expression, with the smallest hint of a smile on her lips.

They ran for the camp, Taryn holding the chip triumphantly, and Dow shouted for the stunned Defenders to get out of the way.

They stormed up the stairs, rushing into the main cabin. The complex Aguirre machine was charged up and spread out across the table, screens displaying regions with little dots across the screen. Four in Court Illegia, One in Kennedy, another in Liberty... or was that two in Liberty? Two Council Members in Liberty? Taryn obviously hadn't noticed the change, and she gently removed the crystal chip from the back, holding it up to the computer screen light.

"Okay, Linc," Taryn said, turning to him. "Your turn."

He took the chip gently from her, examining it. The craftsmanship was beyond anything he'd ever seen, even above the tech in Imperial. The little information wire ran through the glass, pulsing like a heartbeat with light.

A heart. The chip was the heart of the machine. Miriam and Taryn hovered close. "I need space," Lincoln said, shooing them off. He set his bag on the ground.

He tapped the screen, brushing away the tracking maps. "Lyell Aguirre worked with DNA tech, right?"

"Yes," Taryn said.

"And contact tech." He tapped the chip against the screen. The screen glowed red. Lincoln set down the chip, drew up another code screen, and slid over the hologram keyboard. This was a little more challenging than what he was used to, but he got the swing of Lyell's rhythm quickly.

The screen clicked green.

Lincoln grabbed the chip, waving away the keyboard, took a deep breath, and slammed the chip in the base of the machine.

"Lincoln!" Miriam shouted. "What the—"

The machine burst to life, alarms going off like crazy, the two side maps ringing with red dots and alerts.

"It worked," Taryn breathed, stepping forward, placing a firm hand on Lincoln's shoulder.

On the blank screen, a message appeared. *The NMA Files Downloaded.*

"NMA?" Miriam frowned.

Taryn swiped it away, pushing past Lincoln drawing up the maps. A gasp escaped Miriam's lip. "Serg! Court Illegia!"

Miriam was right. Taryn zoomed in on the region. Thousands of small purple dots were racing across the screen. "Someone call Nigel!" Taryn cried. "The Oquelite are in Court Illegia!"

The room erupted into chaos.

Lincoln didn't wait around for a thank you, he grabbed his bag and slunk out of the cabin. An Oquelite attack in Court Illegia wasn't any of his business, all except for three certain people.

He slipped through the border of the camp, breaking out into a run through the path toward the mountains, the pine trees growing thicker around him, the grass catching on his boots, as he ran through the snow.

An attack on Court Illegia wasn't any of his business... but the people there were. He fished his Comm out from his pocket. Agent Lopez wasn't the one the Oquelite were looking for.

Lincoln would not be too late this time.

He dialed Cole's ID.

Cole made three dreadful discoveries in the span of three seconds.

One) They were in mortal danger in a burning building due to him. Two) *He'd* been the impulsive one. And Three) The Oquelite had arrived in Court Illegia.

He struggled to his knees, hopelessly trying to catch a breath in the thickening smoke. He tucked his Comm back in his pocket. The Oquelite were in Court Illegia. They were coming for the Council Member, and Cole had destroyed their only lead.

A scream caught Cole off guard, a heavy crash following, and an explosion of flames knocking him off balance.

"Iracema!" he cried out.

He jumped to his feet, hopelessly drawing his shirt over his nose, and tearing through a gap in the flames, which licked his arm. He looked around, his eyes stinging in the heat and smoke. "Iracema!"

He caught sight of a figure trapped under a table, clawing at the ground.

"Cole!" Iracema cried out, her face covered in sweat and drenched in tears.

He ran to her, slipping his arms under the table, and pulled it upward. Iracema slipped out, gasping for air, and Cole dropped it, flames catching onto the wood. He grabbed Iracema's arm, and looked around.

Where were Lawrence and Tabitha?

"There!" Iracama cried.

Cole's heart leapt with hope before it faltered, seeing the unblocked emergency exit door. He shoved her toward it. "Go!"

"What about you?" Iracema said, her eyes full of fear, her entire frame shaking.

"I'm going to find the others!"

She nodded, not daring to argue, and ran for the emergency exit. Cole tore back into the flames. The tapestry of the red mountains was up in flames, the bookshelf had fallen over, its flammable components littering the floor. He rushed past them, avoiding a lick of a flame that crawled into the exposed pages of a thick book.

The boxes of unpacked artifacts had been toppled. Clay masks, books, weapons, and furniture had collapsed, fire raging through an oak table, crushing a box of glass silverware.

And then he caught sight of a familiar patch of short, uneven hair. Tabitha was laying stomach to the ground, unconscious, a gash in her forehead with a line of blood trailing down her cheek.

"Tabitha!" he cried out. It was pointless. She couldn't hear him. He didn't care, he ran toward her.

"Stop!"

Someone jerked Cole back right before a box tumbled down, bursting in flames.

Cole whirled around. Lawrence stood behind him, looking untouched besides soot and grimy glasses.

"Tabitha's there!" Cole shouted.

"Yeah! And whose fault is that?"

The words felt like a punch to the gut. "I'm sorry, please. I am." Cole's voice faltered. "I can't prove it right now. We just need to get to her!"

Lawrence growled but nodded, rushing to the fallen wall of fire in their way.

"What are you doing?" Cole shouted as Lawrence reached out.

"Oh, please!" Lawrence shouted. "Have you not been paying attention?"

Lawrence tied his coat around his waist, rolled the sleeves of his shirt up, reaching his hands into the flames against the table, and pushed. The table groaned and creaked under the force. A small path formed.

"Go!" Lawrence screamed. "Before it grows!"

Cole dashed between the gap, running to Tabitha. He shook her. "Tabitha!"

She moaned.

"We don't have time!" Lawrence shouted. "Grab her!"

Cole didn't hesitate. He scooped Tabitha into his arms. "Cole?" she grumbled.

"Hang in there," Cole pleaded, turning to Lawrence, who was guiding flames away for a clear path.

"I'm sorry," Tabitha choked. "I'm so so sorry."

He couldn't be angry with her, but all at the same time, he was. He was enraged with himself that he'd let it get this far.

He ran through the path Lawrence had created.

Whatever doubts Giles had had when he'd heard the other Members say Lawrence's essence had been powerful were destroyed right then and there.

Lawrence moved the flames like inanimate objects which had no other choice but to conform to his will. They ran toward the emergency exit and burst into the hall, now clogged with smoke and heat. The door was open, fresh air seeping into Cole's lungs as they burst out from the flaming building.

They were not greeted alone.

Iracama sat shamefully on the hood of a Defender patrol car, one of many, and Nigel Lopez stood front and center, arms crossed.

"We need a Medic!" Lawrence cried, ignoring the angry Defender, leading Cole past him. A Defender with a white arm band ran to their aide, laying Tabitha on a tarp on the ground, beginning immediately to attend to her. Cole couldn't watch. Seeing her clearly would only make the guilt rage deeper in his gut.

Instead he turned and was faced with the disapproving

glower of Nigel Lopez. "You went *back*, directly against my order, and set the place on *fire*?"

"To be fair, Cole tried to stop us," Lawrence said, looking unphased as he dusted himself off.

"We have an Oquelite attack on our city in moments, and you kids are playing around *destroying* it."

"Sir, they were just trying to find the Council Member," Cole pleaded. "They were trying to *prevent* this all, however impulsive it was. I'm the one who screwed up and destroyed the force."

Nigel's eyes grew wide in conflict. He didn't like the force either, but he didn't like burning buildings, and he wanted the Member found too. "We don't have time. All we can do now is fight the Oquelite off, and hope the Member gets out of here. Finding them was a lost cause."

Cole's face fell and nodded.

"I know who the Member is!" Lawrence said, shoving Cole out of the way to face Nigel.

Cole was taken aback, seeing the rage forming in Lawrence's eyes, his fists clenched. "You can't abandon them!"

"You?" Nigel scoffed. "You've hardly been compliant since Sergeant Hunter found you, and now we're supposed to trust your judgement on the fate of this region?"

"Yes!" Lawrence spat. "It's *Matteo*! Matteo is the member!"

"What?" Both Cole and Nigel shouted in unison.

"Matteo? How could it be Matteo? There is no way! No signs, *nothing*." Cole threw his hands up.

Lawrence was growing agitated. "That's because he's really good at making people ignore him. Have you noticed? I bet you didn't notice he was the first one to approach the feather, and that's when *you* reacted. He's the one who touched it and made it burst to life, but you all were focusing on other things! You didn't even notice how he wasn't phased by our abilities!"

Everyone grew silent.

"Matteo knows he's the Member, and he's hiding it!" Lawrence drove it in like a stake.

Nigel staggered back, looking from Iracema to Cole. "Williams, that could all merely be a coincidence."

"Trust me!" Lawrence begged. "Let me find him!"

Nigel growled. "You're an impulsive, stuck-up child, who's been nothing but trouble. I'm sending—"

"No," Cole said, stepping forward. "This was my mission, Agent Lopez, and I'm in charge of Lawrence and Tabitha by the order of Sergeant Jessica Taryn Hunter of the Curatrix Team. And I screwed up, and I take responsibility for that, but don't blame him." He looked to Lawrence with a firm nod. "I—I trust you. Find Matteo, and bring him back to North Cordell safely."

Lawrence smirked. "Sure thing, boss."

Nigel looked ready to explode. Cole knew that bringing up Taryn would remind Nigel that technically, he wasn't the authority. "You dare touch a hair on that boy's head, and I come and kill you personally."

Lawrence rolled his eyes.

"If you're looking at places to find him, I know he likes to hang out in the other theater," Iracema said from her perch on the car hood. "Top level."

Lawrence pulled on his trench coat. "Got it."

He looked to Cole with another nod and a two-fingered salute, and ran off.

Nigel stifled a cough.

A two-fingered salute was reserved for high reverence and respected persons, which after the events of tonight Cole was nowhere near, but the gesture still made his heart quicken.

Now all they could do was wait. Their fate now relied on Lawrence Williams, as much as he hated to admit it.

Lawrence ran down the streets, already erupting in chaos, the Court Illegia Defender force already quick at work. People were being evacuated from the Skyline. Some were lost and confused, others picking fights with the Officers.

Lawrence didn't stop for anything. He just needed to run... could he go any faster? The stupid voice in his head had called themself "The Lady of the Universe," and when he'd tried to reach out to feel Matteo, all he got was the horrible pain through his body.

It couldn't be a good sign.

The air echoed with a boom, the ground trembling. Lawrence glanced to his side, seeing one of the giant ferris wheels burst into flame, beginning to fall over. He pumped his legs faster.

Old museum. Old museum. He had to get to the old museum.

Now people began to panic. Crowds pushed their way through the streets. Defenders tried to keep them under control. Lawrence slipped between their barricades as the guards were distracted by the heavy crows pushing against them.

He burst into the empty cobblestone street, the air smelling of smoke, trash rolling in the winds picking up. In the corner of his eye, he caught sight of a tall, weathered brick building, a sign labeling it "THEATER," and another one nailed "CURRENTLY CLOSED."

This had to be it. He ran up the rickety stairs, broke through the front door, and into the main lobby. He took off toward a staff door, leading to the dark, moonlit shaft with spiral metal stairs reaching high up to the top of the building.

"Matteo?" His voice echoed.

He ran up the stairs, his footsteps clanging on after another, bouncing on and off the walls. Faster. Faster.

He reached the top, and burst through another door. He searched through dusty, dark dressing rooms. Nothing.

He wasn't here. Lawrence's heart sank. Had he been wrong?

A small creak brought his attention to a slightly ajar door, labeled "ROOF."

Lawrence slowed his breathing. Of course. He took the handle in his hand and pulled it back, revealing the roof littered in crates and tarps.

And a boy, wrapped in a blanket at the edge, headphones over his ears.

"Matteo!"

The small, huddled frame of a boy sat near the edge of the roof, bulky headphones over his ears, a blanket pulled tightly around him.

"Matteo!" Lawrence cried.

The boy didn't respond.

Lawrence rushed to him, grabbing Matteo by the shoulder. "Matteo! Come on!"

Matteo jumped, jerking from Lawrence's grip, scrambling

backwards. His eyes narrowed, his breathing hardened, and his headphones fell to his shoulders.

Lawrence froze at the terror trembling in the boy's eyes.

"Matteo," he said, brushing it off. "We have to go!"

Matteo flinched. He didn't respond, turning away, wrapping his blanket around himself.

What was he *doing*? Could he see the flaming wheel on the horizon? Lawrence's jaw clenched.

"It's not the time to be stubborn!"

Matteo nodded.

Lawrence let out a harsh sigh, reaching his hand out to him. "Get up! Come on!"

Matteo closed his eyes.

"No."

Lawrence's heart skipped a beat. "Matteo, you have to come."

Matteo squeezed his eyes, a tear slipping down his cheek. "No."

Lawrence's hands began to shake. What was going on? He dropped his extended arm, and took a seat on the roof. "Is something wrong?"

Matteo shook his head, hiding his face. "Please. Just—just leave me alone," he croaked.

Lawrence opened his mouth, struggling to find a gentle word. "You could die. I'm here to help."

Matteo's body stilled. "I know."

Lawrence's ears rang. The words rang in his ears. *I know.*

No. Lawrence's stomach rocked, forcing its way up his throat.

No.

Familiar thoughts crept to his mind. A locked closet, darkness closing in on him, his breathing ragged and burning. Everything in his body in pain, slicked with blood. His glasses missing from his face, lost to the blurry darkness where no one could hear his screams. Snorts and scorns echoed against his skull. Echoes of a bloody chain.

"Matteo, don't do this to yourself."

Another tremble took the earth.

"Leave me alone," Matteo choked. "There's no point." His body shook. "They're supposed to kill me."

"This isn't the way," Lawrence stammered, his throat

choking up. "If you think this is your fate, then you've already given up. You don't have to give up."

"There's nothing else!" Matteo cried, looking up tears streaming down his face. "I don't know what to do! I can't keep going on and on. I can't do what they want me to! I can't be a hero." He stopped, gasping for air, wrapping his arms around himself. "Please. Please don't make me."

Lawrence's face softened. "I'm not going to force you to do anything I know you can't do."

"You don't know me." Matteo began to sob now.

Lawrence reached his hand out. Matteo slunk away. "Matteo, please let me help you."

Matteo stared at Lawrence's hand, before his watery eyes fell to the flaming horizon.

Lawrence's throat clenched up. "Matteo. I—I don't—" He squeezed his eyes shut, and took a deep breath. "I know this probably doesn't mean anything to you. But I want to tell you, I know what it's like to think there's no other option."

He opened his eyes, feeling them burn.

Matteo's face had turned back to him.

"But I *knew* people cared about me. I knew I cared about people... even if they were just two darn people." Another shaky breath. His voice threatened to break. "If you feel like no one cares about you, please let me."

Lawrence's face fell, letting a shameful tear fall. His heart ached, his mind taunting him. But he didn't care. He couldn't leave him there. He wouldn't let someone suffer like he had. He couldn't dwell on his pain forever. He needed to heal, and he wanted to help. But what if he couldn't? What if he hurt him even more? What if he caused even more pain and torment in the world? What if she had been wrong about him?

A cold hand grasped his.

Lawrence's head jerked up, seeing Matteo's tear brimmed eyes staring into his.

Relief shuddered Lawrence's body. He pulled Matteo to his feet. Matteo took a deep breath before collapsing against Lawrence. Lawrence steadied him.

"I don't want to die," Matteo whispered.

"You won't die," Lawrence promised. "I'll make sure of it."

54

Lincoln's heart hammered against his chest as he trekked through the rolling hills of the base of the infamous four peaks.

He held Nikki's note in his fist, and the powering up Cube in the other. Was he insane?

Of course he was. No one in their right mind would be out here right now.

But it was his only hope. He let out a harsh breath, watching it spiral in the cold air. He was being selfish. He couldn't ditch the Council for personal feelings. They needed an Aviduous. It wasn't like full-blooded Aviduous were rare though. Maybe there was another one with essence strong enough to be a Member?

Unlikely, but the thought comforted him a little.

He sat down on a stump, burnt from the attack weeks ago, on top of the hill. He set the Cube down on the snow, its light still blinking as it loaded. He gently uncurled his freezing fists, revealing the worn crumpled piece of paper.

He unfolded it, reading out the words he could recite in his sleep to the empty plain of snow in front of him. "Life will find me. And so will you."

Please, Nik. Please don't be giving me false hope like this. He looked up and frowned.

A figure stood in the distance, their face covered by their long dark red scarf, flapping in the wind. Lincoln jumped to his feet, scooping up the Cube. Still no signal of a living full-blood.

"Hey!" he shouted. "You good?"

The figure looked up.

He strained his eyes. They had a dainty white face, and blood red lips, furling blonde curls peeking out. A woman, he decided.

"Do you need help?" he called out.

The woman only smiled, whipped her scarf, and turned and began to stride away.

A shiver went down Lincoln's spine. Creepy.

He turned away from her, and nearly cried out as his foot landed in crimson red. He scrambled back, running into a tree. A puddle of blood. Where was he?

He whirled around.

The woman was gone.

There had been fresh snow since the attack, and the site had been cleared. He looked back. The puddle was gone. He was going crazy. Maybe he should go back.

He shook off the thought. He was just paranoid. He picked up the Cube. "Load. Come on," he scowled.

It was pointless. If it hadn't loaded by now, that probably meant it never would.

What you search for comes with a price. The familiar youthful female voice pounded into his head. *I do not know your name, young one. Can you tell me?*

Now, he really was insane. Had that been her? Had *that* been the voice? "Get out of my head!" Lincoln cried. "Go!"

I can help you.

Lincoln scoffed. "I can help myself."

I've seen your malfunctions before, boy.

Lincoln swallowed hard, pressing his hands against the Cube, feeling the whir of machinery. "Then you'll watch me succeed. Where are you?"

A moment of silence. *You are stubborn. Strong, aren't you?*

Lincoln didn't answer, making his way down the hill, lifting the Cube above his head. The wind had begun to pick up. *Who are you?*

He squeezed his eyes shut, snow nipping at his face.

I have many names. A sharp laugh. *What is your name, Aviduous? You can only be satisfied through my help. She will not be yours without my help.*

"I don't need your help!" Lincoln shouted, his voice lost in the wind. "She doesn't belong to anyone! I don't belong to anyone! I will *not* give in! You'll have to kill me first!"

The Cube beeped. A full-blood was found.

Lincoln almost cried out. He opened his eyes. The small red dot on the screen was fluctuating. The signal was weak. He smiled, a tear breaking loose down his face. It *worked*. He was right.

He had been right.

The note didn't lie.

Something slammed into the back of his head hard.

The world flashed before his eyes, everything slowly crashing to the ground as he hit the snow with a thud. His vision blurred. A figure stood above him.

His eyes stung, straining to focus on the cloaked face. "Tell her the Lady of the Universe has arrived."

A foot met his face.

The world went black, one thought still rang in his mind.

Nikki was *alive*.

THE UNANSWERED QUESTIONS

BOOK THREE

COMING NEXT WINTER

Glossary

THE JOINED WORLD
95 REGIONS OF EARTH, ALL JOINED UNDER ONE GOVERNMENT AFTER THE EARTHSHAKER

THE EARTHSHAKER — APOCALYPTIC WAR 340 YEARS AGO, WHICH SENT HUMANITY INTO REBUILDING EARTH

THE DEFENDING DEPARTMENT — THE "DEPARTMENT" OF LAW ENFORCEMENT TO KEEP EACH REGION IN ORDER
- **COMMANDER** — IN CHARGE OF ENTIRE DEPARTMENT
- **GENERALS** — IN CHARGE OF MULTIPLE REGIONS
- **AGENTS** — SPECIAL TASK FORCE UNDER GENERALS
- **SERGEANTS** — IN CHARGE OF A REGION
- **OFFICERS** — UNDER SERGEANT'S COMMANDS

THE CURATRIX TEAM — WELL-KNOWN TEAM OF DEFENDERS, KILLED OVER A DECADE AGO
- AGENT REYNA WENTS AGUIRRE, AGENT LYELL AGUIRRE, SERGEANT JESSICA HUNTER, OFFICER AARON OUTOWN, OFFICER ZITA KLIRKPATRICK

COMMON TECH
SCROLL — UNRAVELING DEVICE THAT CONNECTS TO NET AND CAN PROJECT HOLOGRAM
TELE — GLASS DEVICE THAT FUNCTIONS AS A SMALL SCROLL AND COMM
COMM — GOVERNMENT ISSUED COMMUNICATION DEVICE

THE IMPURE

OVERALL NAME FOR THE SUPERNATURAL BEINGS AND HAPPENINGS OF EAR

ILLIAH/ESSENCE — THE "SECOND BLOODSTREAM" CONTAINING THE SUPERNATURAL ASPECTS OF HUMANITY

THE IMPURE RACES— THE SEVEN "TYPES" OF ESSENCE, WHICH ADAPTED TO A CERTAIN WORLDLY ELEMENT

EWYON — ILLUSION, APPEARANCE

AVIDUOUS— EARTH, STRENGTH, CREATURES

OQUELITE — ESSENCE ITSELF?? (UNKNOWN)

YWONDIE — FIRE

AGUARIOUS — OCEANS, WATER

SUBLINIGHT — EMOTION, FEELING

WINGOR — SKY, WEATHER

HUMANIC — TECHNICALLY "PURE" AS THEY HOLD NO SUPERNATURAL ASPECTS IN THEIR ESSENCE, EVEN IF FULL—BLOOD

MYTHICS— SUPERNATURAL CREATURES, CREATED BY IMPURE

SHIFTERS — MYTHIC CREATURES THAT CAN SHIFT BETWEEN A HUMAN FORM AND ANIMAL

LYNTOX— SHIFTS TO MAMMALS

REPITOX — SHIFTS TO REPTILES

THE EVERGROWING WOODS — WOODS, CONTAINING SUPERNATURAL CREATURES AND STRUCTURES, THAT IS RAPIDLY GROWING ACROSS THE CONTINENT (HOW?? WHY??)

The Council

LEGENDARY GROUP OF 12 DESTINED MEMBERS

Members

Ewyon   X
Aviduous X
Oquelite
Ywondie
Agarious
Sublinight
Wingor
Humanic X

illuminate Holder – Holder of the illuminate blade; representation of light X

Shadow Holder – Holder of the Shadow Blade; representation of dark X

Keyper – hereditary role, can form/bare key??

Guardian – representative of the Mythic

X = found

ACKNOWLEDGEMENTS

The fact I'm actually writing acknowledgments *again* is a miracle all in itself.

I was a freshman in highschool when I first drafted this book, and I remember the distinct thought of "no one is going to read this." But here we are, by the grace of God, at it again.

I owe all thanks to my Creator who gave me the will and passion to write this story through an painful grieving period, and carrying me through the whole way through and hearing my desperate cries for help when I really needed it.

This story wouldn't have been as great as it could've been with You.

- To my parents, who've raised me and all my... uniqueness. Thank you for dropping me off at various coffee shops, and being willing to hear character and plot rambles (no Mom, Nikki and Lincoln are *not* that awkward, I promise).
- To my beta reader crew, Joseph Ellis (for ALL those hilarious comments), Emerald (the reason Nikki uses her wrist correctly ;)), Julie Mozart (for that brief camp AU in the comments), M.T Zimny (for your faith in both Lawrence and Felicity), Luna (for not only the fanart, but encouragement!), Anya (for many things things, and your encouragement and belief in this book from the start), and finally Samantha Crago (one the biggest Tabitha-Cole stans). And Gee, who wasn't part of the beta team, but no less persisted with my bilingual questions.
- I probably would've released a quite flawed OTCC and had half the confidence if it wasn't for you all!!
- Ellie, for unknowingly being there for TUQ when I hit a huge low. Seriously, what is it with you and saving these characters??

- To the crew of my readers at my school, and to Minnie Giles (**wink wink**) and Gianna Hanson, who can't come to an agreement who really named OTCC.
- To all my author friends, especially the author fam Naomi Kenyon, MC Pending, Julie Mozart (again!), and Naomi King. Y'all make life so much brighter, and totally made OTCC worth finishing.
- To another author friend who just needed her own bullet point: Ariana Tosado. I still can't beleive how blessed I am God placed you and your books into my life.
- To the team behind making OTCC a book worth reading: Beck Micheals (for the beautiful cover design!), Anna (for delivering a SECOND gorgeous cover illustration), Micheala Bush (for being my DREAM editor. There is no one I would've rather had edit this book), and Benita Prins (for the formatting! <3).
- To the family I babysit, for helping me out financially and providing a LOT of inspiration. Miriam, here's the mention you asked for. :)

And finally to YOU, dear reader. The readers of TUQ have created such an amazing little base online, and I'm always surprised by the amount of sheer love and support you all pour out. And if you've gotten this far, means you've read not one, but TWO TUQ books and are probably angry with me. I'll get on Book 3 right away, don't worry.

Lauren D. Fulter is an young American fiction author, after publishing her first book at the age of sixteen. After learning the word 'author' at age five, she's been captivated by the art of storytelling, and the little people roaming her mind. Though she longs for the cold, she lives in the desert with her large family, spending her days drawing, dabbling in fictional dimensions, and attempting to make something edible.